D0408909

This
Is How
It Really
Sounds

❖

Also by Stuart Archer Cohen

The Army of the Republic

Invisible World

17 Stone Angels

Stuart Archer Cohen

❖

This
Is How
It Really
Sounds

❖

ST. MARTIN'S PRESS

New York

THIS IS HOW IT REALLY SOUNDS. Copyright © 2015 by Stuart Archer Cohen. All rights reserved. Printed in the United States of America. For information, address St. Martin's Press, 175 Fifth Avenue, New York, N.Y. 10010.

www.stmartins.com

Designed by Kathryn Parise

THE LIBRARY OF CONGRESS CATALOGING-IN-PUBLICATION DATA
IS AVAILABLE UPON REQUEST.

ISBN 978-1-250-04882-0 (hardcover)
ISBN 978-1-4668-4997-6 (e-book)

St. Martin's Press books may be purchased for educational, business, or promotional use. For information on bulk purchases, please contact the Macmillan Corporate and Premium Sales Department at 1-800-221-7945, extension 5442, or write to specialmarkets@macmillan.com.

First Edition: April 2015

10 9 8 7 6 5 4 3 2 1

For Suzy:

No one brings me closer to how it really sounds.

Acknowledgments

﹡

One great joy of this book is that it was usually hard to separate "doing research" from kicking back with really interesting people and talking about whatever.

In Beijing: Jane Zhao and Gary Song were always generous about opening any door they could, and there were many. Also Cecilia Han and Michael Pettus.

In Shanghai: thanks to Vivian Chow and Debbie Cheung. In Suzhou: Xu Xingfang, who has walked with me through an infinity of gardens.

In New York City: Rachel Templeton and Jamie Freundlich, Danny Kramer and Judy Mogul, Whitney Tilson, Jon Jacobs, and Jim Prussky, for their insights into the financial world. A big thanks also to Adam Shore for breaking down the music business for me.

In Los Angeles: Maybe I'm stupid for not seeing the deception and superficiality that I'm told Hollywood is rife with, but what I found was thoughtful, busy people willing to help someone who could offer them nothing. Thanks to Amy Zvi of Throughline, Howard Bragman of 15 Minutes, Eric Kopeloff, Steve Jensen, Vicki Hamilton, Rich Silverman, and Marc Cantor. A special thanks to my agent, Matthew Snyder, for his wisdom and his sardonic laugh. And to Jed Cohen and Paul Lance, who not only put me up when I'm in L.A. but put up with me, year after year.

In Juneau and Haines, Alaska: Elijah Lee, former Free Skiing Champion of Bulgaria (and North America). Dane Harlamert, my snowboarding guru. Lucas Merli, for proofreading the backcountry parts (and generally being awesome). To the Dawn Patrol—Dr. Powder, Aroma, and Fuzzy Bear (known after 8 A.M. as Peter Otsea, Andy Romanoff, and Ray Imel). Thanks also to Bruce Griggs and Herky Deppner, and SeanDog Brownell, of Alaska Heliskiing.

In New York: great gratitude is due to skiing supervillain and tireless agent Markus Hoffman, of Regal Literary, and to George Witte, of St. Martin's Press, for his steadfast support and his agile editing. Also Jill Haberkern and Josh Morsell, of the Mintz Group, Bill Newlin, Brett Dillingham, and Leigh Huffine.

A few people deserve extraspecial mention:

The late Sid Woodcock, whose extraordinary spirit slyly crept into this book and started pulling all the strings, as was his way.

Bob Martin, whose kindness, hospitality, intelligence, and amazing wee-hours tours of 1930s Shanghai shaped this book decisively.

David Perk, who with a single sentence made this book feel possible, when it had been feeling pretty damned impossible for a very long time.

The way that can be spoken of
is not the constant way;

The name that can be named
Is not the constant name.

—LAO-TZU

I

❖

Harry
Goes to
Hollywood

❖

In those days Harry didn't recognize that the price of admission to the life he wanted was surrendering his tickets to all the other lives he might have had.

He was, according to the few measures that existed at that time, the greatest extreme skier in the world. His first year on the circuit he won at Crested Butte and then won at Kirkwood with a separated shoulder. He took the King of the Hill prize in Valdez, Alaska, then went to Verbier for the European championship and beat the locals on their home mountain in a competition where one skier was paralyzed and another was killed. He was nineteen years old.

It was a sport that had no rules and no set course. A few dozen skiers climbed to the top of a steep mountain and hurled themselves down one at a time by whatever route they chose. They popped back flips off cliffs and made desperate cuts to avoid boulders. They raced along beside hissing avalanches. The judges scored them on their grace and creativity. For six years he won every single one of the tiny competitions in Europe and North America that defined the sport, not simply ranking highest, but awing the young men who competed against him, leaving them in despair that they would ever be that fluid, that brave, that beautiful.

He'd met Mitch skiing up at Tahoe. Mitch was a few years older and was obviously an outsider. He drove a two-seat Jaguar XKE with a tiny ski rack, wore a white puffy with a fox-fur ruff. He made music videos in Los Angeles. Some of the inner circle of ski bums joked behind his back about his brand-new, top-of-the-line gear, but Mitch loved to ski, and he could more or less keep up on the lines without cliffs in them. That made it possible for him to see up-close what Harry did, and it astounded him. At the end of the day, when they sat down for beers, he took Harry aside and said quietly, "Do you have representation?"

Harry looked at the smooth face, which even with its skier's stubble and matted hair still seemed astute and worldly in a way his other friends' didn't. "What do you mean?"

"An agent. Do you have an agent? Because I think you've got something that very few people have."

By then, Harry was twenty-five and a legend among the few thousand people in the world who knew what extreme skiing was. The prize money in competitions where people were frequently hurt and sometimes killed might be several hundred dollars and some free helicopter time. The best skiers had sponsors that kept them in gear and paid for their stays in cheap motels, but even the top dogs had to work in the summer, and he spent the warmer months working construction with his dad and fishing out of Bristol Bay.

Harry smiled slowly. The idea of an agent had never occurred to him. "What would I do with an agent?"

"You'd just be you. Your agent will do the rest." Now Mitch leaned in to him. "Don't get me wrong: I'm not an agent. This isn't about me. I don't want to sound weird, but what I saw today blew my mind. I make music videos, and I can say that what you do: it's music. You deserve to be rewarded. I mean, what do you make from skiing in a year, winning every competition: a few thousand dollars? A couple of new pairs of skis? Basketball stars get millions in endorsements, and what they do doesn't have one-hundredth of the risk and spectacle of what you do."

Harry wasn't sure what to say. "Well, a lot of people play basketball."

"It doesn't matter. You're the best in the world at a high-end sport. You shouldn't be sharing a room at a Super 8 Motel. You could be endorsing liquor, or luxury items like Swiss watches or cologne. It's just wrong that you do something so amazing and no one knows about it."

Harry hadn't thought about it much. All the skiers knew that the big names in the Olympics and the World Cup tour were making real money, but nobody had shown much interest in extreme skiers or even made specialized big-mountain skis that they could promote. Mitch went on, "Why don't you come down to L.A. with me this week and I'll introduce you to some people. You can stay at my house. Have you ever been to L.A.?"

He had already finished up a photo spread for *Ski* magazine and happened to have a few days before shooting a part in a low-budget ski movie. He asked Guy about it and his old friend liked the idea. "It's good," he said. "You'll bring honor to the hometown." So he left his skis and winter gear with Guy and tucked himself into Mitch's tiny Jaguar. By the time they'd made the long drive down out of the mountains, he'd stripped off his fleece to end up in a T-shirt in the spring heat of Los Angeles.

Mitch lived in Hollywood, which Harry hadn't realized was an actual physical place with houses and palm trees. He was used to mountain towns, with their inclined streets and scruffy inhabitants. This place was flat in every way a place could be flat. That was the weird thing about L.A.: on its surface it was the most nondescript set of strip malls and parking lots he'd ever seen, but, even so, you were always on the lookout for some kind of glamour, some movie star that was just out of reach.

Mitch started calling around that very night, and Harry listened in, intrigued by his new role as a commodity. *He's the best extreme skier in the world. In the world! He's a legend. Yeah. I've seen him: he's amazing. And he's from Alaska! He wrestles grizzly bears, man.* Silence. *Yeah, yeah, he's a good-looking guy. You could shine him up a little bit, but I don't know that you'd want to.* By the next morning, Mitch had set up appointments with two management companies, and soon had a roster of lunches, meetings, and cocktails that stretched over the next three days. The *Ski* piece hadn't hit the newsstands yet, but Harry had a prerelease copy with its glorious cover shot of him sailing into space. Mitch showed it at every meeting.

The people he was introduced to were friendly and relaxed, like it was just a social visit. They asked him about his sport, and they tried to compare him to downhill skiers whose names they'd seen, like Jean-Claude Killy or Billy Kidd. He ticked off the competitions he'd won, making sure to add the words "World" and "North American" and "European" to each of the titles, as Mitch had instructed him. He had a hard time explaining to them that these weren't races exactly, that he just went down mountains.

Mitch took over for him. "Four words," he said. "Incredibly beautiful. Extremely dangerous."

"Have you ever come close to dying?" one agent asked him.

He thought about it. "How close is close?"

"Close, like, you thought, 'I may not make it this time.' "

The time he'd been swept over a cliff band by his own slough. The time the slope had given way on his left, then he'd cut right and that whole piece had dissolved beneath his feet, and somehow he'd managed to dig his skis into the bed and watched a couple megatons of snow go roaring to the bottom below him. "No. I never think that. If you spend much time wondering if you're going to make it, you're probably not going to make it."

Mitch intervened. "Just describe some of the hairier situations you've been in."

"Oh." He mentioned a couple of things that had happened, telling them in a detail that would start to feel a little stale by the time he left Los Angeles. "But . . . I wasn't, you know, afraid. I was concentrating."

Mitch finished for him. "He races avalanches and he goes off fifty-foot cliffs and he makes it look beautiful. It's like ballet at seventy miles an hour. If you can capture that, you're going to have a best-of-class talent that blows people away. It's a hell of a lot more interesting than watching a guy go around a track in a Formula One car."

They watched the VHS tape that Mitch had put together from a couple of movies he'd been in. There were some runs from Chamonix, and a clip from Alaska where he'd dropped five thousand vertical feet in a minute and a half. He looked good in that one, disappearing into a cloud of his own slough and then reemerging just when it seemed like he was gone forever.

"Holy shit," the agent said. "You were inside an avalanche! What's that like?"

Harry felt like saying it wasn't a full-on avalanche, just some slough, but that would take too much explaining. "It's all white. You're pretty much blind, so you just go by feel and try to straight-line out of it."

The man seemed to have suddenly figured out where it all fit. "You know, I've got a client who's working on the screenplay of the next Bond movie. A sequence like that would be a great opening." He looked at Harry. "Think you could be James Bond's stunt double?"

Harry was too surprised to answer at first. "Not a problem." He grinned. "Do I get the girl?"

Mitch went over the products they could promote with his skiing, and how well the sport lent itself to television commercials, and the agent added a few ideas of his own, and then they left with a handshake and a smile. Like all the meetings, it always felt exciting and positive to Harry. It was only afterward that Mitch would comment on how it had really gone, that such and such person hadn't really been interested, but that another had implied that there was a chance for synergy with his other clients. "What he said about James Bond was good," Mitch strategized afterward. "His brother-in-law works for the producers that do the Bond movies, so he's not just blowing smoke." Harry didn't understand any of it, but he sensed that he was on the verge of breaking through to something big and unexpected, like when the wind shifts and a massive new mountain appears out of the clouds.

They went out to dinner every night. Mitch took him to one restaurant that was particularly hot. "Last week Mick Jagger came in with Jerry Hall and sat right over *there*." He had to take that on faith: he hadn't seen a star since he'd arrived in Hollywood, though he kept expecting to. Mitch picked up the tab, as he did at the bar they went to afterward, where they drank cocktails Harry had never heard of before. Mitch had a lot of friends there, and he always introduced Harry as "the best extreme skier in the world," and then he'd add: "In the *world*! He's from *Alaska*!" People were impressed, though none of them knew what extreme skiing was. They kept asking him if he'd won a medal in the Olympics. He'd gotten tired of explaining what he did, because his descriptions had started to sound shallow and phony. How do you explain about rock and snow and air and speed and having serious pain, or death, right at your elbow, and you don't even know exactly why you do it? He could talk about snow with another skier for hours: corn snow, blower pow, crust, graupel, mashed potatoes, boilerplate, surface hoar, wind pack, sastrugi—a patchwork of constantly changing surfaces all over the mountain, and every change affecting your speed, your ability to turn away from a cliff edge. The vocabulary of terrain was equally wide: there were roll-overs and wind lips, bowls and chutes, cliff bands, pillows, spines, gullies, kickers, rollers. Even avalanches were specific: slab avalanches and powder avalanches, sloughs and glide cracks, crowns and beds, ski cuts, runouts, and terrain traps. But there wasn't much to say to these people, all smooth, sophisticated people with good haircuts and jobs in the industry that enabled them to have long, intense discussions about points and back-end deals and syndication—stuff he didn't understand but that he figured was their version of talking about snow.

Mitch created the tiny bubble of Harry's glory in Los Angeles. He treated him like you'd treat the world's best at something, and years later, he still appreciated it. On the last night, when Harry joked he hadn't gotten to meet anyone famous, Mitch thought about it for a minute. "Okay." He made a call and they climbed back into his Jaguar. He wouldn't say where they were going, except that they were visiting a friend.

"Is this someone I've heard of?" Harry asked.

"Most definitely."

"Man or woman?"

"You'll see."

"But I'll recognize them."

"Oh, you'll recognize them. No question about it."

"Come on! I don't want to end up standing there with my mouth hanging open."

Mitch just smiled. "C'mon, man. You're the greatest extreme skier on the planet. What do you have to be shy about?" He pulled out a joint from under the dashboard and they smoked it as they rode down Sunset Boulevard, which was as L.A. as you could get, in Harry's mind. It was his last night there and a couple of the agents had already called back. The James Bond guy had asked for a bio and a copy of his video footage, which Mitch said was a *very* good thing. They passed several bars with people milling around under the brightly lit awnings of Whisky a Go Go and The Roxy.

"This is the Sunset Strip," Mitch said. "Heard of that?"

Harry thought, *I'm riding past the Sunset Strip*, and his own life was suddenly completely marvelous to him. They turned left and began squirming up a canyon, and in the harsh pink lights above the road Harry could see the dry, sparse landscape interrupted by the irrigated gardens of the houses. As they climbed, the road got twistier and the houses got farther apart, their long brick or iron fences clawing down over the steep terrain.

They reached the top of the canyon and Mitch pulled up to a metal gate and leaned out to an intercom next to his window. A woman's voice came out. It was a drunk-without-any-clothes-on voice. *"Hey, there!"*

"It's Mitch. Pete told me to come by."

"Hold on. *Pete?*"

There was a silence, then the gate swung open. Harry felt a very pleasant sense of expectancy: he was in L.A., it was night, he'd had a couple of beers, he was about to meet someone famous. Everything was lined up perfectly, as if he'd dropped into a hidden line of untouched powder, and all he had to do was lean in and enjoy it.

The door was opened by a girl with long dark-brown hair wearing cutoff blue jeans and no shirt. It was as if her nipples were staring at him, and he had to force himself to look up at her eyes. Much later, when he barely remembered her face, he'd still have a clear image of her pear-shaped breasts and how they'd hung. Her skin was moist and glistening and gave off a sense of sex as a very common, easy event. "I'm Holly!" she announced, and she gave his hand a comically exaggerated shake. He couldn't think of anything to say. Of course she was Holly: this was Holly-*wood,* a place named after a woman who came to the door dripping and half-naked. He wished all of a sudden that he and Mitch hadn't smoked so much weed a few minutes ago. "Everybody's in the hot tub."

They followed her through the living room, in which all sorts of musical instruments were scattered among a couple of big, overstuffed couches and a coffee table covered with abandoned beer bottles. An electric guitar leaned against the wall, and huge black stereo speakers sat in the corners, putting out a steady empty hiss. The place smelled like stale bong water and cigarette smoke. Shirts and pants were laid over the backs of chairs or in piles on the floor. A sliding glass door on the far side of the room was open. He squared up his shoulders as she led them through it. People considered him the best extreme skier in the world; that had to count for something.

The porch was lit with several hanging lamps, and off to the side, where it was darker, a cluster of people were sitting in a cedar hot tub. When he got closer a voice came from the group, an easygoing, uncaring voice. "Mitch, my man!"

Mitch leaned over the tub to shake hands, and Harry couldn't believe it was him at first: the long spirals of white-blond hair, the handsome, square jaw. He'd seen the face on posters and album covers and magazine stands. He'd seen him in music videos dancing across the stage or propped against his guitarist as they leaned into a harmony. It was Pete Harrington.

Everything felt instantly unreal, and he watched in amazement as the rock star and Mitch exchanged words that suddenly seemed hyper-real.

"Pete! How goes it? I saw the new video!"

"What'd you think?"

"That's it, man. It's Pete Harrington! Nothing else need be said!"

Harry knew, like everyone, that Pete Harrington had just come out with a solo album after leaving the DreamKrushers, and he'd heard the lead song all winter long on the radio in Denver, Salt Lake, Taos, and even Chamonix. "Wreckage." He couldn't believe Pete Harrington was sitting six feet away from him without any clothes on. Naked girls were sitting on either side of him, and though the bubbly water made it hard to tell, it seemed like one of the girls was reaching between the singer's legs. He stretched his hand toward Harry. "I'm Pete."

The others in the tub were all watching them, except for a couple that was making out. Harry touched the wet wrinkled fingers. He thought of telling him his whole name, but it would sound stupid. "I'm Harry," he said.

"Pete, this man is the best extreme skier *in the world*! He's from *Alaska*!"

"Cool," Harrington said. "What's an extreme skier?"

"Well . . ." Harry wanted to explain, but then he got stuck. The singer's reality seemed to far outstrip his own, and he stood there looking into that dream face, holding his hot damp hand and saying nothing at all. This was Pete Harrington!

The singer tried to help him out. "Were you in the Olympics?"

But he was just lost, buried under the weight of all the images of this man, and all the times he'd heard his voice, a voice that had been magnified across the globe at the cost of hundreds of millions of dollars by radio stations and satellites and television. He felt like his sense of self was being sucked, whirling, end over end, into the black hole of the other man's fame.

Mitch jumped in. "No, Pete. It's not a race. You climb up to the top of the biggest, scariest slope around and you go down one at a time, going over cliffs, doing flips and helicopters, and whoever does the best line in the best style wins."

The star was intrigued, nodded his head gently. Even in the tub, every curl on his head seemed perfectly placed. "Right on, man." His hand disappeared beneath the surface of the bubbly water and he turned to the girl. "Not now, honey. I'm trying to have a conversation." He looked back at Harry. "It sounds dangerous."

What could he say? *I cracked a vertebra dropping a sixty-foot cliff? A powder avalanche can move at a hundred-twenty miles an hour?* He cleared his throat. "Can be."

Pete Harrington was still looking up at him, waiting for more, but Harry couldn't think of anything to say that wouldn't be like boasting. In the face of the singer's deafening reputation, his own life had been reduced to silence.

"He's the best in the world," Mitch was saying. "He's won every event he's competed in for the last five years. It's not even close. And you should see his movies."

"Cool," the singer said. "What's it like? Describe it for me."

"Well," he said, shifting from one foot to the other as he looked down at the ground next to him, then looked back into that perfect television face. He was acutely aware that everyone in the hot tub was listening to him. "For instance, the last competition was at Mammoth." He told them about the run he'd made, from the tight near-vertical chute at the top to his forty-foot jump from one narrow spine down to another, where a mistake would mean landing in a jumble of boulders at sixty miles an hour. He described how he'd been surprised by the crustiness of the snow on the lower spine, and how he'd had to fight to keep from sliding over the edge, then he'd clipped his ski on a rock, and he'd briefly been on one leg before he got control again, and somehow got down the spine and onto the easier part of the run. "So"—he cleared his throat again. They were all looking at him. "It's kind of like that."

Harrington broke the silence. "I'd be shitting bricks."

"Well, we're even then, because I'd be shitting bricks if I had to stand up in front of twenty thousand people and sing."

"No, man, you'd be laughing your ass off. It's a trip! You should come backstage sometime and check it out. You know, I'm a skier, too."

"You are?"

"Yeah, I'm from Seattle. When I was a kid, I was up at Crystal Mountain every weekend. When I got a car I started hitting Mount Baker."

"Baker! You've gotta be a tree skier."

"I'm known to ski the occasional tree run."

They talked about Alaska. Harrington's band had toured Anchorage and Fairbanks before they'd been signed, and they put it together and realized they'd both been in Chilkoot Charlie's in Anchorage on the exact same night in 1988.

"Yeah, I really like Alaska. I want to have igloo sex, man. That's one of my dreams." One of the girls beside him laughed. "No, really, think about it: You're in that igloo inside a pile of furs. It's fifty below outside and the wind's howling. There's just the light from an oil lamp, and you're with some babe. That's like . . . *yeah!*"

"Sounds like a song!" someone said.

Harrington wrinkled his eyebrows in concentration, singing, "*Ice Queen! Unfreeze my dick. Ice Queen! Come bury my pick!* You ever have igloo sex, Harry? Tell me the truth."

"No. We're a thousand miles south of where they make igloos. We have mountains and glaciers and big trees."

"Cool," the rocker said. "Hollow-tree sex. That's hobbit shit! Yeah!" The people in the tub laughed and the singer looked around at them. It was turning back into the Pete Harrington show. He looked up at Harry. "We should go skiing sometime, Harry. Do you ever ski Tahoe?"

"I ski Squaw Valley quite a bit. I have to be there this week for a photo shoot."

"I've been wanting to get up there. Why don't we meet up and do some runs? You can be my guide. Take me down some of the lines you do. I'll hire a helicopter. Okay?"

Harry looked at him, not completely believing what he'd just heard. "You want to do my lines?"

Mitch broke in. "Pete, trust me: you don't want to do his lines."

"Come on, man! Fucking jumping out of a helicopter, Nam style, and ripping down some big-ass mountain—I could totally get into that!"

Harry thought of some of the recent heli-runs he'd done for movies. They would be difficult even for an expert skier. For a weekend skier, who knew nothing about moving snow and slope stability, they could be fatal. He could start him off slow, he supposed. Do some in-bounds runs with him to gauge his ability, then take him on some easy lines in the helicopter. It would be a kick in the ass. Skiing with Pete Harrington!

"Okay. Let's do it!"

"Mitch? You in?"

The producer shook his head wistfully. "I'm shooting something for Aerosmith on Friday. I can't."

"So it's you and me, Harry." Pete turned to the girls. "Either of you two want to go?" "I'll go," one girl said, and Holly echoed, "I'll go." She looked up at Harry and then smiled at her friend. "He's kind of cute. Skier guy!"

And instantly, he was swept into that imaginary world. There would be Pete and Holly and her friend, the four of them, and that math was easy to do. They'd ski all day, and at night they'd sit in the hot tub and smoke a couple joints and, well, nothing at all wrong with Holly.

They were interrupted at that moment by the arrival of someone new: a short woman in a black evening dress with her brown hair piled up in some sort of formal style. She was all of about five feet tall, and she didn't look happy.

"Pete!"

"Hey, Beth. How was the, uh, *event?*"

The woman glared down at the two girls beside him in the tub as she answered. "The event went well." She looked directly at Holly. "And you are . . . ?"

"I'm Holly!" she said cheerfully.

"And you're CeeCee," she said to the other in a menacing voice. "I already know you."

Harry felt uncomfortable, but Mitch waded straight in.

"Beth!" he said, putting his hand on her shoulder. "I want you to meet a friend of mine. He's the top extreme skier in the world. His name's Harry."

With great effort she pulled a glittering smile to the surface and said, with an East Coast accent, "It's a pleasure to meet you, Harry. I'm Beth Blackman, Pete's wife."

Before, it had been stardom that had taken Harry's voice away. Now it was embarrassment. "Nice to meet you."

She turned back to her husband. "Could we talk for a minute? Privately?"

Harry looked away as Pete got out of the tub and grabbed a towel. As he disappeared into the other room, the singer looked back at Harry and said, "You and me, Squaw, Wednesday: it's on! Mitch'll give you the details."

"I'll be there," Harry said.

"I'll be there, too," Holly said from down below them.

After that the shouting started, and he and Mitch eased out the front door.

. . .

Back at Squaw Valley, he was quietly elated, but he didn't mention it to anyone except Guy. The plan was to finish the movie shoot early Wednesday morning, then rendezvous with Pete Harrington and the girls at noon at the lodge. He'd tentatively arranged for a helicopter on the following day, Thursday. Harry rounded up an extra avalanche beacon and arranged for Guy to join them, because, let's face it, if he got buried, he didn't want to be under there waiting for Pete Harrington to dig him out. Guy, on the other hand—he'd been trusting his life to Guy since they were ten years old. It was an insanely good prospect: ski with a rock star, party with him at night. Mitch said it was a good thing for his career, too: word would get around that Pete Harrington skied with him, and that would give him some extra buzz. He'd call some paparazzi to try to get some shots of them for the tabloids.

He was busy Monday and Tuesday with the movie: shots of him on things that were steep and dangerous, or throwing front flips off cliffs, upside down in the deep-blue Tahoe sky. They got another six inches Tuesday night, and Wednesday morning came up bluebird. They got out early to take advantage of the light. The movie people had dug out their credit cards and hired a chopper to get him over to another peak, and they had a one-hour window to get the sun exactly where the photographer wanted it. An hour for the setup, one run, and then he'd head back to the lodge to find Pete and the girls. It went faster than they thought, but they'd already booked the helicopter time and the photographer had one more idea, so Harry said he'd do one more line if they hurried. The cameraman pointed out the run and then took his post. It was only eleven: they could shoot it in ten minutes and be back to the lodge, no sweat. To his surprise, it didn't play out that way. By noon Guy was dead beneath a hundred tons of snow and he was lying in the hospital under heavy sedation. A week later *Ski* magazine came out with a cover photo of him soaring endlessly through the sky and the caption: "The Greatest Extreme Skier on the Planet."

He never saw Pete Harrington again. Mitch advised him to lay low until his leg healed; clumping around Los Angeles in a cast didn't project the kind of image they were trying to promote. But the heat went away. Mitch

tore his ACL and had to take the next winter off, and that was also the season Harry started to lose competitions. Not lose them, like doing badly,
because even at less than his best, he was better than almost anyone. But he
wasn't winning them. He got a greeting card from the James Bond agent
the next Christmas, but when he called the agent he never heard back, so he
let it drop. That was it. When spring came he made his annual move up to
Alaska, but when the snow fell again he didn't go back Outside. He was
done. He didn't even talk about it. The memory of that last run and Guy's
death floated in and out of his mind along with Harrington's album-cover
gaze like the saddest, slowest song anybody had ever written. And for the
next twenty years, he never stopped hearing it.

II

❖

Fugitive
in
Shanghai

❖

1

Fugitive in Shanghai

✥

The ironic thing for Peter Harrington was that for an entire decade of his life people teased him about his not being the other Pete Harrington. He was the Pete Harrington who worked at a bank, not the rock star, and he'd heard every witticism that could possibly be crafted around the idea. How dare he cheat on America's sweetheart! Was the baby in that paternity suit really his? It was a joke because, obviously, he wasn't the famous one, he was the pale balding one, the Wall Street underling, the nobody working seventy hours a week in a Brooks Brothers suit. That was kind of funny all by itself, right? Then one day he wrote himself a check for three hundred million dollars and cashed it, and the jokes stopped. He had his own big life now.

"We arrive at the Bund," Camille said in Chinese, and he repeated her words, struggling with the tones. The whole of Shanghai's night was wrapped around the gleaming black body of his car. The driver opened the door for him and he stood for a moment and eyed the street as one of the young women on the sidewalk took a few hesitant steps toward him. Then Camille emerged, her smooth thighs tight with the flesh-colored sheen of stockings. Her arms were small, almost girl-like, and her shoulders and waist were fine-boned and delicate. A distant and acquisitive part of him recognized

that she was something worth possessing, at least for a while. She stood on the sidewalk and brushed her white linen dress flat as the woman backed away.

Camille said a word in Chinese under her breath, and Peter Harrington repeated it. "*Prostitute,*" Camille explained sweetly.

He'd never been out with Camille before, and technically, they weren't really "out." She was his tutor, a setup from Mr. Lau, the Hong Kong financier he and Kell had been working with. Lau had described her only as a good English speaker and "very intelligent," and Harrington had been reluctant until the moment, a month ago, when she'd shown up at his door with a grammar book. Mr. Lau was a subtle man. Camille had a wide, smooth face, with pale, clear skin and long glossy hair. He guessed her age as late twenties, but it was hard to tell with Chinese women. Her smile was occasional, ironic, detached. She spoke with the vague condescension of someone who knew that her people had been weaving silk when his own ancestors were still wearing animal skins. He liked that about her.

Camille's role in the evening was, allegedly, to help him practice his restaurant skills, and he'd made it clear that she would be on the clock the entire evening. He'd taken her to Franck, a bistro in the old French Concession, where the Chinese waiter spoke English with a perfect French accent, right down to the mocking Gallic attitude. They sat in the low-ceilinged dark restaurant and Camille kept puncturing their conversation with little grammar hints and vocabulary: *butter, bread, glass, water, cigarette.* He dutifully repeated each of them. He knew she was from Suzhou and that she had other corporate clients, but she always deflected the conversation back to him or to things about China in general, so she remained as opaque as so much else in Shanghai. He was curious to see what Kell would make of her.

The Bund was a strip of grandiose European presumption stretching for a half mile along the Huangpu River. Garnished with columns and cupolas, the old Customs House and banks dated from the days when Shanghai had been divided among the Japanese, the French, the British, and the Americans, a beachhead for foreign business and intrigue. That Shanghai fascinated Harrington. It was Victor Sassoon's Shanghai: the real-estate tycoon had built nearly all the signature buildings of the era. His dark art-deco skyscrapers still gathered a sense of strange gothic foreboding about them. Now the Bund had emerged again as a sparkling necklace of international wealth, which was being funneled through the booming city. The most prestigious of the global jewelry and designer names were here, along with nosebleed-expensive international restaurants and bars. It was so new-century and yet so 1930s that whenever Peter Harrington pulled up to the curb he felt he should be getting out of a huge black Packard instead of a Benz.

They moved across the wide sidewalk to the door of what had once been the Chartered Bank, now a minimall selling diamonds and Ferraris, silk scarves and Swiss watches. They moved past the doorman and waited for the elevator. A young Chinese woman came hurrying past them and began climbing the six flights of stairs to the roof, probably a bar girl who'd snuck in the back way. Camille didn't even look at her.

"Have you been here before?" Harrington asked as they stepped into the little cubicle.

"Of course," she said. Then she said something in Chinese as the girl disappeared up the stairwell.

He repeated it after her, then translated, tentatively, " 'The prostitute goes to the Bar Rouge'?"

"Very good!" Camille said.

He laughed at her. "You are so wicked!"

That elicited a smile from her.

A wall of techno music tumbled over them as the doors opened into the bar's scarlet-lit interior. Harrington thought it was less music than a relentless procession of electronic tones and drum rhythms calculated to produce subliminal discomfort and desolation, but that was the Bar Rouge. "Rouge" like on the face of a 1930s prostitute, the financier thought, but maybe he'd just done too much vocabulary. The walls were mirrored and the darkness was alleviated only by washes of red from the hidden recesses of the ceiling. A dance floor made of frosted glass glowed in the middle of the room, empty, while crow-like men and women gathered around low black tables along the perimeter.

"They're probably outside," Harrington said, touching Camille on the back of her arm to guide her.

As they moved into the room, Harrington brushed against a group of Russians drinking a toast, stepped between a trio of Italian businessmen chatting up two Chinese girls. The men eyed Camille as she passed, looked questioningly at him. *That's right. And she's not a hooker.*

They stepped through the sliding glass door out onto the roof, and the dull buzz of the city replaced the music. The warm air had lost its summer moisture and felt exciting against his skin. The view was stunning: the eighty-story obelisks of Pudong were washed with intense neon tones of green, fuschia, violet—all of it glistening on the silvery back of the Huangpu River. A world-class view by any standards, looking down on a world-class crowd. The feeling came over him again, as it always did, that he was standing in old Shanghai, with its spies and opportunists and global riffraff. There were Japanese executives in sport coats and ties, a couple of dark-skinned Africans, and some men who might be Indian or Pakistani. French tourists, Israeli backpackers, flight crews, trust-fund babies, Communist elites in designer clothes. Sprinkled in: the Chinese bar girls with their fake Prada handbags and Hermès scarves. So old Shanghai. "Whenever I come in here I feel like I'm stepping back to 1935," he murmured to Camille. "It's so sordid and elegant at the same time."

She smiled at him, and he couldn't tell if she was agreeing or if she thought he was silly. He shouldn't have waxed quite so poetic. Maybe he'd overplayed it. "Let's find my friends," he said, and they pushed further into the crowd.

The Bar Rouge was a slightly dangerous place for him to be seen with Camille. A lot of Nadia's friends came here: models from Eastern Europe trying to work their way up to New York or Paris. If a friend of Nadia's spotted them he would have a hard time explaining Camille away as his tutor. Although, to be honest, he was tiring of Nadia. Beneath her beauty she was a girl from a small town in the Czech Republic with a high school education, and her three years of modeling hadn't left her particularly wise in any field other than names on clothing. In her best photos she was exquisitely, impossibly beautiful, and it was that image he was trying to possess, the impossible one. In real life, without makeup and stylists, she was a pretty girl of twenty-three with a taste for brand names and the good sense to stay quiet and let her beauty speak for her.

He spotted Kell across the roof and started toward him. Kell was shorter than most of the people around him, but his wide body radiated a muscular density. With his thick auburn hair and combative South Philly accent, Harrington saw him as the kind of Celtic horse trader that two thousand years ago would have sold the Romans horses during the day and stolen them back at night. He was talking with a dark-haired man Peter didn't know and a couple of Chinese girls that Kell had probably picked up. Kell had a taste for the bar girls that wallpapered the Bar Rouge and the M1nt Shanghai and the Yongfoo Elite Club. They were always here, though they could have been excluded easily enough. They had varying degrees of institute English, except for a few university girls who spoke well and could just about put over the idea that they had real careers. They weren't all prostitutes, exactly. Some were simply girls trying to cobble together a relationship with a rich foreigner from which would spring money, gifts, meals in expensive restaurants, and, the jackpot, a marriage proposal and a permanent round-trip ticket to the rest of the world. Kell always said that if you called them prostitutes, he could make a very good case for calling a lot of the women he'd known back in New York prostitutes also. "The bottom line," Kell said, "is that we all make the best deal we can with what we've got. Money makes me more interesting. A pretty face and hot body make a woman alluring and mysterious. If you put Nadia in an ugly body, would you give her a second thought? Don't answer, because I don't want to hear you lie to me." That was one thing about Kell: you didn't like what he said, but it was hard to prove him wrong.

Now Kell was motioning to him, and to Harrington's surprise the unknown man waved to him as if they knew each other. Harrington was still drawing a blank on him, smiling daftly as he got closer, and then finally, just as they shook hands, the face snapped into place with a surprise that made him rear back a few inches.

"Paul Gutterman! Is that really Paul Gutterman?"

The newcomer beamed at him. "Peter Harrington! The rock star! Kell told me he had a surprise for me, but I didn't expect him to pull you out of his hat!"

"Kell's got a big hat. What the hell are you doing in Shanghai?"

His eyes flickered slightly to the side. "Just seeing the sights, Peter! Everybody talks about Shanghai, and I had to see for myself." He noticed Camille and turned to her. "I'm sorry. I'm Paul Gutterman. Peter and I started at Goldman Sachs together, back before he was notorious."

He hadn't seen Gutterman in at least ten years. He was stuck in his memory as a slim young man with pale skin and dark wavy hair. Slightly nervous, slightly intense in his manner. They had indeed started at Goldman at the same time, but Gutterman had always been just a step or two behind him their entire six years together: his accounts a bit smaller, his access to the bosses less fluid. He didn't live in the city, like the other young fellows out to conquer the world, but instead commuted in from Long Island, always eager to get back to his heavyset young wife. Gutterman was the specter of the going-nowhere career that inspired Harrington to work extra late and extra hard. Now his old rival had gained weight, no longer the reedy man with the boyish face of fifteen years ago. "So what's going on, Paul? How's . . ." He miraculously pulled down the name of Gutterman's wife. "Diane?"

Gutterman's pallid features lost their shine. "We're separated now, actually." An uneasiness took hold of him. "You know"—he shrugged—"things happen. People change . . ." He recovered. "What about Sheila? Is she here in Shanghai?"

"No, that's over."

"Yeah," Gutterman said. "I guess I read about that." His next words were almost smug: "You had a kid, didn't you? A little boy?"

A sharp and familiar sense of dread swept through Harrington's body. He could feel Camille looking at him. "Conrad. He's thirteen now. They're living upstate." He shuddered. "So what brings you to wicked, wicked Shanghai?"

"Well . . ." A weakness undermined Gutterman's voice. "This is supposed to be where the action is, right?"

"Did Goldman send you over? I mean, are you still with them?" Harrington could see Kell behind Gutterman's back, drawing his finger across his neck in the "Cut!" sign.

"Not exactly." Again, Gutterman's eyes flicked to the side. "I'll tell you later. What are *you* doing here?"

Harrington let it go. "Me? Not much. Kell's got a couple of schemes going, and I help out a little bit on that."

"Your last scheme got you number three on *New York* magazine's list of 'Ten Most Deserving of Indictment.' "

Harrington fielded it perfectly. "You mean I've slipped to number three?"

"Hey!" Kell defended him loudly. "Peter here just helped some boys with very pricey educations find out exactly how smart they really were. They should be thanking him."

Camille had moved closer into the group. "Tell me about this."

"It's complicated," Kell said.

"I understand complicated things," she answered calmly.

"It's so complicated," the lawyer lied, "that even I don't understand it, and I'm his partner."

"Let's just say Peter and Kell had a few unhappy counterparties when they closed down their last venture," Gutterman explained.

"Hey. Hey!" Kell raised his arms. "Everything I did was completely legal at the time I did it."

Camille smiled. "I can see you are a man of great virtue!"

"And I can see you're an excellent judge of that."

He tilted his empty glass to his mouth, and his eyes watched hers above the rim.

"Thank you, Kell." Harrington turned to Camille. "I'll explain it later, if you're interested, but it's a fairly boring story. I'll get us some drinks. Kell, you're having water, right?"

"Yeah, with a side of scotch."

He took their orders and wove through the crowd to the bar at the roof's center. This had been a mistake. Kell could be the earthiest, most magnetic man you'd ever met, but tonight they'd gotten the other Kell, the foulmouthed

Irish drunk from South Philly. Gutterman threw him, too. There was something furtive and broken about him, and having him bring up the *New York* magazine story didn't feel accidental. He'd buy the drinks and get Camille out of here in fifteen minutes.

"Helluva scene, isn't it?"

The American voice came from behind him, and even without seeing its owner, he could tell it belonged to a different time. He turned to find himself staring slightly upward into the visage of a very old man. It was a face that didn't fit in at the Bar Rouge, a square, aged face made large by its receding line of snow-white hair and eyes slightly yellowed by a vast number of years. He had to be at least in his late seventies, dressed in an old-fashioned-looking tweed sport coat and a tie held down by a clip with some sort of regimental insignia on it. What was he doing here? Harrington had lost his father a year before, and the stranger brought on a pang of nostalgia. "Yes, it *is* a hell of a scene. Is this your first time in Shanghai?"

The old man smiled. "Not exactly."

"Oh? When were you here before?"

The old man smiled. "Well, to give you an indication, the last time I stood on this roof it was the Chartered Bank."

Harrington looked at him. "You mean, like . . . sixty years ago?"

"Sixty-four. I was here off and on from forty-six to forty-nine. I left a few weeks before Liberation."

The financier cocked his head. "No!"

"I wouldn't lie to you."

Harrington laughed. "That's amazing!" The old man seemed to be alone, and the line to get drinks was a long one. It wouldn't hurt to chat him up. "Let me buy you a drink and you can tell me what you were doing here sixty-four years ago."

The man had been in Shanghai on some other business after the war and what was then called the Chartered Bank had hired him to keep an eye on their staff. "They were having some irregularities, so they put me on as a teller. We had a little table and chairs set up on the roof, and we'd come up and have some drinks after closing time. Of course, the view was a little different then"—he motioned toward the giant picket of rainbow-lit skyscrapers across the river from them—"but it was nice."

"Did you find the thief?"

"Oh yeah. It was a Chinese teller, but it turned out he was put up to it by one of the British vice presidents. He was keeping a girlfriend in high style at the Grosvenor. They put the Chinese guy in jail and sent the British guy back to England. Never prosecuted him." He grinned. "Funny how that works."

Harrington imagined the bank as it had been back then, with brass-barred teller windows and secretaries behind big black typewriters. The old man had traveled through that most distant and exotic land, the Past, a place he could never visit no matter how much money he had. "What was Shanghai like in 1946?"

"Hard," he answered. "Real hard. Communists fighting the Nationalists. Everybody scrambling to pick up as many pieces as they could before things settled down, or fell apart. Whatever you wanted, you could get it: opium, women, a passport, a brand-new Packard. You could hire a killer for ten bucks." He added cheerfully, "A hundred bucks for a really good one." He tapped Harrington's sleeve and nodded toward the bartender. "You're up."

Harrington ordered drinks for his group and a Manhattan for the old man, then turned back to him. "So . . . I'm sorry, what's your name?"

"Ernie."

"I'm Peter. Ernie, what brings you to Shanghai again?"

"The Chinese government's getting together a bunch of World War Two vets next week in Beijing, and they want to give me a plaque or something. Last hurrah, I guess."

"Are you here alone? Didn't they assign someone to look after you?"

"Yeah, but he's not much help. He just wanted to park me at the hotel. I thought I'd come up here and see what's new."

"And what's new?"

The elderly tourist raised his eyebrows. "Everything!" Then he smiled. "Nothing."

Harrington was beginning to hope the drinks wouldn't be ready too quickly. Ernie had been in the War, that last righteous war that was really worth fighting, so that six decades later its few survivors were sainted by an aura of heroism and sacrifice. Ernie told him he had trained for winter warfare with the Tenth Mountain Division. "Then, once I got really good at skiing and climbing, they sent me to the jungle in western China. Go figure that one."

The old man answered Harrington's questions about the war as if he was describing a package tour of Europe and Asia. He'd worked around Kunming for a time, training Dai tribesmen to kill Japanese, then raided with Merrill's Marauders in Burma. He'd done a stint in Indochina before they transferred him back to Yan'an to help the Chinese irregulars harass the Japanese rearguard. He'd had lunch with Mao Zedong. Twice.

Ernie went on, "After the war, things were all mixed up here. We were backing the Nationalists, but we wanted to maintain some ties with the Communists in case they won. Discreetly, you know. I had a lot of relationships with the Communists from my days in Yan'an, so Uncle Sam sent me to keep an eye on things."

"For the CIA?"

"This was before the CIA. It was just a bunch of OSS guys who were kept on in a group called External Security Detachment Forty-four. The CIA picked us up when it was chartered in forty-seven."

Harrington examined the old man carefully. The OSS had been the agency of commandos and counterspies during World War II, parachuting behind enemy lines, assassinating Nazi officials, training partisans. He realized that he was standing in the presence of a rare and precious object, rarer than a thirty-thousand-dollar watch or a limited-edition luxury car. He had met plenty of artists and models and billionaires and bankers. But he hadn't met any spies. He hadn't met any living legends—that is, real legends, and not just men who were "legendary" on the Street because they'd made a lot of money or ruthlessly built a company. He'd met his share of those, and they were depressingly like him. He glanced over at his group. Kell was gesticulating with great animation to Gutterman and their two Chinese dates, while Camille was looking slightly bored with all of them, gazing out at the synthetic aurora glistening off the twisting tin sheet of the river. The whole scene on the rooftop felt suddenly cheap and empty. He heard the old man's voice behind him.

"So what do you do, Peter?"

He usually enjoyed answering this question, or, more usually, half-answering it, as if he was too modest to claim his identity as the notorious Peter Harrington. Now, the query seemed almost like an accusation. "Oh, it's actually rather stupid. I had some good luck in the bond markets." He shrugged. "It's not like winning World War Two."

The bartender turned to them, the last cocktail in his hand. He put them all on a tray, and Harrington dug out eight hundred yuan to cover them, waving off the change. He thought of inviting Ernie over to meet his friends, but as he imagined Kell's drunken prognostications, or Gutterman's edgy laugh, he couldn't bear to do it. At the same time, he didn't want to let the man go. He slid the Manhattan over to the elderly spy. "How long are you in Shanghai, Ernie?"

He wasn't sure, he said. He was supposed to be in Beijing next week. If he felt up to it, he might fly out to Kunming. He had an old friend there . . . Tomorrow, he thought he might kick around the Bund, take a look at some of the old places, see what was left. He'd like to hire a driver who spoke English. How did one go about doing that here?

"One doesn't," Harrington said. "One uses my driver, who not only speaks English but is a native-born Shanghainese."

It took Ernie a moment to understand. "Peter, I didn't want—"

"No! Absolutely. You're taking my car. In fact, why don't we do this: I have to get back to my date right now, but why don't you let me take you to lunch tomorrow? I'll pick you up at your hotel and we can have lunch at the Peace Hotel. That was the Cathay back then—"

"The *Cathay,*" Ernie repeated. There was something about the way he said it. "I know the Cathay well."

"You'll have to tell me about it over lunch. We can take a walk along the Bund, eat lunch, and then you can have my driver for as long as you want. How would twelve noon be?"

Ernie started to protest one more time, then just smiled modestly. "That'd be swell!" They exchanged contact information, and Harrington threaded his way through the crowd to his group. When he turned back to look, Ernie had moved to the edge of the roof and was staring out at the view, alone.

Kell had already gulped down most of a whiskey he'd cadged off a waitress and had wrapped his arm possessively around his date. "You took long enough!" he said. "What's the story with Grandpa over there? Did he lose his tour group?"

"Grandpa is a very interesting man. He was telling me about Shanghai right after the war." He suddenly became possessive of the old man and didn't want to say more. "But that's another story. What did I miss?"

"Paul was telling us about your Pete Harrington obsession. Buddy, I had no idea."

The financier glanced over at Gutterman, trying to hide his irritation. "I was never obsessed."

"With whom?" Camille asked.

"The rock star, Pete Harrington," Gutterman said. "Peter was completely obsessed."

"I was not obsessed!"

"Come on!" Gutterman turned to the others. "I shared an office with him. He had all his albums and he went to see him two consecutive nights when he played New York. I'd call that a minor obsession."

Harrington choked down his irritation and smiled. "What's your point here, Paul?"

"Nothing, really. I just thought it was kind of funny."

In truth, Pete Harrington had loomed large for a while. They shared a name and were roughly the same age, but Harrington had become world-famous for making shallow, irresistible music and pinballing through a succession of starlets, strippers, and lawsuits whose reportage always included a picture of him grinning, even when being led to jail. Whatever happened, he *just didn't seem to give a damn!* And people loved him for it.

To this he had compared his own life. Measured and measuring. Risk-averse. Calculating. By all appearances a midlevel banker with a perfectly orderly life. But to himself, inside, he was the other Pete Harrington. He just needed a way to prove it to the world.

"Peter," Camille interjected, "it's so nice to meet your friends, but I actually have to go. I promised a friend that I would come to her party."

All the electricity seemed to depart from the roof. He'd meant to get her away from Kell and Gutterman, but he realized now that to her eyes he was just like them. Fair enough. She'd mentioned something about a party when he'd asked her out, and he couldn't blame her for using her escape hatch. He tried not to sigh. "I understand. I'll walk you downstairs."

They pushed through the crowd to the elevator, and as they got in she said, in Chinese, *"elevator,"* and he repeated it: *elevator.* She gave an embarrassed little smile and said *"down,"* and he mimicked her: *down.* When he stepped out of the building, several women moved hesitantly closer to him, then backed off when she emerged. *"More prostitutes,"* she said. *Prostitutes,* he echoed, numbly. *Pointless,* he thought. *It's all so pointless.* The whole farce of learning Chinese, of trying to be at home in Shanghai, when the only point in being here was to not be someplace else.

He looked at his watch, hiding behind his business persona. "It's eight thirty now, and we started at six, so that's two and a half hours I owe you."

She leveled a look at him. "Don't be silly. I won't accept any money for the night. We are friends. Besides, you can come with me. Unless you want to stay with your companions."

"Oh!" He felt his chest swell. "I'll call my driver."

"No," she said. "We will go by taxi."

"Why?" He was already taking out his cell phone. "I'm sure he's close."

"Because he's your driver. Your car. Your life. It's too easy for you. This way it's *our* night." She said it in Chinese, and he repeated it: *our night.*

A cab was already idling at the curb, and they climbed in. Camille said something to the driver and he grunted and they rolled out onto the Zhong-shan Lu, past the opulent lights of the Bund. Peter glanced at Camille's profile. Everything he wanted was contained in this motion and the opacity of

the evening in front of them. Life was a song about a beautiful woman in a
cab in Shanghai on the way to a party. What else did he need to know?

He had a subtle sense of things changing, accelerating. Camille produced
a tiny silver flask from her purse and offered it to him, a move that was un-
typical for Chinese women, but somehow very elegant. Flappers, the 1920s.
Shanghai, 1947. He took a drink. It was *bai-jiu*: Chinese white lightning. It
burned down his gullet, then burned back up again, like a mushroom cloud
in his chest. He gave it back to her and watched her put the bottle to her
lips. They were on an adventure together.

"Your friends are really crazy," she said.

"They are crazy. I think Kell just has too much money. If that's possible.
I don't know what the story is with Paul. I always thought of him as sort of
a loser. I haven't seen him for years, and then he pops up here, in the middle
of a divorce. Something's up."

"Goldman is being investigated." She saw his surprise. "I have a friend
here who works in their Shanghai office. Everyone knows about it."

Harrington laughed. "Let me tell you how this plays out: they 'investigate' it, the government issues some press releases and makes some speeches,
then Goldman agrees to pay a fine with no admission of wrongdoing. A
couple of guys get fired; everybody else gets promoted."

She pulled out her phone. "Should we check your friend's name and see
if he is one of those to get fired?"

"I'm enjoying the evening too much to do that."

"He envies you. It is clear. He is in trouble, and *you* are famous."

"I'm not famous."

"Yes, you are. I searched your name on the Internet. Crossroads Partners."

So she knew about Crossroads. That always happened sooner or later.
"Well, I'm flattered that you searched me on the Internet."

"Some people are very angry at you."

"Let them be angry. Everyone knew the risks and everyone played the
game. I didn't do anything illegal. Does it change your opinion of me?"

She looked at him across the width of the backseat. "No," she said breez-
ily. "Just don't ask me to invest any money with you."

He shook his head at her. "You are something!"

"Yes, people tell me I am too honest. Were you really obsessed with Pete Harrington?"

He tried to minimize it. "I liked his music. I actually met him once, believe it or not."

"Really?"

"Really." The awkwardness of that brush with fame felt quaint now that he was famous in his own right. "It was probably about 1996, and I was at a club called CBGB in New York and he came in. He was sitting at a table with some friends, and I couldn't resist going up to him and saying hello. I think I said something stupid like, 'I really like your music!'"

"What did he say?"

"He said, 'Thanks, man!'"

"That's all?"

"That's all. And I just stood there. I'd just gotten the news that I'd made vice president, and I'd had a few drinks, so I was feeling pretty pumped, kind of like, *hey, we're all rock stars here.*"

The idea amused Camille and he could see her smiling in the car's shadowy light. "Tell me more. Who was he sitting with?"

"I don't know. A couple of girls, a guy in a suit. Duffy, who was the lead guitar player in his band. And I'm standing there, I've already blown my big, brilliant line, which was, *I really like your music!* I mean, seriously, that was my best line! And suddenly everything was just sucked out of me. Like he had all the gravity and I was just the satellite, orbiting around him. And I felt like if I walked away, I'd go spinning out into the nothingness of my own little life. So I just stood there, as if he was going to invite me to sit down and have a drink with him. In English they call that being starstruck."

Her mouth opened into a silent laugh and she covered her teeth with her hand. "I'm sorry." She reached over and touched his sleeve. "What did he do?"

"You know, I gotta give him credit: he was incredibly gracious. He'd probably had this experience hundreds of times. After this incredibly long—no, not long: *timeless* pause, which to other people was probably ten seconds, he turned back to me and said, 'Hey, man, what's your name?' and I told him, and of course since we have the same name he probably thought I was completely *crazy,* but then he said, 'Listen, Peter, we're kind of in the middle of something, so I can't hang out with you right now. But I'm glad you came over to say hi.' Then he shook my hand, and I could walk away and not feel like a complete zero. He was actually very decent."

"Maybe I would be the same way as you. He's very famous here, you know."

"I've noticed that. Why?"

"He was one of the first foreign bands to come over for a tour after the Tiananmen incident. At his show in Shanghai, he said, 'This is for the heroes of Tiananmen,' in Chinese, and in a few minutes they had closed his show and canceled all his concerts. Now he is known for that."

The former banker remembered hearing about that. Nobody knew why he'd shouted it or who had put him up to it—he sang about getting drunk and getting laid, not politics—but ever since then he defined to some degree what a real rock star was for the Chinese. His rock star face had worked its way into their art like a Warhol image: the intersection of the superficial and the desperately important. At least, that's how one of the gallery owners at Moganshan 50 had put it.

But he was tired of Pete Harrington. "Tell me about yourself. You've been tutoring me for two months and I still know almost nothing about you."

"My life is so boring!" Camille said. "I grew up in Suzhou. Very boring. I went to Suzhou University. Also boring."

"Why did you move to Shanghai?"

"I always wanted to live in Shanghai."

"Why?"

She didn't answer immediately. She looked out the window at the passing river and then turned to him. "From the time I was girl, Shanghai seemed so exciting, and so filled with interesting things. I imagined wrapping Shanghai all around me, like a beautiful coat." She cocked her head and smiled. "And now I am wearing it."

She offered him the flask again, and he poured more of the raw liquid down his throat, then shook his head like a dog. She laughed at him, then took a delicate sip before screwing on the cap.

"Your description of Shanghai reminds me of why I went to New York. But I always thought of it as the Other Life."

"The Other Life."

"I didn't know what else to name it. This will sound stupid, but I think everything I've done in the last thirty years is based around that idea."

He'd never explained it to anyone but Kell, who had ridiculed him. The Other Life was something he'd discovered when he went to New York from Pennsylvania. At first he associated it with the clubs: the famous ones like CBGB and the Palladium. They had a line outside and a rude doorman looking like he wanted to give you a shove, and you stood in the line and watched people try to break in front of you, or just walk up to the bouncer and glide past him, and the only reason he could think that so many people would subject themselves to such brutal selection was that there was some sort of hidden world inside, people who knew something you didn't, girls who would fuck you in some special way, like in movies, except they'd be the person in the movie, and make you that person, too. And invariably the places were hot and loud, filled with people who were just like him or despised him for his ordinariness because he was, at that time, just a Wall Street flunkie, and after five hours of drinking and shouting over the music until his ears rang, he always walked out and he wasn't a rock star or a person in a movie, he was still himself.

Which didn't stop him from chasing his other life all over New York. It stopped residing in the hip clubs and glimmered anew at the restaurants that had once been too expensive for him, and in the executive dining room, and on the fifty-seventh floor, where the senior executives had their offices. It glowed darkly among the grandiose ambitions of his imagined bond fund and the idea of making vast amounts of money, far more than he would ever have thought he needed to be happy. It swelled and became more exclusive, something shared by people who flew private, who had waterfront mansions in East Hampton and apartments in Paris. It was the big money, the completely unreasonable money, where restaurant menus and airfares and automobiles and all the expenses that most people reckoned carefully against their income became so insignificant that they were no longer even noticeable. It was like traveling in a country where the currency had been devalued beyond all sense, and one of your dollars was worth a thousand of theirs. He wanted to make the whole world that country, and Crossroads would be his passport. He left Goldman and struck out on his own.

There were countless meetings, a thousand nights spent calculating risk and profit depending on a hundred variables. The first few backers were the most difficult, but by the end, when he was already well-known within the smallish circle of Wall Street players, people came to him and couldn't wait to invest their money. For ten years he'd been utterly absorbed in chasing the Other Life, chasing it in polished cars and private jets, chasing it to a diner in rural Pennsylvania, to dinners in the Hamptons, to the runway at Paris Fashion Week, in and out of a marriage, to Aspen, to his father's deathbed, where he received the first intimation that the Other Life was bigger than he'd guessed. Finally, he walked up to the vast wood table of the world's second-largest financial firm and signed a pile of documents, and when he turned away from the table three hundred million dollars richer, he felt at last that the Other Life was finally his. He stumbled home in a daze, alone, with nothing to do but enjoy the fat-headed barbiturate of pure satisfaction.

For a short time, he'd had it. He was making more in interest each day doing nothing than most people earned working all year, and if that wasn't a win, what was? He could charter jets and read admiring profiles of his success in magazines. He could see awe in people's faces when they were introduced to him. But having it, he didn't know what to do with it.

He lived in a loft in Tribeca, the entire top floor of what had once been a factory. His day revolved around going to the gym and puttering around with various museum boards, or eating out with friends, or going to the office he still kept at Crossroads, since he still held a large interest in it. Dinner parties kept him busy, too. New York City was an aquarium of interesting personalities, and he filled his time with a parade of new acquaintances. This person who wrote for *The New York Times,* another who was a Rockefeller, the famous artist, the Russian banker, the fashion impresario, the Internet billionaire, the gorgeous waitress, the Columbia professor . . . New friends, new galleries, new restaurants, new bands, always new things in buildings, until the occasional feeling began to steal over him that it was all just more of a uniform commodity called "newness."

Everything pleased him but nothing inspired him. All the stories of his life—where he'd grown up, how he'd made his fortune—began to feel stale. How many times had he deflected questions about himself in the exact same pseudo-modest way? How many times had he refused comment on the market, as if he was far beyond it? He read Ecclesiastes and then got sick of hearing himself talk about it. Then came the dissatisfaction about insignificant things. The coffee at a hundred-fifty-dollar lunch was lukewarm. The service at the hotel was lackluster. The window of the limo had a tiny chip right at eye level, and his gaze was always drawn to it.

Camille listened to this story without interrupting. Now she tilted her head to the side in a show of mock sympathy. "It must be sad to be so rich."

He laughed, and then she laughed with him. "I know," he said. "The man who has everything but isn't satisfied—it's not very original."

"That's so Western, to worry about being original. In China, we don't worry about original. It's not important to be original. Kongzi, Lao-tzu, Han Shan—they didn't care about original, they cared about the Way, or about the Mountain. So, here in China, don't worry about original." She leaned back into her corner of the seat. "You haven't told me about the women."

"What women?"

His deception amused her. "Of course, Peter! Do you think I'm a baby? If you look for your other life in a nightclub or in a private jet, of course you were going to look for it in women!" She was holding him expectantly with her eyes. "You wanted to tell me about your other life—okay! But you have to tell everything about it, not just the parts that you want to tell." She laughed. "I'm sorry: did you think that this was your car and your driver?"

Harrington felt shame at being caught out, because in fact the women had been an integral part of what he'd thought was the Other Life. He smiled down at his lap, then to her. "You are *something*!"

"Yes, yes: you already told me that. Let's hear it!"

He liked being toyed with. It felt the same as when she demanded he pronounce a phrase a dozen times until it sounded right. It amazed him that he was talking about these things with her. He'd been seeing Nadia for four months, and had never mentioned any of it. Nadia was more slow and receptive, like a beautiful sculpture.

"Okay. As you can see by looking at me, I'm not the most handsome man in the world . . ." He couldn't help waiting a fraction of a second for her to jump in and politely disagree with him, but she merely watched him in the shifting lights of the car's interior. "But suddenly, I had several hundred million dollars and I was fairly well-known. Not like a rock star, of course, but with profiles in the major print media in New York, *The Times* and all that, and when you put that together in an Internet search, it gives you a certain e-fame—"

"And you had three hundred million dollars."

"Actually," he corrected her, "that was the liquid part. When you count the stake I still held in Crossroads, it was more like six hundred million. Which is not as neat as the word 'billionaire,' but when your date can google you and find your net worth—"

"Six hundred *million* dollars!"

He laughed. "Okay. Point taken."

"*My* car and *my* driver. Now"—she crossed her arms—"what kind of women did you like?"

"Well," he offered, knowing Camille would get there anyway, "there was my wife, I suppose."

The former art student turned waitress. That was before the six hundred million. By all measures, she was a good woman. Pretty, but not exotic. Extremely kind, though, with an earthy gift for mothering that transcended the urban environment of Manhattan. Seeing her with Conrad was magical, like being in the presence of a Renaissance Madonna. But as Crossroads began to reveal the lineaments of his new life, it became clear that she didn't fit. She wasn't charming with clients and she didn't like leaving the baby with a sitter. Even if she'd kept up her artwork, she didn't have the ambition to compete for agents or gallery space. She seemed to want him to just stay home every night with her and the baby. If they'd been living up-state, where she was from, or he'd been a small-town banker in Indiana, she would have been ideal; they could have done the old farmhouse, the pony for the kids—all of that. But not this life. Not the one he wanted. In this one, she felt like Paul Gutterman's wife.

He summarized the whole thing to Camille with the arid phrase: "It didn't work out."

Camille wasn't fooled. "Of course not. A wife is the life you have, not your Other Life. What about the ones after that?" She grasped his arm and pinched him gently. "Tell me! Tell me everything!"

What he'd gravitated toward, after his marriage, was actresses and mod-els. Their printed images conveyed impossible states of being: sexuality and innocence, coldness and availability, aloofness and hunger, and that was what intrigued him. In their portfolios, fugitive combinations of light and expression were shot a hundred times from a hundred angles to snatch that unreal instant of beauty and name it into existence, and it was that image that he wanted to possess.

She laughed. "You're very shallow, Peter."

"You wanted me to be honest, right? I know how shallow all this sounds, but how shallow is it, really? Glamour, fame: on one hand they're shallow, and on the other, Who wouldn't want a piece of them, if they could get them on their own terms? Wouldn't you rather be riding in a taxi with the other Pete Harrington, the rock star, than me?" Her discomfort pleased him and he laughed. "You don't have to make a choice here. I'd like to ride in a taxi with Pete Harrington, too. But I'm telling you the truth. I'm saying I chased that experience all the way to its furthest extreme, all the way to the photo shoots and the parties that you imagine when you look at the ads. I've had dinner with Calvin Klein. I sat on a yacht in Marseilles and had a drink with Allegra Versace. I mean, the fact that I'm even bragging about that, as opposed to bragging about having a drink with Paul Gutterman ten years

ago in New York, and that you would find that more interesting, shows that
it's a real phenomenon. And it's not that they're not interesting people, and
even quite nice people, but do they hold some mysterious knowledge, the
way it appears in their photos and publicity? Is any model as beautiful as
she appears in that one instant when she's made up and it's the perfect exposure and there's no stupid remark or tiredness or sweat or any of those
things that make up real life? I can tell you: no! I tried to go all the way into
that experience to make it real, and, finally, the answer is *no!* So if that's
shallow, I'm shallow."

"But Nadia is a model." She said it with just enough feeling that Peter
sensed it was more than an abstract observation, and he felt a tiny, quiet
pleasure, even though it flew in the face of what he'd just professed.

"Nadia is a very nice woman who is kind and intelligent and also happens to be a model. And if I met someone else that I had more in common
with, Nadia's profession wouldn't matter at all." It seemed coldly disloyal
hearing himself say it, but things had already shifted in the few hours since
they'd met for dinner.

Camille heard him out, then dismissed it. "Yes, she's very nice."

At that moment the cabdriver turned his blunt crew-cut head toward
her and asked her for directions. Harrington could see nothing familiar
around them. They could be anywhere in China. Camille settled back into
her seat for a moment without saying anything, then turned straight to him
and looked in his eyes for a few seconds before she spoke. "Do you want to
try something?"

She dug into her purse, then opened her hand, which she held down below the level of the seat, where the cabdriver couldn't see it. Two pills like
aspirin tablets sat on her palm. Harrington became wary, but excited.

"What is that?"

"It's Ecstasy," she answered.

He looked into her half smile. "You mean, the drug Ecstasy?"

She nodded very slightly, without a word.

He'd done X a few times in New York, so it didn't scare him in and
of itself. He liked the buzzy little errands it sent his mind on. But to do

it now, in a foreign city with a young woman he barely knew, on the way to an unknown destination . . . He felt a little thrill. His driver was far away, he didn't know what part of the immensity of Shanghai they were in. He had no control. Who knew where that rabbit hole came out? "I'll do it if you do."

Her fingernails poked his skin like cat's claws as she put one of the tablets on his palm, then she looked at him as she stuck the little white circle on her outstretched tongue and flicked it back into her mouth. He frowned and tipped his head at her, then ate his pill. They washed it down with the fiery *bai-jiu*.

"There," she said, "now you have done something illegal."

"But I swallowed the evidence."

She put her hand on his leg. "So do I, sometimes." When she said it, his brain went thick, even though the drug hadn't yet hit his stomach.

"Go on," she said, inquisitorial again. "You found that your other life was not in the women. What happened after that?"

The Other Life. It felt close right now, as close as this woman and this confession. As close as the end of this taxi ride, or wherever she was taking him. He felt the urge to keep talking, to tell everything.

As New York became unsatisfying, he'd begun to chase the mystery in a wider arc. He flew to Venice for the Bienniale and lingered in Italy for another month, driving through Tuscany with one of his model-girlfriends. He came back and talked about it until he was sick of it—the castle they'd stayed in, the rare wine. After three tellings, he was done with it. After that he went to Peru and toured the ruins of the Sacred Valley, half-amused at the novelty of being robbed at gunpoint in the sacred acropolis of Pisac. That made for a good story also, but he felt increasingly weightless, as if he were standing in a swimming pool up to his neck, and his feet didn't press very hard on the bottom. He wanted to get away. Not just from New York, but from all his anecdotes and exploits and professed wisdom about the financial markets dispensed in luxurious interiors. People assumed that because he was young and rich, he knew some hidden secret, but, in fact, he hadn't discovered anything.

He booked a condo for three months in Aspen and went skiing every day. He'd been skiing for fifteen years, usually in Vermont, but that winter he got good enough to feel free. He could choose his line and go almost anywhere he wanted, and it was refreshing to be someplace where the only thing known about him was that he was a guy from back east who skied okay but could never land the drops. The only friends he had were other skiers he met on the slopes, and most of those were transients there for a week or else part of the local world of waiters and rental-shop workers who were living their twenties and thirties in a shared limbo of snow and easy good times. These were the people who knew the good spots the tourists never found: which roped-off areas were filled with hidden powder stashes and which would send you over a sixty-foot cliff. They were a clannish bunch, subtly ranking each other in a meritocracy of skiing ability and back-country savvy. A juvenile scene, in some ways, but also one that valued phys-ical toughness and bravery, like tales of the Yukon gold rush he'd read as a boy. He had no reason to want to be part of it, but he did, and sometimes, when one or two of them might take him to a forbidden area of the moun-tain and show him a route with a warning like "Whatever you do, stay away from that roll-over on the right." *What's there?* And what was there, on the right, was disaster, death on a ragged spike of rock far below, in terrain that one out of a hundred thousand skiers could negotiate. He could whip past right next to it and look down and feel the Other Life there, or see it high overhead in the smoky slopes that crouched beyond the ski lifts, the ones that you needed special gear to get to, leaving in the dark of the night with a headlamp and climbing for hours to a highland of cliff bands and moving snow where everyone descended on his own, singly, so that an ava-lanche would only kill one of them. It was there in the mist, far away, a place he could only imagine. He wanted to go there more than anything he'd wanted in a long time.

He bought the gear, all brand-new and top-of-the-line, getting advice from his friends on climbing skins and *randonnée* bindings. He bought an avalanche transceiver and a special backpack to keep him on the surface if things cut loose under him. Then he spent a week skiing his new gear in-

bounds and wearing his beacon strapped to his torso like it was the shini-
est piece of bling in the universe. His friends wouldn't take him until he'd
practiced with the beacon, and he became adept at reading the numbers on
the display and following the arrows to the target that simulated a buried
skier, though it was impossible not to imagine that buried skier as himself
and to marvel at how long it took to find someone, let alone dig them out.

He did a shakedown run with Dave, one of the locals he'd befriended.
They climbed for two hours to a nearby peak and skied it carefully, and a
few days later they climbed a steeper one. He learned how to use an ice ax
and practiced self-arrests by hurling himself backward down steep slopes.
He did well enough that Dave invited him to join a trip to a much higher
peak. It was a three-hour climb from the road, and in flat light or low visibility could be, in Dave's words, "sketchy." They'd go with two other young
men that Harrington had heard about and seen but never met, big dogs on
the local extreme-skiing circuit. Harrington drove his rental car to the closest viewpoint, but it wasn't something you could see from the road. He mentioned it to another friend at the bar who knew how he skied and the fellow
had looked at him with raised eyebrows. Along with its thousands of feet of
untouched powder, the peak was well-known as an unstable south-facing
area filled with narrow chutes that sucked you in and then cliffed-out disas-
trously when there was no longer any chance of retreat. "You're going there?"
he said, then gave a single piece of advice: "Don't go first." Harrington felt his
heart speed up.

He never made the climb. A storm came in, and the snowpack became
too fragile. They waited a few days for it to consolidate, but one of the men
caught strep throat, and then it snowed again, and while they were waiting
for that new dump to consolidate, a slide of another sort had begun.

He had spotted the possibility of Crossroads's collapse several months
before, not as something that would necessarily happen, but as something
that could happen given a confluence of various unlikely events. Despite its
gigantic paper assets and its worshipful mentions in the financial press,
Crossroads owned nothing and produced nothing: it derived its value from
the arcane relationships it created between hypothetical streams of income

that were cut and repackaged and repackaged again like a shipment of co-caine at a dockside warehouse. Vast flows of future money were claimed and in turn promised to others, minus a tiny percentage, while those others in turn shunted the flow in another direction, taking their cut along the way. It was a trillion-dollar balancing act, so highly leveraged and brittle that a few taps of precisely placed doubt could shatter its immaculate structure. And in that case, no one would escape alive.

A journalist at one of the lesser financial papers called to interview him for a story on the fund, and Harrington dismissed the man's assertions with a show of good cheer that had the reporter apologizing for his mistaken assumptions. Fifteen minutes after he hung up, Harrington quietly called his sister and mother and told them to sell their stakes. They rushed for the exit the next day, but most of the big entities, the ones that mattered, that could bring down the whole financial system, were locked into a kind of suicide pact with counterparties on the other side, and to them he preferred to say nothing. Sounding the alarm would itself precipitate the end, but as much as that, it simply embarrassed him. How could he admit to his investors and all the people who had lauded him for his brilliance that the whole foundation of their profits was, from another view, a gigantic greed machine? The fund was perfectly designed to prey on certain people's presumption that they should be able to flow millions of dollars their way, not because they had done something useful, but because they could, in turn, prey on people equally presumptuous further down the line. So he kept quiet, and waited for the avalanche.

When it came, it was nearly instantaneous. On Monday Crossroads was a trillion-dollar fund. By Friday the doors had been padlocked. With a swiftness that Pete Harrington the rock star might have envied, Peter Harrington the financier suddenly became famous. Not e-famous: infamous.

"Why?" Camille asked. "Simply because you guessed wrong?"

"Not exactly," he said. "I think the bigger issue was that I hedged."

After he'd cashed in the first time, he explained, he'd wanted to protect his remaining investment. "Don't forget; I still had a lot of money invested in Crossroads." And so, knowing better than anyone the exact composition of his bond fund and its weaknesses, he began to take out insurance against its failure. Not a lot, at first, not something that could be called "betting against it," but finally, as things began to change in the world and his partnership with Kell became closer, the hedging became a business venture of its own. When word came out that he was leading the charge against his own creation, Crossroads collapsed with a violence that shook financial markets all over the world, and he made more money on its failure than he had made on its success.

In the space of a few days, he became one of the most reviled figures in the country. The day his picture appeared on the front page of the *New York Post,* a busboy dumped a tray of dirty dishes into his lap, and within twenty-four hours he had changed all his phone numbers and hired a bodyguard. An army of accusers confronted him in every public place he showed himself. He learned the telltale signs: the change of expression as they recognized him, the angry conference with a nearby friend, the moment of hesitation, the determined crossing of the room. Even his bodyguard's cold glare wasn't always sufficient; he couldn't very well hammerlock a sixty-year-old sales clerk or a middle-aged woman who'd lost her retirement. He stopped going out publicly, relying on an assistant to do his shopping for him and cruising from his loft to each appointment in the safety of his limousine. The charitable organizations were still happy to have him around, but the dinner invitations became fewer, and the dinners more contentious. There was always the offhanded joke or the unexpected insult when he met someone new. At first he tried to defend himself, pointing out that he had merely hedged his remaining Crossroads holdings, just as any prudent investor would. It was useless: in some people's eyes, the fact that he still had a fortune was a mark of disgrace, rather than achievement. Month after month, a relentless assault was waged across the Internet and the financial pages. On late-night comedy shows, his name became a bitter one-liner about bottomless greed.

"Then you felt ashamed?" she asked him.

"No! I felt angry. I played the game according to the rules. They shouldn't blame me if the rules were inadequate."

So when Kell relocated to Shanghai, and invited him to join him in his new venture three months ago, he'd jumped on it. Shanghai fascinated him. It reminded him of New York in its mixture of exquisite manners and rude hustle. The Chinese businesspeople he met were friendly and sophisticated— either they hadn't heard of him or they were too polite to mention it. The culture was strange and fascinating; the feel was fresh. The Chinese had never taken the advice of Wall Street's eminent pitchmen, so the global financial collapse was a distant shudder in Shanghai. He had over eight hundred million dollars, and few were worried about how he'd made it.

"So that's my whole shallow story," he said.

"You don't hear stories like that all the time," she said, nodding. "Thank you for telling me."

He was starting to feel the Ecstasy now, a subtle rushing between his temples. He looked over at Camille, who sat in her white dress, watching him. He wasn't sure exactly how long it had been since either of them had said anything. "Where is the Other Life now?" she finally asked.

"I was hoping you could tell me."

"The mountain is massive. The mountain is mist."

"What's that mean?"

She leaned over and squeezed his arm, and her touch seemed to travel up to his head and make it vibrate for a moment, like a xylophone bar being struck. "It's just a poem. From Han Shan."

She smiled at him. They were coconspirators now. He had no idea who Han Shan was, or who she really was, and he didn't want to know at the moment. The city had rearranged itself behind its façade of street scenes and traffic and become a secret world that they coursed through together, full of electric and alluring pleasures. He had a sense of distant hilarity, unattached to anything in particular. This girl, this taxi, these ringing, bending, liquid lights: this other life.

The Ecstasy was creeping up to his head now, giving everything a burnished feel. Ernie's black-and-white Shanghai of 1946. *Whatever you wanted, you could get it: women . . . opium . . . a passport.* Camille was that woman, and the cabdriver, with his big, crew-cut head, was actually a rickshaw driver, yes, from the last century, transmigrated into this car and this Shanghai. Peter had no idea which Shanghai that was anymore. Once he left the three or four neighborhoods and highways he frequented, every section of the endless city was interchangeable with any other. The driver dropped them at a street closed off by food vendors who had begun to pack up their stalls for the night. Steam was billowing from pots of boiling water, luminous in the lights that hung above the carts. The secret panting of a beast disguised as lumpy old women waving ladles through their bubbling cauldrons. He could have looked at the steam for hours, but he felt a tugging on his arm as Camille plunged them into the narrow file between the cauldrons and grills, past the skewers of barbecued pigeons, past the rows of glistening candied crab apples on sticks. The dumplings . . . and they were beyond it all, floating down the sidewalk within the clicking of her high heels.

The street seemed typical of nonforeigner Shanghai, small-scale shops selling hardware or food or inexpensive furniture, no logos in sight. The façades were brown brick or concrete, dulled by decades of pollution and resonant with the million small transactions of lower-tier lives. A strange place for a party. The line of buildings ceased and was replaced by a low white wall, which they followed for a long time before Camille stopped in front of a brown wooden door. She took out a set of keys and unlocked it, then pushed it open for him.

The space inside was dark, as if the light from the street couldn't enter. The only illumination in the murky little courtyard was a paper lantern glowing above them in red and white, and when he saw it there against the dark it seemed suddenly intensely important, like the original red and white lantern of the entire universe. As his eyes adjusted he could make out shrubs and rockeries. They stood in a tiny white-walled courtyard the size of a small living room.

"What is this place?"

"This is the Nan Lin garden," Camille answered. "This was the estate of a very rich man during the Qing Dynasty. Like a hedge-fund manager. Like you. If you lived at that time, this would have been your life."

The courtyard was bounded by pale white walls, and she led him through an opening shaped like a crescent moon, into another courtyard lined with jumbles of oddly shaped rocks rising as high as his chest. Their shapes suggested birds or strange animals. They made him uneasy and claustrophobic.

"Camille, what are we doing here?"

"*Shhh* . . . You wanted the Other Life."

They passed through an opening in the wall like a giant teapot, a narrow passageway, and then another door shaped like a vase. They were deep in the garden, among the teeming rocks and the fronds of bamboo and shrubbery that rose over their heads. He could hear, strangely, the sound of jazz, and he wasn't sure if he was really hearing it or if it was in his head.

"Do you know where you're going?"

Camille looked at him and her mouth twisted out of shape and her eyes narrowed. "This will be new for you," she said, and she took him straight toward a high barrow of rock whose center collapsed into a vague black emptiness. A stab of dread went through him. He had a feeling that she was leading him to his death.

She felt him resisting. "Oh, are you afraid of the dark? Poor little boy! Hold on to me." She grasped his hand and he entered into her shroud of jasmine fragrance as they plunged into the darkness. She seemed to curve to the left, and in seconds they had both disappeared. The smell was of moist earth and dead leaves, as if they were deep inside a cavern, or a grave. She stopped and stood there silently in the pitch darkness. Soft bursts of color and swaths of light swarmed across his vision. "Where are we?" he asked. He just wanted to hear her voice.

"Are you frightened?"

He didn't know how long he hesitated before answering, tumbling headlong through her question. It might have been one second or it might have been a minute. In the dark cave, there was no way to measure anything. "No. I trust you."

"Good."

She started moving again and took a turn to the right. He thought he could make out a change in the quality of the darkness, and with every step it seemed to become less uniform, to break into different shades of black, then charcoal, and then, to his surprise, they turned left again and were facing an opening whose large expanses and yellow luminosity seemed, after the cave, to be the most brilliant vision he'd ever beheld.

They were at the edge of a pond, and on the other side, rising from its own reflection, was a pavilion adrift in glowing light. Dots of red and white lanterns curved off to the sides, mimicking the upswept roofs that rose into the darkness. A confetti of gay voices wavered from across the water, the sound of jazz that he'd heard before, nicked by a shred of laughter, or an expression of surprise. Amid the glow were elegant men in ties and women with their shoulders wrapped in silk or cashmere shawls. It seemed less a party than a dream that he was entertaining.

"How do you like it?" Camille asked him, still holding his hand.

"I don't believe it."

They walked around the small lake and into the middle of the gathering. A jazz sextet with a black saxophonist and a white pianist played with their Chinese cohorts, all of them in white dinner jackets and black ties. He could see fragmentary pieces of a huge buffet along one side of the room, and servers weaving through the dancing crowd with silver trays of champagne. The strange sight of it, and the brief caress of Camille's fingers on his hand as she released him, made him lose track of where he was and who he was and go tumbling through the night garden.

He felt a swiftly moving stream of electrons coursing from the nape of his neck and through his brain, and a giddy sense of excitement. He was so ripped! He wished Kell was here. *Kell, I am so ripped! I don't even know what year this is!* He was at a party in a Chinese garden with a woman he barely knew, and his whole life felt incomparably grand and wondrous. As they ascended the steps of the pavilion he became acutely aware of all the expressions in the room: the sudden laughter and the polite smiles. He sensed the somber alienation of the people at the edges, the earnest incomprehensible arguments made and received in avid conversations. He ricocheted through a dozen tiny fragments of other people's lives. The middle-aged woman over there, in the olive-colored blouse and black skirt: pondering something. The young man speaking too eagerly into the face of a pretty young woman, who listened and subtly withdrew at the same time, as if looking for more distance.

A waiter came by and Harrington pulled a glass of red wine from his tray. The wine had a chalky, cheap taste. He sensed this was some sort of art event. He spotted a bar in one corner of the room, where a white-jacketed bartender was mixing cocktails. "Can I go get a drink?"

"Of course," Camille said. "You are the guest of honor."

He examined her ironic, narrowed eyes. "Thank you. Can I get you something?" He left her there and wandered toward the bar. The hall was warm in the autumn air and many of the women had bare shoulders, slender carvings of smooth skin rising toward their black hair. He could discern now that some of the people were younger, less wealthy looking but often with earrings or creatively colored hair. He supposed they were the artists, nonconformists in a country that had only lately adopted the Western tradition of admiring the rebel.

He reached the bar and ordered two gin and tonics, then leaned his elbow on the white cloth and looked through the crowd. Necktie knots glided past, shoulder straps, a gold earring, the smell of nicotine, crisscrossed bits of Chinese conversation. He'd lost sight of Camille. She wasn't standing where he'd left her. A little shudder of fear went through him. Would she bring him all the way to the center of this dark garden just to ditch him?

His eyes came to rest on a giant photograph, easily ten feet long, mounted on the wall behind him. The cardboard placard beside it held some Chinese characters and the words "Buried City #46: Hero in the Island of Forgetting." Next to that was another placard in both Chinese and English, telling about the artist, Xu Ruoshi. It seemed the artist came from one of the cities that was flooded by the Three Gorges Dam and had dedicated himself to photographing his city in its death throes. In this picture, that city had already been almost completely abandoned, but a few old people still refused to leave, and little signs of life appeared among the empty buildings. Laundry on a line. A tiny dumpling stand with one steaming pot. The artist had colored the photos in washes of blue-green, so even though the city had not yet been flooded, it seemed to be underwater already. It was beautiful, and Harrington found himself lost in it, imagining that its life continued to go on magically at the bottom of the dammed-up river. He could be that dumpling vendor, standing there before the abandoned movie theater. The show would be over, the people gone, and him left standing there remembering a crowd that would never return. Harrington stared for a long time thinking of the man, his tiny home, his son far away from him in a distant city, beyond his help. He felt a deep sadness. The Ecstasy . . .

Two drinks sat fizzing on the bar and he lifted one to his cheek, could hear the radio-static sound of the carbonation. He felt the sour bubbles bursting through the sweetness on his tongue. A woman's sudden laugh, a tray of rice noodles stuffed with shrimp, a flat note from the saxophone, a shawl draped across a shoulder. Far down, in the drowned city, laundry was hanging on a line.

"Do you like it?"

Camille was next to him again.

"It's very moving."

She pointed across the crowd toward a thin young man with long hair wearing a black suit cut so strangely that it seemed almost like a caricature of a suit. "That's Xu Ruoshi," she said. "He is the artist. He just won a very important prize, and this party is to honor him. If you like, one day I can take you to the gallery where his works are on display."

The prospect of having her as his guide again made little sparklers start to sizzle softly in his brain. "I'd like that."

Suddenly another woman appeared beside them. She seemed around forty, alluring as a spider in her tight black dress and feather-covered vest. Her hair was braided stylishly against her head like an African. She could be someone in the background of an Italian fashion exposition. She greeted Camille with a kiss, and they exchanged a few words in Chinese, at the end of which the woman raised her hands with surprise and turned to Peter.

"So you are Peter Harrington! It's a pleasure to meet you! My name is Diana."

So she knew him. He struggled to retrieve that silly Peter Harrington who was a financier and had a history. "And what do you do?" he asked her.

"I own the Phoenix Gallery. Xu Ruoshi is one of my artists."

"Lucky you!" He had meant it to be sincere, but he suddenly wondered if he sounded flip or sarcastic. "Congratulations . . ." *African Chinese woman . . .*

"He is very talented."

Camille laughed and said something in Chinese, and Diana answered her in a tone of mock indignation, then held out her hand. "So very nice to meet you, Mr. Harrington. Camille is afraid I will kidnap you and make you come to my gallery."

"Don't worry, I will take him," Camille said. "But now we must go. Good-bye!" She took his hand and began pulling him through the crowd. He noticed with surprise that he'd almost finished his drink, and he left it on a tray as they exited the pavilion.

She led him out into the dark. Sets of people like softly waving flags swayed in the buttery halo that surrounded the windows of the party, and farther away, where the light began to fail, he could see dark couples sitting on the railings by the water. He imagined he could hear their voices in soft, cricketlike murmurings. The moment felt vast and mysterious, expanding infinitely out into the world without need of a past or future. Only this moment existed, rushing off to the ends of the earth and into every room in the universe, out past the moon and sun, into distant galaxies, clustered around him and Camille and this garden and the blooming of the creamy white flowers that spewed a dizzying phosphorescent softness into the dark. *Just this moment.*

She led him through the garden, over tiny arched bridges and along the sides of miniature lakes that gleamed like slabs of onyx. They never seemed to cross the same space twice, as if everything was multiplied not by mirrors, which create identical images, but by a single idea in countless variations. They passed through another wall, and then she stopped in another of an infinity of courtyards, again with its gnarled trees and rockeries. Before him was the three-part entryway of a building, beautiful, like the others, with its upswept roofs and its intricately cut latticework windows. Camille unlocked one of the doors as Peter stood behind her. Small flashes like fireworks blossomed and exploded soundlessly against the charcoaled interior, but he knew they were just in his eyes. She picked up a small fluorescent lantern inside the door and switched it on.

They stood in a traditional Chinese reception room of two hundred years ago, with its stiff cushion-less wooden chairs arrayed before a wide, throne-like wooden couch. In the colorless luster of the lamp, the room seemed like an ancient photograph.

"This is where you would have received visitors," Camille explained. "Your other rich friends, or some government officials. This is Cold Mountain Hall."

The Ecstasy directed his attention briefly and fiercely toward one object after another, each crackling with its history and its potential. An inkwell and brush. A large ceramic vase on a stand. Behind the couch hung a large slab of marble whose gray and white swirls formed a series of indistinct peaks and valleys, lost in clouds. Camille approached it with the lantern and read the four gilded characters below it in Chinese, then translated them:

" *'The mountain is massive. The mountain is mist.'* Han Shan."

"Your poem," he said, staring into the undulations of the stone. He thought of standing there, in his skis, ready to push off into a luminous fog. Then he felt her take his hand, and he was being swept past the screen and deeper into "his" house, through another open space and then down an uncomfortably narrow corridor whose white plaster walls swallowed up the meager effort of the lamp. In a moment they were outside again, walking in a latticed gallery beside a courtyard. He could hear the jazz again, faintly. Bushes and jagged rockeries teemed around him, and beyond them he knew there were other unknown courtyards and corridors and caverns multiplying through the garden.

"This is the Courtyard of Sighing Winds," she said. "This is where you might greet your daughter or your son."

Again, the dreadful overtone. He refused to hear it. "You sound like a tour guide."

"I am a tour guide." She squeezed his hand. "Or perhaps I am a ghost."

She pushed open another door. "In Qing times, the master's children lived in this house." The lantern's chalky glow spread over the room. There were several desks, each with the classic ceramic ink tray and brushes. A shelf held volumes of paperbound books, like those he'd seen in the Shanghai Museum. An eerie sense of other people's lives came over him.

"This is where your son would study. The four classics: he must memorize them for the Imperial Exams, so you hired a Confucian gentleman to teach him."

Without meaning to, he pictured his own son here, sitting at a desk. Himself in an old-fashioned robe, putting his hand on Conrad's shoulder: the proud father. Protecting and preparing his son. If only it could be like that. "Is this a museum? Are we allowed to be here?"

He could see her smile in the soft light. She put her finger to her lips to hush him. "Quiet. This is *my* other life."

She took his hand again and walked him through the room into a slender corridor, then to a tiny steep stairway, almost a ladder. He watched her ascend to the ceiling on a chorus of wooden creaking. He followed her up, his stomach fluttering, as if he could feel the spirits of the building's old inhabitants behind him in the hallway.

The gallery upstairs looked over the courtyards below them and the tops of the trees. Off to the side he could see the lights of the party and hear the piano like something borrowed from a different time. He felt her brush up against his side, like a cat.

"There's more."

He followed her white dress through the shadowy spaces, to a large room with furniture in it. He recognized a traditional Chinese bed, its four posters draped with cloth that was pulled aside at the front. He could make out the dark outlines of a mattress and a down comforter. A small sink was bolted to one wall beside a small table. Next to the sink was a night table with some toiletries and a clock. Beneath it, a ceramic chamber pot. A wardrobe stood half-open, filled with hanging clothes that were monochromatic gray in the dim light.

"Who lives here?"

"I do." She smiled at him.

"You live here?"

"Of course!"

He put hand to his head, amazed. "I can't believe this. It's a dream."

She laughed softly. "Of course it's a dream. Why would you think it was anything else? Sit down on the bed."

She motioned him over to the bed, and his heart started to pound. Was he supposed to kiss her? He didn't feel any sexual desire for her, just a desire to understand this moment, to encompass all of it. He was in her room, but also lodged in the lingering afterlives of dozens of people who had inhabited this house over hundreds of years. She turned away from him and took a long embroidered turquoise coat out of the wardrobe. The rustle of the silk as she slipped into it sounded like static electricity. She turned her back to him and took a strangely shaped object from a case, then pulled over a small stool. She sat down, and he could see she was holding a Chinese lute. She turned off the lantern and the bright turquoise of the robe went colorless, like everything else in the room. The jazz band must have finished, because there was only silence now.

She started to strum the lute, tuning it, and then the idle strumming took shape in a rhythmic, pulsing beat. Strange music, its beautiful harmonies always rubbing against flats and sharps. She began to sing over it in a thin high-toned voice he didn't recognize, loosing long opaque verses that swooped away from and back to the soothing ground of the lute strings. Sometimes she would stop playing and insert a few spoken words against the silence in the same sharp voice; then the lute would begin its scratchy melody again, and she would continue to sing. He didn't know how long she went on: he thought it was only one song. When she stopped playing it took a few seconds for the sound of the strings to lapse into a silence that seemed alive with the memory of her playing.

"There," she said at last. "Now you know a little about me. I'm from Suzhou. I teach Chinese. I live in this garden. I play the *pipa*."

She had changed utterly during the course of the evening. He had a thousand questions, but on one side were the questions, and on the other was this simple, unspoiled moment, full of everything still unknown and unnamed. He allowed the quiet to flow around him, looking at her, at the shadowy room and its scattering of simple furnishings. He could ask those questions anytime.

At last she rustled her heavy silk robe. "Do you know that it is two in the morning?"

He gave an amused grunt. "That would never have occurred to me."

She turned on the lantern and hung the robe up again in the wardrobe, then found a lightweight black cardigan to button over the top of her dress. In half a minute she was leading him through the interlocking passageways of the garden to the gate that they had originally come through, with its single lantern. *The lantern at the center of the universe.*

"How do I get home?"

"Look." She opened the door and the same taxi was waiting for him. "I told you: *my* car, *my* driver. He knows where to go, but you'll need to pay him three hundred renminbi. No more than that. I will say good-bye now."

"Camille. Thank you." He put his arms on her shoulders. The top of her head came to his nose and he could smell the breadlike odor of her hair along with a lingering trace of jasmine.

"Camille?"

She looked up at him. Her face was inches from his. He could feel her breath, then the touch of her nose on his eye, and on his cheek, then her lips against his own, neutral-tasting and alive, and he thought of sea cucumbers, alive. She pulled away from him and stepped back. She seemed completely self-contained again, as if they'd just concluded a lesson about Chinese grammar. "Good night, Peter. I will see you Tuesday."

He couldn't bring himself to get in the car. "This was an amazing night."

"I enjoyed it also."

He stood there for a few seconds, desperate for a way to narrow the distance he felt swelling between them. His own words surprised him. "I don't understand any of this."

She laughed at him, then touched his shoulder. "Peter. You are so silly. Why do you think you are supposed to understand it?"

She gave a few last instructions to the cabdriver, and as the car pulled away he watched the door to the garden swing closed behind her.

2

The Afterlives

⁑

The next day Peter Harrington looked at the exquisite little machine that he wore on his wrist and calculated that he'd arrived fifteen minutes early. His brain wasn't hazy, the way it would be after a big drunk, it just felt slightly tired, like an athlete who had run a marathon the day before. He'd had only a few hours of sleep, and the events of the previous night had left him confused and excited. It felt like the offer to take Ernie to lunch had been made by a different Peter Harrington.

The hotel was a decent one, Chinese-owned: you could tell by the marble in three different colors, arranged in that glossy, grandiose style the government seemed to favor for its lobbies. The old man was sitting in the reception area looking hapless and tentative, as if he'd been left there by a caretaker. He smiled when he saw Harrington and carefully rose to his feet. Once standing, he loomed over his host.

Harrington had searched his name an hour ago and had been pleased to get a couple of hits on World War II and veteran sites. He'd found him on the Merrill's Marauders page; he even thought he saw a face that resembled him among the hundreds in the company picture, but it was hard to tell with such an old man, so long ago.

They shook hands and Harrington guided him to the car, listening to the details of the hotel's breakfast buffet and Ernie's difficulties communicating with the front desk. He had arthritis in his ankle, he said, and it was bothering him this morning. The middle-American patter made Peter wish he'd never made the lunch appointment. The old man had seemed so interesting when they'd met at the Bar Rouge. Now, he looked antique and outdated, like an old watch he'd found in his father's drawer. Mr. Ma opened the door and Ernie fitted himself carefully into the backseat. The businesslike traffic noise of downtown Shanghai spattered their windows as they pulled into traffic.

"You know, your name seems familiar," the old man said. "Isn't there a ball player or something named Peter Harrington?"

Harrington hesitated. People Ernie's age didn't run Web searches on acquaintances. "There's a musician. Pete Harrington. He had a band called the DreamKrushers."

The old man slapped his forehead. "*That* must be it. Gee whiz, I thought I'd heard it somewhere before. People make that mistake often?"

"Once in a while. If the restaurant host looks disappointed when I show up, I know they were expecting the other Pete Harrington. So—" Little pieces of the garden kept glinting in his mind: that moment in the cave, the party reflected across the black water, the sense of one space being replicated a thousand different ways. He searched for a question to ask Ernie about Old Shanghai, since that was their reason for getting together. "How many years were you here after the war?"

"Off and on, the four years after the war. I left just after the Nationalists abandoned Nanjing."

They chatted about conditions at the time: Ernie got stuck trying to dredge up the different varieties of currencies issued by the teetering Nationalist government. "Let's see: there were still some Japanese dollars floating around, then the gold yuan, and after that the silver yuan, then Communist paper money from the Liberated areas. Wait a second"—he grimaced—"I might be wrong there. Maybe the silver yuan came first, then the gold yuan."

They turned the corner onto the Bund and Ernie took out a bulky, outdated camera and pointed it through the glass at the line of buildings. He made an exasperated sound as he lowered it. "I hate these digital cameras," he said. "I've got a perfectly good camera at home, but you can't get the film developed anymore. Who'd have imagined that?"

Harrington felt a little sorry that a man who'd once been so formidable was so completely adrift with his digital camera. "Just tell me when you want a picture and I can take it for you. Is this a good place to start walking?"

They were in front of the building that held the Bar Rouge. Ernie lifted his camera again, sweeping it far down the street. "Yeah. This place brings back a lot of memories."

A few seconds later, Mr. Ma opened Emie's door for him to get out. He was still fussing with his camera as Mr. Ma drove off to find a parking space.

They began walking and Ernie named the buildings, reeling off the forgotten purposes of the 1930s streetscape. The Customs House, the Russo-Chinese Bank building. He stopped in front of the Waldorf Astoria Hotel. "This was the Shanghai Club, where they had the Long Bar. They claimed it was the longest bar in the world. I had a friend I used to meet there that ended up getting killed by headhunters in New Guinea in 1947."

Ernie's memory wasn't perfect. He mistook some of the most famous buildings, even though they had plaques right on them. And most of his information wasn't particularly interesting. Every tourist already knew that the Shanghai Club had the longest bar in the world. He found himself dropping out of Ernie's discourse to reflect on things Camille had said. *It must be sad to be so rich!* The affection in that ridicule. *What makes you think you are supposed to understand it?* He should call her this afternoon. He also had to read that material about the Akron sewer system. They were planning to take it over and they had an important meeting with Shenzhen Red Dragon in two days to talk about it. There was a lot at stake. With Red Dragon's infusion of capital and credibility, the whole project would quickly reach critical mass. He was supposed to get together with Kell and David Lau later this afternoon to get ready. He never should have made this appointment.

"Excuse me." He took out his cell phone as if he'd received a call and stepped off to the side for a half minute. He mumbled a few phrases then approached the old man again. "Ernie, I'm afraid something unexpected came up and I have to go in a few minutes. I'm so sorry about lunch. I'll take a cab and Mr. Ma can stay with you and drive you around. And lunch is on me, of course. Mr. Ma will take care of it."

The tall man looked at his watch. "Sure! Not a problem. But you know, there's just one more thing I want to show you—" He looked around the street, squinted, and to Harrington's frustration, began to walk in the opposite direction of the Peace Hotel. He stopped, seemed about to say something, then started walking again. Harrington trailed beside him helplessly. They continued a few hundred feet to an alley and then Ernie stopped, raised his hand to his forehead, and looked to the side. "It was back here somewhere . . ." He started walking along the alley, seeming to hunt for something.

"Ernie!" Harrington called to him, then reluctantly followed.

He had stopped where a small awning covered the doorway of a restaurant. "This was a shipping office. The owner was a German Jew who'd escaped to Shanghai in 1937." Ernie went silent, staring at the door, then turned toward the banker with a strange, mild look of remembrance on his face. "Actually, he wanted to hire me to kill someone."

Harrington examined the aged features in front of him, which no longer seemed bumbling and uncertain. "He wanted to hire you to kill someone? Why?"

"There were a lot of scores to be settled after the war," the old man said slowly. "Scores that can't be settled."

He turned back to the freight office, gazing at it in a way that seemed to bore through the upscale façade into an interior that had been entombed there for more than sixty years. Harrington waited, wondering what was going through Ernie's mind. Then the old man looked at his watch and started walking back toward the Bund. The financier tagged along, lost in the deepening story. "Who did he want you to kill?"

Ernie didn't answer until they had arrived back at the luxurious entryway of the Waldorf Astoria. He stood in front of it.

"The Shanghai Club was members only. I used to come up here to smoke cigars. I had a South African acquaintance who was a member, by the name of Vorster. The old-timers used to tell me he never would have been allowed through the door before the Japanese Occupation. He was Afrikaaner: those guys never were big supporters of the Allies. This Vorster had finagled permission from the Japs to stay in Shanghai during the war with some sort of bogus Red Cross cover story, and he used that to make a fortune for himself in the black market. He was an operator. Into everything: gambling, currency speculation. One of those types, you know? When he's buying you drinks he's the swellest guy in the world, but if you got on the wrong end of one his schemes, by golly you'd want to put a bullet in his head. Of course"— he smiled faintly—"he just might have someone put a bullet in yours first." Ernie turned to Harrington. "Kind of tricky that way."

"Was that the man you were hired to kill?"

Ernie raised the camera and took a picture of the doors, then turned to the street and pointed it in that direction. At last he lowered the camera from his face. "I said he *wanted* to hire me. I didn't say I accepted the job. The war was over, and despite what you see in the movies, Uncle Sam doesn't take kindly to that kind of moonlighting."

By now the financier was beginning to forget all about his other obligations. He'd entered a different Shanghai. An illustrated-novel Shanghai he'd imagined but never gotten this close to. "Why did this refugee want to kill Vorster?"

Ernie frowned. "Big-time operator. Probably double-crossed a lot of people—nature of the business. I'll bet he had a dozen people that wanted him dead." He put the camera back in the pocket of his sport coat, smiled playfully. "But it wasn't Vorster."

At that moment Mr. Ma came up, signaling his presence to his employer then dropping back several yards. The old man eyed him for a few seconds, then looked off down the street toward the old Peace Hotel. It had recently undergone a massive renovation by a global luxury hotel chain, and its gothic darkness had been somewhat alleviated. Now the veteran motioned toward it. "That was the Cathay Hotel, as you know. Sassoon's place. That's where the guy was staying. Right under Sassoon's nose. That's how I ended up hearing about it."

"You knew Victor Sassoon?"

Ernie shrugged. "Met him a few times. Just like a couple hundred other people who 'knew' Sassoon. He was rich, he was famous. Half of Shanghai claimed they 'knew' him."

"But it sounds like you actually *did* know him. How did you meet him?"

Ernie shrugged. "He wanted to buy some scrap metal."

"I don't understand."

The older man laughed and looked at his watch again and waved his hand. "It's a long story, and I don't want to keep you. I know you're busy."

Harrington began to panic. "No, really, this is fascinating. Let me see if I can rearrange my schedule." He took out his phone and walked fifteen feet away, then faked another phone call. He returned a half minute later. "Okay," he said. "I pushed my other meeting back. We're all clear."

As transparent as it was, Ernie accepted the lie with an innocent gratitude. "Gosh, that's nice of you. I'll tell you what: it's just about lunchtime. Why don't we go over to the Cathay, like you suggested, and I'll tell you the story over lunch."

Not the Peace Hotel, the *Cathay.* That's where they were headed, no question about it. This man had known Sassoon! How many people alive could say that? Harrington had thought the city was something fixed in place with names and numbers—this club or that restaurant—but it had suddenly become much more than that. As in the garden the night before, he sensed the afterlives of Shanghai's denizens in the throng of people who surrounded him on the broad walkway. Taxi dancers and bar girls, bankers and businessmen, traders, veterans, hustlers, police: people who at this moment looked as modern as they had looked in 1946, still unexamined by the curious backward gaze of the future. Ernie was one of them, and he realized that he himself was one of them, coursing along through the black-and-white past, a figment of someone else's imagination.

"One second," Ernie said. He stopped beside the formidable bronze lions of the old Hongkong Bank and fumbled with his camera. He aimed it into the distance, muttering something about the focus, when there, in a sight so strange and wonderful that Peter Harrington thought at first it was a hallucination, there was the unmistakable head of curly blond hair, the famous face, the entourage of Chinese onlookers soaking him into their cell phone cameras. Closer, until there could be no doubt about who it was, nonsensical on the Shanghai sidewalk. He was approaching, his expression intense and focused solely on Peter, as if he somehow remembered him from that bar in New York all those years ago and realized that they were both rock stars after all. Straight toward him, as if his other life had finally arrived: it was Pete Harrington.

III

✢

Kickin' It
with The
Man

✢

1

The House at Wilksbury

⁂

The bus had broken down somewhere outside Wilksbury, Pennsylvania, after a gig in Cleveland. Pete Harrington remembered that because, when he was a teenager, his grandfather had told him that as a young man drifting through Wilksbury he'd met the most beautiful girl he'd ever seen, and that if he'd had half a chance to win her, he would have stayed on there the rest of his life. That was 1932, and a pretty girl didn't have much interest in a twenty-year-old hobo offering to do chores for food. Pete never understood why the old man was still telling the story fifty years later: he thought maybe Gramps had run out of things to talk about. Then, between a gig in Cleveland and another in Philadelphia, he'd been drifting off to sleep when he saw a green highway sign for Wilksbury, and he remembered his grandfather and the girl. The next thing he knew he woke up and the bus was silent and stationary. Everyone else in the band was sleeping.

The gas station sat far from the highway. An old one, with white clapboard sheathing and a solid wooden garage door that swung up on springs. Christmas-tree air fresheners in little packets. A glass-doored vending machine with pale white-bread sandwiches in it. It had nothing interesting about it, but at the same time its antiquated presence buzzed with mysterious lives whose contours he could almost imagine.

It was five A.M. They were wrapping up the *Wreckage* tour, so it must have been autumn. It had been raining around there; it seemed like it would start raining again any minute. Behind them, the highway cars were hissing into the bleached-out dawn sky, and big trucks groaned and gunned their engines to climb the grade, bouncing their machine voices off the rock cuts.

The owner of the station had just arrived wearing a pair of blue coveralls with a little white oval on the breast that said LES, and he dumped some coffee into a frilly filter and set it gurgling. Les and the driver and Bobby talked over how long it would take to get parts from Pittsburgh, and could he find them transportation to Charleston? Pete wandered away to the edge of the parking lot to take a leak and looked out over the fields that floated through the mist down below him. A red barn sat at the bottom of the slope, and, far off on the other side, he could see a farmhouse with a wide porch and a tree in the front yard. For some reason he thought about Gramps again and his half-century-old story about the house and the girl, and he realized that this must be that house. He scrambled down through the litter and the wet bushes to check it out.

The barn was open at the sides, and there were big yellow leaves hanging all around from the rafters, which he realized, to his amazement, was tobacco. Bales of hay formed a little fortress in one corner; some had been broken down into a big soft pile that smelled so sweet and grassy that it went to his head, the best thing he'd ever smelled. He saw a pitchfork, a tractor attachment of some sort. There was a faint odor of diesel and lubricants. He was startled when something moved. Then he heard the snuffling and dense breathing of a horse. He felt uneasy all of a sudden, and he stepped out again, into the field.

The house sat some two hundred yards away from him, and he could see that a light was on in one corner of the ground floor, probably the kitchen. Someone was making breakfast; he was sure of that. Supermarket coffee percolating on the stove in an aluminum pot. There'd be oatmeal. Bacon. Three fried eggs, like the "truckers' breakfast" in the truck stop, except this

was the "home" of all the promised "home cooking" at every highway restaurant he'd ever been to. Who lived there, at home? He dreamed a middle-
aged couple, maybe with a few kids. The mother was the first one up, with
an apron on, presiding over the salty smell of morning. Maybe they had a
daughter, a beautiful eighteen-year-old daughter, the most beautiful girl in
western Pennsylvania, fairy-tale beautiful. He'd knock on their door, and
they'd open it and look him over. He'd say, *Hi, I'm Pete Harrington and my
bus broke down on the highway out there.* They'd invite him in and offer him
something to eat, not knowing who he was, and the beautiful daughter would
come downstairs to stare at him and he'd stay around for a few days in the
guest room, doing some chores around the place, helping in the fields, chopping wood, and before he knew it, it would be home, and she'd be his, and
they'd be living this gorgeous green life of hot black coffee and waking up
on autumn mornings in a world that was antique and crisp and uncluttered
and luminous. That whole life transpired in a moment as he stood there,
from lying naked with his new wife to walking with his grandchildren, just
a feeling, but so strong and possible that he felt he could make it real, just
by reaching out and touching it.

He made a few steps toward the house. The field was filled with stubble,
and he could feel the cold dew soaking through his velvet tennis shoes. The
earth was soft and rich. The rectangle of light on the other side of the mist
seemed to pulse almost imperceptibly.

Pete! Where the hell are you going? Get your stoned ass up here!

Bobby's voice. He turned around and his manager was up at the top of
the slope, at the edge of the gas station parking lot. Duffy and Cody were
standing next to him and they probably thought he was still spaced from the
mushrooms. Maybe he was. He turned and looked at the farmhouse again,
the window with light in it, the dark ones where people were still sleeping.
His other home. Cody: *Come back up here before you get shot, man! We can't find
another lead singer!* The others yelled, too. He stopped and let their voices wash
over his shoulders. The farmhouse was vibrating there, across the field.

He'd never reach it. His life had caught up with him, with its news-
papers and its clothes all his size. He'd never reach it and he'd never be able

to explain it and he tried writing a song about it afterward that never came
out right, no matter how many words he added and subtracted. The song was
about the house near Wilksbury, and the girl he never saw, but if it was the
story of that girl, how could it not be the story of that gas station and the
barn and the night before and the mushrooms they'd eaten? The rain in
that place that had just turned to mist, but not the rain of the other place that
they had left behind, the light in the window, the little cloud of darkness
beneath the tree, the horse snorting, the grass breaking, the old man dreaming
of a life he'd never lived, the trucker passing northbound on the turnpike
strung with towns reaching for his thermos, thinking *Six hundred miles. Six
hundred miles. Six hundred miles . . .* The best ones always got away.

2

Thanks for Your Support

⊕

The problem, he thought, was that you only had one life, when really you needed three or four. You should be able to say, okay, boss: done being me! Ready to be, say, the president, or maybe this guy in the liquor ad sailing out into space on a couple strips of fiberglass. That looked insane! Hanging with the snow bunny by the roaring fire, sipping a . . . what was it . . . Hennessy cognac? A gig he could handle!

He sensed the waitress beside him with the tray and he draped the copy of *Vanity Fair* over his laptop. He hadn't gotten any songs written, but he'd probably work better after breakfast, with better blood sugar. It was only eleven, and he had plenty of time.

"Here you go, Pete. One 'Healthy Choices Breakfast.' One double vodka and mango juice." She said it without irony: she'd been on the scene that long. Pete Harrington looked up at her over his red-tinted reading glasses and smiled. "Thank you, gorgeous." He remembered her bartending at the Whisky twenty years ago, when she was young and hot, and, though he couldn't place it exactly, it seemed like he'd fucked her in a closet during one of his gigs there, unless that was some other blond chick. He always wondered about it when he saw her in here, but he hadn't figured out a good way to ask. She's still not bad: a tad heavier at the waist, but a nice rack to make up for it. Face a little harder, but he'd come to like that in a woman. Live this life, and your face damn well better be a little harder, or you haven't learned a thing.

Reading the fan mail that came in through his Web site. On a good day he'd get twenty letters, anything from fortysomething women sending naked pictures of themselves to hard-core fans asking about the drum kit used on the East Coast leg of the *Wreckage* tour, after Cory fucking offed himself by drinking a bottle of 151 in one gulp. Sometimes he got letters from China; he could always tell by the bad English and the little chicken tracks along the bottom of the page. Bobby said they still remembered him from that whole crazy tour in 1992, but it was all pirated, so who cared? Some letters asked prying personal questions. *How many women have you slept with, Pete? When was your first sexual experience?* Yeah, like I'd tell you. A lot of them were still cheering him on about the thing that happened with the bassist from Uncle Sam's Erection. He had an antenna for the losers, the ones who were way too into him. Others looked like pretty well-balanced people who just liked his music. "When's your next release coming out?" Or, better, "I saw you in Detroit on your last tour, and, man, you've still got it!" He usually didn't answer them himself: Bobby said it lessened his mystique, but once in a while, when someone sent something that really made him feel good, like someone who said they really liked one of his later albums, or maybe if the woman in the picture looked young and pretty, he'd send a short little reply, like, "Thanks for your support. Keep rockin! Pete."

He looked down at the oatmeal and the packet of green tea beside the mug, then took a long sip of the cocktail. Fifteen minutes to eat breakfast, then he'd get to work. The tour was in three or four months, so he had to write the songs, get a band together, and nail them down, not to mention rehearsing his classics, which is what everybody came to hear, anyway. Bobby'd been pretty clear about that fact, over and over. *They want to hear the hits, Pete. You captured that moment for them, and only you can bring it back.*

He mixed some diced dried fruit into his oatmeal, then dumped some brown sugar and cream over it. Healthy fucking choices. He gulped down the rest of the cocktail.

The tour. So far it was Old Nevada Silver Days, in Elko, followed, probably, by a week at a Harrah's. The Harrah's in Reno, not Vegas, but Bobby claimed it was a foot in the door to Vegas. After that the Fresno Harvest Festival, and then the convention center in Anchorage, Alaska, which Bobby claimed was becoming the next Pacific Northwest underground scene. "It's like Seattle just before Nirvana broke," Bobby said. "Believe me: you want these people to hear your new songs." He'd played Anchorage before: he wasn't seeing Nirvana there.

He turned the page past the skier. It was a perfume ad, which meant that it was more or less a lingerie ad and an evening-dress ad. The black-haired woman, probably Chinese, in soft-focus gazing out at him from the seat of a limousine, a white sleeve with a cuff link resting on her bare thigh, where her cocktail dress had gotten mysteriously hitched up. What was the message here? *Buy this perfume and you will be sexy. Sexy and elegant. So sexy and elegant and in-control that millionaires will feel you up in their expensive cars. And what could be better than that?* He'd screwed this model, hadn't he? During the *Looking for the eXit* tour? The DreamKrushers had just hit the cover of *Rolling Stone* and she'd spotted him at a party in New York. Stalked him like a game animal. They ended up in his room, and in the half-light after she'd done everything he asked, she'd looked up at him, in that same soft focus, with the same look.

Crap, that was twenty years ago. That woman was probably this model's mother. And now he was just another sucker, like millions of others who saw the ad, plugging himself into someone else's story. He might as well be out there in America somewhere—sitting in a strip mall beauty salon in Fargo or walking into some hardware store in Alaska wearing oily coveralls—see this picture on the counter, and think, "This is the woman I should have had, not fucking *Maybelle*!" And there'd be some proprietor type behind the counter named Luke or Jimmy or Arnie, saying, like, *We've got a special on reversible screwdrivers, Harry!* And Harry'd just be, like, *I wonder if I can shoot myself six times in the head?*

He could feel the glimmer of a song. A sort of Mellencamp anthem about small-town America, their faded dreams, the unpretentious value of their simple lives that they can't recognize because they're longing for something in a magazine. He picked up the pen and paper he always kept with him and jotted, *Staring at a model in the hardware store, she's looking right at him, she's asking for more . . . You were supposed to be mine, not this faded time . . .* Something, something, something, *Vanity Fair.* Because it was, like, people's vanity that stood between them and happiness, and the media stoked that vanity and kept it just out of reach at the same time.

Maybe there was something there. Already he could see himself finishing the song, cutting a quick demo. Some quiet acoustic guitar riffs and just a bass drum to give some shape to the silence in the background . . . His own voice repeating, *"Vanity Fair."* Then the fucking label guy saying, "Too Mellencamp."

Fuck them. He tried to add on to *Vanity Fair* in his head. What came next, after the magazine? Some lost love? Lost opportunity? *Used to go to the races, with the roar and the lights,* something, something, *feeling all right . . . You were supposed to be mine, not this broken time,* something, something, something, *Vanity Fair.*

It was stupid. *Feelin' all right* was the most overused phrase in rock, and besides, Joe Cocker had squeezed everything out of the words that was worth squeezing. *Go to the races,* yeah, that was original! We're off to the races. A day at the races, it's a horse race, a rat race—never heard any of those before! The whole thing: some guy longing for a different life, shinier than his own: how many songs had been written about that? What the hell did he have to add to that wide, sorry genre?

He leaned forward and rested his elbows on the table and his forehead on his fingertips, staring down at the unfocused furrows of black-and-white print over his laptop. When the label guys got in your head, you were fucked. Period. It's what they did: they killed shit with their labels, hung a word on it that dragged it down like an anchor.

He hadn't finished a song in two years, just a bunch of fragments that he always told people were waiting for some overdubbing, like a new album was going to be popping out next Thursday, or maybe the Thursday after that. He didn't even call up Duffy to work on things anymore. Duffy'd gotten a regular gig with Face the Cobra, and though he'd never actually say no, he always had a scheduling problem, and even when he did come over they ended up mostly drinking and talking about old days, or he'd bring his wife and she'd bring a friend and they'd just hang out by the pool and drink gin and tonics and whatever. Because what they both knew was that even if Pete Harrington wrote a good song, it didn't matter anymore. A song was just a shell. You needed the backing that would put it in heavy rotation all over America and send it ringing through the buzzing electric field that hung above the earth, and from there into people's ears and into their brains, where they made it something private and glowing of their own. That energy took promoters and publicists and aggressive management. It took money, and nobody was going to put that money into a forty-five-year-old lead singer without a band whose main gig now was doing covers of his twenty-five-year-old self.

He drank the last of the mango and vodka cocktail and pushed away his Healthy Choices oatmeal, wished he'd ordered bacon instead. He flipped the page of the magazine. More noise about the financial crisis: some billionaire who bet against Mom and Pop and won big when the show collapsed. Read about that shit in the papers, the Wall Street guys walking away with millions while all these other people lost their houses and their retirements. At least he'd ducked that one. That's what he hired money guys for.

Which was why the whole thing with the Boxster didn't make sense. It was probably his fault for not putting it in valet parking, but there was a space almost right in front of the Rainbow, so, like, why not? When he paid the tab and got to the street, there was a large light-brown man getting into his car.

"Hey!" Pete ran up and grabbed the edge of the door to keep the guy from closing it, and for a second he regretted it as the big man slowly got out of the driver's seat and stood up in front of him. His chest and belly formed a bulging slab of black polo shirt underneath his gray sport coat, and the overall impression was of immovable bulk, detailed out by an over-size face with a razor-thin beard running along the jawline. "Pete Harrington," he said.

Pete felt that little positive charge that he always got when he was recognized. "That's right. What are you doing with my car, bro?" He tried not to let it sound whiney, but it was hard, because the man was so damn big. Big men and sexy women messed with your perspective whether you liked it or not.

The guy pulled some papers out of his coat and spouted a bunch of noise at him about no payments for sixty days and the leasing company and re-possession.

Harrington looked at the form. It had his name and address on it, even his social security number. Then a bunch of legal stuff. "That's bullshit! It's paid on the fucking"—he wasn't really sure when it was paid, because Lev always paid it for him, but he took a swing at it anyway—"the fucking seventeenth of every month!"

"You gotta settle that with them. *Here . . .*" He handed the musician the leasing company's business card. "Call this number." The man seemed to sense that Pete wasn't going to push it, and he squeezed himself back into the tiny front seat. He started the engine and looked up at him. "I love your music, Pete! You're on my favorites list."

"Awesome! Which cuts?"

The man put the car in gear and it started to roll forward. "Everything up to when you went solo. It was all downhill after that."

The tires chirped and Pete Harrington watched the yellow Boxster disappear over the hill toward Doheny. *Thanks, man,* he thought. *Thanks for your support.*

They met up for lunch at a restaurant he'd read about in *Los Angeles* magazine, the latest French-sounding place on Avenue of the Stars where a lot of the Creative Artists agents took their clients for lunch. Table for four for Mr. Harrington. The valet showed the proper professional respect, *Hello,*

Mr. Harrington, even though Pete thought he saw a glimmer of surprise at the Volkswagen he drove up in. It was the extra car he kept around for out-of-town visitors. "Mine's in the shop," he explained, and he gave the valet a twenty-dollar tip, just to show him he could. The hostess was a nice-looking brunette, probably thirty-five, professional hostess-actress type you found in the high-end restaurants. She recognized him and told him she liked his music and she looked like she just might be doable if he took her out to dinner and a club. He ordered a vodka and mango cocktail as she led him to his table. "Bring it quick!" He smiled as they came into view of the three men. "It looks like I'm going to need it."

Bobby was sitting next to his investment guy, Jason, and across from them was Lev, his accountant. He could sense a weird energy: the three men weren't chewing over the menu or bullshitting about little stuff. They were huddled together talking something over, and Bobby was saying something low and sharp-sounding to Jason as he and the hostess reached them. There was an orchid on the table and sweating glasses of sparkling water with lemon wedges next to the plates.

"Hey Pete!" Jason came halfway to his feet and stuck out his hand like he was grabbing on to a life preserver. He had a sickly look of welcome on his face that hung like a stink in the space between them. He was about ten years older than Pete, a small man with thinning hair that was badly dyed to an army-boot black. It never worked on those older guys, like, *Hey, your face is all wrinkly and you've got the hair of a twenty-year-old? I don't think so.* Jason wore a suit and tie, as always, because the financial guys always wanted to show how permanent and conservative they were, and how carefully they were watching your money. He didn't put out a lot of confidence at the moment: he was cringing in his corner of the booth, avoiding contact with Bobby's heavy body as if Bobby was an electric fence. It looked like he'd been brought here at gunpoint.

Bobby and Lev both stood up and gave him a serious greeting. Lev, his accountant, was wearing a short-sleeve silk shirt with royal flushes on it that he'd picked up in Bangkok. He had about a dozen from the same store. He'd told Pete all about it one time, but Pete had forgotten what it was that

made them special. Same as the hipster goatee reduced to a half-inch patch
of beard on his chin, a style that had been around for a while but that he
must have figured was still current. Bobby was as usual: a big curly head of
black hair, a dark T-shirt over his gut. Over six feet tall. He'd been a road
manager before he took on all the management duties and he still had that
roadie vibe. The guy who could heft an amp into a semi at two in the morning and still stiff-arm some late-night autograph seeker when necessary.

Except for the weird vibe, this wasn't so different from how things were
supposed to work. Usually, when some little money glitch came up he'd get
a call from Lev giving him a little lecture about not pissing away his money
quite so fast on shit like coke and racehorses, and then he'd have Lev call
Jason and they'd talk to each other and the noise would go away. So what
were they all doing here?

Nobody was drinking, which was unusual for Bobby. A couple of people
at the tables nearby were staring at him, and he carefully ignored them,
though he pushed his blond hair a little to the side. Pete slid in next to Lev
and opened up his menu. The hostess showed up with his drink and he
called her an angel of mercy and took a couple of gulps.

"What looks good?" The other three picked up their menus like an
afterthought. He went down the list of entrees. He was rigid about what he
ate, because lately he'd noticed that it tended to stick to him if he wasn't.
He was good at refusing things, though. At least, things other than co-
caine. Or women. Or, gotta face it, booze. Crazy menu. He didn't even
know what half this shit was. Radicchio? Why couldn't they just call it a
radish? You needed a fucking special assistant just to order for you. Radicchio, radicchio . . .

"So . . ." he drawled in a leisurely voice, without looking up from the
menu. "Some guy repo'd my Boxster yesterday."

He dropped it in and then peered up over his reading sunglasses at them.
Jason looked like the menu was the most interesting thing he'd seen his
whole life. Bobby looked annoyed, and for a few seconds the only sound he
heard was the João Gilberto tune playing in the background. The safe choice.
Classy in a completely generic way.

"Jason . . ." Bobby's voice had that overly friendly tone that meant he was ready to start yelling at someone. He pulled down the menu that Jason was looking at. "Why don't you explain it to him?"

Jason swallowed. His voice was quavering a little. "Well, first of all, I want to say I'm really sorry about how this all turned out."

"*You're* sorry? That's my Boxster, man. Why is some three-hundred-pound Samoan guy showing up with a fucking court order and telling me I haven't made my payments? Do you know how embarrassing that is?"

There! He'd fucking laid it out there for them and they'd better have an answer.

Nobody said anything, and then Bobby nudged Jason with his elbow. "Go on, Jason, tell him."

Now Jason picked up a piece of paper and held it out to him. It was shaking.

See, Pete, we've got some liquidity issues at the moment . . .

He started into one of those long Jason-type speeches that Pete tuned in to and then out of, but still looking like he was thoughtfully following it all. He put on his reading glasses to look at the piece of paper Jason had given him, looked over them to see if he could spot the hostess, took them off, and wiped them. He really liked these glasses. He'd picked them up a few months ago when he left his Versaces on an airplane. These were Gucci: slightly pink, very cool. He'd had the original lenses taken out and replaced them with the tinted bifocal ones. This way, if some paparazzi caught him off guard, it'd look like he was wearing sunglasses, not reading glasses. They *were* from last summer, though. Maybe he should pick up a new pair. That could be tomorrow's mission. Get mirrored lenses, or maybe black, like a limo window. Flip 'em down below his eyes: *climb right in, sugar.* Those'd be some kickass reading glasses! Meanwhile, words kept popping up over and over again from Jason's little speech: *bond, derivative, liquidity.* He might as well have been speaking Egyptian. This was shit that he paid people like Lev and Jason to think about. Why were they bothering him with this? He waved his hand upward in a little spiral of dismissal. "*Whatever,* Jason! Just take care of it. That's what I pay you and Lev for."

Jason looked at Bobby and Bobby glared back at him.

Lev took over. "Pete, Jason invested most of your money in a bond fund called Crossroads Partners. They bought a kind of bond based on people's mortgages. Jason thought they'd give you good income without any risk."

"I was told they were fixed-income—"

Lev cut him off. "But you didn't read the prospectus."

"When the biggest banks on planet earth are selling it as fixed income, you don't read the prospectus!"

Lev turned toward the musician. " 'Fixed-income' means rock-solid investments that don't fluctuate in their rate of return, like municipal bonds. You're a retired businessman with a million dollars in the bank and you buy bonds at five percent and live on the fifty thousand a year. They never lose value."

Jason wouldn't let it drop. "Their guy stood up in front of fifty financial advisors and said they were fixed-income! Fixed-income that paid nine percent! How else was I going to keep Pete afloat? You know how much he spends! Do the math!" He turned to Bobby and said angrily, "Do you mind if I get up to take a piss?"

Bobby slid out to let him pass, then got back in.

Lev said, "That's the last we'll see of that idiot."

"Fuck, man." Pete laughed, lifting his empty cocktail tumbler. "I'm dry already. And I definitely need another one."

Lev talked some more. Pete listened to him, but he kept getting distracted by the poker hands on his shirt. All royal flushes. But if everyone has a royal flush, they split the pot, right? So what the shirt was really saying is, even when you think you're holding a winner, life's a goddamn stalemate, so fuck you. Maybe that's what was so special about that store in Bangkok—fucking *irony*.

". . . And the first thing is, do you want to take the deal?"

"What deal?"

Lev looked annoyed. "One of the big banks is offering to buy out what's left of Crossroads' bonds for five cents on the dollar, and you have to decide whether to take it. You'd clear about four hundred thousand."

"Four hundred thousand. That sounds pretty good."

Lev looked over at Bobby, who put his hand to his forehead and looked away. "Pete! It's not good. It's what you have left out of eight million."

The singer took off his reading glasses. There was something really serious about this that he didn't like.

Lev went on in a soft but insistent tone. "Let's try it again: if you take the offer . . ."

He was listening now. Listening harder than he'd listened to either of them in a long time. It was like there was a messenger on horseback wearing a red coat, coming from far away over the hills, reappearing around each bend a little bit closer, a little bit bigger, that red pennant, the pounding of the hooves: he's coming. *If you take the money, you'll have enough to live on for a few months at your present level. Otherwise, there's a class-action lawsuit you can join, in which case you might get a payoff a few years down the line, but maybe not. In these kinds of class-action lawsuits . . .*

He put his hand up in the accountant's face. "Hold the noise for a second, Lev. You said, 'enough to live on for a few months.'"

Lev stared at him for a second, looking annoyed. "Pete! You're broke!"

"What do you mean *broke*? I can't be broke! Jason told me I had eight million dollars of assets!" Actually, he couldn't quite remember how much Jason had said he had, because Jason always gave such complicated explanations about assets and liabilities when what Pete really wanted to know was: can this go on? And if it could, then he didn't need all that static about liabilities and cash flow and etc., etc., etc.

Now Lev started in on him again. "You had eight-point-three million in *assets,* but you also had liabilities. Unfortunately, your assets are worth about one tenth of what they were before. But your liabilities are the same. And when that happens, and you miss payments, people start wanting your assets. That's what happened with the Boxster. I've been telling you this for six weeks. Didn't you read my e-mails?"

Bobby was actually trying to be gentle with him. "You're broke, Pete. That's the bottom line."

Message delivered. He was still taking that one in when the hostess came up to them. "Would anyone like a drink?" She looked like she was giving him a special smile as she glanced around the table and finished looking directly at him. Yeah, she was definitely available. Probably thirty-five, nice body tone, all the parts still in place, and with a whole lot of experience at making them work together. He stretched his gaze up at her over his reading glasses. "What's on offer?"

The messenger in the red coat had moved on now; things were back to normal. Bobby and Lev knew better than to cramp his style, and he had a nice little exchange with the hostess before he ordered another vodka and mango. He watched her walk away, then turned back to Lev. "So I'm broke." He shrugged. "I've been broke before."

"Exactly," Bobby said, comfortingly. "It's nothing you can't deal with. You've been up and you've been down, and, either way, you're still Pete Harrington and you've got millions of people every day who listen to your music and love you. Meanwhile, we have to do some streamlining."

Lev pulled out some papers to explain exactly what "streamlining" meant, which was sell the house, sell the place in Montana, sell the race car, take the deal offered by the bank. Get an apartment and keep his living expenses under five thousand a month. That would look good to the judge when he got to bankruptcy court.

"Bankruptcy court?"

"Yeah, Pete. A couple of banks are getting ready to foreclose on your houses and they're going to want your song catalog, if they can get it."

"The banks?" He remembered the article he'd looked at in the magazine the day before. "You mean the same banks who just pulled off the biggest heist in the history of the fucking world? Those banks? The ones who held the whole fucking galaxy for ransom when they needed a bailout? Where the *fuck* do they come off foreclosing on *me*?"

The hostess showed up at that moment with his second drink, and they all went silent as she put it on the table. She started with a big smile, but then she glanced at the faces and left without a word.

Lev said, "Maybe you ought to hold off on that drink until we're finished."

"I could use one," Bobby said suddenly, putting his hairy fingers around the tall glass. "That okay, Pete?"

"Fucking *whatever*, Bobby!" He let the annoyance pass. "Lev, I'm about to go on tour in three months. Can't that raise enough money to take care of this?"

Lev looked at Bobby, then back at him. "Pete, we looked at the income side, and I'm not seeing salvation there. We could sell your catalog, but that wouldn't save much and would leave you without any income stream in the future. I don't want to see you go there." Lev went back to the list. "I guess the Boxster's taken care of. Then there's three Harleys. Anything left in the wine cellar?"

Another one of his hobbies. He still got the Sotheby's catalogs. "Nope."

Lev raised his eyebrows without looking up from the list. He started to go into more detail, including an action plan for each item: call a Realtor, fix the driveway, sell the horses—crap he wouldn't know how to do in a million years. Look for an apartment—was he serious? Lev was still rattling on with various tiresome shit when his order came: a twenty-five-dollar hamburger made with meat from some special farm, cheese from some special village in the French Alps. They should have called it *hamburgicchio.*

"And, uh, Matthew's got to go."

"Matthew! That's ridiculous! What am I going to do without Matthew?"

"Let's see . . . Go to the supermarket? Answer the phone? Take your own clothes to the dry-cleaners? Not to be snippy, Pete, but most of us do that every day."

"Well, I'm not most of us, Lev, and I would think you'd have figured that out by now! Everybody has an assistant! I mean, you're a fucking accountant, and you've got an assistant!"

"Show some respect, Pete," Bobby cut in. "Lev's just trying to help you out here."

"Hey! You're right. I'm sorry, Lev. My head's all messed up." He put his forehead in his hand and squeezed his temples. He could see his Gucci reading glasses sitting on the table, but they didn't look cool anymore. They just looked like reading glasses. "What happened here, Lev? Is it my fault? Is it

Jason? Because if it's Jason, I'm going to track his silly ass down and beat him with a fucking seven-iron!"

He expected Lev to get all over Jason's shit, like Bobby had, but Lev's voice was strangely gentle. "Jason never should have put eighty percent of your assets into one instrument. And he should have read the prospectus, just like thousands of other people should have. If you want to go after Jason, you have good grounds for a negligence suit. But you wouldn't get anything out of him. Jason's ruined. He lost his house and his FA license." He shrugged. "And he deserved to. But the fact is, Jason got conned by experts. There was fraud every step of the way, but the guy at the top walked away with hundreds of millions of dollars, and he'll never be prosecuted for anything. You want to track somebody down with a seven-iron? That's who you ought to go after."

"Who is he?"

"His name is Peter Harrington."

"Yeah, Lev, that's really funny. I really need sarcastic morality shit right now."

His accountant smiled. "No, really! His name is Peter Harrington! If you were ever ego surfing, you must have run across him."

He tended to consider those other Peter Harrington entries on the Internet interlopers on his fame, but, come to think of it, Crossroads did sound familiar. "The fucker even ripped off my name?"

"That's ironic," Bobby said.

"No, man, it's not ironic," Pete answered. "It's *seven*-ironic! Yes!" He curled his fingers, and Bobby responded with a congratulatory fist bump at the pun. "I'll deal with Mr. Peter Harrington later." He motioned toward Lev's list. "Go on. Because every item on that list I'm taking out of that guy's ass."

As they went over the accountant's plan, it began to dawn on Pete that things really were about to change. When he left this table, he'd be walking into a whole other life, a sort of underlife that had been secretly waiting for him beneath what he thought was his real life. He tried to put it out of his mind.

The bill came, and they all stared at it for a moment. Close to a hundred bucks for a burger and a couple of sandwiches. Pete waited a few seconds to see if anyone else would pick it up.

"We can split it," Lev said.

"Forget it!" He reached for the check. "It's still a business meeting." He threw his gold card down on the little black tray. A few minutes later the hostess came back with an awkward look on her face. Pete knew why she looked so embarrassed. This was her last chance to hook up and she had to figure out how to make her play in front of everybody. He smiled encouragingly at her. No use making her beg.

"Mr. Harrington?"

"Angel of mercy?"

"I'm sorry. Your card's been declined."

He laughed out loud. It looked like that date wasn't happening.

Bobby picked it up and they all left. The same valet fetched his car, a young Mexican guy who looked just about right driving up in the old Volkswagen. The Gardenermobile. "Here you are, Mr. Harrington."

He felt like pretending the car was someone else's, but there it was, served up with his name on it. He folded up a fifty and put it into the valet's palm, who thanked him smoothly, without even looking at it.

He was on the computer within five minutes of getting home. Matthew was on his laptop, posting messages on the boards, or some shit like that, and he started to tell him about his phone calls, but he walked right past him, "Not now, Matthew," and went straight into the studio, which, since it hadn't been too active lately, he'd fitted out with a massive TV screen. He reached into the minifreezer for a bottle of vodka and was pleased as always to find it so cold that it was almost syrupy. He poured some vodka in a glass and shot it, then poured some more and flopped onto the couch. He put the keyboard on his lap and searched his name and "Crossroads." He got over a million hits on the wall-sized monitor. Shit! This other Peter Harrington was as big as he was.

He clicked on the pages, and the story started to come out. First, most recently, the fallout: journalistic crap about the collapse of Crossroads and how it had laid waste to a butt-load of banks and pension funds. Everybody shaking their heads, like this Harrington guy was Satan's fucking ethics professor. It didn't mention any bankers or pension-fund guys losing their jobs—that wasn't how those guys played it—but they did manage to find some Moms and Pops out on Main Street who'd seen a big chunk of their retirement get vaporized. They looked old and wronged, in that sour, hurting way that kneels down at night and prays, *God Almighty, grant me the serenity to accept the things I can't change, the courage to change the things I can, and a large-caliber handgun filled with fucking magnum rounds to blow this greedy motherfucker's balls off. Amen!* Or something like that. A prayer that never got answered. Even the government was crying foul, ponying up $160 billion to stabilize some insurance company, another couple hundred bil to rescue some banks. The funny thing was, searching back a few pages, all the same fuckers were saying just the opposite! Ass-kissing write-ups in *The New York Times* and *The Wall Street Journal*. Harrington's a genius, a rock star! *Rock star!* Nothing remotely "rock star" about him: that pasty skin, the high forehead and wispy brownish hair. His face was shaped like a peanut, for Christ's sake!

He kept moving backward in the search engine, where relevance to the terms "Peter Harrington" and "Crossroads" began to drift. Now the foreign-language entries began to surface, in German and Chinese. He translated a few, but most came out too garbled to understand. A bunch of hits to the Metropolitan Opera and the Museum of Modern Art, and a half dozen other charities the shithead seemed to mess around with. Showing up at parties with his picture next to unrecognizable people who must mean something in that world. Hey, there he was with Al Pacino! And again next to some model chick, and Calvin Klein. *Livin' large, on my money.* Further back, the traces of Harrington's earlier career were floating around. Promoted to vice president of Special Purpose Vehicles at Goldman Sachs, something about extreme skiing. He skied? Something fired in Harrington's memory, and he clicked on the link.

It was an old back issue of *Ski* that someone had scanned in, and the cover said "The Greatest Extreme Skier on the Planet," with a picture of some dude just completely launching into the ether, the edge of some ungodly steep mountain behind him and a mountain range far off below him, flying over it on his skis like gravity had never been invented. Unreal. He looked at it a few seconds, imagining himself up there, hanging effortlessly in the sky, and then he remembered. This was that skier he met that time! The guy from Alaska! Mitch's friend: he was in L.A. trying to be somebody, or maybe Mitch was trying to make him somebody, but when you looked at the picture, it was pretty clear that he was somebody all by himself. He'd been supposed to meet that guy in Tahoe. That was it: they'd been all set up to do some runs in Tahoe and then Beth unleashed fucking World War Six on him and that ski trip was the least of his worries. He couldn't reach the guy to cancel, and Mitch told him later he'd snapped his leg or something. Never saw him again, and he hadn't seen Mitch in about ten years either.

He looked at the picture again. In some other life they skied together, and he taught him how to fly like that. To jump and be free from all the shit that dragged a person down: time, losing your audience, losing your money, just the whole thing about the world's interest that moved on, and you really had no control over it. Where was that guy now? Still flying? He wondered if his offer was still good.

By the time he came out of the room, dusk had come down. Matthew had gone, and he went out alone to the pool and sat by the blue rectangle that looked out over the city. This would all be gone soon. All of this that he'd worked his whole life for would be gone, and he'd be living in an apartment somewhere down there, back where he was twenty years ago when he'd first come to L.A., except that twenty years ago he'd been young, and all this had been ahead of him: a big magical future. Things are so fresh when they hit you the first time. Your first lunch where the suits pick up the tab, *cool,* your first deal, like, *yeah, of course!,* your first person going absolutely speechless when they meet you, your first model slipping you the tongue, your first two-on-one, your first time walking into a party and realizing everybody is staring at you, your first trip in a chartered jet, your first stadium crowd cheering so loud your whole body shakes. Then the other stuff. The first time your buddy kills himself with a drug overdose. The first time you play to a half-empty house. The first time your name isn't on the VIP list. Not being invited to the party, not having your calls returned, not having your contract renewed. That stuff wasn't behind him. That shit was still in front of him.

Because what Harrington had taken away from him wasn't just money, it was possibility. Money was like water in L.A. With money you could hire a publicist, you could wear the right clothes at the right events, the thousand-dollar sunglasses, show up in the nice ride that was definitely *not* a late-model Volkswagen. You could throw parties and invite people who mattered, make donations to charity and issue press releases. In other words, you could do all the career-maintenance bullshit that he'd never had to do the first time around but that he realized he'd have to do now if he was ever going to get on top again. But Peter Harrington had ripped that chance away from him, just before he realized he needed to grab it. According to Lev, he couldn't even afford an assistant!

Screw Lev's action list! What he needed to do wasn't call a real-estate agent or pavement resurfacer. What he needed to do was track down Peter Harrington and beat the fucking daylights out of him! He's kicking it in a limo while I'm selling everything I have? He's living in a penthouse somewhere while I'm looking for a two-bedroom apartment? It was time to settle a score here, and not just his. Everybody's! All those working stiffs and old folks and middle-class dupes who thought they'd make a little extra in the stock market, like the big guys, or thought they had a safe retirement. He'd find him, spin him around, say, *Hi, I'm Pete Harrington and you owe me eight million dollars,* and then just deck his silly ass. Give him a few stiff kicks while he was down. That was something worth doing! Fucking curling up and dying in a two-bedroom apartment in West Hollywood . . . Fuck that!

He imagined that peanut-shaped face. That grinning, smirking self-satisfied overeducated punk with his schemes and his millions! Thought he was The Man, didn't he? Well, he'd just go and kick it with The Man for a little while and see how he liked that.

That was a song right there—Kickin' It with The Man! Some untouchable money guy in a tuxedo getting the boot from one of the little people he'd ripped off.

Pete hummed a few chords, imagining them as guitar licks. *You think you got it all and you can't be reached. I got news for you: your fortress is breached.* Something, something, *a line in the sand.* Something, something, something, *now I'm kickin' it with The Man!* He laughed. *Fuck yeah!*

He felt a sudden surge of joy, a boundless power rising from within him and smashing all the doubt and bitterness of not only the last eight hours, but of the entire soggy decade of failure that had preceded them. He laughed at the incredible clarity, the lightning-like truth of it. The song, the knowledge that he'd practically been appointed by God to find this dirtbag and beat some fucking enlightenment into him. Yeah! You're fucking with God now, motherfucker! You're fucking with Right and Wrong and Justice and whatever your Wall Street buddies told you when they made the fucking rules in their own image doesn't mean shit anymore! You're guilty—you stole my name and I'm *fucking* going to make you pay!

He jumped up from the table and rushed into his studio. Two hours later he called Bobby. It was all different now. The mist had cleared. Shit was *on.*

Bobby had shown up with a bottle of tequila, and they'd already killed a quarter of it by the time the doorbell rang. "Look out," Bobby said, "that'll be Beth."

His ex-wife. "You called her?"

Bobby raised his hands helplessly.

He opened it and there she was: streaked brown hair, quick blue eyes in a round face, five feet, one inch of nuclear-powered New Jersey womanhood. She gave him her full body scan. Like at the airport, but more thorough: she could tell how much he'd drunk, how much he'd fucked off instead of

working, and the age of the last girl he'd slept with, all in a one-second
glance that she irradiated him with every time they met. It was that last
little vestige of ex-wife wariness. Although, realistically, she could probably
do that with anyone.

She gave him a quick kiss and one of those sympathetic sad-puppy looks.
He could tell she'd already talked to Lev and Bobby. Definitely knew about
the Boxster et al.

"Don't look so serious, Beth. Everything is awesome!"

"Awesome . . ." she repeated, because her mind was unquestionably like,
Crap, Pete's more fucked up than I thought! She shook it off. "Ira says hello. He
had to stay with the kids."

"Good man!" Thank God for Ira. Ira'd been his ticket back to her good
graces after their marriage liquidated, or, really, after he basically put a brick
of C-4 under it and pushed the plunger. He'd had to crawl on his stomach
over broken glass for years before she'd even talk to him. In a moment of
supreme inspiration he'd dropped Ira on her, and, to his amazement, they
could go on to being what they should have been in the first place: friends.
And in the clinch, you definitely wanted Beth Blackman as your friend.

She turned down an offer of tequila and sat on the couch to hear him
out. He explained the whole thing to her: who the other Peter Harrington
was, his Crossroads scam, and what he was going to do about it. When he
finished, she slid an empty shot glass toward Bobby. "Give me about a half
inch of that stuff, will you?" She and Bobby traded looks, then she started.

"Let me make sure I understand this, Pete. You're going to find this financier, punch him in the face, and you're writing a song about it that you're
going to use as the theme of your tour. And this plan has all developed in
the last eight hours."

"Don't try to talk me out of it, Beth. It's fucking righteous and it's what
I have to do, for me and for the thousands of other people who got ripped
off in this bankster's game."

"Fair enough." She looked over at Bobby again, who was flopped backward on the couch like a walrus on an ice floe. "I won't try to talk you out

of it. But let me just put a couple of things out there. First of all, there's a word for what you plan to do. It's called assault. And that little incident with Uncle Sam's Erection a few years ago? That's called a prior offense. You could get a lot more than sixty days this time."

"I don't care."

"You don't care." She nodded her head slowly. "Okay. What about the song? Have you written this song, or is this a song you're *going* to write?"

"Ha ha, Beth. Very funny. As a matter of fact, I wrote it today. And it's not some wimpy protest song—" His voice became nasal and cloying. "Wall Street bigwigs, we want justice, boo hoo hoo. No, it's, like, I'm finding this guy and I'm kicking the crap out of him! Because that's fucking *justice*!" He stood up. "This is hero shit, Beth! It might be too *epic* for you to understand!"

"But Jason's the one—"

"Jason's just the puppet! This guy's the puppeteer!" She started to say something but he talked over her. "Don't you get it? These guys fucked over an entire country! People lost their savings, they lost their houses. This fucking asshole made a fortune off other people's misery! Do I just kick back and let him get away with it?"

Beth patted the place on the sofa next to her. "Sit down. Okay? That's it. Put the glass down and look at me." She put her hand on his knee. "Pete. I'm your friend. Right? I've always given you the best advice I could. Isn't that true?"

"Yeah."

"I know this is all a shock, and when you're shocked, you want to fight back. But you can't fight when you're in quicksand. Lev says you're spending fifty thousand dollars a month, and you have to cut it to five. That's where your focus needs to be. Plus, you've got a tour you have to get ready for, right, Bobby?" Bobby nodded. "You need a new place to live, and there's going to be lawyers and forms to fill out and a lot of other things that aren't very pleasant. But you've got to be the grown-up here. This is the part where you save your own ass."

He gave a long exasperated breath. "I *am* trying to save my own ass. Don't you understand that?"

"Pete! It's a fantasy!"

"That's my life, Beth! Everything good I ever did started as a fantasy!"

"This is insane! Bobby—?"

The walrus roused himself. "She's right, Pete. It's insane."

He looked from one to the other, both of them so comfortable in their successful lives. And him. The failure. "There comes a time," he began in a low voice that got steadily louder, "when you get to the edge of the cliff, and you either back off, or you fucking launch it. And I will always, *always* launch it!" He jumped to his feet. "I'm going after this asshole! He stole my money. He stole my fucking name! He fleeced the whole goddamned world, and he thinks he's fucking untouchable! Well, he's not! I'm going to beat this guy down and I'm going to write a fucking anthem about it and the whole world's going to stand up and cheer!" He was shouting now. *"I'm touching the untouchable!* And if you can't understand why I need to do that, then you are *fired* as my manager and you are *fired* as my ex-wife! I'll do it without you!" He stormed across the carpet to the hallway, then turned around and threw back in a painful, enraged shout: "Fuck you!" He rushed into his bedroom and slammed the door.

Fuck it! In the end it always got down to this anyway. You were on your own and you had to do it for yourself and not for anyone else, and the more impossible it seemed, the more worth doing it probably was. Okay. He was alone. If nothing else, this whole Boxster thing and then being basically abandoned by Bobby and Beth brought everything full circle again and stripped away the illusion that he was anything but alone. Hell yeah! He was happy about it! There was nobody left to desert him now.

He heard Beth's and Bobby's voices coming from the living room. They were talking about something, and the volume kept creeping up around some argument Beth was making, answered by Bobby's sleepy croak. Then Beth's voice sawed away for a longer time, and Bobby croaked back, and then Beth said something short, then Bobby answered her kind of sharply, and he thought, *No, Bobby, no!* because then Beth went Jersey on him in a big way, and God help the SOB: he knew what that felt like. It wasn't just that she got loud: Beth could harsh a decibel until it was like having some dude caning you in a Singapore jail. It was quiet for a while, then Beth knocked on the door.

"Pete? Will you come out here, please? Bobby and I want to talk with you."

Bobby was sitting there like a house that had just had its roof ripped off by a tornado. Beth had refilled her glass of tequila.

Bobby started first, kind of slow and serious, like he didn't want to say the wrong thing. "Pete, I understand how you feel. You want to take this guy down a notch—"

"Not a notch, Bobby. I'm taking this guy all the way off the fucking totem pole!"

"Okay. He's off the totem pole. I understand. You want to do this? I'll help you."

"We'll both help you," Beth added.

This was a fucking attitude adjustment. The singer examined them both, looking for some trace of an angle. "What do you mean?"

Bobby answered. "For starters, you need to train for this. And we need to find out where Peter Harrington lives, stuff like that. And it all has to be done confidentially. It's complicated."

"But doable!"

"Doable," Bobby conceded.

"And worth doing," Pete insisted.

Beth spoke up. "It *is* worth doing. Bobby and I sat here after you left and we thought about it and we realized, Pete's right about this. Something really wrong happened here, and nobody was punished except the people at the bottom. That's wrong. When the system is rigged, maybe somebody needs to act outside the system."

"I told you," Pete answered calmly. "It's hero shit."

"It *is* hero shit," Beth agreed.

"It's superhero shit," Bobby said.

Now Beth took over. "So here's the deal, Pete. You take care of your

financial situation, which means all the things Lev told you to do, and
Bobby and I will try to find someone to help you on this project. But you
have to keep it quiet, and you have to keep us out of it. This is all *you,* and
nobody should think otherwise. Is that a deal?"

"Deal."

All three of them stood up and shook hands together. The singer felt a
swelling of joy and relief. The untouchable was getting closer.

3

Tiger Claws a Tree
A Precious Duck Flaps
Its Wings

✢

Knowing Bobby and Beth were backing him up made it marginally easier to see his life dismantled piece by piece. It went fast. The meeting with Lev and Jason had been on a Wednesday. By Friday he'd signed for a new apartment and some organizer woman from Panama had come over and put little colored stickers on all his shit: blue for stuff they were moving, green for stuff they were selling, and black for shit they were throwing out.

Like when his mom had moved into the nursing home and everything had to be cleared out. He'd been getting ready for the *Wreckage* tour so he hired a service to take care of it, but his sisters still got on him for not helping. The single day he'd shown up, one glance into the Dumpster had destroyed him. The blue ceramic mixing bowl, the one Mom used to make cookies in, sitting there on the heap with the crack finally broken completely open, and he'd started to tear up, and Cody was like, *Forget it man, it's gone,* and it was gone: his childhood, his father, the kids in the neighborhood. In a few months, Cody would be gone, too, stupidly. Chugging that rum, and everybody too wasted to know they needed to call 911. That was some fucking wreckage, all right. The show went on, everybody saying shit like, *Cody would want us to go on,* but the reality being that it was their first big tour and *they* wanted it to go on. It had that weird dead-friend vibe, beneath all the blow jobs and the interviews and the parties, like Cody was looking over their shoulders all the time, not disapproving, but insistent, and it gave a weird dimension to the tour, one he never talked about except with Duffy and Bobby. He never wrote a song about it, never knew how, just like he'd never write a song about the mixing bowl in the Dumpster or that house outside Wilksbury. It didn't rock.

He was supposed to be helping the process of closing up his house, but on the last day he just lay on a couch with a bottle of Jägermeister and watched it all wash away. Moving guys in and out for three hours. A couple of them asked for autographs between hauling his stuff. The stereo equipment, the pool furniture, the chrome floor lamp, the guitars. Fifteen years of his life turned into yellow tags at a secondhand store. When the only thing left was the couch he was lying on, he stood up, stepped into his sandals, and walked out.

This is what it came to. Two years in Tacoma with his high school band, then a couple more in Seattle, then three more in L.A. before the Dream-Krushers got signed. Everyone thought rockers appeared on the scene after a few months of club gigs; they didn't see the humiliating grind that led up to it. Asking for favors from people who owed you nothing, building mailing lists of potential fans, begging people to please come to your next show, please keep on liking you, because somehow you might be able to turn all that liking into a better gig, a bigger spotlight, a contract, a million dollars, a future of parties where you hung with people you couldn't quite imagine but that were somehow better than the ones you presently knew. A little bit like the perfume ad, where you thought you were going to be elegant and in control, when what you were really aspiring to was having some unseen rich guy feel you up in his limo. Which was kind of funny, actually.

Once he got into the new apartment, Bobby was the one who got him focused. They still had to find the Crossroads guy: he'd fallen off the charts a while ago, and they needed to know where he lived and where he hung out. Bobby would look into that, but if he was going to find this fucker and beat him down, he needed to prepare. "It'd be a shame if you tracked this punk down and got your ass kicked," Bobby said. "Plus, he might have a body-guard, so you can't dink around. I've put together a list of some martial arts teachers. You just have to pick one."

Bobby would always call ahead and make sure the instructors knew he was coming. There were some fans out there; a few autographs got signed, and one of the instructors told him that "Looking for the eXit" was one of his favorite songs. But mostly he was treated as no big deal, which made him a little uncomfortable amid all that sweating and kicking and shouting.

The different schools were like different styles of music. The big tae kwon do studio had rigid files of identically dressed students in white paja-mas, each kicking and shouting in unison, banging the heavy bag with jump-ing, spinning motions that would probably go over well in his act.

The kung fu class did most of their motions standing in place in a deep, wide stance—straight, powerful punches and big circular, whipping mo-tions. He liked their outfits, too: black pajamas with little frog closures. But when he tried a class, they set him in place and told him to hold a horse stance for five minutes. Legs wide, knees bent. After one minute, his thighs were shaking, and when he went to sit down, the instructor came and gave him a lot of noise in that Chinese accent. He walked out, just to show him he didn't have to take his shit, no matter what kind of master he was.

Bobby took him to some sort of Hsing-Yi-Bagua thing, with a fat, middle-aged instructor who wore his gray hair in a ponytail and looked about as dangerous as the Stay Puft Marshmallow Man. They spent the first twenty minutes standing still with their arms out in front of them in a cir-cle, breathing. Then they moved to a different position, and breathed some more. Then they walked around in a little circle moving their arms, like a little dance. Then they did some more breathing, just in case. Nobody looked particularly athletic: there were some stocky housewives and a couple of older guys. The master had a huge potbelly, which he said he used for Jujube gut. "Here," he said, "punch me in the stomach as hard as you can."

"Isn't this what killed Houdini?"

He insisted, so Pete punched him as hard as he could, a big wide swing that seemed to sink into the instructor's fat belly as if into a tub of Jell-O. The instructor never lost his smile. It was impressive, but he wanted to learn how to hit people, not how to absorb hits. And that belly? Seriously! That's what lipo was for.

He tried Muay Thai, but after one session with a personal trainer his shins were bruised and the muscles in his hips hurt. The Shito Ryu class was in a storage unit in Pasadena. They'd shoehorned a locker room and a tiny reception area into some raw space lit with fluorescent bulbs. The instructor was a tiny Japanese man who spoke bad English and obviously hadn't heard of him. The style itself looked businesslike and effective, but he couldn't see driving all the way to Pasadena to work out in a storage unit. At the boxing gym, they looked at him like they were just waiting for the chance to hit him in the face. The Brazilian jiujitsu class: no way! They'd break him in half!

He went through a dozen schools in three weeks, until it seemed like Bobby had run out of styles. "Pete, you're going to have to get serious about one of them. You can't keep blowing them off."

"I just don't feel it, Bobby!"

"I got one more guy," Bobby said. "I don't know too much about him. I heard about him through a bodyguard friend of mine. Evidently, he's got a lot of experience at the kind of skills you need. He used to be some kind of spy, or assassin. I'm not sure what, but it supposedly involved killing people."

Pete was in the tiny exercise room of his apartment, walking on his treadmill, but he stopped and let himself be carried backward to the floor. "Don't you think that's a little harsh?"

"I'm just saying, this is the guy's background. His name's Charlie. He's a war veteran and he helped train the Navy SEALs. I don't know anything else about him. Just that he can teach you what you need to know and help you find this guy and get close to him."

An assassin. At the very least, it'd be an interesting conversation. He'd never met an assassin before. "Set up a meeting."

"Evidently, you don't set up a meeting with this guy. You let him know, and then he'll set up the meeting with you."

They agreed, and the musician began to wait. With the imaginary assassin on his way, he began to train harder to be ready for him. He didn't want to look like a pussy. He hit the treadmill every day and started upping his time and speed. He started going to the gym again, eager to get to the weights and start lifting them, looking in the mirror afterward at his swollen muscles and imagining how intimidating it would be for his adversary when he finally confronted him.

But lifting weights was so boring! In fact, every day he seemed to do a little less weight lifting and a little more magazine reading. Or steaming. Or hanging out at the juice bar and scoping out the talent. Then he'd hit the weights for a few reps and call it good. Some days he spent half his time in the lounge, reading magazines. He had to keep current on the music business, not to mention reality shows and stuff so he could make good career choices once his new song took off.

He often thought of the man he was waiting to meet, picturing him in his forties, with dark hair and eyes and a navy-blue sport jacket, like James Bond. Or else he pictured him as a sort of human vulture, tall, pale, and bald, with aviator sunglasses that he never took off and a grave demeanor through whose lengthy silences blew the monotonous music of death. Or something like that. He'd have a low voice, be kind of slim but wiry, never smile. He'd be a good character for a song. *Hit man, do not follow me, with your graveyard voice and your little bag of time. Hit man, do not follow me, I had no choice and I* something, something *blind.*

But the hit man didn't seem to be following him. Two weeks passed, and he started to suspect that Bobby had been bullshitting, or that someone had been bullshitting Bobby, or maybe, and this depressed him, that a real pro just wasn't interested in working for a washed-up front man. The Pete Harrington name still impressed people, at least the little people. For people in the business, though, Pete Harringtons were the cheapest commodity around, used-up artists who'd had their day and didn't have enough talent or charisma or whatever it took to keep that day rolling out to new horizons.

Maybe this assassin had talked to some industry people or just put two and two together.

The whole thing was starting to feel empty. He still had no fight training and no plan for just how to do this. He didn't even know where Peter Harrington was! New York? Kickin' back in the Caymans with all the other tax dodgers? Bobby said he'd handle it, but maybe he was only going through the motions after all. A different future was starting to unroll, one where the other Peter Harrington kept on living large in some unknown place on his ripped-off fortune while this whole dream of justice went colorless and shapeless and dead, leaving him just another dumbass at the gym training for something that would never happen.

So when the word came down, he wasn't ready for it. He'd done his first set of reps, or actually half a set, then decided to take a break and have a cold soda. He eyed the room to see if there were any good-looking babes who recognized him. There was one he'd been seeing the past couple of weeks: former vixen but, shit, probably older than he was. He sat in his usual chair in the lounge and picked up a copy of *Rolling Stone.* Wedged into the table of contents was a white piece of paper. It said:

YOUR MAN IS IN SHANGHAI

He stared at the message. Was it for him? It seemed like it might be, but maybe it was for a woman whose boyfriend was traveling in China. Maybe Shanghai meant "trouble" in some sort of new gang talk. Some drug dealer's runner was in trouble with the law or with another gang. *You're in fucking Shanghai now, motherfucker . . .*

He decided to be cool, to keep pretending to read the magazine while he looked around. There were a dozen other people in the lounge, the usual mix of young people wearing sweat clothes or leotards. The older woman was watching him. *I have so made you, hit man!* Or hit woman. Whatever it was.

He'd noticed her watching him the past couple of weeks. She had blond hair and a thin face, an older woman's body kept in near-mint condition by some kind of fiendish exercise program. A little bit worn, but wearing it well. Maybe she was forty-five, fifty. Of course! If you're going to be a hit man, what better way to conceal your identity than to be a woman! Take away the leotards, and *definitely* the kind of chick who'd put a snubby in your kidney and pull the trigger. When he caught her eye, she smiled at him.

He got up and walked over to her, brandishing the note. "Okay. You got me!"

She said, "I guess I did!"

He put out his hand. "Pete Harrington. It's a pleasure to meet you."

"I know exactly who you are. I know all about you. I love your music!"

"Cool. I'd be a little intimidated if you didn't like my music." He was getting a weird vibe off her. "We should probably talk someplace with a little more privacy, don't you think?"

She looked at him carefully then raised her eyebrows. "We could do that."

He managed to find an empty massage room and lock the door behind them. He turned to her. "So . . . How did you find out he's in Shanghai?"

The woman kept her smile but tilted her face quizzically to the side. "Who's in Shanghai?"

"Peter Harrington. The guy I'm looking for." He held up the piece of paper. "*This* guy."

She laughed softly. "You were always very mysterious, Pete."

"You didn't leave this note?"

"No." She looked at it, then at him, licking her lips. "If I'd left it, it would have said something else."

"Oh!" Getting the vibe now. No mistaking it. "So . . . Do we, um, know each other?"

"Actually, Pete, we do. I was with you for five days on the *Looking for the eXit* tour, between Denver and Phoenix."

He searched his memory for her face, tried to put a younger version of it into a vague hotel room or backstage, but he couldn't pull up anything. Fucking eighteen years ago. "How was it?"

"Unforgettable." She was looking earnestly up into his face. She was completely available, and he instantly felt his cock beginning to harden.

It had been awhile since he'd done this. Years. Now it took more wining and dining, more "relationship," instead of girls who just wanted to chock you up as someone they'd done and brag about it to their friends. Those girls had other people to brag about now; they were sucking other dicks in other dressing rooms.

"Well," he said, more softly. "Here we are."

She raised her eyebrows. "Here we are. Again."

He was as hard as a stallion now. He put his arms around her and kissed her. In another ten seconds he had one hand under her sports bra, kneading her breast; then she went to her knees and pulled down his pants.

He was getting into it, forgetting where they were, forgetting about the note, when he heard voices pass by outside the door. He froze for a second, feeling vulnerable: she stopped to listen, and then the voices passed and she started in again. Now, though, they'd gotten in his head. Sure, he'd locked the door, but plenty of people had keys. What if someone was scheduled for a massage? He'd never used to care about that before. He'd been caught a half dozen times, but he'd always laughed it off and kept on going, maybe tossing out a "privacy, please" to whoever'd blundered in. Now, though, it bugged him. And what about that note? What if whoever had left it had seen him come in here, was standing outside the door right now? What if this was all some sort of weird sting operation?

He noticed a skunk streak of gray in the middle of her dyed-blond hair. Christ, how old was she? Somebody's mother? *Grandmother?* The woman seemed to sense his wandering mind and redoubled her efforts, but the more she sped up, the less he seemed to feel, and now a new and more disturbing thought occurred to him. What if he simply went soft? What would she think? What would she tell other people? *Wow, Pete Harrington can't even keep it together for a quick blow job anymore! And I heard he lost all his money, too!*

In seconds he was completely soft. He pushed her head away.

"I'm sorry!" she whined, as if it were her fault.

"It's been a crazy day," he mumbled.

"Sure!" She suddenly looked ugly to him, her face wrinkled and eye-shadowed, her body overstuffed with breast implants. "We could do this some other time," she said. "I mean, we could go out to a club or something. Why don't you give me your number?"

The sound of a key burrowing into steel, and suddenly the door swung open and one of the masseurs was there with an armload of towels.

"What is going on in here!" the attendant said loudly.

"Just leaving," Pete mumbled, and he bolted past the masseur into the hallway, followed by the aging groupie. "Pete!" she called. "Pete, wait up!"

He strode quickly toward the entrance, ignoring her. He streamed past the front desk, banged into the release bar on the plate-glass door, and stepped out into the exhausted sunshine, away from the horny grandma and his failed workouts, from his half-finished songs and his idiotic dead career and his grand gesture of revenge, from the whole silly, stupid idea of what it meant to be Pete Harrington. He would never go back!

Except his car keys were in his locker. House keys, wallet, credit cards, fucking cigarettes. All the shit that made up his nice modern life. He stood there in the morning sunlight, a beautiful Hollywood morning, stunned into confusion and shame. He stood there for a long time. If he went inside, they'd smirk at him. The woman would find him and chase him through the hallways hollering his name. He looked up at the sky and then back at the door, stuck there beside the passing cars.

"Would you like me to go in and get your things for you?"

The voice was low and foggy, and when he turned to his side, it was logical that its owner was old, extremely old, with snow-white hair and deep wrinkles radiating like ripples from his pale blue eyes. He had jowls that hung down slightly at his jaws and a small wattle of flesh below his chin. He was taller than Pete, and even if his shoulders slumped a bit from the years, there was still a certain power lingering there.

Pete didn't answer, and the man smiled at him, showing parchment-colored teeth. "C'mon. Why don't you tell me your locker number and give me the key, and I'll take care of this for you."

"Who are you?"

"I'm Charlie. I heard you're looking for someone to help you with your Crossroads Partners situation."

Pete stared at the ancient face before him and its little slit of smile. Did he know what had just happened in there?

The man went on in a pleasant, unhurried way. "I did a little research on my own about your problem. I thought it'd be fun to spring it on you like that."

"You put the note there?"

"Let's say I had it put there. That was an easy one. You conk out halfway through your workout and go and sit in the same chair every day, or the one next to it. Today you found two magazines: *Modern Maturity* and *Rolling Stone.* That was your choice. If you'd sat someplace different, I would have put it in your locker. As far as the rest . . ." The old man deepened his smile and shrugged. "Do you want me to get your stuff?"

Pete Harrington gave him the key to his locker and watched the old man make his way through the gym's shiny glass doors, walking slowly, with a slight limp. He was wearing a checked camel-colored sport coat and baggy brown slacks, old man's clothes that weren't either in style or out of style. He came out with Pete's belongings in a plastic bag with the gym's logo on it and handed it to him. He lifted his chin toward the traffic. "There's a place across the street I like."

When Bobby'd said he was hooking him up with a war veteran, he didn't say the Spanish-American War. The man's eyes looked like they'd been bleached from whatever he'd been looking at the past eight decades, and he seemed more likely to put you to sleep with a bedtime story than a garrote around your neck. He'd hoped this day was done getting weirder, but that didn't seem to be in the cards.

Pete had eaten at Canter's Deli a thousand times: the band used to go in there after gigs and drink in the lounge. It had a 50s thing going, right down to the waitresses that looked like your grandma, if your grandma was old and hard and too broke to retire. They weren't part of a scene, like at the Rainbow. They were just hard. He waved one down from across the room and she came over to them like a bad cloud. He'd had this waitress before:

she was so impersonal that by the time the meal was over, you felt pretty damn sure it was personal. Now, though, Charlie turned on the smile, spoke to the crabby waitress in some secret, old-guy cadence. To his amazement, a long-lost young woman seemed to flutter up to her skin. And for that moment, he could go back in time forty or fifty years and say, yeah, definitely, might have been babe material. He tried turning the clock back on Charlie's face, to unwrinkle and unsag it, to put the hair back and color it black or brown, but it was pretty much impossible. He felt like saying to Charlie, *Dude, you've still got it,* but he didn't know him too well so he tried to keep it buttoned down. "So, you've been watching me for the last two weeks?"

"I like to learn a little bit about prospective clients before I agree to work for them. It helps avoid problems."

Pete didn't want to be one of this man's problems. "Was that lady one of your . . . ? You know . . . the blonde?"

He waited for the old man to answer the hanging question, but Charlie just kept looking at him. Then he said, "Let's talk about your problem."

The possibility that the girl hadn't really been after him, that she'd just been paid to give him a blow job, bothered him. "Yeah. My problem. Well, you know, there's Crossroads."

"I'm familiar with Crossroads. They built some sort of bond fund and then went bankrupt. The top guy, Peter Harrington, got out with several hundred million dollars eight months before it collapsed."

"Yeah, and I was one of those people that got left without a chair when the music stopped. This Peter Harrington dick made hundreds of millions, and I lost everything."

"And you want revenge."

"Basically."

"How far do you intend to go?" the man asked calmly.

Pete swallowed. He was a bit unnerved by the question, but he didn't want to look like a lightweight. "Well, I don't intend to kill him."

"Good!" Charlie smiled. "I don't intend to kill him either."

That was a relief! "Yeah, basically . . . What I want to do is find him, get in his face, and then pretty much punch the crap out of him."

Charlie didn't seem surprised or disapproving, just practical. "And you understand that's a crime, don't you? That would be assault with premeditation. You're not going to get a self-defense plea there. Once the lawyers get started, you might end up losing whatever you've got left after Crossroads."

"I don't care, man. I'm beyond that now. This is something I'm doing."

Charlie waited about ten seconds, watching the singer, then smiled again. "Except, if it takes place in China, they've got to prosecute you in a Chinese court. And I imagine that China's judicial system probably has better things to do than prosecute a foreigner for a petty assault charge. Especially when they don't have an extradition treaty with the United States." He tossed his head lightly. "As long as you don't seriously injure the guy and you get out of the country right away, I don't see a problem."

The old man had obviously scoped the situation already. "How did you find out he's in Shanghai?"

"Your man's a squash player. If you spell his name with an *e* and go twenty-two pages back on an Internet search, he turns up as an entry in a squash tournament in the Portman Hotel Health Club in Shanghai. Tells you something about the quality of his security."

"Do you think he has a bodyguard?"

"If he's smart."

"So, how do I get past the bodyguard?"

It seemed like Charlie was smiling, but this time there wasn't really a smile there. "I take care of the bodyguard. If we decide I'm taking the job."

He looked at the neutral features in front of him, the ancient blue eyes that merely watched him, but with a calm intensity that felt like a challenge. "Man, who *are* you? I mean, seriously. Bobby said you worked for the CIA or something. Like"—he leaned in and lowered his voice—"taking care of business."

He reached into his sport jacket, and Pete saw a flash of black leather shoulder holster beneath his arm. He pulled out a business card and handed it to him. CHARLES PICO CONSULTING. Harrington took out his tinted reading glasses to make out the fine print. BALLISTICS. EXPLOSIVES. PERSONAL PROTECTION. EXPERT WITNESS.

Charlie began a brief and unembellished overview of his professional experience.

Incredibly, he was a veteran of World War II. He'd enlisted at the age of seventeen in 1942 and served behind enemy lines in Europe, western China, and Burma. After that he'd been a day agent for the CIA, working in various Eastern European and Latin American locales. Czechoslovakia, Yugoslavia, Ceylon, British Honduras. Countries, Pete noted, that didn't even exist anymore. He'd been an investigator in the Kennedy assassination, verifying the accuracy of Oswald's rifle.

The singer couldn't resist. "What did you find out?"

"People always ask me that," he said in an unhurried way. Pete waited, but Charlie went on with his résumé. He'd set up and run corporate security details in twelve countries, trained special forces at Fort Bragg, cowrote the CIA handbook on improvised weapons, and was a seventh-degree master in Kodokan judo and Chin-na. He stopped and gave that slightly wolfish smile with his sepia-toned teeth. "I think I can deal with your problem."

"It sounds like you could deal with a small revolution."

He shrugged. "Done that, too. Here's how I work. I already found out that your guy's in Shanghai. That was a freebie. If we go forward, I'll have his address for you in a couple of days and a workup of his routine in ten days: where he goes, what time he goes there, and how deep the grass is on his front lawn. I have contacts in Shanghai who'll do that. You'll pay their fees: figure on about three thousand dollars, paid in advance, and more for their assistance when we get in country. I train you for one month in martial arts and physical fitness. I go to China with you, ground truth our information, set up the interception, and neutralize the bodyguard when you have your conversation with Mr. Harrington. Then I make sure you get out of the country in a timely manner. In exchange, you never mention my name to anyone or write it down anywhere. Does that sound like it meets your needs?"

He liked this guy's style. Charlie was old, but he knew his shit. The episode with the note was primo. *Modern Maturity*! "Yeah, it does."

"My fee is twenty thousand dollars, plus all expenses. That's cash. Half in advance, half on completion."

Pete wasn't sure what to say. He hadn't done a lot of comparison shopping for this kind of service. It was weird: the dude was so old, but there was something sort of brisk and scary about him. If anything, he seemed like he should be dropping into Havana to ice Castro, not helping him track down some financial dirtbag.

"I guess it's reasonable."

"It'd be a lot more reasonable to just let it go. Punching a man in the face may not be as pleasant as you imagine."

"It's not about having a pleasant experience, Charlie."

The old man considered his words without responding, just looking carefully into the musician's face. He put a five-dollar bill on the table and they both got up to leave. "It wasn't the girl," Charlie said. "It was a guy with glasses and maroon sweatpants."

"I don't remember seeing him," Pete answered.

"That's how it's supposed to be."

4

Wreckage

⊹

As Charlie drove down La Cienega toward West Hollywood, forty-five years as a day agent were telling him that this was a bad job. It had all the signs: the shaky client, the bullshit objective, a whole operation that boiled down to somebody's petty personal grudge being worked out on a bigger scale just because they had the money or the power to play it out. He'd turned down a dozen jobs like this over the years, chickenshit assignments where the top guy had no idea what they were getting into. Sometimes you got stuck with them; you woke up in some beauty spot like Tegucigalpa or Vodochody realizing that you weren't a knight on the global chess board; you were just on some bureaucratic fool's errand that might get you killed. This one had that air about it, but without the danger. The only gun that would get pulled on this deal was one of those clown pistols where a little sign popped out that said, "Bang." Or maybe, *"Fucking* bang." Charlie smiled to himself.

No, twenty years ago this job would have been a definite walk-away. He was still getting good work back then. Some high-profile terrorism cases. Consulting on the blast pattern in Oklahoma City. It had gotten pretty thin the last few years. He got the occasional surveillance job, since a man his age was basically invisible anyway, but all his best contacts at the Agency were dead or retired. He spent too many days sitting at home browsing through his books on chemistry and ballistics, trying to stay fresh, trying to keep his mind from letting go of all those details. Even so, he wasn't modern anymore. Now everybody wanted to read satellite images and do electronic penetration. Then this came up, and he found out the target was in Shanghai, and it all made sense. He'd started his career in Shanghai, and he still had some unfinished business there. At this age, Pete Harrington was the last excuse he'd ever have for making the trip.

Charlie rolled up to the address Harrington had given him and rang the bell. The singer came to the door wearing a black tank top and a gold chain around his neck, his hair all poofed out, like he was fresh from the hairdresser.

Charlie! Come on in!

He instinctively took in Harrington's bare arms and shoulders. Strength only meant so much, but it did show a certain willpower if they'd acquired it, and that meant more than the strength itself. This man's arms seemed fleshy and weak, and he didn't like the skull tattoo. Or the dice. Or the barbed wire etched around his bicep. The fashion in this crowd, he guessed. They thought etching barbed wire on their arms showed how tough they were, but what it really showed was how little they knew. He'd seen his share of barbed wire.

Harrington was walking him in, offering him a drink at eleven in the morning. The apartment looked cluttered, with towers of cardboard boxes that said things like DISHES and AWARDS. The kitchen counter was a nest of empty takeout containers and plastic bags. Pretty much what he'd expected when the manager hired him. He noticed an empty bottle of vodka and a couple of dirty glasses sitting on a coffee table. This client would need a lot of babysitting, and he wasn't a babysitter. There were guitars and keyboards, microphones and other musical paraphernalia around, mixed with posters that hadn't been hung and a couple of gold records in black frames lying on top of a pile of laundry. The man's life had been packed up and tossed into this apartment in a hurry.

He smiled at the musician. "Are you ready to start?"

"Let's do it!"

Harrington wasn't in particularly good shape for a man his age. He had a little potbelly, probably from drinking too much, and though he said he used to do high kicks in his act, he couldn't kick above the waist anymore. In his heyday he must have been fairly muscular: he said he'd had a personal trainer who went on tour with him. The definition was gone, though. Charlie asked him to throw a few straight punches, and they looked girlish and awkward. He held up a pad he'd brought and asked him to hit it as hard as he could, any way he wanted, and Harrington drew his hand down to his side and then swung in a wide arc that only ended up clipping the top of the pad. Charlie worked at not letting his disdain show.

"Let me ask you something, Mr. Harrington—"

"Pete"

"*Pete.* I read on the Internet that you got in a fight about three years ago."

The musician looked a bit wary. "With the bass player from Uncle Sam's Erection."

"What happened there?"

"I was doing a gig at the Tacoma Dome. Actually, it was me and some other acts, and I was opening. And I was like, *Me?* Opening for punks like Uncle Sam's Erection? I should have just said, like, *No, I flush turds—I don't open for them,* but Bobby had already set it up, and I didn't want to make him look bad."

"How did it start?"

Harrington's energy level rose as he recounted the story. "Well, he had his bass sitting out blocking the stage left entrance, where I always come in, and I'm supposed to come running out, that's kind of my thing, and it's time, and I say, *Dude, your bass is blocking the entrance.* And he says, *We're the top billing. Work around it!* I was, like, Am I really hearing this from this punk? But I had to go on, so as I was getting ready to run out, I accidentally knocked his bass over, and he starts cussing at me, and I was already partly on stage, so I turned around and gave him the finger . . ."

"Hold on—how accidental was it when you knocked his bass over?"

The singer looked sheepish. "I guess I could have been a little more careful."

That was good. He'd started it. It was the first glimmer of good news since he'd taken this job. "Go on."

"So he comes roaring out . . . I think he was pretty wasted. And I'd had a few drinks myself. So he comes roaring out, barking at me, and I said *Bitch! Go back to your kennel!* And I'm, like, mic-ed up! So everybody hears me call this guy a bitch!"

"How many people were watching this?"

"The house was around seventeen thousand that night."

So, Charlie reasoned, the guy had to fight. You don't let someone call you a bitch in front of seventeen thousand people. "How big was your opponent?"

"About my size. Some young guy, full of himself. Thinks he's the next Flea. Except Erection's last album completely tanked, so what's he putting on airs for, you know?"

"Go on."

"So he comes out to where I am, at the edge of the stage, and he, like, takes this big swing at me and clips me on the cheek, and I have this kind of ventriloquist raven on my shoulder, you know, it's part of my act, for 'Raven at My Window,' and he knocks it off, and then it's just . . . you know, game on! You can't fuck with my raven."

Charlie managed to stifle his laugh into a smile. He'd heard a million fight stories, but none quite this funny. "So he landed one on your cheek. Did he hurt you?"

"Not at the time, but it looked pretty bad the next day. Anyway, he clips me, and then I swung back at him, but I kind of ended up hitting his shoulder, and then he comes charging at me and pushes me down. Now the crowd's screaming, and a lot of these are my fans, you know, and I can't just let this guy fucking knock me down in front of my people. And besides that, I'm super pissed. So I get up and I come running at him, like"—Harrington put up his fists in front of him as if he were a child pounding on a wall—"but then, somehow, the guy gets away and hits me a couple more times in the head."

Charlie reasoned that the other musician must have been nearly as incompetent a fighter as Harrington. A good fighter would have dropped him in seconds.

"Then we were sort of wrestling around, and then I got free, and this guy was still coming after me! He was crazy! I said, 'Just chill, guy. It's all good!' But he came at me again, so I saw this, like, flute sitting around, so I grabbed it, and I, like, did a *Seven Samurai* kind of thing on him, like"—he moved his arm in a cross-body slashing motion—"and the second time, I caught him in the face, and there was blood and stuff. That kind of ended the fight." He shrugged. "I can show you the whole thing."

The musician walked over to the computer, and the next thing Charlie knew, there was a stage with two tiny people on it, blown up onto a huge flat-screen television. He'd seen a blurry cell-phone video of the fight, but the figures in it had been very small. Now the camera zoomed in. The blond one was wearing red leather pants and a black muscle shirt: his client. He looked a bit thinner than the present-day Pete Harrington. His opponent was slightly bigger and moved much more quickly than Harrington. Both men were off balance, lurching around and swinging amateurishly without a specific target. It happened just the way his client said it did, probably because he'd watched this video over and over again. When it was you, and it was your first fight, you usually got some of the details wrong. What struck Charlie about it, though, wasn't the fight. It was the crowd. When Harrington shouted, *Bitch! Go back to your kennel!* their voices ballooned into a white roar, and at the first blows they exploded into a jubilant howling, the like of which Charlie hadn't heard since seeing an adulterer get stoned to death in Pakistan back in the fifties.

It got weirder, though. Harrington whacked his adversary with the flute. The guy staggered, blood gushing out of his nose. Then, amazingly, Harrington started waving the flute around like a baton, signaling the drummer to start the beat along with him and going straight into his act, cueing the guitar player to slam out their first earsplitting attack, and then he jumped into the middle of the stage and let out a long, loud scream, a cry of exultation that Charlie understood immediately and completely. Amazingly, it was the first note of his song, and he went right into the show, the crowd so beside itself that they nearly drowned out the music. He could see now that there was a reason Harrington had been a star. In some ways, he was fearless. Harrington watched himself sing another ten seconds of the song, then he seemed to remember Charlie and stopped the video.

Charlie stared at the screen for a few seconds. He looked up at the musician with a faint smile. "Never seen one like that before," he said.

"Yeah, I was originally going to start with 'Raven at My Window,' but under the circumstances I changed it to 'Wreckage' on the fly."

"Looks like it went over pretty well."

"Are you kidding? They practically tore the place apart. My downloads went through the roof. My sales are still feeling it three years later. Look at this . . ."

He pointed to a number on the screen, among all the disconnected commentary and phrases in black, red, and blue. It was 12,874,311.

"That's how many times this video has been viewed."

Twelve *million*! "Holy smokes!"

He could see now why the manager wanted this to happen. He'd never dealt with show-business people before, but underneath their smooth exteriors he sensed there were some characters as slippery as any double agent. And the ex-wife was a piece of work! She'd have made a good station chief.

So Harrington had a few of the ingredients. He'd started the verbal attack, which meant he could do it again. And he'd responded as soon as his opponent attacked, instead of standing there in a little cloud of disbelief, which was what a lot of people did. Best of all, he'd improvised a weapon and used it, which meant he could escalate if things went that way. And he wasn't going to crumble if he got hit.

He'd already thought about how to train him. It would take a long time to turn him into a real fighter, in the sense of someone who could spontaneously attack or defend with a variety of techniques. At the monastery they figured a year to make a decent fighter, minimum—decent being someone who could defeat a stronger, larger, untrained opponent. That was training for hours, every day. After that, it was just a matter of how many opponents you wanted to defeat, and how good they were, or what weapons they had. At the highest levels it became almost a matter of style. He'd seen monks look at a flock of chickens, point to one, make a strange, high-pitched guttural sound, and have the chosen chicken jump up in the air and fall down dead. Harrington wouldn't be killing any chickens.

"Here's how we're going to do it," he said. "I'm going to teach you one technique, and you're going to practice it every day. Two hours in the morning, two hours in the afternoon. With both sides of your body. You get that one down, I'll teach you one more, and so on. As long as I see improvement, I'll keep teaching you. You start sandbagging me, I'm done. And you'll still have to pay me."

"Okay."

"Rule number two: no drinking on the days we're training. If I smell alcohol on your breath, we're done. And you still have to pay me."

There was a longer pause before he answered that one. "Okay."

"Let's see your heavy bag."

He brought him into one of the rooms, and the big black cylinder he'd sent over was hanging there from the ceiling with its dull leathery sheen like an electromagnet in a junkyard. As always, part of him instinctively wanted to hit it—that's how heavy bags were. The red bag gloves were still sitting in their plastic wrapping on a chair. Nearby was a treadmill that probably didn't get much use either. "I have some weights in the other room, too."

"I saw them." The disassembled stack of chrome-plated disks in a corner. "You won't be needing those." He'd thought about this, too. "I have some exercises that will build your strength and your flexibility at the same time. I learned them in China a long time ago. They work." He showed him Tiger Claws the Tree, a Farmer Lifts a Cart, Opening the Bow, and a Precious Duck Flaps Its Wings, all of them performed slowly with all the muscles tense. "I'm going to test you every three days, and if you don't show improvement, I'm done. Same rule as before. Let's see how many push-ups you can do. On your knuckles. Back straight."

Harrington managed to do four, and even those he had to do on the carpet because he kept whining about how his knuckles hurt.

"Today you'll do four push-ups every hour. Tomorrow, when I come here, I want you to do five. The day after, you'll do six, then eight, and so on. You're going to work up to forty an hour, every hour you're awake. On the wood."

The idea of the push-ups wasn't really to build strength—it was to train his mind. A man who could do four or five hundred push-ups on his knuckles every day was a man who knew he had the will and the fist.

He had him put on the bag gloves. "Hit the bag a few times. Not too hard. Keep your fist tight." He watched him throw a couple of roundhouses that were supposed to be hooks, then jabs that glanced off the hard bag, even though they'd been thrown straight at it.

He put him in a boxer's stance and showed him how to twist his hips while he punched, then spent ten painful minutes watching Harrington try to imitate his hip twist in every way but the correct one. It was awkward, and Harrington tried to make it better by speeding up, which made it even worse. Charlie went on watching him with his arms crossed.

The guy punched like a pansy. No, that wasn't fair, because a lot of pansies could actually punch, when you got right down to it. He'd seen it in the service: queers who'd gotten picked on their whole childhood beating the crap out of the barracks bully when he wouldn't lay off. And Phil had been a queer. He could punch like a sledgehammer, and a damn good man. Phil had saved his ass in Prague, because he hadn't trusted the girl, while he himself had been trying to get her in the sack. Then the Stasi set him up with the boy and wrecked his marriage and his life when he wouldn't turn. The agency paid his loyalty back by furloughing him. Claimed he was compromised. Nineteen fifty-eight. That was how they did it back then. Last time he'd seen Phil he'd been drunk at a queer bar in Denver. Sometime in the eighties. A weird scene. Phil wanted to talk about the old days, and he'd walked into that bar with no idea what kind of bar it was, but he couldn't leave the guy: Phil had saved his life, so he sat there with the old fairy drinking whiskey while Phil drank Pink Cadillacs, as if Charlie represented the

Agency and he was going to show Charlie he didn't give a shit—he could drink a ladies' drink if he felt like it. Once in while you'd see flashes of the frightening old steel underneath. Then some young buck would come up, and Phil would fawn all over him. And he wanted Charlie to put a good word in for him if they needed a day agent, somebody who could do the queer thing, because that could be another cover: nobody suspects an old queer. Phil ended up crying, and he wished he could cry, too, just because he wanted to show Phil he understood, deeply, and that he'd never stop being grateful to him, but it was too late for Phil. He was an old man with dyed-blond hair. Just too late. That was the last time he saw him, twenty years ago. Wreckage.

What was it that made a man's life disappear behind him, anyway? With Phil, you could argue that he'd made a mistake by being queer, and, supposedly, that could be a reason for losing his wife and his family and his profession. But what about everybody else? Your friends moved away or died; your jobs dried up. You spent all that effort making sure nobody put a bullet in your lungs, only to find out sixty years later that your lungs were shot anyway and, instead of matching wits with the Czech StB you were trying to train some puffed-up has-been to hit a bag.

"I'm going to show you your attack," he told Harrington. "Put up your arm, like you're protecting your face." Charlie gently pushed the arm down a few inches as he shuffled in and threw a slow punch toward the musician's face.

"That's your attack. You're going to walk up to him, say his name, tell him whatever you need to tell him, and then, if he lifts his arm up defensively, you'll rest your hand on it and push it down, like this, just a few inches. That's the trap. You've got to hit him before he realizes what's happening. Hit him right in the bridge of the nose, as hard as you can. That way, you'll stun him. His eyes'll tear up and he'll probably start bleeding. If you do it right, you'll break his nose. At that point you can continue your attack or walk away, whatever you want to do." He watched the musician's face as he explained it. It was one thing to train for violence. It was something very different to actually carry it out. The singer didn't flinch, though. He peeled off a piece of athletic tape and stuck it to the bag at the level of Harrington's nose. "You're going to do two hundred of those on each side, every hour, every day, with the trap and the shuffle and then hitting this piece of tape. Get it to where the trap and the hit are one motion. Let's try it."

He held his arm up, and Harrington clutched it and punched, too far away to reach him.

"Step in as you punch."

He stepped in, but ended up crosswise to him.

"No. Shuffle in. Don't take an actual step. Just shuffle. Your feet don't cross."

Now he shuffled in, and suddenly Charlie felt a stab of pain at the floor. He recoiled silently, and for a second he thought he was going to fall. When his head cleared and the sharp misery of his bad foot had died down, he realized that Harrington's hands were wrapped around his upper arm. "Sorry! Is your foot okay?"

Charlie looked down at the hands, and the musician pulled them away. Then he limped over to the stool and settled on it with a small groan. He inhaled and then let out one long single breath. "That's my bad foot."

"Shit, Charlie! I'm really sorry—"

"Just keep hitting the bag."

Harrington hit the bag, clumsily. He hit it again.

This was feeling all wrong. Some jobs were wrong, and the sooner you sensed it and gave it a pass, the better off you were. Like when he'd gone down to San Salvador to help Colonel Quintero set up an off-the-books intelligence network, then figured out pretty early on that what he was really setting up were death squads. Hell, he'd figured it out before he even went down there. Bill Casey's baby. Not that the Cubans weren't running around whacking their share of people, but he should have pulled out. Instead, he read about his work two years later under an ugly headline in *The New York Times*. Stuff that would turn your stomach. They called Quintero a mad-dog killer, which showed how full of crap they were, because Quintero was actually a sly, manipulative killer, a proficient liar who'd given him enough lip service about due process and rehabilitation that he could pretend it was all for the better. Even the ruling families couldn't control him, and when the story hit the *Times*, the CIA sent him back to solve the problem, since he and Quintero were such good buddies. He put Quintero crossways with the military, killed his top guys, froze his finances. Finally got him by watching his bank in Panama and picking him up there when he ran out of money. Closed the book on a bullshit job that got a lot of people killed in bad ways, which in El Salvador in those days was like the afternoon rain. Never should have taken it, but he'd had a whole other pile of problems: Millie in the nursing home with Alzheimers, savings running low, and, to be honest, at sixty-five years old, he figured if he turned down this job, they'd find someone else for the next one, too. Permanently.

Now look at him! Him, a man who'd been a soldier for his country for sixty years, playing to some guy's petty vanity. He wanted to show that he was still on top of his game, and all it did was provide incontrovertible proof that he really was finished. It was stupid. The whole thing. He'd call the manager and give back the deposit. Tell Zhang in Shanghai to stand down. Whatever he'd left unfinished there was finished all by itself, on its own terms, which he couldn't dictate. That ticket had been canceled a long time ago.

"Is this right?"

The client was still whaling away at the bag without doing much damage. As likely to hurt himself as whoever he was up against. It was just an overhand right, for Christ's sake! "Okay," Charlie said, putting his hand on the younger man's shoulder. "I think that's enough."

His foot was killing him. He carefully climbed off the stool and limped back into the cluttered living room.

Harrington followed him. "You want a beer or something?"

"Nope. Thanks. I've got another appointment." That always worked well for a quick exit. He picked up the hand pad he'd brought and moved toward the door.

The client could sense his mood. "So, how'd I do today?"

He turned to him. It might as well be now. "Let's talk about that." He saw the worry go across the singer's face as he stood before him, about three feet away. "Mr. Harrington, I have to step away from this project."

"Why?"

The man looked so genuinely hurt that he didn't have the heart to say, *because it's chickenshit.* "It's just not a job I feel comfortable with."

"But you knew what the job was when you took it."

"That's true."

"Is it me? You think I can't do this? Because I can."

His voice got a little thinner as he lied. "I know you can do it." He swallowed. "Mr. Harrington, what is this all about? Really."

"Really?"

"Yeah. You lost some money just like everybody else in the country. Why do you want to push this?"

The singer dropped his usual puppylike air. He actually seemed to be considering what he said. "Okay. Let's be straight up, Charlie. You spent your life going to dangerous foreign places and doing complicated scary shit that only one out of a million people can do—why?"

Charlie answered flatly. "I was serving my country."

"And I'll bet when you say that people usually just kind of widen their eyes and say, *Oh, wow, thanks, man!* But, see, I think you're laying back on me here a little bit, Charlie. I'm not doubting your patriotism, but you could have been in the Peace Corps and served the country. You could have been in the IRS. That's like me saying I became a rock star because I wanted to give the world great music. I like singing, yeah. But I wanted the girls and the bucks and the excitement and the people standing on their chairs and fucking howling my name for an encore."

"I'm not sure I understand what you're getting at."

"On some level, you wanted to do shit that would scare the crap out of most of us. Why? Because it makes you feel like your life is about something other than the mortgage and the bills and going to the supermarket and getting older. You wanted to do hero shit, not punch a time card. Am I right? Straight up, now."

Charlie nodded slowly. "There's something to it."

"So, sure!" Harrington continued. "I could kick back and be reasonable about this dirtbag ripping off the world. It's not my job to be, like, global policeman, and when you get screwed by someone rich, the deal is you kick back and accept it. But there's a whole world of shit I don't accept, Charlie. I don't accept getting old. I don't accept being a statistic. I don't accept that my life means nothing. I don't accept death. And I realize all that stuff may happen to me, but I do not accept it. And I don't think you do, either. That's why you're still going for it at the age of . . . fucking a hundred and fifty, or however old you are! I don't see you sitting in a rocking chair." His face lightened. "And admit it, Charlie, you like the game. Fucking *Modern Maturity*!" He laughed, shaking his head. "Dude, you played me like a two-year-old!"

Suddenly, Charlie couldn't help laughing. He laughed for a while, and then he thought about Pete Harrington and started laughing all over again. The singer laughed with him, muttering, *It's true, man, like a child!*

When he'd settled down, Harrington clapped his hand on his shoulder.

"It's okay, Charlie. You've lived the life and reached an age when you've earned the right to do anything you want to do. You're sacred, man. You really are. You want to drop me? That's completely cool. A lot of other people have. But I will do this. Even if I have to learn karate from a fucking comic book, I *will* finish this."

"You couldn't even finish your workout two days ago."

"That was then. Now I'm alone. It's me against the fucking universe, and when it gets down to that, I say, 'Universe! Me and you' "—he pierced the air with his finger—" 'it's fucking *on*!' "

Charlie smiled. For the first time, he actually liked Pete Harrington. He opened the door and stepped outside before turning back. No sign of disappointment on the singer's face. He looked solid. Almost serene.

"Keep training," Charlie said. "I may just check in on you down the line."

"I'm already there. Trap and hit. A Precious Duck Flaps his Fucking Wings. I've got the faith, man. Even if you don't."

Charlie nodded, then turned his back on Harrington and made his way through the underground garage to his car. Give him a couple of weeks. See how much he trained. See if it really was "on." Then they'd find out who had the faith.

5

The House in Columbus

✠

It had been somewhere in southern Indiana. Near Columbus. He'd been looking for investors for Crossroads, to get it going, and he'd gone there to do a presentation to a man named Simon Schloss. Schloss had made a lot of money marketing a putty used in repairing dents in car bodies and had a global sales network that he ran from an office in Columbus. In Washington, D.C., inside men in the administration had just crushed efforts to regulate the secondary bond market, and those few who understood the ramifications knew that the gold rush had begun. Schloss knew that: he was a bald, fat, coarse man who'd built his auto-putty empire through a relentless marketing effort that had consumed two wives and the last thirty years of his life. He'd educated himself about finance and had scored enough small wins to risk a couple of million on the fund. Later, he'd multiply his money by a factor of seven and get out before the bust. He didn't have expensive taste, and because he, Harrington, was the one asking for money, he didn't have to pretend he did. They met at a modest restaurant near the highway whose menu Schloss had obviously memorized, and Harrington sold him the deal over a BLT on whole wheat and a cup of watery coffee in a white ceramic mug with two green pinstripes along the rim. Schloss left a ten-dollar tip and called his lawyer to have him prepare a memorandum of understanding. He left first to draft the papers and suggested Harrington take the scenic route back to his lawyer's office in Columbus, along the old highway. He sketched it out on the back of the place mat and took off. While Harrington was in the bathroom the waitress crumpled up the place mat and threw it away.

He started down the rural route. It had rained that day and the tires made a wet sound like radio static as he swooped through the corridor of cool air between the trees. It was autumn, and the big hardwoods were letting go of orange leaves and yellow leaves. The countryside was rural: old-looking little farmhouses and occasional smallish fields. What did these people do? Where did they work? Did they commute the half hour to Indianapolis? What crops could they grow in these fields that would make them enough money to live? How could they compete with the huge farms in Ohio and Iowa and California that measured their acreage in the hundreds? Red or white barns glistened in the wet gray air. Pickup trucks rusted quietly. Metal mailboxes: THE PRICES. THE MARTINS. There was something mesmerizing about the road and the feeling of people who weren't at all attached to his world, or anything he knew of the world. This is how he'd thought of The Country when he was growing up, before everything around every city was a vast suburb of swallowed-up towns.

He soon became lost. Schloss had mentioned Old Post Road, but when he actually reached it, he could no longer remember whether he was supposed to turn on it or cross it. He'd expected to see signs with an arrow pointing toward Columbus, but the poles only said Springdale Road and Old Post Road. *Old Post Road. Old Post Road.* He imagined a stage coach, a man in breeches holding a whip, the dark trees, the houses far apart. He thought the interstate lay somewhere close by, but he couldn't see it.

He saw a farmhouse nearby and decided to ask directions. He pulled the car into the long dirt driveway. The house looked old, with a wide porch, and as he approached he saw a panel of stained glass above the door that had probably been leaded by a German immigrant in the last century. The afternoon was fading, and the rain made it even darker, so even at four o'clock the windows of the house had a pale yellow light coming out of them. Off to the left stretched a long field, anchored by a red barn with wide-open doors and yellow leaves hanging from the rafters. What did these people do? Could they live simply by this one field? He rolled down his car window and waited to see if a hound would come barking out at him, but nothing happened, so he got out of the car. The driveway was hard but still muddy, and the mud looked yellow against his black leather shoes.

He was in their world now, and every object in it suggested something deep and forgotten. He climbed the wooden steps, painted and overpainted in a flaky gray, resounding with each footfall. A child's tricycle sat curled up in the corner, and a two-wheeled girl's bike, colored red. The wide screen door had a small hole that had been mended with another piece of screen. Behind it the wooden door was closed. Narrow glass windows flanked the front door on both sides and he couldn't resist looking in.

A dark wooden stairway rose up in front of the door, with coats hung over the balustrade. Off to the side was a living room with wallpaper like an old-fashioned calico dress, an outdated style, perhaps from the thirties. The coats were made of cloth: one was the kind of tough gray-green wool used by hunters. Another was cotton duck lined with red and black plaid flannel. He saw a pair of men's work boots on the floor by the window, and next to it a nearly identical pair, but half their size. Two baseball mitts sat on the stairs: one an adult's, one for a child.

He pushed on the round black button and heard a buzzing ring coming through the glass. Nothing happened, so he pressed it again. He called out timidly, "Hello?"

He was puzzled. The lights were on, and he thought he could feel the footsteps of someone inside vibrating through the drumlike wood beneath his feet, but no one came. He moved to the side and looked in the window at the living room. The furniture looked slightly old and not stylish, things that had been gathered together over time. A couple of upholstered wooden chairs with claw feet, a field of nondescript tweed stretched over a square-shouldered couch. The potbellied stove in the corner of the room looked like an antique, as old as the house. A little square of embroidery was framed on the wall. Several old family portraits in black and white. Nothing from beyond the year 1970 intruded: no computer or television. The light came from a floor lamp near the back of the room, while from the ceiling hung an old light fixture of frosted glass. The small room had a feeling of intense hominess, of lives that were tightly bound together, and he imagined the husband in the wool jacket sitting by the woodstove with a cup of coffee in the morning. In the evening he would read the newspaper while his child or his teenager sat jackknifed on the couch with a piece of notebook paper and the *Principles of Trigonometry* textbook that was sitting on the end table.

He stepped back from the window and rang the doorbell again. Who would go out and leave the lights burning? He moved around the house toward the back door, the big furrowed field on his left, and a dark-red barn on the other side of it. He climbed a set of concrete steps, and then he was standing at the kitchen window. There was a note on the glass that said,

Honey, look in the front closet. Not to be worn at school! You are such a beautiful young woman! I hope rehearsal went well.
PS: Please turn off heat under Dutch Oven. See you at 6. Love, Mom.

He knocked on the door and called out again. "Hello?"

A denim jacket hung over the chair at the kitchen table, draped by a pink gauze scarf. The table was set for four, complete with water glasses and folded paper napkins. In the center of it was a blue ceramic mixing bowl. The wallpaper had some sort of American Revolution theme, with muskets and tricorn hats. There was a black cast-iron pot steaming on the avocado-colored stove and a coffeemaker half-full with coffee. A few children's drawings in crayon hung in frames, slightly faded. He called out. He knocked on the glass.

Who were these people? The beautiful young woman, the manly father, the wife who so obviously wove them all together in that house. They were as remote from his world as if they lived in Inner Mongolia. He twisted the knob, and to his surprise it turned with a soft click. He pushed the door open two inches. He called into the inner atmosphere of the house. "Hello?

Hello?" The air was savory and rich with the aroma of the evening's dinner cooking on the stove. He could smell meat, and carrots and the peppercorns bouncing in the simmering broth. He could sense the white starchy scent of the potatoes, the honey-flavored coffee cake. There was cold milk, and warmed-over black coffee, and bubble gum. He smelled the tang of the dishwashing soap and the moist leather bacterial odor of a boot. He smelled the manure in the barn, diesel, freshly sawn wood, chimney smoke, the dying leaves, the snuffling of the horse, the cold of the quilts, the sparks of the harvest bonfire going high into the stars. He smelled all of it.

He opened the door wider and called out once more into the house, then slowly took his first step inside. The concentrated aroma of the dinner overpowered him, and he was transported into a future when the plates on the table would be full, when all would be seated discussing the day's events, then go and sit by the stove and eat dessert from little plates that they held on their laps. What would it be like to be that father? That strong man in the wool jacket? What would the wife be like? Maybe she'd be handsome and strong, climbing into bed at night with a flannel nightgown and then hiking it up under the dark, cool covers, in that alien world.

Strangely, more than anything, he wanted to live this mysterious life, to lie in the dark with the wife, to clean the barn, to chop wood, to know the children and their faces. Because whatever happened with Simon Schloss and Crossroads, whether he signed or didn't sign, and whether the venture fizzled or made him vastly wealthy, this was one secret he would never unravel. He didn't understand what made it seem so beautiful.

The pot was steaming, and a steady trickle of moisture was flowing from beneath the lid and down the side of the pot, hissing into the gas flames beneath it. He called out once more, then he took four quick steps across the kitchen to the stove and turned one black knob a quarter-inch counterclockwise, to OFF.

He rushed to the door and closed it quietly behind him, then walked briskly back to his car. He didn't want to run. He'd done nothing wrong. He got back on the road and started driving, straight through the intersection, which turned out to be the correct way after all.

6

Kickin' It

✣

Pete really just wanted to get this one song right: "Kickin' It with The Man." One song. Not an album, not an EP: just one track, and do it fast, like the old days. With the DreamKrushers, he'd worked really fast, writing songs in a half hour and roughing them out together in one session. You catch it on the fly, he always said, because you could always tell the ones that you caught after they'd rolled to a stop. For a long time, though, he'd stop them himself, tear himself apart with all the voices, like he was playing in a third-rate bar and the crowd was heckling him about his age. *Loser!* Now, he just flicked a cigarette butt in their faces and said *fuck you!* An essential skill for any artist. He'd worked out some chords and laid some background tracks in on the Mac, but he wasn't really much of a computer guy, and he needed someone live to bounce things off of. Duffy being his first choice, of course. Face the Cobra had just come off a tour and they weren't rehearsing anything, but as usual Duffy didn't sound so eager to work with him on a song. "I'd rather just hang out, Pete." Pete got the message that, in Duffy's mind, his career was over. Sure, he was still Pete Harrington, immortal—sure, and an old friend—but not really happening. He didn't have a band or even a label, so why not just hang, have fun, instead of keeping up the whole façade that he still had a career? He'd picked that up.

But this time, Duffy showed up with his guitar.

"C'mon, Duff. I just want to get this one song down. This is a song about payback, man. About banksters who steal all your money and then skate away in their shiny business suits."

He'd dug up some pedals and a fuzzbox, and Duffy hooked them together. Then the guitarist slipped the strap over his head and tuned it up, looking faintly bored. It was the first time Pete had heard the thin, amplified sounds of a guitar in his place in a long time. "How does it go?" Duffy asked him.

"Kind of like, C, A minor, C." He splayed his fingers across the keyboard and pushed out the chords. "Then it goes . . ." He tapped out a few more notes, and Duffy immediately picked it up and played it a couple of times on the guitar. "Let's try it a little more like *this*"—Duffy reached down and twisted a knob on the stomp box, and when he played the notes again they were dirtier, more threatening. He went through it once, staring down at the floor as he played. "I'm thinking maybe a little more, kind of, ragged, you know?" He riffed through it again, and this time the notes ran into each other, were slightly off-key.

"Yeah, I like that," Pete said. "Then the bass drum comes in: *bowm bowm bowm b-bowm!* And the drummer starts, kind of like, sneaking up on the high-hats, kinda jazzy, but you know, driving. Here, I laid this down yesterday." He played the percussion line he'd worked out for it, and it was a computer, and he wasn't really a drummer, but Duffy could hear it, too, that there was something in the opening, something wicked and determined and exciting. "Let it run." He bent over the neck of the guitar and started toying with the lead line, pushing past what Harrington had first given him, into a melody that began and ended with the compelling beat of the bass drums and the high-hats. He played it a few times and then looked up and smiled. *"That's* a hook!"

"It's you, Duffy!"

"No, man; you came up with that one. What's the opening?"

He started playing again, and Pete bobbed his head with the beat, then started singing softly. "You got some woman in Shanghai, silky, silky, silky, silky! And you run around in your big black car—" He sang the lyrics he'd written for the first time with music in the background, and for a moment he forgot all of the other things of his shabby career and just lived in the music. He was Pete Harrington again, the old Pete Harrington, the young one, and then there was no Pete Harrington between him and the song at all. Just in it. Duffy started lacing it with some riffs, skittering away from the melody but always pulling it back just enough to keep the song moving forward, to build it. "Okay," Pete said, "then there's a change, here. You go *bowm bowm bowm . . .*" He sang out the notes. "And then I go,

> You think you got it all and you can't be reached,
> I got news for you, your fortress is breached.
> I'm finally gonna draw a line in sand,
> 'Cause you think the world's your football, but now I'm kickin' it with
> The Man!

Duffy smiled when he heard it, a smile of pure joy at something being right, and he immediately continued his friend's voice with a string of luminous notes. "Sing the chorus again!"

In a half hour they'd worked it all out, the chorus, the bridge, miraculously, as easily as their best songs for the DreamKrushers. Duffy's mood had changed. He was upbeat, celebratory.

"I got another one, Duffy. It's a little more downbeat. It's called 'Vanity Fair.' Listen . . ." He played a few chords on the electric piano and sang the first verse and the chorus."

"I like it. It's a little like Mellencamp, but you could give it more of an edge. Make it more real. Play it again . . ."

They worked on the song for forty-five minutes, then ran into a dead end at the bridge. "I'm stuck, Pete. I think we need a rhythm guitar here."

"This is where Cody'd come in handy."

"Cody. Wow. I haven't thought about him in a while."

"I think about him a lot."

"Yeah, you came down to L.A. with him. That's right. You two grew up together."

"Yeah. Hey. You remember that time our bus broke down outside Wilksbury, Pennsylvania? And there was that barn, and that field, and that house?" Duffy looked foggy. "We'd played Cleveland the night before and ate some mushrooms, and then we woke up at this old gas station in the middle of nowhere at, like, five in the morning. And I started walking across that field, and you and Bobby and Cody hollered down at me . . ." He waited for Duffy's face to change, but there was no spark. He sighed. "Shit gets away from you, doesn't it? Forget it." He changed the mood. "Hey man—good day's work! An hour and a half, a song and a half. It should always be this easy. We could do a whole album in a weekend."

"Let's crack open a beer!"

Just then the singer's cell phone started beeping, and Harrington flopped himself on the floor and counted out twenty push-ups. He struggled through the last three, slower and slower on each one, until he stalled halfway through the twentieth and then managed to fight his way to the top. He stood up again, red in the face, breathing hard. "I'm in training."

"For what?"

He led him to the other room, where the big black cylinder of leather loomed from the ceiling.

"What's up with the punching bag?"

"I told you, I'm training."

"Boxing?"

"No. Ass kicking."

Duffy looked unsure of what to think. "You're getting in shape. Good man."

Pete knew Duffy well, and right now Duffy was thinking, *He wants to make a comeback, and that's cool in some ways and it sucks in other ways, because he's probably just too old, too past it. Who needs a forty-five-year-old front man?* And Duffy was thinking, *Crap, I hope he doesn't tap me, because I've got a good solid gig with Face the Cobra, and I don't want things screwed up. It was a good song, though. It was an excellent fucking song!*

Duffy pawed at the bag a couple of times.

"Like this—" Pete stepped in and hit the bag with a satisfying smack, then another.

"You're really into this! Are you planning a rematch with the bassist from Uncle Sam's Erection?"

"No. I'm planning for a rematch with Crossroads Partners."

"Who are they?"

"The ones who lost all my money. Created by a guy named Peter Harrington—yeah, I know, ironic, let's move on. He cooked up some sort of bond fund and sold out for three hundred million. Then he bet against it, and when the crash came he walked away with another four hundred mil. Fucking betting against the people who'd just bought him out."

"That's fucked up."

"Yeah, but since he and his buddies basically wrote the fucking laws, everything he did was legal."

"Been a lot of that going around."

"No shit. But in this case, I know exactly who did it and where he lives, and I'm training to go kick the crap out of him."

The guitarist raised his eyebrows. "Would that place he lives by any chance be Shanghai?" Pete smiled, and his old friend laughed. "You're really going to go all the way to Shanghai to get this guy?"

"I'd fucking dive down to the wreck of the *Titanic* and bitchslap this punk on the quarterdeck if I had to! Bankers, bond traders, hedge fund vultures: they think they're fucking untouchable. I'm going to show that they're not."

"Right on, Pete. You're still an American hero." The singer flinched inside at the American hero tag, but Duffy rolled on. "So, you've got, like, a personal trainer?"

No use lying about it. "I'm doing it myself, right now, actually."

Duffy looked at him queerly, because to be doing something alone, without even an assistant, was suspect. This was L.A., and you were supposed to have your team: your assistant, your stylist, your publicist, your manager. If you didn't have a team, it was because you weren't worth it.

Pete headed him off. "That's right, man. Old-style. Alone. Fucking *Taxi Driver* shit. But I did get some help from this guy who used to be a CIA assassin."

Duffy raised his eyebrows, impressed. "That's kind of heavy. Where'd you find him?"

"I didn't. You put the word out and he finds you."

"Sounds like a drug deal."

"Payback *is* a drug." He put his finger in the air: "Song title! Anyway, I'm training."

"Are you going to, like, *stalk* this guy? In China? What if he's got a bodyguard?"

"I don't know, Duffy. But it's on. I *will* give that fucker his day of reckoning."

His friend nodded his head gently as he looked at him. "Cool. You're fired up. You're going it alone. You're flipping *crazy*! But that's what makes great rock and roll."

"Just climbing the mountain, my man. Climbing the fucking mountain. You still want that beer?"

This was where, if he'd been back at his old house, they would have kicked back by the pool and Matthew would have brought them a few beers and they would have drank until it was time to go get dinner, then drank some more. As it was, he got Duffy a beer and himself a diet soda, and they sat in his living room listening to Robert Johnson while Duff told him about the tour with Face the Cobra. He'd been sorely tempted on that one: the girls in London had been more outrageous than usual, and his wife was running out of forgiveness. The tour had gone well and the houses had been good, though by the time the tour manager finished charging them for their expenses, who knew how much money would be left? The fucking suits at the label were trying to renegotiate their contract, downward of course, complaining how the music business was dying, so bad these days that even parasites like them were having trouble making a living. Duff went on like that for a while, and Harrington would have been bothered to hear about someone else's successful tour, even Duff's, except that today they'd actually roughed out a new song. A great one, with real single potential, and he felt like he was in the game again, even without a band. Duff would come along, if he pushed him. They'd hit the big time together, as kids. That still counted for something. There'd be a lot of crap for Duffy getting permission from the label. But that didn't matter. He'd written a song. A good one, and he could feel that old power running through him, the current that got a man up on stage across from twenty thousand people to shout, *Hello, Akron! Hello, Seattle!* Nothing to hide behind but eyeliner and a microphone, throwing out his chest and screaming to cut through the darkness and blast away everything that had ever been sensible and finite and reasonable and confined by rules and protocol that fucked you over and made you old. *Hello, New York! Hello, Los Angeles! Hello, Shanghai!*

By the time a month had passed, he'd written six new songs. "Kickin' It," "Vanity Fair," "Never Grow Old," "Cold, Hard, and Dangerous," "Buried Alive," and "Perfect." Duffy had worked on all of them, and they shared the songwriting credit, which was good, because with songwriting credit came publishing royalties, and that was where the money was. Duffy had a stake in it now. And Bobby—for the first time in years Bobby didn't seem to be sleepwalking through his career. Bobby would check in with him every week or so or stop by the apartment and listen to the latest cuts. He'd firmed up another date on the tour, and actually seemed to be working the phone a little harder to line up more gigs.

He was also up to thirty push-ups. When he hit the bag, he moved it. Not with a little push, but with a loud smack and a little shock wave that made it flex around his fist, like the bag was taking a little tiny bow. He'd done the trap and hit at least twenty thousand times, by his count, and when he finally worked up the nerve to go back to the health club, a trainer there taught him how to throw a hook and do a front kick, and he incorporated those motions into his routine. He went to the club every day now, worked with the trainer, rode the exercise bike, did the strange exercises Charlie had taught him, even though everyone stared at him, and finally, drenched in sweat, he'd sit down to read a magazine. He still didn't know how he would find and confront Peter Harrington in Shanghai. He tried to put together an MO from various private-eye shows he'd seen on TV. He'd enter a squash tournament and punch him out on the court. He'd charm the receptionist at the Portman Hotel Health Club and get the dirtbag's address. He'd follow him on the street with his collar turned up and one of those earbud radios talking with some dude on the other end of it, saying shit like "I've got a visual!" or "The package is moving." If he had to, he'd fly to Shanghai and make it up as he went along.

He missed Charlie a little bit, since he was the one whose routine he was following. Even though Charlie had dumped him, Pete reasoned that maybe that was just what had to happen. Charlie thought he couldn't do it, but Charlie was all the people who'd ever told him he couldn't do something, whether it was moving to L.A., or hitting it big with the DreamKrushers, or going solo. On and off during his workouts he'd think of the old man, thinking, *Check this out, Charlie!* In a way, Charlie was present. He didn't know how present until he sauntered into the cool-down area one day and sat in his usual chair. On the table next to it was a copy of *Modern Maturity* magazine. He looked at it, on top of a stack of other magazines; then he glanced around the room. A couple of people noticed him—he was still Pete Harrington—but he knew better this time. He picked up the magazine. The note was inserted next to the first page:

65 WU LI LANE. LET'S TALK.

He found the old man waiting patiently outside the club. He felt like hugging him. "Charlie, man, you punked me again!"

Charlie, smiling at him, reached over and patted him on the shoulder. "You gotta have a little fun in this business or it gets you down. I heard you finally learned how to throw a punch."

"Don't make me drop you, old man!"

Charlie raised his eyebrows amiably; then his face suddenly changed and he gave a guttural snarl and slowly reached for Harrington's throat with both hands. The musician reflexively reached up and grabbed Charlie's wrists, and before he knew it, without feeling anything but a gentle insistence from Charlie, he found himself somehow turned around backward and hunched down with his wrist at the breaking point and his arm locked stiffly out to the side. He was pinned in place like an insect, looking at the lower front door of the health club.

He heard Charlie laughing again up above him; then he was turned loose. The old man's yellow wolfish teeth were exposed in an expression of pure joy. "Oh, that was funny!"

"What the hell did you do?"

"Just a little Chin-na. You may need more than a month of training to drop me."

"Teach me how to do that!"

Charlie started walking down the street, and Pete followed him. "I'm sure you wouldn't find it very interesting."

"No, seriously!"

"It's old-guy stuff."

"C'mon, Charlie! Cut me in on the good shit!"

Charlie turned to him. "Maybe later. How many push-ups can you do?"

"I'm up to thirty an hour. I can do forty, max."

"On your knuckles?"

"Does this answer your question?" He made a fist in front of Charlie's face, hearing the joints crackle into a solid ball of bones and muscle. The knuckles were covered with thick yellow calluses.

"Let's see."

"Here? On the street?" They were on the sidewalk between a law office and a kosher deli. At any given moment there were three or four people passing by.

"Right here. On your knuckles."

Pete dropped to the ground. He could feel the pebbly surface of the concrete, but the skin was thickened enough that he didn't feel any pain. He knocked out thirty push-ups quickly, slowed down progressively on the next six, labored heavily on the following three, then stalled halfway up on his fortieth before fighting his way to the top. Just before he finished, Charlie said, "Do one more."

He went down again but there was nothing left in his arms. He could see people's ankles slowing down and halting around him. He pushed as hard as he could, but his body didn't rise from the pavement. His arms began trembling.

Charlie's voice came down to him, harder than he'd ever heard it. "Do it!"

He summoned everything he had and focused all of it into his arms. It was the entire universe squeezed into one gesture of will, there on the Fairfax Avenue sidewalk with its pedestrians and its litter of car horns and paper cups and plastic bags and stray music. If he failed, he would fall on his face. He rose a quarter inch, then an inch, and with that movement he seemed to build some unlikely momentum and shivered slowly to the top and held himself there. He hesitated a moment, and then, when Charlie said nothing, he bent his knee underneath himself and stood up, breathing hard and feeling the blood swelling in his face. He faced the trainer, who looked at him levely, his slightly cloudy blue eyes unyielding. "Are you still going to Shanghai?"

"Yeah," he puffed.

"That's a coincidence. Because I've been thinking of going there myself. I've got some loose ends to tie up."

Pete grinned. "Let's do it!" He lifted up his fist for a bump, but Charlie just looked at it.

"What's that for?"

"It's a fist bump, Charlie. We bump knuckles."

The old man carefully raised his fist and moved it gently toward Pete Harrington's until it touched.

"*Hell yeah!*" the musician said. "I told you I'd keep the faith, Charlie."

"So you did. Let's head in here and get something to eat." Charlie pushed the door of the deli open. He turned back to the singer and said in a lower voice, "I think the waitress has her eye on me. And I kind of like it."

IV

❧

Cathay
Hotel

❧

1

The Buried City

⁜

The trip to Shanghai was the longest flight Charlie had taken in two decades, and he wasn't really sure he was up to it. After the first two hours, his
back had started to hurt, and by the time they got to Tokyo, nine hours
later, he was squirming in his seat like a two-year-old. His bad foot started
to throb from all the blood pooling in it, and he had to go to the bathroom
about a dozen times, waiting in line beside the tiny cubicle and trying not
to fall down. He had to lean against a seat, and the woman in it kept giving
him dirty looks. He felt a bone-tiredness that bordered on the painful, as if
all the muscles that held his spine together were too damn beat to do the
job and everything was going out of alignment. In Tokyo he managed to
find a rest lounge and lie down to sleep for an hour, so deep under the darkness that when Pete woke him up and he rose to his feet, he was still dreaming of Millie and the old farm in Washington, before their son died. The
way those dreams always went. Nothing really happened in them, it was
just the presence of his son, but all so much more vivid than he could ever
re-create in his waking life. It wasn't like when he tried to remember him,
it was just *him*, with the clothes and the smell and the haircut, all of him
instantly there and alive. They were in the house. Eddie was about eight,

standing in a white T-shirt like kids wore back then, and he was so over-
joyed to see the boy, he'd gone straight to him and thrown his arms around
him and said, "Eddie! I miss you so much!" and the boy had hugged him
back. Then he'd felt someone shaking his shoulder, and there was Pete, telling him to get up, that they'd called their flight to Shanghai, and the only
thing left was that furry rotten taste of sleep in his mouth.

He had to force himself to get back on the plane for the last three hours
to Shanghai. He managed to doze off, his mouth hanging open and his
snoring so loud that a man across the aisle finally poked him and said something unpleasant in Chinese. The lights in the cabin snapped an obnoxious
glow into the cabin, and useless little hot towels were handed out with tongs,
as if you could actually get your hands dirty in a sealed corridor thirty thousand feet above the earth. They watered the passengers with pots of green
tea, brought a breakfast of noodles and red barbecued pork, which blocked
up the aisle when he desperately needed to piss. He waited until he was
practically salivating with the need to go, then begged them to let him pass
and managed to reach the bathroom just as his bladder started to give out:
he was only a little wet but he sprayed urine all over the bathroom floor and
wiped it up as well as he could out of embarrassment and shame. He dried
his pants and tried his best to cover himself as he made his way back to his
seat. It was nine at night when they got to Shanghai.

He recognized absolutely nothing. The Shanghai he'd known had disappeared as completely as the sixty-odd years since he'd last been in this city.
The airport back then had been more like an oversize airstrip, mostly military traffic. Some DC-3s, C-40 Constellations cashiered from the war. The
world was still clearing rubble from the streets, and people had better things
to do than tour around a country like China in the last phases of a civil war.
Nineteen forty-nine. The Nationalists were leaving town with everything
they could carry: crates and crates of stuff from palaces and mansions, military ordnance, fancy prewar automobiles. He still remembered a maroon
and white Bugatti limousine a half a block long being backed into a wooden
crate while an army officer held a loaded pistol on the owner. The damn
.thing was probably sitting in a museum in Taipei now.

Zhang met them at the airport and took them to their hotels. They'd traveled on opposite sides of the plane and were staying at separate hotels, just in case somebody looked into it later. Zhang had gotten gray in the twenty years since they'd last seen each other, when Charlie'd come over to Beijing on a trade mission for Hughes Aerospace. Zhang shook hands warmly, but he looked tired, and Charlie realized he must be close to seventy now, a lifelong smoker. He'd been the chief of the Shanghai branch of the Public Security Police in the eighties and early nineties, then retired to make a lot of money in the new China. Still had enough *guanxi* there to coast along for the next decade doing little odds and ends like this. Zhang was doing him a favor more than anything else: Charlie'd saved his father's life in 1944. He'd given Zhang the financier's name, and Zhang called back a week later with a whole dossier: names of his business partners, both Chinese and American, entries and exits, photos, right down to the girl he was seeing. The beauty of a police state.

They dropped the musician at a name-brand hotel in the center of Shanghai. Charlie didn't want to go in because of the security cameras, so he said good-bye in the car. Pete clapped him on the shoulder. "You okay, Charlie?"

"I've felt better, but I've felt worse, too."

"We'll be up and running after a good sleep."

He watched through the glass doors while Zhang's driver helped him check in. It was funny traveling with Pete Harrington. He always looked around as if he expected to be recognized, and, surprisingly, he often was. Even in the boarding line at the Tokyo airport, a young Chinese girl had come up to him and asked for his autograph.

"I'm a cult figure in China," Harrington announced to him.

Charlie chuckled. "Why is that?"

"Who knows, man? Wayne Newton is a major draw in Slovakia. Guns N' Roses is still huge in Argentina. Something hits at the right time and you've always got that moment. I toured here in 1992, one of the first big Western acts, and it, uh, created a little stir." The singer lingered on that memory, then left it quickly behind. "The girls on that tour? I don't even want to talk about it. They were all like little geishas."

"That's Japan."

"Yeah, whatever, Charlie. Don't bludgeon me with facts. I'm a big-picture guy."

Now Harrington was getting shy looks from a little cluster of young Chinese workers behind the reception counter. He saw one of the boys work up the nerve to ask for his autograph, which the singer gave him with a little flourish that so cowed the kid that he stepped back a few feet and stared incredulously at the piece of paper.

They drove off to his hotel, a couple cuts below his client's, but Zhang could get him checked in under a phony name here. A lot of polished stone and brass, an updated version of the better Chinese state hotels he remembered from twenty years ago. A camera over the reception area, another over the door. The guy in the black sport coat talking to the bellhop looked like security, but maybe not. The place wasn't that expensive.

By the time he got to bed it was eleven at night, and he lay there for an hour, wide awake. Something in the airplane food had given him a bad stomach, and his gut was rumbling until two. He had to go sit on the toilet every twenty minutes. His goddamn foot was still throbbing from the flight. If he didn't watch it, he'd end up in the hospital with a blood clot. Wouldn't that be fun to explain to his client? Charlie'd crossed the Atlantic in the gun turret of a B-17, dropped into Burma, into Kunming, into Germany. All so long ago. Like Pete Harrington's great career. They were both trying to salvage something here.

The next morning it took him a few seconds to figure out where he was, and then he could barely get out of bed. His foot was killing him. His asshole was raw from the diarrhea. He had that doped-out feeling from jet lag and exhaustion, but this time he didn't have any uppers to snap him out of it for the mission. He dragged himself into the shower and let it run over his head, massaging the back of his neck until he could at least move it to one side, and he put his knees together and moved them in big circles to try to loosen up the tendons, the way he'd learned to sixty years ago. The damn things were shot, too much jumping out of perfectly good airplanes, but it helped a little bit. That's how it was now. He spent a half hour every morning loosening and stretching his old-man's body, and when he was all finished it was only twenty percent better than when he started. He did his back exercises and twenty push-ups and then he did the strange stretching and strengthening movements he'd picked up in China. Tiger Scratches the Tree. An Archer Opens the Bow. The Bear. Back when he'd had real muscles, he'd used to like looking in the mirror when he did these. Now he did them as he looked out at the city. After that he sent a quick e-mail to Beth Blackman and told her everything was on target.

It took him an hour and a cup of tea to get rolling. He got down to the cafeteria at 6:30 and surveyed the copper chafing dishes of the buffet. Bleached-out sausage, runny scrambled eggs. A halfhearted nod to the few Western travelers who'd gotten marooned here. He found a big cauldron of rice porridge, something he'd developed a taste for in his old Kunming days, when they'd gone sneaking through the jungles and a cup of cold porridge was a damn feast. The tribesmen used to put insects in theirs, when there was nothing else, but he'd never been able to do that. He spooned some out and stirred in a few pickled vegetables.

At 7:00 Harrington still wasn't answering his phone. He didn't really need him today—he wasn't the person to take along when you didn't want to be noticed—but the lack of discipline brought all his old doubts back, too. The singer had trained hard, and he'd trained lonely, but that didn't mean he'd pull it off. He went outside to make sure the driver was waiting for him, and then he left a message at Harrington's hotel. "I'm going out to look around. Keep your cell phone handy. I'll see you this afternoon." It was Thursday morning in Shanghai.

Zhang had hired them a car: a white Audi, Chinese-made. The most forgettable car in the world. Also two cheap local cell phones that they'd tested during the ride in from the airport. Zhang had found him a man he'd worked with before who spoke decent English and had the necessary experience, including keeping his mouth shut. Zhang had written out the relevant addresses for him in Chinese and English. They were headed to the financier's home. On the way there he tried out the little bit of Chinese he remembered from the war, but his pronunciation was all off, and he didn't want to use up the man's good humor on it.

Peter Harrington lived in the old French Concession, and he remembered it as one of the calmer areas of Shanghai. At least it was still recognizable as the same place. The plane trees with their mottled pale-green bark, still lined the streets, and the high white walls sealed the houses off from the road. A good area for running, which was one of Harrington's exercise routines. From his house to his health club, five mornings a week. If the target was like most people, he could probably trace out his running route just by downloading a map from the Internet.

He loved to study people: what routes they took, what stores they stopped in to pick up a coffee or a newspaper, where they really went when they were supposed to be somewhere else. A person's life was built up out of habits like that, and once you knew the habits, you could move them around like a chess piece. If a man had a secret, you could ruin him, or control him. If someone wanted him dead, you could whack him, easily. It was almost mathematical, most of the time. Like that arms dealer in Mexico City: he had a crew of six very capable bodyguards trained by the East German government, all attached to the embassy. But he *loved* German food. So Charlie's team opened up a restaurant a few blocks from the embassy: brought in a chef from Germany, advertised it, made sure they got a few glowing reviews in the papers. They were doing land-office business. The embassy crowd was in there every day. A month went by, then another one. The place was actually making money, which kept the guys back in Washington happy. Life was fairly normal, other than that he was down there to kill someone. A couple more months went by, and finally the target showed up with his security team. They sprinkled a little ricin in his Wiener schnitzel, and he was dead in twenty-two hours, a fact that would have hurt the place's reputation if the East Germans hadn't tried so hard to make it go away. The place was still in business, last he heard.

The address they had for Peter Harrington was 65 Wu Li Lane. The house was tucked away in a little rabbit warren of alleys and small connected homes, built in the early thirties when Shanghai was booming, and the whole maze of tiny streets was closed off with an iron gate and a guard in a blue uniform reading a newspaper. You could spend twenty minutes bumbling around trying to find the place and be seen by a dozen people. He pulled out a real-estate broker's card that he'd asked Zhang to print up for him then had the driver hand it to the guard. Brokers always had a reason to be snooping around. "Ask him to show us where Sixty Wu Li Lane is."

The guard let them in and walked them into the elegant little enclave, with small trees and plantings framing a narrow brick walkway, a dollhouse sort of neighborhood. There was no number 60, of course, but the guard walked them right up to Harrington's residence while he looked for it.

"Ask him if there's another entrance. Tell him maybe we were supposed to meet another broker there."

The guard dutifully led them to the back entrance and opened the gate onto a mossy little alley that was closed off by a pile of old paving stones. Pretty clear Harrington would be using the front entrance. So much the better: the place even had a café across the street where he could sit by the window and wait for Harrington to exit.

Christ, this was easy! During the bad old days, if you weren't careful, you'd be the one to end up with someone following you, or they'd make you and never let on, just let you chase your own tail for weeks. In some places, of course, it could get you killed. Not this job. He ordered a pastry and settled down to wait.

At 8:34 the gate opened and Harrington walked out. Light brown hair a little thinner than his pictures. A high forehead. A little bit heavyset, but he looked like he was in decent shape. Moved fairly well. Have to tell the client that. This might turn out to be interesting after all. He wasn't dressed like a businessman. He was wearing a sweatshirt that said Shanghai University and running shorts, and he was carrying a racquet. Just as Zhang's surveillance had said: played squash every morning at nine thirty. Better not to stage it when he had the racquet with him: he'd have a fairly good chance of breaking the client's face with it if the first blow wasn't decisive. Harrington waited there a few seconds, and then, just as he'd expected, the man's driver got out of a black sedan parked nearby. The driver doubled as his bodyguard, an athletic-looking Chinese man in a sport jacket, midthirties. He already knew the bodyguard practiced Hung Gar and carried an expandable baton in a belt holster. Zhang had told him that. He'd have to figure out how to take him out of the picture for fifteen seconds. Charlie snapped a couple of shots with a telephoto lens as they made their way to the car.

They followed him to the health club, arriving at 8:52. Harrington went inside, carrying his gym bag. Charlie noted it in his book. He told his driver to find a parking space: and they went around the block and double-parked down the street. His driver stepped out of the car and lit up a cigarette, leaning against the hood.

He'd get his client his best shot at him. Fine. But he'd need more than that to complete this job. That's where Zhang's other men came in. He wasn't sure how he was going to make it happen. Like a lot of jobs: you made it up as you went along.

He called Pete Harrington on his cell phone.

"We're going out tonight."

"Cool! Where?"

"I don't know yet, but don't get your hopes up. You'll be staying in the car. I want you to get a good look at this guy so you know what you're up against."

Harrington sounded disappointed. "You don't think I can take him?"

"You can take him. But I want you to see him first. I want you to set your mind. Did you work out?"

"An hour and a half."

"Good. That'll help you stay loose. I'm going to try to get next to him tonight and see what I can set up."

"Got it."

"Are you still sure you want to go through with this?"

There was a pause. "Yeah. This has to happen."

"Why?"

The line went silent for a long time before the musician answered. He sounded tense. "I think you know why." Charlie could interpret that one a lot of ways. He went on, "Once in a while somebody's got to kick the crap out of greed. It's my turn."

Now Charlie went silent. He didn't know how pure Harrington's motives were. How much of it was kicking the crap out of greed and how much was just to make himself feel like he was still somebody, or to get a better class of girl? Sixty years in the spy business and he knew all about motives: there was the one you admitted to, and then there was its ugly sister, and you always had to take both sisters along on the date. That other Shanghai was coming back at him again. "Well, okay then," he said at last. "You'll get your chance."

He hung up and melted back in the seat as a wave of exhaustion rippled through his chest and head. He let his head loll to the side and his gaze drifted out the window to a long wall of beige plaster and, behind it, the top of a Victorian turret, one of the walled mansions that dotted the residential neighborhoods of the French Concession. Slate roof shingles hung above dark exposed eaves. There were the Tudor beams. *Wasn't it . . . ?* He sat up and studied it, and then it seemed as if a bell started ringing in his head. Christ! It was Abe Benjamin's house! He felt like saying it to the driver: *That was Benjamin's house!* Nineteen forty-six. Benjamin and Sassoon sitting there in their jackets and ties in the hot afternoon parlor. The sweat on a glass of gin and tonic. Benjamin, the guy who owned the racetrack. Sassoon, the real-estate magnate. Jews who'd sat out the war in the Bahamas or under Japanese protection, now liquidating their assets and tying up loose ends. *You're in the import-export business, Charlie. We'd like to buy a load of scrap metal.*

Not stupid people. They'd made his cover pretty quickly, then let it be known that they'd be interested in buying all those surplus weapons still hanging around the South Pacific. *Gentlemen, do you honestly expect me to believe you want those weapons as scrap?* Sassoon smiling as he gave a little tilt of his head: *Do you expect us to believe you're in the import-export business?* He didn't have the authority to pull that one off, but he hooked them up with Stanton Rogers, and it got hazy after that. He heard rumors later about a load of dismantled tanks being shipped to Tel Aviv.

He closed his eyes. Lots of side deals available back then, but you had to watch your step. It suited him. As much as he'd hated the war, he'd enjoyed it in a strange way. The comradeship, the excitement. He hadn't been ready to go back to the family farm, and Donovan begged him to stay on, offering him a hundred bucks a week and a flat in Shanghai in the days when Truman was starting to have second thoughts about pulling the plug on America's only intelligence service. He was only twenty-two years old, but they must have seen something they liked. Supposedly an import-export broker, he was really there to check out the Communists and see if there was anything to be done with them if they won. That was the start, anyway, making friends with the Commies who were underground and trying to figure out how much loyalty they still had to Uncle Sam for all the nice weapons and explosives he'd given them during the war, most of which they'd stockpiled to fight against Chiang Kai-shek anyway. After the bit with the surplus armaments, other people started bringing him propositions. Mostly off-kilter business deals that traded on his war connections. Not interested. The French wanted to send him back to Indochina to finger some of his old allies. He gave that a pass, too. But the problem of Hermann Maier and his daughter was different. It wasn't business, and it wasn't his job. It had nothing to do with money or rank or prestige. It was something that nobody but a tiny circle of acquaintances would ever know about, and those people wouldn't talk.

He'd been thinking about the Maiers ever since he'd found out that Peter Harrington was living in Shanghai. People he'd put aside for decades. And though he knew it was useless, some part of him couldn't help expecting to walk the Bund and see Vorster, Richter, and Anna Maier, or hear her piano music streaming through the quiet lanes. He felt a moment of deep loneliness. All that was gone now, covered up by the modern, like those buried pyramids in Mexico City that you saw underground when you rode the subway, except now all of Shanghai was that subway, and he was its only passenger.

He was woken up by the sound of his driver opening the car door. The financier was moving again. He noted the time, 10:37 A.M., noting it again when they arrived back at Harrington's house, 10:59. Harrington went in, then came out an hour later wearing a business suit, and they followed him from there across the river to Pudong, a new area crowded with modern-looking office towers and condominium stacks. He went into a small Western-style restaurant beneath one of the buildings, a pricey one, judging by the corner location and the wraparound glass walls. This was all so ridiculously easy: he had his binoculars and he could watch the target sit down right next to the window. Charlie noted the address of the building: it was just out of habit, at this point. He was already coming up with a plan. A second man sat down across from Harrington: short and broad, with a sort of belligerent look about him. Probably his partner. With these binoculars he could practically read the menu. "I'll have a black coffee, boys, while you're at it." He took a picture with the telephoto lens. It sure was good to work again. He hadn't had this much fun since that trip to Panama. The target stayed there an hour and a half, then came out with the short wide guy and talked all the way to the open door of his car. The bodyguard didn't look too alert. An ex-cop, according to Zhang. A glorified driver. Might be fairly competent once things got going, but from the look of him, he wouldn't be spotting it too far out. Which was good. That's all he needed: a head start. The financier shook hands with his lunch companion and then climbed into his car.

Easy life . . . Play a little squash, have a cup of coffee with your friends. Tinker away at a business deal. No need to work too hard when you're sitting on six or seven hundred million. He knew the type, had done personal protection for some of them. They got bored. This Harrington would have a handful of expensive restaurants he ate at regularly, his favorite nightclubs, where the doorman knew his name. A string of girlfriends. Tonight was Saturday night. Could be a dinner party, could be a restaurant and a couple of clubs. That seemed to be his routine. Zhang had tailed him for a few days and verified that. He liked the Hyatt and a place on the Bund called the Bar Rouge. Not a care in the world. Except when you walk away with six hundred million of other people's money, someone was liable to punch you in the nose someday. Nothing personal: that was just how it was.

They followed Harrington back to his residence. Charlie hadn't intended to sleep, but the jet lag finally overwhelmed all the coffee and he dozed off in the car with his mouth open. Occasionally he would surface again and catch a glimpse of the modern city: the Huangpu River below them as they crossed the bridge, the anonymous doorway of some modern new building. Also, sometimes, the brown brick of the older city, with its dark, ominous skyscrapers only thirty stories tall but more imposing than the new ones that were twice their height. When they got back to Harrington's place, his driver touched him on the shoulder. He noted the time, then took out a piece of spearmint chewing gum to swab away the taste of sleep. The financier went inside. He probably wouldn't come out until around six, for dinner, and the driver could sit on it until then.

Charlie unlatched the car door. "I'm going to stretch my legs. Call me if his driver comes back. If he moves on foot, stay with him and call me."

His knees were feeling creaky from sitting in the car so long, but at least his foot was behaving itself. Even his back didn't feel too stiff, considering the flight yesterday. He stood next to the car and surveyed the street, erasing its pedestrians and its automobiles, scrubbing away the neon and the posters and the light posts and the noise. He knew where he was now. He could see through all the shiny new businesses to where he really was, not just geographically, but within all the different Shanghais that had stacked up over the course of his life. He was trying to remember how that music sounded.

He started off past a drugstore, glancing in the window at vitamin supplements and crutches, then past a Bank of China and a bakery and a store that sold Tibetan goods. *This one . . .* He stopped. *This was the French laundry.* Madame Fortier, with the husband that went back to Vichy to visit family and got conscripted by the government. Poor bastard got killed defending the coast on D-day. He walked another half block to a brown brick storefront with an expensive-looking little café in it. *Hapgood's Stationery Store.* He could still see the black-and-white tiles, the glass cases. *Used to stock Parker pens. Dispensed a little opium under the table to foreigners who wanted to stay clear of the Triads.* Charlie felt as if he were walking downhill now, drawn toward the subterranean world of the past, toward something in his memory, a place that existed there so fiercely that it dulled the present-day illusions around him. Past coffee shops and cell phone vendors, past an appliance store and a travel agent. This was it: Rue Lafayette. He burrowed down through the modern street, by a notions shop and a milliner, an auto dealership selling DeSotos, Buicks, Packards. There was the hat shop and Chen's Fine Tailor for Men, the dull interior of the billiards hall and cigar store. The season seemed to have gotten warmer, or maybe it was just the walk. Then he saw the little sign at the entrance to the little alley. LANE 37.

He turned into the narrow road, and the noise of the avenue disappeared behind him. So peaceful here. High cream-colored walls lined either side of the roadway, a little canyon broken by wooden doors and wrought-iron gates. The smooth bark of the plane trees peeled into greens and grays and tans, as if they'd been painted by numbers, and their roots humped up the sidewalks. He could hear his footsteps. The light was getting yellow now.

He reached number 116 and peered through the bars of the black metal gate. A bougainvillea scratched at the wall of the little garden inside. Overhead, the wind blew and the wide flat leaves rustled against each other. A lone rickshaw hustled past behind him. He could hear the driver panting softly as his feet padded by. Not many of those left these days. He looked at his watch, the little gold hands pointing at the dots of radium, now dull yellow-green in the sunshine: punctual to the dot, a habit he'd honed during the war. He rang the bell and waited. The servant came, a Chinese woman in a blue dress and white apron, with a white cap on her head. It was spring, yes, definitely a warm day in spring. The jasmine was in bloom and the perfume of it damn near made his head swim.

"I'm Charles Pico. I'm here to see Mr. Maier."

The servant must have known he was coming. She opened the gate and led him along the red tile walkway. The steps to the small porch loomed in front of him, and he mounted them slowly. He glanced in a side window and saw the interior of a room: a slice of credenza, the tops of armchairs, a painting of some sort. The big wooden door swung open, and he found himself looking down a dim hallway lined with flowered wallpaper and a wooden banister leading to an unseen second floor. It was all in dark greens and gray, somber colors that he figured had come into vogue before the war, when he was still on the farm.

It wasn't a mansion, but in a city where land was at a premium, any free-standing house was a luxury. As she led him down the hallway he looked at the accoutrements. Some Chinese cabinetry, done in the old style, occasional expensive bric-a-brac made of ivory or ceramic. Through the dining room, with a fine mahogany table and chairs, past a piano with a metronome, a sofa upholstered with striped silk, and a coffee table holding a copy of the *Hamburger Zeitung* neatly folded and waiting to be read. On the piano was a stiff, unsmiling wedding picture of a slight, bookish young man and his rather more attractive blond wife. The maid motioned to the couch and offered him water from a glass pitcher, which he turned down. She turned on the table fan as she left the room, and Charlie watched the propellers accelerate in their wire cage. He heard footsteps approaching from the back of the house, a few words of muttered Chinese, then Mr. Maier came into the room.

He was a small man with silver wire-rimmed spectacles, and the first impression he made with his mildly stooped shoulders was of physical weakness. At that time Maier must have been in his fifties, which had seemed old to him then, when he was only twenty-two himself, just getting into his present line of work. Maier's hands had a slightly skeletal tension to them and his hair was thin and white. He'd seemed frail, but the truth was that he was still alive, where a lot of stronger guys were dead, and after seeing so many powerfully built men killed by little pieces of metal, Charlie's image of strength had undergone an evolution in the past few years. Charlie stood up as he came in, and they shook hands. His grip was cool, soft.

"Mr. Pico, please, there was no need to get up!" He extended his spotty hand toward the couch. "Can I offer you some American whiskey?"

Maier poured him some Old Grand-Dad from the cart and sat down across from him in a chair. Charlie noticed it was a brand-new bottle.

Mr. Maier was wearing a brown tweed sport jacket with a bow tie and a white shirt. He spoke English with a strong German accent. The man radiated cunning the way some people radiate sex appeal or physical strength, but it was complicated by a nervous sadness that collected in the droop of his shoulders. Before the war, Mr. Maier had been in the shipping business in Kiel, had gotten out of Germany in 1936, bounced through Singapore and Bangkok, then landed in Shanghai in 1937. He'd spent six years watching the Nazis cut his country into perfect little swastikas, and then another six watching them set it all on fire.

He tried to imagine Maier's life in Kiel. A nice house by a canal, a family, relatives. Years of worry, standing by as the worst people in the world slowly get the upper hand, and then one day you wake up in Shanghai with diamonds sewn into the hem of your overcoat praying for a letter from Argentina, Bolivia, Palestine: whoever hasn't slammed the door shut yet. He noticed a photo on the piano that had a younger Maier in it, in a schoolboy's outfit, surrounded by parents and brothers and sisters. He didn't ask where they were now.

They chatted a bit about the United States: Mr. Maier had visited America on business in 1930, so he'd been to the East Coast. He had a first cousin in Los Angeles. "And you?" he asked. Charlie told him he'd grown up on a farm in Washington State. By way of explaining his presence in Shanghai, he threw the import-export cover at him, but the old man just waved his hand at him, smiling. "I already talked with Sassoon," he said.

Charlie returned the grin, though he wasn't completely happy about it. He didn't want his identity to be an open secret in Shanghai. Mr. Maier seemed to anticipate that. "Don't worry," he said, "it's a very small group of us. And besides, I take no sides in that argument. The Communists will crush everyone sooner or later, as they did in Russia, or the Nationalists will run a gangster state, as they are here in Shanghai. Either side will one day take notice of me. I'm moving to the United States. I want to be somewhere I don't have to flee again."

He had no idea why this meeting had been set up. He'd only gotten a message from Benjamin, saying call this man at this number, he wants to make a proposition to you. Sassoon had finally gotten his properties back from the Japanese and would be clearing out for the Bahamas. Maier, too, having fled Germany, would be hightailing it out of Shanghai before long. One step ahead of the Fascists, and one step ahead of the Communists. He was a nimble man.

"That's the advantage of shipping," he said. "Your assets are movable. Most of them."

They talked a bit about Charlie's service record behind the lines in Germany and western China and what it was like to parachute out of a plane at night. It seemed like small talk and it seemed like an interview. Maier asked him if he was a spy in the war, and he said no, he didn't know anything about spying, but if you asked him to blow something up he had a moderate degree of competence. Still, the man wasn't revealing anything.

"I'm at your service, Mr. Maier," he said at last. "But I'm also at a loss here. Is there something specific you wanted to talk to me about?"

He had just opened his mouth to speak when someone came in the front door and called out, "Papa!"

Maier answered her in German and she came into the room. A young woman of perhaps eighteen, dressed in a schoolgirl's outfit of a white blouse and a blue and white checked skirt down to her calves. Tendrils of her ash-blond hair were swept up over her forehead and cascaded down in curls to one side like Veronica Lake. She stopped short when she noticed Charlie sitting there on the sofa.

He stood up for her. She was a living version of the young bride in the photograph. It threw him off a little.

"Anna," Maier said, "this is Charlie Pico. He is a friend of ours from America. I'm asking him to help us."

She shook his hand cautiously.

"Anna!" her father said, "have a seat. Don't be shy. These are things you should know about. You are old enough." The girl sat down, quietly radiant. "Anna is the one who plays the piano," Maier said.

"Very poorly," she said.

"So poorly that she was asked to play three of Chopin's Nocturnes for Princess Elizabeth when she visits next month."

"Papa!" She rolled her eyes toward Charlie. "They couldn't find anyone else. Do you like Chopin?"

"I've never met the man," Charlie said.

She smiled for the first time. "You're very funny, Mr. Pico. I'll play you some Chopin one day and then you can give me your opinion of him."

Hermann Maier began again. "I'll tell you my story, Mr. Pico. It's not a unique story, not for you, who I am sure has seen many terrible things in the last three years."

Nothing surprising about the story, as Maier had promised, given the sad state of affairs the world had been in. He'd arranged for the whole family to get out of Germany. It had taken him nearly a year of bribes and arrangements, and he'd had to sign over much of his business to various third parties who stood in for prominent Nazis. The problem was that his wife was a beautiful woman. "Anna gets her looks from her mother." From her time at *Mittelschule* she'd had an admirer, a Karl Richter. Richter had come into her orbit because their mothers had grown up in the same neighborhood; they had been playmates from a young age. But Richter's mother had married a drunken, brutal man, a stevedore who had long bouts without work during the chaos of the Weimar Republic. It was due to his own oafishness, but he blamed it on the bankers and the profiteers, and in his mind that meant Jews. Richter took after the father. He was a rough, simpleminded adolescent with dark hair and a wide Slavic face, far from the Germanic ideal, like most Nazis. That was the funny thing about the Nazis, Maier said, the top ones never measured up. Goebbels, a cripple; Göring, a fat buffoon; Hitler himself, a dark-haired misfit. It was as if they'd invented an ideal they couldn't possibly meet so that, by naming it, they could possess it. Richter enjoyed sports like boxing and rugby and was constantly having trouble at school. Unfortunately, he had also had an affection for Lille, Maier's wife, and as he reached the age of eighteen, the affection grew into a mania. She rejected his advances, and though he was hurt, Richter's attitude toward her was still solicitous and courteous, in his brutish way. As time went on, though, his attentions began to have a slightly sarcastic tone to them. After she married Maier, Richter became bitter and abusive toward her, emotions that were given a new articulation when he threw himself into Fascist politics. By 1931 he was an important person in the Kiel Nazi Party, a prominent speaker about the "stab in the back" and the Jewish bloodsuckers. On those occasions when they had the misfortune to meet him in the street, he would insult them. *It's so nice to see you with an animal of your own species!* he might say, favoring them with a grand smile. *And what a charming little brood of rats!* Always with a gleeful and venomous flourish. Hatred had devoured him completely; it had become a kind of joy.

The unfortunate thing was that the path to an exit visa ran directly through him. He had extracted everything he could: offices, warehouses, even their residence. He was convinced that Maier had a large fleet of ships, just because he was a Jew and Jews always hide their true wealth, and it was only through the intercession of a sympathetic Lutheran minister that he could be persuaded to release his hold. They received their visas the morning their ship was to depart, though they had been stamped a week earlier. They rushed to the port with whatever they could fit into their suitcases, and he and the children passed through Immigration first. At that very moment, just as their papers had been stamped with all the officiousness that the Reich could muster, Richter appeared with his usual vicious pleasantry, and he told them to go ahead, that his wife would be with them shortly. When he hesitated, Richter screamed at him. "Go now, or you will never leave!"

Charlie glanced at the girl, Anna, who stared down at her lap as the ugly words rolled through the room. Her shoulders were hunched like a child's, as if she was still cowering.

His wife was no longer the object of youthful fantasies that Richter had desired. She was near forty, a mother of two, immersed in a life that had long ago cast off from whatever dreams Richter might have harbored. His goal was not to possess her but to take revenge on the fact that there were things he would never possess, no matter how much he wanted them, no matter how vaunted his new role as a high Nazi official. Maier knew this, but he was trapped. If he left, he didn't know what would happen to his wife, but if he stayed, his children would be caught, too. In the way that was particular to the Nazis, Richter controlled the situation with another lie. He'd smiled and said, "Do not worry, Herr Maier. I am just saying good-bye to a childhood friend."

To his shame, this lie had been enough. He'd gone with the children and checked into their stateroom. The purser, a Frenchman, seemed to know they were escaping and treated them sympathetically. Maier had waited five minutes for Lille's knock on the door, then, at the blast of the ship's horn, rushed to the gangplank just as the crew began to raise it. He hurried off to find the purser, but then the horn sounded again, and he felt a slight lurch as the ship began to move. He dashed through the passenger lounge and the ship's bar, finally spotting the purser and grabbing him by the arm, demanding to know of his wife. The purser told him, with alarm, that his wife was not on board but that they had been ordered by the highest local authority to cast off. Maier had to be helped back to his cabin, where his young daughter and toddler son were waiting for their mother. Richter had won.

That was the last time he'd seen her. He'd written her letters, but they were never answered. From his Lutheran minister friend he heard she'd been deported, but she hadn't appeared on any of the lists of survivors that the Red Cross had issued. He'd made every kind of inquiry in every Displaced Persons camp; nothing had turned up so far.

Charlie listened to the story. There were a lot of stories like that. Few of them had good endings. "I could make some inquiries for you. I have some friends in the service who are working with DPs."

"She is lost!" the older man answered. "I know that! She would have contacted my cousin in America to look for us. Only one thing can keep a mother from searching for her children. She is lost!" Maier was leaning forward in his seat, a frail and ferocious little man, but now, in a motion that indicated to Charlie the degree of self-discipline he had, he calmed himself and leaned back, then said offhandedly, "But Richter is in Shanghai. He's alive and enjoying the clean air of freedom."

Footsteps crossed the ceiling over their heads. The maid rattled some pans in the kitchen. "And you'd like to see that situation change."

Maier nodded. "Of course."

"I'm not a hired assassin, Mr. Maier. I'll bet if you ask around you can find a Chinese guy who can do the job quite well. It's a buyer's market for that stuff these days."

"Mr. Pico, I have no connections to the Triads, and I do not want any. Men like that may come back and ask for favors. I know you are someone I can trust."

Killing somebody wasn't really his line of work—at least, not unless it was a war. Once the war was over, the rules changed, for some reason. Ten months ago parachuting into Germany and killing Richter would have gotten him a medal. Today, it would get him a murder rap. Was Richter less guilty now that an armistice had been signed? Was he any less deserving of dying, or of living?

The three of them just sat there. Maier probably offered him another drink or a smoke. It seemed a little odd that the shipper would have his daughter sit in on his attempts to hire a killer, but she had a right, he supposed.

Charlie knew already he wasn't going to take the job. The idea of clipping an ex-Nazi didn't bother him too much, but he was busy with his other work in Shanghai, and the government didn't look fondly on side jobs. Those kinds of deals were a slippery slope. He'd seen it plenty during the war and would see a lot more of it afterward: you start out using your connections to do favors, and the next thing you know you're a black marketeer or a mercenary.

The problem was, he couldn't ignore the girl. It had been a long war, with the closest thing to romance being the whorehouses in Rangoon and Kunming. Anna was the kind of pipe dream he'd hung on to in the jungle, when he'd imagined someday turning the misery and fear into stories he'd tell to impress someone intelligent, civilized, beautiful. He wasn't any of those things himself: he was a dumb farm boy from Washington State that got demolitions training because he knew how to blow up stumps and then got pretty good at killing people, yet here she was, like the secret reward he had earned by being a "hero": A hero's wife. A spy's mistress. There was something about the unknown, the endlessly possible that she represented. And at the same time, beneath all that, she was a young girl who had been grievously wronged.

"Just for the sake of discussion, Mr. Maier, what's this Richter doing in Shanghai?"

This wasn't known, Maier answered. He had arrived several days ago and had taken up residence at the Cathay Hotel, directly below Sassoon's offices. The day manager at the Cathay was from Kiel, and he had recognized him immediately.

At this Maier's face burned slightly brighter. "Right below Sassoon, the most prominent Jew in Shanghai. As if he has done nothing wrong and can never be punished! He is mocking us! He is mocking the very idea of justice!"

Charlie didn't answer. Lots of Nazis had stood trial at Nuremberg that year; if this Richter was traveling freely, he might have been investigated and cleared. Which didn't prove anything. He'd heard through the grapevine that the geniuses at Military Intelligence were letting a lot of Nazis off in exchange for promises of future help against the Soviets. But to stay at the Cathay . . . "Maybe it's because he wants you to know he's here. Can you think of a reason he might want to contact you?"

Maier let his gaze roam out the window, then linger on the wedding portrait. "I cannot allow myself to hope anymore, Mr. Pico."

Charlie doubted that was true, but he said nothing.

The shipper collapsed slightly. Without any further answer, he walked over to the liquor cart and opened the ice bucket as if to make himself a drink, then closed it again. He and his daughter looked at each other. "Let us do this, Mr. Pico: let us say you are not hired to kill him, only to watch him and find out why he is here . . ."

"Mr. Maier, I'm up to my ears in other business right now—"

Maier smiled and held up his hand. "Only to go to the Cathay and watch him and learn a little more about him. Find out why he is in Shanghai. Anna will go with you. I have no picture of him, but Anna will know him."

He turned to her. She seemed extraordinarily calm and adult and expectant. "Are you sure you'll remember him? You must have been eight years old when you last saw him."

"Nine," she said, and her next words felt cold. "I have not forgotten his face, Mr. Pico."

In the quiet, cultured interior of the house, the gazes of Maier and his daughter held him in place. Part of him had known as soon as Anna walked into the room what he was about to say. "I'll give it a few hours. But you can't pay me. Consider it a favor."

At six the next morning he and Anna were both sitting in the hotel bar with coffee and French pastries, at a table that afforded a view of the lobby and the coffee shop from behind a dark wooden balustrade that screened them. The bar was closed, but Mr. Maier had cleared it with Sassoon beforehand. It should be easy to spot him. People tended to leave hotels in the morning and return before dinner to freshen up, so morning or late afternoon were both good times. Would Richter make the girl, if he hadn't seen her since she was nine years old? A Nazi on the lam would be wary, but a Nazi who'd been cleared and checked into Shanghai's foremost hotel owned by its foremost Jew didn't seem like a man who was worried about his past. Anna wore a black pillbox hat with a lace veil in case Richter glanced over at them.

They chatted awkwardly as they waited, like two people out on a date. She was shy, as an eighteen-year-old girl talking to a war veteran might be, and tense because she was about to lay eyes on the man who had taken her mother away from her. At the same time, he detected a thread of curiosity.

"Where are you from, Mr. Pico?"

"Call me Charlie, please."

"Charlie. How did you grow up? What was your home like?"

"I grew up on a farm in western Washington. That's in the northwestern corner of the United States."

"How was it? Did you have cows and a . . . a house for the cows?"

"Yes, we have a house for the cows." He smiled. "It's called a *barn*! With a couple of horses and chickens and ducks and a pig." He told her about the crops they grew: corn, alfalfa, mustard, wheat. Different crops depending on the year. Vegetables for the family and a few extra to sell. "We have a little white house, with a porch and a glider, and a big black woodstove to heat it, because there's a lot of forest around, and we have a creek on the property. It's in the foothills of the mountains. Really, Anna, it's one of the most beautiful places on earth. For a home."

"It sounds wonderful."

"It *is* wonderful, Anna." He thought of his mother fetching water from the well and his sister coming back from the barn with a tin pail of milk. He thought of the dinner bell ringing, of firewood popping and a spark rocketing from the open stove when he stoked it. What you knew on the farm was that you had everything a man really needed. You had your family close by, right beside you, and food and milk and fire. The whole beautiful world revolved outside your windows, and it was the only world that mattered. The snow fell. The leaves turned green. You found a good wife and you loved up your children: "I'll probably be going back there when this Shanghai thing is over."

She pursed her lips into a little smile, her eyes lively, as if she already knew his whole life. "Will you?" Now she changed the subject, as if embarrassed at her presumptuousness. "My father says you are a hero."

He had thought he would impress her with the things he had done in the war, but as he looked at the young woman in front of him, his stories seemed base and violent, like something that would dirty her. "A lot of people did more than me," he answered. His throat became thick, and he cleared it so he could continue. "It's all mixed up, really. Bad becomes good; good becomes . . . weakness. But then, mixed up in all of it, there's evil. And that's what you hope you're fighting."

As if reminded, she turned to look through the balustrade at the lobby, and he followed her gaze. No one in sight yet. He asked her if she had any idea why Richter would come to Shanghai, just in case she gave away something her father hadn't, but neither of them seemed to have anything hidden. He quizzed her about the details of how to do foot surveillance that he'd given her the day before. When to follow, when to drop back. He went over the diagram with her in his notebook. He would have liked to have a couple of Chinese men for that, but he didn't want to get his friends in the

KMT police involved because it might be inconvenient later. He had a driver waiting outside in case Richter got into a taxi.

Just after seven, Richter came down the stairs and made his way into the coffee shop. Anna was flustered, turned her face down and away, as if he might see her through the balustrade. "That's him." There was an old fear in her voice.

He looked around fifty, with cropped, graying hair and a frame that had become fattened and gnarled, though it still had some of the raw energy of the athlete lingering in it. He'd probably been SS; he didn't have the look of a man who'd spent time on the eastern front, and most of those guys never came back anyway. He'd probably stayed at home keeping things under control for the Party, dealing out favors in exchange for money and women, fingering stray Jews or anyone else uncooperative for deportation. He'd seen guys like that when he'd been in Berlin in 1944: cruel, fat, vicious men romancing a string of desperate hausfraus while their husbands froze to death in Leningrad and Narva. Now he was wearing a charcoal pinstripe suit and a checked silver-colored tie, a proper businessman. In his gut, Charlie knew he was selling something. He could feel it. So who was the buyer, and what was the sale?

Richter ordered a large breakfast and ate it quickly, his head bowed down toward the plate and his jaws moving rapidly to keep up with his appetite. Not a wary man. An arrogant man, who probably reasoned that if the world hadn't seen fit to punish his crimes, they hadn't really been crimes in the first place. A stupid man. Even at twenty-two, just beginning to get into his field, Charlie knew this would be an easy job. Richter finished his breakfast and lingered over another cup of coffee as he read a German newspaper he'd picked up from the rack. He wasn't hiding anything: he was flaunting it. He made his way through the lobby without dropping off his key, and they had to hurry after him so that they didn't lose him. To Charlie's relief, he didn't get a taxi but went walking straight down the Bund, past the Customs House and the Hongkong Bank. He crossed the street and let Anna follow him for a block or two, then he gave her the sign, and she dropped back and he followed. Richter wasn't cautious. No glances behind him. No stopping at a newsstand to pick up a magazine and inventory the street. He'd spent his life doing what he wanted, and there'd never been any consequences. Why should he start worrying now?

Surprisingly, he turned in to the Shanghai Club. They'd be serving breakfast at that hour, though one would think that an ex-Nazi wouldn't be the most welcome guest. Of course, anyone could be anything in Shanghai. Richter could pass himself off as a Catholic priest if he wanted.

He signaled Anna to catch up with him, marked the time in his notebook, then retreated across the street.

"Do you know anyone at the Shanghai Club he might be meeting?"

"No."

"Let's wait here for a few minutes, let him get settled. Then I'm going to go in, and I want you to stand over by that delivery truck and wait. Change that hat for your other one and put on that scarf. If Richter comes out before I do, follow him."

"What will you do if you see him inside?"

"I don't know! Maybe I'll walk right up to him and introduce myself!" He laughed at her puzzled expression.

He waved at the doorman and passed inside. The club was still cool and sluggish in the early morning. The long bar was untended, and the restaurant was empty. In the front section a Chinese waiter with a silver coffeepot was moving among the leather armchairs and couches. Richter had to be there among the high-backed chairs that faced the other direction.

Charlie took out a cigarette and moved quickly toward the waiter. "Say, have you got a light?"

The waiter pulled out a lighter, and, as Charlie looked past it, he noticed Richter's back. Facing him, now impossible to ignore, was Matthias Vorster, the Afrikaaner who'd spent the whole war in Shanghai. He could see a brief flash of annoyance cross Vorster's face. They had no choice but to greet each other.

"Charlie! Good morning, my friend!"

"Matthias!" He stepped over to shake hands with Vorster, then nodded cordially at the Nazi. Vorster introduced him as a friend from Holland.

Richter stood up and shook his hand heartily, smiling. *"Amerikaner . . ."* He gave him a thumbs-up: "Number one!"

Vorster spoke for him. "Karl had a tough time during the war, Charlie. All the Jews did under the Nazis."

That was a hard one to swallow, but Charlie kept a straight face. "So I've heard."

Richter seemed to pick up a word here and there. "Nazis—!" He scowled. "Bad!"

He hadn't wanted this job, but Richter was tipping the balance here. He spoke directly to the German, knowing Vorster would translate. "What brings you to Shanghai, Herr Richter?"

The query went back and forth between Vorster and Richter.

"He's looking for some relatives. They escaped Germany in 1936, and he heard that they arrived here. He has news about one of their family. Maybe you know them. The man's name is Hermann Maier."

Charlie grimaced and shook his head from side to side. "No. I can't say I do know a Hermann Maier. But I'll bet the Jews have got a club of some sort where you could ask. That'd probably be a good place to start. They all know each other."

Vorster relayed it to the other man, and a short conversation went on between them. Of course Richter couldn't go to the synagogue. They'd make him in five minutes. Vorster was likely his bird dog on this. Probably old business associates during the war.

"What kind of news is it? Good news?"

"Very good news. The mother of the family was separated from the others. But she survived the war."

That was it then: some sort of shakedown to separate Maier from some more money in exchange for the whereabouts of his wife. Except the wife was certainly dead. He could see that by one look at Richter's swollen, stupid face. "That's news anyone would be glad to hear. It's very kind of Mr. Richter to make the trip all the way to Shanghai to find him and tell him."

"He is joining relatives in Australia, so it is on the route."

"Well, I know a couple of fellows of the Jewish persuasion that I can ask. Where is Mr. Richter staying?"

"It's easiest if you just tell me, Charlie. Karl is at the Grosvenor now, but he wants to change. And thank you, my friend."

He'd found out what he needed. "It's a pleasure." He stood and stuck out his hand. "Mr. Richter: Good luck."

When he came out he glanced across the street at Anna and then walked a block before waiting for her to catch up. He told her what had happened, and the expression that came across her face was haunting. A mix of childish happiness, flooded instantly by tides of suspicion and hope and pain. "But Anna, he's lying."

"How do you know he's lying?"

"I just know. It's his type. He's trying to squeeze your father for more money."

He explained the same thing to Maier that night and saw the same mix of emotions as with his daughter, made more pathetic by his gaunt, pale face.

"If there's even the smallest chance she's alive . . . !"

"I don't believe she is, Mr. Maier. She would have contacted your cousin, as you said. She would have found—"

"But if she *is*!" he hissed. The man was in agony. "We must find her! We must make Richter tell what he knows!"

This was going exactly the way he had thought it would as soon as Maier had told him Richter was in Shanghai. "Mr. Maier, I'm sorry. This is out of my—"

He had come to his feet. "I'll pay you ten thousand dollars! In any currency you choose! In gold! I'll deposit it in Hong Kong, if you like. Or America. Anywhere!"

Anna interrupted him. "Charlie," she said softly. "Please. It's my mother."

He looked at her green eyes. It wasn't that she was promising anything; she didn't have that kind of guile. There was nothing playful or coquettish about her but, on the contrary, something very elegant and reserved and sincere. He wanted that part of her, that part that he'd always thought was unattainable for a farm boy from western Washington.

"Okay. But we're not going to kidnap him."

"What do you suggest?" Maier asked.

"I have another idea. Let me take care of it. And don't worry: he won't leave Shanghai until he's found you."

Charlie's cell phone went off. He was *here* again, in this Shanghai, standing at the gate of a house on Lane 37. He'd been staring at the front door some time, but all the staring in the world wouldn't make it open and release its missing people. He took the cell phone out. It was Pete Harrington.

"Charlie! How's it hanging?"

The joviality of Harrington's tone annoyed him. "It's fine. What have you been doing?"

"Just walking around, checking out the whole scene here. I was here in '92, and I don't remember *anything*! I've still got some fans, though. I was recognized twice. It was freaky. Like, these big crowds of Chinese people just surrounded me and stared!"

"Glad you're enjoying yourself."

"Yeah, that's what I called about." Charlie heard a soft woman's voice in the background. "Umm . . . I met a girl, and"—Harrington lowered his voice to a near whisper—"I'd say I've got a pretty good shot, you know?" His tone returned to normal again. "We're supposed to meet up tonight. She's coming by the hotel. So this is kind of a scheduling thing. What time were you and I going to go out?" He added quickly, "I mean, I can cancel, Charlie. No problem. But you just want me to ride in the car for a little while and get a look at this guy . . . Right? You don't need me all night."

"Are you serious?"

The singer hesitated at the sound of his voice. "Well, yeah, I mean . . . Yeah, but not really—"

"Because if you're serious, I'm done here. I'm getting on the next plane to L.A."

"No, man, definitely, it's . . . you know, I've got my priorities. We're here to do this, so—"

"No!" Charlie cut him off savagely. "*You're* here to do this! I'm here because you're paying me! And you're paying me whether I stay or go. Understand?"

"I do, Charlie."

"Is she with you right now?"

"Yeah."

"Get rid of her. Right now, while I'm listening. So I can hear it!"

Harrington's next words were distant, spoken past his phone. *No, not tonight, but maybe—*

"Get rid of her!"

"*Yeah, sorry. No time. Good-bye! Gotta go! No, don't come with me! Sayonara! Bye-bye!* I'm walking away from her, Charlie. It's done."

"What is it with you? Do you just compulsively have to screw off? Because I have to deal with the bodyguard, and right now I don't see why I should be getting ready to throw myself on a grenade while you chase a piece of ass around Shanghai!"

The plea coming through the tiny speaker was twisted with pain. "*Please,* Charlie. Don't give up on me!"

"You were the guy who was going one-on-one with the universe! Who was going to kick the crap out of greed."

"I still am!"

He let the assertion drop into silence. It took a while for Harrington to muster the courage to venture a question. "It's still on, right? Just tell me that."

Charlie looked around the quiet walls and tree branches of Lane 37, and through the gate at house number 116. This was his now, too. "It's still on."

He closed the phone and started walking back toward the car. Why was he still in this? There was a good chance his client would blow it and an even better chance he himself would get hurt in the process. That'd be a little piece of hell: stuck in a Chinese hospital with a broken hip and anybody but Zhang seven thousand miles away. Crappy way to end a career. All the people who looked at him as a living legend would see him instead as a silly old man hanging on to one last client, no matter how ridiculous. *Of course,* and this made him smile as he walked back to the cross street, if he *did* pull it off . . . Well, he'd studied Peter Harrington's business dealings fairly carefully, his rise through the bank and his double-dealing with his bond fund. If Pete Harrington really did punch the banker in the face, it was going to make a lot of people very happy. There'd be a loud noise, and then word would get around, quietly, among those who knew, and some of those men who'd turned him down for jobs, who'd put him out to pasture, were going to say, *Holy smokes, it's Charlie Pico!* They'd know that the living legend was still *alive.*

The bells of a nearby church rang three o'clock, which left him very little time to reconnoiter and get back to the financier's apartment before he went out for the evening. It took him ten minutes to get back to the car, then he pulled off the surveillance and had the driver take him down to the Bund. The place had been considerably spruced up. Used to be for international banking and trade; now it was all fancy restaurants and chain stores stuffed with overpriced jewelry and clothing. The old resonance wasn't coming back to him. Too many people around, and, besides, he was working, searching for just the right spot. And there it was, just like he remembered, with its roaring bronze lions and its stately columns and steps, the old Hongkong Bank building, now the Shanghai Pudong Development Bank. Perfect. Looked like a Bank with a capital B. Crowded but not constricted. Room for three or four people to get a view from different angles. Easy access to the escape vehicle. He could walk him around and tell him a few stories to get the timing right, if necessary; then Pete Harrington could come from the direction of the old Cathay. Things were getting clearer.

"Pull over here." They double-parked, their police plates making them invulnerable, and he walked the terrain and planned out their trajectory. "This is where we're going to do it," he told the driver. "You'll put one man *there.* He's going to follow our client with a cell phone camera, like he's just recognized him and is getting a souvenir. Put the second one over *here*. Start him at ten meters away, and then he can move in. He should keep the lions in the background and make sure he gets the bank sign. Get somebody who's not afraid to get physical, because if the bodyguard gets past me and chases our client, your man will need to get in his way and slow him down without creating any suspicion. And I want *you* over *there*." He indicated a place a hundred yards down the street. "You'll be parked. Use a cell phone with a good zoom and keep an eye on everything; then get him out of here afterwards. Our client should have a ten-second head start, and he'll come straight to your car. Have the motor running. Got it? From here, you take him straight to the airport."

Charlie could tell by the man's questions that he understood. Zhang worked with good people. He felt okay at the moment. Not too tired, and his foot wasn't so bad. He had a plan. He just had to get the financier to this spot, and that was what he'd try to set up next. Now all he had to do was go back and sit Harrington's house, take a little nap in the car. But it was the time of day when the late-afternoon sun burnished everything with a film of dusty golden light, like the whole avenue was trapped in honey. And here he was, again. "Why don't you wait here for a while," he told the driver. "Give me ten minutes."

He walked a few hundred yards along the Bund. The sidewalk was filled with well-dressed Chinese people, heavily salted with foreign tourists gaping at the porticos and columns. All so different now, so lousy with cappuccinos and jewelry stores. *Where was that place, anyway? Was it this block, or the next one?* He came to the alley and walked away from the river, and at first he couldn't recognize it, because there was a fancy Russian restaurant with a striped awning. He stared for a long time, taking away the awning and the brass menu holder until he saw it once again. Maier's shipping office. He took a deep breath, then walked farther down the alley to the backstreet that ran parallel with the Bund. It was much quieter here, as it always had been. Three-story row houses somebody was trying to lease out as restaurants, architecture offices. More of an alley than a street. He turned left and walked along the back of a building. There was the window, now bricked

closed, and the doorway sealed shut with a barrier of gray metal. No sign on
it, but there hadn't been a sign back then, either. Not in the telephone di-
rectory, either. A guy like Vorster didn't necessarily want to be located. You
could find him, or else you probably had no reason to find him. Charlie
could find him. Still could.

The operative piece of information in that whole encounter with Richter
and Vorster at the Shanghai Club was that Vorster knew all along who and
where Hermann Maier was. His office was virtually around the corner, and,
moreover, an operator like Vorster who dealt in shipping on a regular basis
would have run across Maier sometime in the past eight years, by name if
not in person. They might even have done business. He arranged to meet
Vorster at his office one block in from the river. The black marketeer rented
a ground-floor office in a building built in the boom of the thirties, with
pink and black tiles on the floor and a sleek black telephone and intercom system imported from America. On the walls were pictures of Vorster
standing over the bodies of various dead African game, taken in the twenties, from the looks of the clothing. Vorster offered him a cigar and some
brandy, joking that he liked to be on the ground floor because in case of an
unwanted visitor one could always climb out the window.

"Interesting business," he told him.

Vorster took out a knife and clipped the end of the cigar. "You know my
business, Charlie. I buy. I sell. I try to be a little bit smarter than the next
man. Is that illegal?" He shrugged. "Who makes the rules? The people who
profit the most. The Generalissimo only shoots the smugglers who don't
give him his share."

He passed the knife over to Charlie, who trimmed the end of his own
cigar. It was a dark heavy Cuban leaf. He looked at it as he spoke. "I'm curious about your friend Karl Richter."

"Oh, Karl! Quite a sad story, isn't it? But maybe with a happy ending."

Charlie laughed. "You're a hell of a smuggler, Matthias, but you're no
Olivier. You know very well Hermann Maier has an office right around the
corner from where you and Mr. Richter were having breakfast."

Vorster became slightly less jovial. "Why are you here, Charlie? Has the export market gotten slow these days?"

His tattered cover story. "Isn't anybody buying that one?"

"No one important."

He shrugged. "That's the guys in Washington for you. I'd have made a great feed and grain salesman, but there's not too much call for that here." He put the open penknife down. There was a leather-covered desk lighter about the size of an eight ball, and Charlie flicked a blue and yellow flame out of the top. "Who do you think's going to win this war, Matthias? Communists or Nationalists? I'm putting my money on the Commies. The Nationalists . . . Chiang . . ." He paused to ignite the cigar. "There's just nothing much to save there."

"I give the KMT two years."

"But the Communists still need materiel. Artillery shells, radios, M-1 cartridges. They're sitting on a bunch of Arisaka Type 99s. I don't suppose you've got a line on some old Jap ammo lying around that maybe got stranded when the war ended."

"It's an interesting thought."

He was conscious as he spoke the next words that he was straying far over the line of what his bosses would accept from him. "How would you like to meet a couple of Communists with the wherewithal to do some business?"

"Is that before or after they shoot me for being a collaborator?"

"Oh, hell, Matthias! You don't have to worry about that until after Liberation. And by then you'll be in some other war zone. Here's the deal: I'll introduce you to a couple of interested friends of mine in exchange for some information about your Dutch pal, Herr Richter. Is he a business associate?"

"*Ex*-business associate."

"From the far eastern part of Holland, I'll bet. The part that's Germany. Around Kiel."

"Are you working for Hermann Maier?"

"Does it matter who I'm working for? We have a deal, right? What's Richter's story?"

Vorster reached for the lighter and lit his cigar as he looked down at the blotter on his desk. "You know about Maier's wife, don't you? Terrible. Sassoon told me, but I never knew it was Karl that was involved in it." Vorster recounted a briefer version of what Maier had already told him about his wife. A sudden pall of philosophy came over him. "They went too far," he said. "I have no love for the British. That's not a secret. But the Nazis went too far. It's inhuman. I had no idea until after the war ended."

Vorster seemed genuinely disturbed, but it was hard to tell how real it was. He wasn't here to find out. "Richter seems to be fat and happy these days. Walks the street like he hasn't got a care in the world."

"Your people let him go, Charlie. That's what he told me. They arrested him, they gathered evidence, and when the evidence was complete, they freed him and gave him a job with the police. You Americans have an interesting way of punishing people."

Charlie didn't react. Just as he'd thought: Richter must have gotten a second life as an anti-Communist.

"So what's he really doing in Shanghai?"

"Karl is crazy. He says Maier sold him his business but never turned over all his assets. He talks about it as if Maier stole his property, instead of how it really was."

So Sassoon had told him that, too.

"Now he thinks he can sell him information about his wife in exchange for what he claims Maier owes him. It's an obsession. He wrote from Germany and I tried to ignore it, and then a few days past he showed up at my office."

And now Richter was a problem for Vorster. He probably had something incriminating on the black marketeer that kept Vorster from giving him the air. Charlie realized he'd been stupid to offer Vorster the arms connection. Vorster probably would have given him up for nothing. "Is the wife alive?"

Vorster hesitated. "No. He said she was gassed at Dachau in 1942. He kept her name off the lists of the dead because he thought he could get money from Maier someday." The smuggler raised his eyebrows and glanced briefly at the table. He spoke with an air of confession. "He's a very evil man, Charlie. I am not so very good, I know. But I look at Karl Richter, and I see something different."

Sure. Everybody wanted to see some daylight between themselves and Karl Richter. At least, now that the Germans had lost the war.

So the wife was dead. Richter was just back here to extract some money and inflict more pain. He felt a wave of disgust for the German. He'd seen a lot of ugly things in the war, and he'd done some of them himself: prisoners being shot, fine young men having their throats cut in their sleep. Wars were made up of millions of individual crimes, but they all got smoothed down by some sense of purpose, because it was for your country so it was okay, whatever your country was. This had no purpose, though. The war was over. Murder had lost its sanctions. Crime was general again.

He said good-bye to Vorster. He'd set him up with Zhou, hoped nothing came out of it. Because if it did, he'd be labeled a traitor by anyone who ever found out, and Vorster would always have that on him. He'd had a hunch the job would turn out like this, and that's why he hadn't wanted it. He still didn't want it. Now he was stuck breaking the news to Hermann Maier and Anna.

The piano was playing when he walked up to the gate of the house on Lane 37. He could hear it flowing out of the open window and across the small green lawn. It was something classical, which was what he'd expect. She must be practicing for her concert. He stood on the sidewalk for a minute, just listening to it. She would break at a part in the middle and then repeat that phrase, trying to get it right. There was something so elegant about it, but someone else's elegant. One that involved music lessons and a quiet home and a world where life's purpose was to create something beautiful. The music swirled out around him. He had the sense of standing there, but at the same time of being somehow in the old house he grew up in, and in the jungle in Burma again, and in a succession of cities whose names were indistinct to him but that scrabbled out into the future in a long string: Berlin, Prague, Sarajevo, Buenos Aires. Others he couldn't even imagine yet. All the places he would someday go, and those he'd been to, existing together in this one beautiful, fragile moment. Someday, he knew, he would be standing and trying to remember this music. This was how it had really sounded.

The maid saw him and came out to open the gate. It was around four in the afternoon, three days after his first conversation with Hermann Maier. He went up the steps and the door was hanging open for him. The music was louder here. Everything was just as it had been, with the dark wallpaper enclosing the furniture in its austere tones of sage green and silver-gray velour. A spray of flowers was in a vase. He could see a pile of Anna's schoolbooks on the chair and a boy's jacket hanging from a hook.

Anna halted her playing when Charlie walked in.

"Don't stop! It's wonderful!" he said, but she stood up and stepped clear of the stool. The maid took his hat and he sat on the couch.

"My father is upstairs. He'll come down in a moment. Would you like something to drink?"

"Just some water." She poured it, and Charlie's fingers touched hers as she handed him the glass.

"Have you found out something?" she asked.

"Let's wait for your father. I'd rather say it once, if that's okay."

"As you like, Charlie." He was impressed that she could put it away like that. "We are grateful for everything that you have done. Or, I should say, my father is grateful, and *I* am grateful. Me, on my own."

"I'm happy to help out."

"My father says you refuse to be paid."

"My employer doesn't like me taking side jobs. It's safer for me to do this as a favor. Besides, I haven't done much. Just talked to a few people. That's nothing."

"I think it is much more than nothing." She closed the cover to the keyboard, then opened it again. "I was thinking about what you said. About your farm. I find it very hard to imagine you there."

He thought of the house with the porch and the red barn across the field where he'd jumped in the hay as a kid. Fresh, sweet hay. Best smell in the world. Always would be. He thought of his parents, waiting there for him. "Lots of good things about farm life. It's peaceful."

"My father says we're moving to the United States. Maybe you can show me your farm one day."

In that moment, he imagined she was inviting him. He should have known she was only an eighteen-year-old girl, that she couldn't make a claim on anything in her future life, but for just a little while he lived it all out. Anna, miraculously, who'd never been to a farm, walking up the wooden steps of the porch to the front door. Her radiance, the surprise of his parents when they met her, her miraculous contentment. And then they would just be there, year after year. They'd have a son whom he'd teach to be strong and brave and a daughter who starred in the school plays. He could imagine the holidays without reckoning that she was a German who didn't celebrate Thanksgiving and a Jewess who didn't celebrate Christmas, and later on he'd realize that they didn't really have much outside Shanghai and that one monstrous crime that went to the heart of her family, and every family. But he didn't know that at the time. At twenty-two. At that age, it was all still possible.

She smiled and began playing again, something bright and joyful, with quick flurries of notes that bounded through his head in bright colors. He watched her, and she looked away from the music for a second and smiled at him, then turned back to the page. They both knew that he was about to deliver the worst news a child could hear.

She stopped playing as her father walked into the room, wearing a gray jacket and a maroon tie. He had a nervous feel to him. "Mr. Pico!" He extended his hand. "A pleasure to see you again! Anna! Didn't you offer Mr. Pico a drink?"

"She's been the perfect host, Mr. Maier. I asked her for water and she gave it to me."

They made small talk about the latest rumors of the fighting in the North, where Chiang was claiming to have inflicted a devastating blow to the Communists, which didn't explain why the remnants of his army were pulling back to Tianjin. The conversation faltered, and Charlie decided to be brief.

"Mr. Maier, I'm afraid I have bad news for you."

Maier blanched and waited. Charlie glanced from him to Anna, whose hands rested idly on the piano keys. At the last minute, he couldn't bear to tell them Lille Maier had been gassed. "I'm sorry. Your wife died of typhus in a concentration camp in 1942. There's no record because Richter used his influence to keep her off the lists. He came here to try to sell you phony information about her whereabouts."

Maier tightened his jaw. "How do you know?"

"There's a black marketeer named Matthias Vorster—"

"I know Vorster."

"He and Richter did some business during the war, and Richter came here looking for his help. Richter told him his scheme and Vorster relayed it all to me. I believe Vorster's telling the truth."

"Vorster," the old man said softly. Because now he did look old. "I suppose it's better to know."

Charlie softened his voice. "Richter can't get at you now."

Anna suddenly let loose a low, painful, feline sound that turned into a sob, then bent her head down toward the keyboard and put her hands over her eyes. "Mama!" She began bawling uncontrollably, and her crying pressed Charlie to the couch like a heavy stone. She could have been a ten-year-old. Her father went over and put his hands on her shoulders, but he, too, began weeping with a soft huffing sound. At that point an adolescent boy peeked into the room, alarmed, and Maier said a few words in German. The son's face fell and he perched himself desolately on a wooden chair at the edge of the room.

None of them said anything for a few minutes. In the grief-soaked room, Charlie was aware that there was a problem. The problem was that Karl Richter had committed any number of atrocities and been cleared of them. The problem was that he had murdered Lille Maier and the happiness of her family. The problem was that there was evil.

He asked Maier to send the boy away, and then they closed the doors to the other rooms. He'd started coming up with a plan as soon as Vorster told him that the wife was already dead. He assumed correctly that Sassoon would be helpful. And he guessed that Richter was still so obsessed with the Lille Maier he'd known in 1922 that he'd let his guard down if he saw her image in the streets of Shanghai. But planning revenge and executing that plan were very different things. One was a fantasy; the other was a crime, and it would feel like a crime.

"Are you sure you can do this, Anna? It's going to be ugly."

It was the next morning, and they were sitting in a pastry shop across the street. Anna was wearing her schoolgirl outfit. The ankle-length pleated skirt. The blue ribbon at her neck. She nodded, but after that neither of them said anything else.

Just after nine, Sassoon's man came out to the sidewalk and started sweeping, the signal that Richter had come down to the lobby. Twenty minutes later, they picked him up exiting the Cathay and heading down Nanjing Lu. Anna went straight for him. Nanjing Lu was always crowded, and it was hard to keep her and Richter in sight from a safe distance. Even from a hundred yards away, though, he could see the shock on Richter's face as Anna caught up with him. They'd fixed her hair up the same as in her mother's wedding picture, and Richter stared at her as if his life had skipped backward to 1922 and all the buildings that were Shanghai had turned suddenly to Kiel. His mouth hung open as she talked to him, and after an exchange the two of them started walking together. Charlie hung behind. Richter glanced behind him at one point, but he didn't seem overly cautious. Anna knew where to lead him.

She walked him two blocks and then turned left and walked him three more. The streets were less crowded here. That morning they'd swapped out one of the brass plaques on a near-empty office building, and as they reached the door Anna motioned toward it and led him inside. He would think it was Maier's place of business. Charlie started running. He reached the door in ten seconds and entered to find Richter and Anna standing together in the dim, narrow hallway while she pretended to fumble with her keys. Richter looked at him, surprised.

"Mr. Richter!" Charlie said as he approached. "I'm glad you two found each other!"

Richter was doubtless trying to formulate an appropriate lie. Charlie kept smiling as he crossed the few paces toward him. In a life-or-death situation, the best actor always won. "Have either of you got a light? I'll trade you a cigarette."

He got the knife out just as Richter accepted, and he'd sunk it in under his lungs before the man realized what was happening. Richter gasped and teetered on his feet. Charlie grabbed him and spun him around, then clamped his hand across his mouth and dragged the knife through his carotid artery. The blood went surging down his neck and ruined the overcoat Charlie had worn. He let go of him, and the heavy man careened against the wall with his hand out, then fell heavily onto the tile floor on his back, with one leg tucked under him and his eyes moving hazily from one point of the ceiling to another.

Anna was staring down at him, transfixed by the sight of the dying man. "Anna," he said calmly, "you'd better go outside."

She looked up at him. She seemed far away, but she marched quietly out the door, imprinting little ovals of blood across the tiled hallway.

Charlie grabbed a huge steamer trunk they'd stashed in the stairwell and pulled out an oilskin tarp. He spread it out and dragged Richter onto it. He was trying hard not to think. He'd taken the lives of at least a half dozen men with a knife, always in situations where he was terrified, inside an enemy base, surrounded by people who wanted to kill him. Now it gave him a feeling of disgust. In half a minute he'd wrapped Richter in the tarp, put him in the trunk, and wiped up the blood with a sponge and a cloth. He threw his bloody overcoat in the chest with everything else. He signaled to the truck Maier had placed outside, and one of Maier's Chinese men helped him get the trunk aboard. He and Anna watched as he drove it away to the docks. One more missing person in Shanghai that nobody was going to be looking for. There were a lot of them in 1946.

"Let's get you home," he said.

They walked back to Nanjing Lu and flagged a taxi, both of them silent.

He'd just killed someone in cold blood, without any government stamp on it. No commendation for this one, no extra bar or star. It was more like he'd just cleaned up a particularly ugly mess, something with a bad odor, and now that it was done there wasn't any sense of accomplishment, only relief that it was finished, and the suspicion that some part of the smell still clung to him.

Anna sat beside him in the taxi, staring straight ahead, glassy-eyed, like she had a concussion. Seeing a man's throat cut at close range, let alone being part of it, would shake up a front-line soldier, and she was just a young girl who played beautiful things on the piano. The taxi let them out and he walked her to the door. Her father was at his warehouse at the docks, taking care of the last details, and he didn't want to leave her alone, so they sat together without saying anything. He poured himself a whiskey, and he poured her one, too. She forced it down with difficulty. She opened up the cover of the keyboard as if she would play something, then closed it again. They hadn't spoken in an hour. Finally she turned to him. Her face had a sort of gaiety to it, like she was trying to make a witty remark, but her voice came out flat.

"Charlie," she said. "I don't think you'll ever go back to that farm."

He thought of his parents again, and of his younger sisters, all together in the living room around the stove, the whole peaceful dream, and then the picture rushed away from him. "No. You're probably right." And what he knew she was saying was that she would never go back to that farm, either. That all of that was gone, if it had ever really existed.

He was sent to Nanjing a few days later. Then to Inner Mongolia and to the Philippines, where the Huks were stirring things up. Sometimes he wondered if someone in Washington had gotten wind of it and wanted to move him to a different locale for a while. He sent Anna a few letters, but he was moving around so much only one of her letters ever reached him. It was as grave and affectionate as she herself was, but he never knew if she'd sent others. He didn't get back to Shanghai for three years. He rang up Hermann Maier that very day, but the number had been reassigned to someone else who didn't speak English. It was 1949 and everyone was clearing out of

Shanghai. Nobody knew what had happened to Hermann Maier. His office was closed. Even Vorster had left.

He couldn't resist going by the house, but other owners were living there, and they looked at him suspiciously as he stood at the wrought-iron gate. There was no music.

He woke up at the sound of a car horn outside his window, not knowing where he was, and instinctively looked at his watch. Five o'clock. That was it: his driver had dutifully followed the banker back to his residence and they were sitting it. A paper cup of cold black coffee was resting in the cup holder and he took a sip. He'd eaten almost nothing all day. He went into the café and got some sandwiches and used the bathroom, then returned to the car. He didn't expect the financier to go out for at least another hour. He called Harrington.

"Hi, Charlie." Even those two words sounded bruised and dispirited.

"Have you eaten dinner?"

"No. I've been here at the hotel waiting for your call. What's the plan?"

"Come on over to where I am. I got you a turkey sandwich. And I got you one of those cream-filled pastry things for dessert. I don't know what it's called, but it's French. Is that okay?"

He heard Harrington warm up. "Yeah. Thanks, Charlie."

"And we changed cars. We're in a black Peugeot now. See you soon."

Twenty minutes later, he heard Harrington knocking at the window. The sight of his smiling face cheered him up.

"How are you feeling?" he asked the singer as he slid into the car.

"Got some jet lag happening. It comes in waves."

"I know." The cellophane crinkled as he pulled the sandwich from the bag and handed it to him.

"So what are we doing here?"

"We're sitting his residence. At some point he's probably going to come out and have some dinner, and then he'll probably go to one of his favorite bars. At that point, I'll try to set something up."

"Okay."

"I want you to take a look at him so you can be sure to recognize him immediately when it's time. I want you to get used to the idea that you're going to walk up to this man, say a few words, and then hit him, like you've practiced."

"Okay."

"This is your show," he reminded him. "You made this happen."

They waited silently. The driver had gotten out to smoke a cigarette. He needed to build Pete up after coming down so hard on him earlier in the day.

"So what was that all about, with the girl?"

"I'm sorry about that."

"No, I mean what was it really about? I can't figure it out. You train for two months, you spend a bunch of money, you fly over here, and just when it's all about to happen, you want to shack up with some Chinese Kewpie doll you met on the street. You caught me by surprise on that one."

"It's an old habit."

"No, it's more than that. It's compulsive."

"Yeah, it is more than that." The singer was looking out the window on the street side, rather than toward the gate. "You want to know the truth? No bullshit? I'll tell you, because I just figured it out myself this afternoon. I mean, I think I knew, but I never named it. You know I toured here before, when I first went solo. 1992."

"I read about it. You said something about Tiananmen Square and they shut you down."

"Yeah, here in Shanghai. We were about halfway through our tour. I got up on the stage in the second act, and I said, 'This is for the heroes of Tiananmen Square!' in Chinese. This was only three years after the massacre, and not something you talked about here. In fact, I think they still don't talk about it."

Charlie spoke without looking away from the entrance to the financier's complex. "You said it in Chinese?"

"Yeah."

"So, some gal with a pretty face used you to rub dirt in the eye of the Communist Party."

"Crap, Charlie!" Harrington chuckled, but there was something slightly self-mocking about it. "Okay! Guilty! She was superhot. She had a brother who was killed at Tiananmen, and I agreed to do it because I felt sorry for her. And, you know, I'm no China expert, but I think we can say that killing a couple thousand students in a few hours is probably a bad thing to do."

"I'll grant you that."

"But I had no idea what kind of shitstorm it was going to kick up. Boom! End of tour! Boom! My ass on a plane to Tokyo! My manager screaming at me and telling me every Chinese roadie on the tour has been arrested to see who put me up to it. Then, boom! Back to the States, and suddenly I'm a fucking hero. The TV networks were on it like I was fucking Solzhenitsyn. I mean, Amnesty International invited me to speak at some banquet in D.C. I probably got asked a thousand times why I'd done it, and I couldn't tell the truth, because it'd get her arrested, which she probably was anyway. So all I could say was, *Because those people deserve to be remembered.* And it was bullshit. I said it because she played me, just like you did, at the health club.

"But man, they rolled out that Hero carpet, and I walked down it. I was the guy who stood up to the Chinese and gave them a big black eye. Bobby put an American flag on my next album. Fucking country music stars wanted to record duets with me. I even got asked to do a gig at the White House, and the president came up and jammed with us. It was all just a big lie. And that's when everything started to feel hollow."

Harrington sighed. "I just didn't want to do that fake rock-hero shit anymore. So I failed my way out of it. But once you get in that habit, it's a hard one to break."

"And now you want to do something real."

"Yeah. This isn't for an audience. This fucker's a predator, Charlie. He thinks he's untouchable. Somebody's got to touch the untouchable." He laughed. "You know what I'm talking about. I know you do."

Charlie didn't answer. *Always the ugly sister.*

The street was dark now. The driver said, "Here is his car," and the financier's chauffeur pulled up in the black Mercedes. Suddenly, Peter Harrington was emerging from the gate.

"There's your man," Charlie said.

"I see him." Harrington watched intently as the financier moved toward the street. "Seems kind of pudgy."

"At least some of it's muscle. He plays squash five times a week. He probably lifts weights. You can't go to a health club and not lift weights."

Harrington seemed to be thinking that over. There were a few more seconds of silence. "Fuck it!" the musician said. "I can take him!"

"I know you can. And you will."

As Peter Harrington moved toward his car, a man walking along the street seemed to approach him. Charlie watched the banker's driver subtly put himself between the pedestrian and the financier. Not too bad, but he seemed more of a crowd-control guy than a serious custodian. "That driver also doubles as his bodyguard."

The singer sounded intimidated. "How do we deal with him?"

"That's my job."

Harrington turned to him. "Seriously?"

"I can get you about ten seconds from the time he sees you as a threat. That's plenty of time if you don't waste it."

"You know, Charlie, if this might get you hurt—"

He cut him off. "I appreciate that. But I've done this before. With a little luck, he'll be off parking the car, and I won't have to do anything. The main thing is, no matter what happens, you have to stay focused. Otherwise, everything we've done will end up being for nothing. I'll do my job. You do yours."

They watched their target get in his car, then followed it out into the flow. Traffic was tight and slow, so it was easy to keep him within sight. The black Mercedes never left the French Concession and pulled over at the entrance to a warren of upscale businesses and restaurants. Charlie asked the driver to follow him, and he disappeared on foot behind their target. A few minutes later Charlie's cell phone rang. The financier had gone to a French restaurant called Franck, where he'd met a young Chinese woman.

He told the driver to wait twenty minutes and then go in and order a drink.

They waited over an hour, leafing through English magazines in the streetlight that came through windows of the car. After a while their driver called ahead and told them the target was moving, and a minute later Harrington came out of the lane into the brightly lit street, walking with his companion.

"She's got some talent," the singer commented.

Charlie didn't want him to empathize with the target. "She should thank you for paying for part of her dinner."

They left the French Concession and headed toward the Bund, as Charlie'd suspected he would. They pulled up to the old Chartered Bank, as he thought they might. Upstairs was the Bar Rouge, which Zhang had put down as one of his hangouts. They watched him go in.

"Now what?" Harrington asked.

"You go back to the hotel. I want you to rest and get your mind right for the next step. I'm going inside."

"What are you going to do there?"

"Well . . ." Charlie almost laughed as he thought about it. "Maybe I'll walk right up to him and introduce myself."

"You're bullshitting me, right?"

Charlie laughed and put his hand on Pete's shoulder. "This is what I'm good at. Just go back and try to rest. I'll come by your hotel in an hour or two."

Charlie'd worked a lot of covers over the years. He'd been a businessman, a scrap-metal salesman, a foreign-aid worker, even a college professor. Now he didn't even need a cover. He was just the old vet.

Not too old for the prostitutes to swerve over to him as he crossed the sidewalk. Thank God for small favors. He took the elevator up, and the door opened. A wall of what passed for music these days slammed into him. A few people glanced his way as he came in, but nothing about him held their interest. He was old, and that made him invisible in this crowd.

He looked around and spotted Peter Harrington and his date in a little cluster of people, two Western men and two Chinese women. He recognized one of the men as Harrington's lunch appointment, probably his business partner, Kell McPherson. He could work his way into the group, but that could complicate things. Better to get Harrington alone. He noticed the financier and his date didn't have drinks, which meant he'd go to the bar or else order from a waitress. Staking out the route to the bathroom could work, but it could be awkward, too. If nothing else, he'd have to get him on his route tomorrow: maybe catch him at the health club and play the lonely old tourist, or "recognize" him somewhere and tell him what a bum rap he'd gotten in the press. That might work. Harrington had a lot of time on his hands and would probably go in for some interesting stories. He only needed a couple of minutes.

He positioned himself equidistantly between the route to the bathroom and the bar and watched his target. He'd already built an identity on some old vet he'd found on the Internet. Ernie Sivertsen, member of Merrill's Marauders and whatever other outfits Charlie decided to sign him up for. He had enough of a trail on the Internet that Peter Harrington would find him, but not enough to show his death date, unless Harrington went all the way to page 18, which was unlikely. The cover story would be easy. He'd spent plenty of time in western China and the border area. He'd barely even be making this up.

The financier didn't seem to be having such a great time with his friends. The short one had the fuzzy motor skills of a drunk: slopped his drink, leaned in too far when he spoke. Harrington tore himself away to the bar, and Charlie moved up behind him and spoke up. "Helluva scene, isn't it?"

He turned around, not very curious. He was being polite to an old man. "Yes, it *is* a hell of a scene. Is this your first time in Shanghai?"

That was all Charlie needed. He'd done this dozens of times. When he'd been a contractor for the Agency, they'd often hire him to get close to people they wanted to recruit or compromise. Sometimes it was to pick up information or to see about doubling a foreign agent. Sometimes it was to solve a problem. He'd set up a couple of people for termination. He didn't lose any sleep over it: they were bad people. Just like it didn't bother him to be setting up Peter Harrington right now. Truth be told, the man was overdue. Maybe not at the top of the list, because it was a very long list, but definitely deserving of some instant enlightenment. Hell—it'd probably make him a better person.

Just like he'd hoped, in the eight minutes it took Peter Harrington to get his drinks, Charlie had already set up a meeting with him the next day. He'd be putting him exactly where he wanted him, when he wanted him. He hung around another twenty minutes after Harrington went back to his group of friends. It could all go wrong, of course. Harrington could change his mind, or get sick, or the driver might suddenly need a day off. And if that happened, he'd figure something else out. Just like always. Christ, it felt good to be working again.

He was dead tired by the time he got to Pete Harrington's hotel, but he called ahead and asked him to come and meet him at a little bar across the street. The musician had ordered a glass of Coca-Cola, as if to show his seriousness. "Are you ready, Pete?"

"Are you going to ask me to drop down and give you forty push-ups in the middle of this bar?"

"No. We're beyond that. But you can still change your mind."

"I'm not changing my mind."

"Okay, then. This is how it's going to happen." Charlie related the conversation he'd had at the Bar Rouge, and his appointment the following day with the financier. "I'm going to drive you past the place tomorrow, and I'll show you where to wait for the driver to signal you. Try not to make too many friends along the way."

"Cool."

"What are you wearing?"

"Well, I thought of wearing some sort of disguise."

"No. Don't do that. Let your hair down, dress the way he thinks of you. If he recognizes you, he'll be confused. You can deck him before he knows what's happening." Harrington seemed to be bothered by that idea. "Pete, this isn't about having a fair fight. Use the element of surprise and act before he understands what's happening. Do it quick and do it right. Otherwise, it's going to get messy with the bodyguard."

"What if the bodyguard chases me?"

"I won't let that happen. Besides, his job is to stay with the client in case there's a second attacker. You stay focused on hitting your target and getting back to the car." The musician looked uneasy. "You're nervous, aren't you?" He patted his shoulder. "That's okay, Pete. It's normal. Just remember why you're doing this. You came here to give him his day of reckoning. This is it."

2

Green-Screen Universe

‡

The jet lag was not working in his favor. When Charlie called about meeting at the bar, he was so tired he could barely get out of bed, but, after dragging himself back to his room, he slept three hours and then woke up ready to charge at two in the morning. All he could do was lie there for three hours watching television and thinking how he should have kept the girl on tap after all. Fuck, man—there he went again! He finally got up, did some pushups, practiced some hits and kicks, and took a shower. He separated the clothes he was going to wear—a leather jacket, white shirt, blue jeans—then threw the rest into a suitcase. He checked his e-mail, saw nothing of interest, then made some coffee in his room and stared out the big picture window at the sun coming up behind Shanghai's skyscrapers. He thought of writing Beth, saying, *fuck yeah, it's* on! Just to let her know he wasn't fucking up again. It was really happening today. Go time. Showtime. Whatever-the-hell-you-called-it time. The weird thing was, he wasn't really that pissed at Peter Harrington anymore. Sure, the guy deserved an ass kicking on general principles, let alone what he'd done to him personally, but looking at it from the rest of the world's point of view, which he usually tried to avoid doing, it did seem a mite extreme to fly across the Pacific Ocean to kick the crap out of somebody. *Reasonable, Pete. Never be fucking reasonable!* That's the death knell: next thing you know, you're a guy wearing shirts with royal flushes on them.

He was the first one to the breakfast buffet, watched as businessmen catching early flights trailed in with roll-on suitcases. Fucking *these guys* is reasonable! It's not my job. Nope: not my job. My job is punching Peter Harrington, dirtbag financier, in the face. How's that for reasonable?

Charlie and the driver picked him up at eight o'clock, and they drove down to the Bund. Charlie didn't want to get out of the car because there were surveillance cameras—and if it ever came to that, he didn't want records of them together—but he pointed out how it was going to go down. Charlie was hit-man cool. "See those lions? That's the old Hongkong Bank. That's where you're going to intercept him. You'll be waiting around the corner and Mr. Chen will be in a car over there, by that cross street. He'll be watching me. We'll be walking toward the bank from the opposite direction, and Mr. Chen here will be watching and he'll text you when I'm a block away. That should be about twelve fifteen. I'll get your man over by this second lion, and I'll delay him there. You should be able to approach, hit him, and then walk directly over to the street by that traffic light. Do not look at me, do not speak to me, do not acknowledge me in any way. If you do, you'll put me at risk. Understand?"

"I understand. Don't let on that I've ever seen you before."

"That's right. It's *very* important. These situations are fluid, and I may have to say or do something unexpected, but you'll ignore me. If I go down, ignore me. Got it?"

"Got it."

"I'll have another man nearby to intercept the bodyguard if he decides to chase you and gets past me. Don't look for him. Mr. Chen will be waiting with a taxi and he'll bring you straight to the airport. You'll have a first-class ticket on Cathay Pacific, and he'll take you through VIP security. Mr. Zhang already set it up. You'll have an hour and a half to make the flight, starting from this point. Now repeat that all back to me."

He went over the whole thing for Charlie, and, yeah, he was feeling it a little. Light in the stomach, pulse running faster.

"Good." Charlie looked him in the eye. "What are you going to say when you walk up to him?"

"I'm going to say, *Hey, I'm Pete Harrington, and you ripped me off for eight million dollars!* Then I hit him."

"I guess that works."

"Or I could say, *You owe me eight million dollars, and I'm taking it out of your ass!*"

"Okay—"

"Or maybe, *Motherfucker—*"

"You mean you haven't thought this through?"

"Well, yeah, Charlie, I've thought about it a lot, but, you know, it's like writing lyrics: it takes a few tries to get it right."

The old man put his forehead down to his hand, shaking it back and forth, then looked up at him again, smiling. "Well, whatever you say, don't get in an argument with him. You're not there to dialogue. Say it; hit him before he understands what's going on; if he goes down, maybe kick him a couple of times; then walk to the car quickly."

"Got it. But there's one thing we haven't talked about, Charlie: how are you going to get away?"

"That's the easy part. I'll give you a call when I get back to Los Angeles."

They dropped him off at the hotel, and he went back up to his room. He had a hard time staying still, half-watched the television as he sat on the edge of the bed. At eleven, he went to the lobby and checked out; then Mr. Chen came for him and put his luggage in the taxi that he was driving now. By eleven forty-five he was in place, two blocks from the old Hongkong Bank building, waiting. The driver would text him when it was time to go.

The morning was cool and his leather jacket wasn't quite doing the job. He was shivering, and that probably wasn't just from the cold. Charlie had told him it would be like this, and he kept calling up Charlie's calm, fatherly face. *Keep a level mind, stay with the job. Get in, get out. You trained for this. You're ready.*

He looked at his reflection in the window of a restaurant, the street reflected in back of him, as if it was a green screen and someone was just projecting him there. A music video, the one of "Kickin' It with The Man," except the video he'd imagined happened in a universe waiting for an avenger to punch greed in the face, and instead some dumbass had green-screened him into a universe that just didn't give a fuck!

What was he doing here? Standing on the street in Shanghai about to go assault some dude—this was *fucking* crazy! He should be back in L.A., working on a song, planning his tour. Why was he pretending to be some kind of hero? He looked at his watch. Another twenty minutes to kill, and now his body was starting to shake. He was freezing out here!

He drifted to the window of a jewelry store. Glittery bits of glass on metal: bullshit fishing lures for the rich. The street front of some sort of upscale shopping gallery. He wandered inside. Men's clothing. An audio shop. He wandered over: those new Bose headphones. Nice. Some speakers. Norwegian shit. It felt comfortable, so he wandered in, and the salesman came up to him. Youngish Chinese guy, casual hipster clothes. He recognized him, seemed embarrassed. "Mr. Harrington! Hello!"

Give the dude a little salute: "G'day." Christ, where'd that come from? Was he fucking Australian now?

The salesman still seemed starstruck, but he went into his routine. He probably didn't know what else to say. Talking about, *Have you seen the new Bose headphones? Very good signal-to-noise ratio.*

And he was like, *Dude, I'm getting ready to assault somebody! That's the only noise I'm hearing!* But he didn't say that, just waved at him and drifted out of the shop, back out onto the street, and he could see the salesclerk talking excitedly to someone else, and then the two of them came over to the front of the shopping gallery, came out the door saying, *Hello, Mr. Harrington. Can I take a picture?* They didn't wait for an answer: whipped out their cellies and started filming him. He waved and smiled, then tried to get some space, but they were following him with their phones, calling out to him, saying something in Chinese. Now other people were looking at him, too, and it was like feeding goldfish: when the first ones come to the surface, all the other ones come, too, until you've got a swarm of goldfish blowing bubbles all around you. He kept a vague smile on his face and tried to fade away, but he really had no place to go, because he was supposed to wait here for the text. In a couple of minutes, he had four or five people taking videos of him, asking for autographs, and when people saw that, they whipped out their cell phones, too, clueless little smiles on their faces, like, *Who the fuck is this foreigner, and why am I taking a movie of him?*

Okay, this is fucking *off* the crazy scale! Did I make this? Did I create this world and this street and this nervous guy waiting to go do violence to someone? And I'm doing this *why*? He felt his cell phone vibrate in his pocket, and he pulled it out and looked at it. It was the driver. The text said, "GO."

He swallowed. He was doing this. Day of reckoning, right? That was it. Fucking day of reckoning. Say it, step in, trap, and hit. Kick him if he goes down. Head for the traffic light.

The sidewalk was crowded but he could see the lions a couple hundred yards off. A few people were walking alongside him with their cell phones out, filming him, silently, but he wasn't paying attention to them. He could see Charlie up ahead, talking to another man, and beside them a third man, the bodyguard. They were staring at the buildings, so they couldn't see him yet. The guard was listening and following what Charlie was saying.

His heart was speeding along. This was stupid! Was he really doing this? Now only a hundred yards away, and he could make them out clearly. Charlie had his camera out and was pointing it at the building. The bodyguard and the financier were all looking that way. This was it. This was the guy who'd ripped him off and cost him his house and his career. The guy who'd fleeced the world and laughed about it. Fucking Peter Harrington! He was only fifty yards away, and now Charlie glanced over and, without actually looking his way, moved so that the bankster saw him coming, too, dragging his little entourage of Chinese celebrity hounds. Charlie moved in between the bodyguard and Peter Harrington. He was twenty yards away. Should he say something now? Was this the time? Wait another few paces? What was he was going to say? Something about eight million dollars? Or six hundred million?

He was only thirty feet away now, Peter Harrington seeming now like just a regular guy on the street standing with an old man and a local. They locked eyes, and then he saw it: the face lit up in that way he'd witnessed a million times. That dumbstruck recognition, that worshipful stupor, that wonder, that amazement, that sense that the whole world had just expanded into something huge and fabulous, like a movie or a video. He was a fan!

Charlie was looking his way. He was supposed to say something, right? Something about owing, or payback or something, but he couldn't remember, because the guy was a fan! For Christ's sake, the guy was smiling! He looked like he's about to ask for a fucking autograph! And now he was only three feet away from the fucker, completely blank-minded, and the guy was reaching his hand out to shake, and the bodyguard was starting to shift a little like he senses something.

"Hey," Harrington said softly, in a flat tone of voice. "I'm Pete Harrington."

"I know you are!" the financier said. "I really like your music!"

He was frozen there, and Charlie was just gaping at him now, five feet away, with this look of anger and fucking horror, like, *How could I go all this way with you, all the way to China, and you're just fucking going to forgive and forget because this guy's a fan?* Charlie was shaking his head now, subtly, but visibly.

"Yeah, well—" He could barely get it out: "You're a fucking dirtbag!"

He saw the expression of puzzlement and hurt on his opponent's face; then the bodyguard started to move toward him. In that instant, Charlie came lurching toward him, saying, *Listen you, who do you think you are!* And then Charlie seemed to trip and go stumbling sideways into the bodyguard. He spotted Charlie's leg wrapping behind the bodyguard's leg, and then both of them went down in a tangle of limbs, with Charlie sprawled out on top of him, swearing.

The financier had a look of disbelief on his face. Pete stepped forward, his left hand moving up to execute the trap, even though the banker was too stupefied to raise his hand. In a motion he'd practiced thirty thousand times, he shuffled in with his left foot, drew his right fist back, and then sent it snapping forward like the piston of a locomotive. He felt the small bones of the bridge of the other man's nose under his knuckles, and heard a faint clicking, mashing sound as he hit. Harrington staggered backward a few steps and then sat down clumsily on the sidewalk.

The bodyguard was trying to struggle to his feet, but Charlie was rolling around on top of him, tangled up with his legs, yelling, "Get off of me! You're hurting me!"

The financier was curled up on the pavement with his hands over his face. Pete stepped in and kicked him a couple of times in the legs. "Remember this while you're spending all that money!"

He turned and began walking quickly toward the car. There were at least ten people with cell phones out, filming him. He glanced over his shoulder and saw Peter Harrington still on the ground, covering his nose, while the bodyguard was still trying to get free. He reached the car and ducked inside. The bodyguard was up now, but it was too late, and as they pulled out into traffic he took a few running steps and then stopped. A million cell phones were out, a million eyes. He had done it. He'd touched the untouchable. He just wasn't sure what he was supposed to do next.

V

⁜

Return
of the
Noise

⁜

1

The House near Monthey

※

When Beth Blackman was in third grade her classroom had featured a poster printed by the Swiss Ministry of Tourism. It showed a steep-roofed chalet floating in a vast green ocean of pastureland. There were flower boxes below the windows and stacks of logs, and she spent hours as the teacher droned away in the distance, wandering into its spaces and imagining who lived there. It never occurred to her that one day she would find out.

It happened when she was thrashing in the wake of her divorce from Pete Harrington. She was trying to put the experience behind her and Nino seemed like the perfect vehicle for that. He was the exquisitely dressed scion of an old Italian family who had come to Los Angeles to be a movie producer. Nino was beautiful and hapless and she knew within ten minutes of meeting him that he would not be successful. He presented no threat to her whatsoever, and that was why she'd accepted his invitation to go skiing in Switzerland. She wasn't really a skier: three days into the trip, she sprained her wrist and was content to sit in the lodge reading or poking through the little villages below the slopes.

They would stay at one resort for a few days and then drive to the next in the 1962 Alfa Romeo that Nino kept telling her was a classic. Somewhere between Gstaad and Monthey the red light on the dashboard of the old car began to flicker. Nino pulled to the side and opened the hood, absorbed in his little drama of the manly and mechanical. She got out and glanced at the engine in a show of support, then turned to examine the landscape.

They were in a wide snow-caked valley that ran along the left side of the road. On the right the mountains sprang directly upward, silhouetted against a colorless sky. It was high, empty farmland, and she imagined that in the summer it was transformed into lush grassy fields with cows and wildflowers. Now, it was a great empty tablecloth scratched by stone walls and leafless branches. Nino declared that they needed water for the radiator, and they got back in the car and drove slowly along, their eyes on the steadily climbing temperature gauge. Soon they came to a small stone house that seemed anchored there among the heaving landscape.

The roof was high and peaked, with deep overhanging eaves, and someone had stacked firewood to head level along the heavy walls. It reminded her instantly of a house in a tourism poster that had hung in her classroom, and in moments she had convinced herself that it was the same house, or, if not the very same, somehow, *the same.*

They pulled into the driveway and turned the car off, opened the hood, and then stood for a moment in the silent landscape. She breathed in the crystalline air. Around them, the sky was stuffed with undulating masses of silver and gray that vaulted over the mountains. She'd never seen clouds like that before. Sets of skis were leaning against the wall, five or six pairs of different sizes, and a snowboard. The ground floor of the house seemed to be a sort of stable for animals, and she could hear the scoffing voices of the goats as they climbed the wooden stairs to the front door. Something exciting was happening. It was that house. She was actually here. Nino rang the bell.

The door was opened by a blond woman who seemed in her forties and wore a sweater and jeans. She looked heavy and strong, in the way of German women, with big breasts and hips, but not ungraceful. More like a very well-made object: strong and in proportion and not liable to break easily. She had a wide, clean face with light-colored eyes. She looked like the kind of woman she might want to be at that age, if she lived here in Switzerland, instead of in Los Angeles.

The woman looked at Nino, and then her eyes moved to Beth, and she seemed more at her ease to see a petite young American in a ski jacket and fur-topped boots. Beth smiled at her and said, "Hello, I'm Beth!" as if it was a professional setting. The woman smiled back and said her name, but it wasn't Marta, or Gertrude, or anything Beth had ever heard before, and she forgot it as soon as the woman finished speaking. Nino started explaining about the car, but the woman didn't seem to know English, or French, or Italian. Finally Nino motioned at the steaming chassis and said *"Wasser? Wasser?"* The woman hesitated a moment, her gaze moving between the two of them. She glanced past them, up toward the mountains, and stared at the heights for a few seconds. She uttered a few words in a language that might have been Polish or Hungarian, and then she pushed open the outer door and motioned them in.

It took a few moments for Beth's eyes to adjust to the interior. It seemed like an old house, with wooden walls interspersed with stone that had been plastered and painted over. There was a cuckoo clock above the sink, and the black cast-iron woodstove in the corner had a kettle on it, gently steaming. She could imagine the woman getting up each morning and lighting the stove and winding the cuckoo clock. A steep stairway disappeared into an upper floor.

The woman offered them coffee and then set a pot of water to boiling before leading her to an armchair by the woodstove. She turned to Nino. *"Wasser!"* she said with great emphasis, and she led him outside.

Beth sat in the armchair, feeling the dry warmth of the stove and looking out the picture window at the white landscape. Her mind wandered out into the vast porcelain trough of snow-covered valley, off past the wooden fence posts that poked from the snow, down toward the faraway clumps of trees and to the neighbor's houses, so small that she could hide them with her thumb.

What did this woman do here, alone each day, hour after hour? There was a family: she could tell by the selection of boots and shoes by the door.

She could imagine their footsteps moving across the ceiling as they woke up. What was her husband like? Was he handsome, quiet? Did he have a pleasant voice, or a harsh Germanic manner? And what about their children? She could spot several feminine coats, and the sort of colorful rubber rain boots that looked like they might be worn by a teenage girl. A schoolbook sat on the bench by the door.

She tried to imagine all the circumstances that had led their hostess to this house in a country where she didn't speak the language. She made guesses about her life: this was a woman comfortable in the cold. This was a woman who could carry things. This was a woman who cooked, who bought gifts for her children. She thought, with a pang of grief: this was a woman whose husband would never cheat on her.

Beth heard footsteps coming up the wooden stairs. The woman knew a little bit of English after all, and she and Nino were trading the few words she had. She seated them by the stove and returned a few minutes later with a tray that held a French press full of coffee and a plate with cookies on it. Nino was eyeing her breasts and her hips as she turned sideways to place it on the table, but Beth suppressed the flash of anger she felt rising. She didn't care enough about Nino to be jealous. That was the whole point of coming on this trip with him.

Their hostess told them with signs and words that she had two children: a girl and a boy, seventeen and nineteen years old. The girl was away at the university in Zurich. The boy, she couldn't explain. She said the word *ski* emphatically, twice, and she motioned out the picture window toward the mountains in a very general way, as if he was in the sky, up above the horizon. She seemed a bit agitated. She tried to explain something about her husband, and they could tell it involved her husband and her son, but they didn't know what. The woman finally gave up trying to explain. They held their mugs quietly as she stared nervously out the window at the mountains, occasionally glancing back to them and giving them a quick uneasy smile.

They finished the coffee and went to the door, thanking her. She walked out with them to their car, scanning the far ends of the road and looking up at the heights, as if she expected to see something there. She mustered a last burst of warmth as she said good-bye to them, then glanced up again. Looking in that direction, Beth saw parallel tracks that made a path up and around the hill until they disappeared from sight.

Beth snapped a picture of the chalet before she got in the car. Nino started the engine and said they could probably reach the next town. As they pulled away Beth turned to wave one final thanks, but the woman wasn't looking at them at all. Her face was turned upward toward the high mountains, gazing as if she could see far into them, at things happening beyond this hill and the next, where the lives she possessed were swirling and burning in secret orbits Beth could never imagine. There were suddenly innumerable perfect ashes hanging in the growing distance between them. Millions of pale white eyelashes, sliding softly from above, like silent messages. Something about the sky, about clouds. The Swiss woman stood in the empty road as they fell all around her, becoming small and indistinct behind the thickening curtain of snowflakes, until she was lost forever in the memory of winter, without a name.

2

Return of the Noise

⁜

The whole operation had gone off better than Pete could have dreamed. The bodyguard stayed with his client, just like Charlie said he would. The driver was waiting at the traffic light, as planned, and Charlie'd clocked the whole thing out so that he arrived at the airport an hour before the flight, breezed through the first-class security setup, and was sitting next to some French businessman without even breaking a sweat. This was hit-man shit, and he felt like he imagined a hit man would feel: bland, detached, moody.

He got in at two in the afternoon, and Bobby called while he was waiting in line at immigration. Charlie must have sent his flight reservations ahead.

"Welcome home. How'd it go?"

"Textbook, Bobby. Direct hit. I sent him to the bottom like the fucking *Lusitania.*"

"Excellent. How'd the footage come out?"

"What do you mean?"

Bobby was quiet for a second. "Footage . . . I mean, did you kick him when he was down, like you said you were going to? Wait, don't tell me anything! I want to hear about this in person. I'm waiting for you outside baggage claim."

Wow! Bobby picking him up at the airport! How long had it been since that happened?

Bobby jumped out of the car wearing a leather sport jacket, soundlessly high-five'd him with a huge grin on his face. "Welcome back, Pete!"

He wanted to hear about the whole operation, from start to finish, and listened to it like it was the gospel. He wanted to know what was said, exactly, and how it got said and how the financier had reacted. Did he kick him when he was on the ground? Where was Charlie in all this? Did he get out of the way? How did they deal with the bodyguard? He didn't get why Bobby wanted to know those kind of details, but in any case he was happy.

"You know, though, Bobby, it kind of bothers me."

"What do you mean?"

He explained about the look on Harrington's face, and then how he'd felt sorry for him when he was on the ground. Defeat was an ugly thing, under any circumstances.

"Pete! He's a fucking bankster! He ripped you off for eight million dollars and the government had to fork over billions to try to stabilize the financial mess he left behind. Where's the moral ambiguity here, man? Because I'm just not seeing it!"

"Well, I think the guy's a fan."

"He's a fan?"

"Yeah. The last thing he said before I hammered him was, *I really like your music.*"

Bobby laughed. "Yeah, Pete. You feel bad about hitting a fan? Send him an autographed copy of 'Kickin' It.' He'll be eternally grateful."

Bobby was right: he was splitting this a lot finer than it needed to be. The man was a bankster. Case closed.

They moved on to the tour stuff. Nothing much had developed in the last four days; still a lot of holes in the schedule, and gigs that Bobby wasn't too specific about. He didn't have the heart to press him on it. They talked about the new songs. Bobby'd already released "Kickin' It with The Man," but it hadn't done much so far. Fourteen hundred downloads from the usual suspects, along with some "positive energy" from the radio stations. Bobby's industry-speak way of saying it wasn't going anywhere. A few months ago he would have bought into it, just said, *Bobby's got this one,* because, basically, he paid Lev to worry about the money shit and Bobby to worry about the career shit. When songs tanked, Bobby pretended to care and he pretended to believe him. That had been the deal. But that deal was no longer in force. "So Bobby, what you're saying is that 'Kickin' It' isn't getting traction."

"Not yet."

"Why don't you tell me exactly what you're doing to make it get traction."

Bobby seemed kind of surprised when he popped him with that one, but he went down the list in a very professional-sounding way that involved incoming links and outgoing links and social bookmarking and a whole bunch of Internet stuff that was like, yeah, whatever. The bottom line: between track downloads and streaming, he'd made about a thousand bucks on the song since it came out two weeks ago. Didn't even cover the studio costs. The strange thing was, Bobby actually seemed pumped about the song. "Don't count this one out yet, Pete. This is different. I've got a good feeling about this."

Bobby dropped him off at home and Pete pushed his key into the lock. He'd only been gone four days. He didn't even have a stack of mail to throw out. And it was over. He'd gone to Shanghai, he'd done everything Charlie'd said, he'd kicked it with The Man, and now he was back in L.A. with a new song going nowhere and a concert tour that had so many holes in it you couldn't really call it a tour. He wandered aimlessly around his apartment, swatted at the heavy bag, read a magazine while he stood in front of the open refrigerator and ate wrinkled grapes. Maybe it was the jet lag that had him down. He hadn't slept in twenty-eight hours and it was four in the afternoon. Fourteen hundred downloads wouldn't even pay his rent for a couple of weeks. It meant oblivion. There were always merchandise revenues, royalties from his catalog. He could keep limping along like this for a while, but, really, if he'd written his best song, and it was dead in the water, where did he go from here?

He tried to tune it out and work on a new song, something with a honky-tonk feel, maybe a guy who had his girlfriend stolen by his best friend, or maybe a guy who stole his best friend's girl—something like that. But it felt stale. He'd written that song already, a hundred times over.

He put on his headphones and listened to the demo of "Kickin' It with The Man" that he'd cut with Duffy. Bobby'd hired some studio musicians to lay in the other tracks, and the damn thing really sounded like a Dream-Krushers song, one of their earlier ones, before all the fights about songwriting credits and royalties started sapping them. The weird thing was, listening to it now, he didn't feel the same juice. He'd dreamed it, he'd planned it, he'd trained for it, and he'd done it. He was finished with it now, something he hadn't figured on when he'd imagined singing it in arenas across the country.

He took some pills and dozed off around six, then woke up at four in the morning. His first thought was that he should be writing something, putting new material between him and whatever despair was on his ass at the moment, but he was too buzzed out, so he went to his computer to check his mail. Weird shit happening: there were four messages from China that had come in over his fan site. He could tell them by the chicken scratchings along the bottom and the fucked-up English, and he'd already deleted the first couple as spam when he noticed something different. Not the usual Chinese fan letter, some Chinglish version of, *I like your music, Mr. Pete Harrington,* but instead, *Very funny video you beating banker! Very good!*

Interesting. And the next one: *I see you hit him strong!*

Damn straight he'd hit him strong! He'd made a couple of people happy, anyway. But how had they tracked him down so quickly? He knew there'd been witnesses: downtown Shanghai at one in the afternoon was a piss-poor place to keep something secret. One of the e-mails had a link to a Chinese Web site, and even though it didn't have a single word of English on it, he could see from the grainy image of the video still that it was him, in Shanghai, with the other Peter Harrington. He clicked the arrow to put it in motion. There were some Chinese characters he couldn't understand, a soundtrack too garbled to make anything out, but he immediately recognized himself walking along the Bund, then going up to the other Peter Harrington, and then—hell yeah!—just hammering the living crap out of him with a single perfect overhand right that sent the bankster staggering backward onto his ass. Fucking nice shot! The guy went down, then scuttled around like a crab trying to avoid his kicks. He watched it again. Shuffle, trap, hit—boom! Charlie'd be proud of him when he saw that. The kicks could have been stronger, but the idea wasn't to damage him, it was to make him feel powerless. And by the look on the guy's face, he'd fucking aced that test.

He watched it a third and then a fourth time. It was all there: the hesitation, then the words, and then the flawless punch he'd honed with thirty thousand repetitions. The only thing missing was Charlie, taking down the bodyguard like a carnival rigger.

He watched it a few more times, then searched his name to see what else was out there. None of the videos came up. He got it: you had to search with Chinese characters or something. So at the moment it was strictly in China. He had a hunch it wasn't going to stay that way.

Bobby called him at nine. He sounded excited. "Have you looked at YouTube? Search yourself on YouTube."

And there he was, walking up to Harrington, saying a few words, then punching him in the face. It was the same as the Chinese video, but better picture quality, like they'd loaded it at higher resolution, and they'd put some English subtitles in to identify the players. But there was a second video, too, from a different angle. Some of it familiar: the startled bankster, the part where he recognized him, the surprise, then the disbelief as Pete punched him right in the nose. He remembered a couple of Chinese fans following him with cell phones. This definitely looked like their work. The sound was better. He could distinctly make out Peter Harrington saying, *I really like your music.*

Bobby was analyzing it. "Evidently it got posted on a Chinese site, and then someone posted it on YouTube. It's got eleven thousand views already, mostly from Europe. That's in eight hours."

"No shit!"

"You look good, Pete. You smoked him."

How do you answer that one? You stack up a huge pile of hundreds, set them on fire, and, just when you've decided it's all been pretty useless, Bobby calls up and says, *Good show, old chap! Eleven thousand views!* And though he should have been all existential about it, all very detached Bob Dylan and shit, he couldn't help saying, "How about the downloads?"

" 'Kickin' It' has been downloaded twelve hundred times since this went up. That's almost as much as the previous two weeks."

He was quiet for a while, holding the phone away from him, until Bobby said, *Pete? Are you there?*

"That's not why I did this."

"I know."

"I'm going to hang up now."

"Cool. We'll talk later. But, Pete, I need you to promise me something: don't say anything to anyone about this. Not your friends—nobody. In case there's legal issues. Just say you can't talk about it."

Not an easy directive to follow. By late afternoon, his phone started buzzing. He didn't pick up, but he listened to the messages. Friends calling to congratulate him. *Pete! That was so badass!* Or, *Pete, I saw you deck that banker on YouTube! Nice!* Duffy called about one of the songs they were working on, and he picked up for that one. He steered him to the video, and Duffy called back a few minutes later. "You did it, Pete! You brought the hard hand of justice down on that guy, just like you said you would. I'm proud of you!" His sister and his mother called. His first cousin in Montana called. The only call missing was Charlie. He'd tried to reach him three times that day, figuring he was jet-lagged, or just old-man cranky, because Charlie could get that way, but he never picked up. What had happened to him? Had he gotten hurt, or arrested? Was he back in the States? Bobby said he hadn't heard from him.

But all the other noise was starting up again: he could feel it. Noise he'd heard when the DreamKrushers had first hit, and then again after that China tour. The kind of noise where people called your name again and again, but even though it was your name it wasn't really you, it was just a name they knew. Because how could it be *you* punching a guy in the face but not *you* with a sense of fear? *You* singing a hit, but not *you* chasing after that song you couldn't write. He went out to the Rainbow for a quick dinner, half-heartedly flirted with the waitress. When he got back he tried to start a new song, that one about the house in Wilksbury, but he couldn't figure out the melody, or what he'd call it. He pushed it around until ten o' clock, then took a couple of Valiums. He went over to the computer to take one last look before the pills kicked in. The video had gone to fifty thousand views.

The Valium only kept him down for six hours. When he fired up his laptop again, he thought at first it had some sort of virus. There were over three hundred e-mail messages waiting for him in a half-dozen languages and every variation of stilted English you could find. A lot were from fans, but there was a new element now. The link must have gone out to some sort of Crossroads-victims mailing list, because dozens of messages had come from people who'd lost a chunk of their retirement or their houses in the collapse. They retold their hard-luck stories and thanked him for what he'd done. Again and again, the stories and then the chorus, in one form or an-other: *You're my hero!* On top of this were the requests for interviews from Web sites and media. Even some of the music labels were on to him now, congratulating him on his new release and pretending that they'd been fol-lowing him all these years, just waiting for a chance to sign him. Sure, pal. You always loved me. He picked up the phone and called Bobby. Even as he surveyed the messages, new ones kept sliding in at the top of the list.

"This is fucking weird, Bobby. I've gotten three hundred thirty-two messages in my mailbox in the last eight hours!"

"It's five in the morning, Pete! You woke up Sandra!"

"Sorry, man. I couldn't help it: it's freaking me out!"

He heard some muffled swearing, then a woman's voice sounding pissed. "I'll call you back, Pete," Bobby said. Then carefully, so he would understand him, "Don't answer any e-mails. Okay? Not even from your family."

. . .

When Bobby called back at ten he was cheerful, as if waking up his bitch wife at five A.M. was no big deal. *No, hey, Pete. Call me anytime you need me. That's what I'm here for.* He was starting to get it now: this was the new Bobby. The new Bobby told him that "Kickin' It" had been downloaded 6,000 times in the last twenty-four hours. That set him back for a second. He did the math, something he'd gotten good at, though with much smaller numbers. With no label to take a cut, that was $1,800. Not only that, he'd had another 7,800 downloads of other tracks, and over 300 album downloads, on which he scored about six bucks a pop. Total take: close to $6,000 in twenty-four hours. Bobby sounded warm and brotherly, like they were in this together, no matter what. He said his phone was ringing off the hook. Industry suits, media people, even major-market radio stations interested in "Kickin' It with The Man." It looked like people were starting to remember who Pete Harrington was.

"So, Bobby, I've got, like, four hundred e-mails. And a bunch of them are interview requests? What do I do?"

"First of all, don't answer them. Second, I think you need a publicist." His tone lifted slightly. "Maybe you should give Beth a call."

"Um . . . Do you really think that's a good idea? It took me twenty years to dig out of the hole I made last time she was my publicist."

"That's ancient history; we're all grown-ups now. And she's one of the smartest people out there. Give her a call and see what she says. She cares about you, Pete."

An hour later he was at her PR agency. The ground floor of a Wilshire Boulevard office building, it was all open and airy, like nobody was actually working. Even the little cubicles were open on two sides to make them feel more humane and egalitarian. Everybody seemed like they were right out of college, looking up at him with that "it's the client!" smile as the receptionist walked him through the space to Beth's office. Framed pop stuff to show how hip they were: a Lakers uniform, an electric guitar belonging to Eric Clapton, and even, no shit, an old Oompa Loompa costume with a signed photo of Gene Wilder next to it. Oompa Loompas: cool! The house that Beth built. Have to admit: the woman was impressive. He'd screwed her over pretty badly when they'd been married, no doubt about that, and rescuing that relationship from a watery grave had taken many buckets of blood. He'd serially messed up at least a million relationships in exactly the same way, but Beth had been different. She wasn't some little bonbon waiting to be unwrapped and eaten: he'd really admired her. They'd finally settled in to a friendship where she and Ira were the responsible couple and he was a sort of wayward son, soaking up dinner and practical advice. Sometimes he called them "Mom and Dad." Their kids laughed at that.

But they'd never had a professional relationship, not after the last one. Now they were going to see if anything had changed.

Her office was pale and expensive, with two big white couches facing each other that reminded him of the kind of fat clouds that you'd see out an airplane window. There was a small conference table and a flat screen on the wall and some kind of thick shaggy carpet that looked like it was the final resting place of about a dozen goats. The potted plants were the kind that had one beautiful bloom on an elegant stem. Beth was wearing a white blouse and jeans and an unbuttoned cashmere sweater the color of lipstick. She was finishing up a phone call, pointed him toward one of the white sofas as she said her last good-byes, then came from behind her desk and planted a light kiss on his cheek. It was good to see her. He hoped she could make some sense out of this shit, because, though he didn't want to mention it to Bobby, the whole thing was a little bit creepy, especially watching the other Peter Harrington say "I really like your music" over and over again before getting punched in the face. What did that mean? After the first dozen times the line had started to crackle with some sinister irony aimed right at him. "I really like your music!" *Wham!* That would freak anybody out. Beth motioned him to the cloud couch, then sat down across from him as he slumped into it. Another assistant came in with a bowl of expensive chocolates and set them in front of him. Nice-looking number, a little extra smile with that smile. Maybe on the way out . . . When he glanced back at Beth, she was frowning at him.

"Keep it in your pants when you're here."

"Wow! Is that the first thing you say to all your clients?"

"You're not my client, and I know you too well. She's my rabbi's niece."

"You know, at this phase of life, I'm thinking more about spiritual stuff. Maybe—"

Beth put her hand up: "Don't even!" Then she laughed, and he laughed with her. "You will never grow up."

"No, I will never grow *old*! How are the kids?"

She grimaced. "Sarah's doing great. Dylan . . ." She sighed and rolled her eyes. "His therapist says he's in a nihilistic phase."

Pete smiled as he imagined the boy. "What do you expect? He's . . . what? Thirteen?"

"Fifteen. But he's tiny. He's got the body of a twelve-year-old. We don't want to give him hormones, but it's hard when you're the class shrimp."

Pete had known Dylan since he was a baby and felt himself smiling as he imagined the face of a toddler changing into that of a ten-year-old and then the Dylan he'd seen two weeks ago. "It'll happen. He's a great kid."

She asked about China, and he gave her the whole story of how they'd found the guy, stalked him, put him exactly where they needed him, and then how eighty-six-year-old Charlie had taken out the bodyguard. "He folded that dude up like a fucking origami!"

"I'm impressed. You really did it. Tell me something, though: was it satisfying to clobber him?"

He didn't have a simple answer. "Let me say this: no man ever deserved to get hammered more than that guy. I still stand by that. From another angle, I trained for two months, and every day of those two months I thought about decking that asshole. Multiple times per day. But when I finally walked up to him, I wasn't really mad anymore. I was over it. It wasn't really even about what he did to everyone else, or the money. It was more because Charlie was there. He went all the way to Shanghai and did all his spy stuff to set it up, and at that point I just couldn't fail on him. Have you heard anything from him?"

"He's back in Los Angeles. He wants to avoid contact with you, me, and

Bobby, in case our friend in Shanghai decides to investigate it. He said he'll get in touch with you when things settle down."

It was disappointing, but Charlie knew his shit. If he wanted to lay low, so be it.

Beth went on. "So now you've got twenty thousand downloads and about ninety thousand views just on TMZ. My assistant found fifty-eight sites with that video on it."

"I also got six hundred e-mails. As of about an hour ago."

"That's the most interest you've had in a long time. How's it feel?"

"Kinda weird. It reminds me of when the *Wreckage* album first hit. That noise. I'm guessing it will be fun soon, but right now it's kind of confusing."

"You've been down for a while. Maybe it's hard to see yourself as successful again."

"Maybe. But I didn't go over there to be successful. I went over to do something."

"Wait a minute. You told me you were going to kick this guy's ass, and write an anthem and the whole world was going to cheer. You used pretty much those words."

"Okay. I did."

"Well, Pete . . . they're cheering."

"Yeah!" he said. "I guess they are."

"So what do you want from me?"

"I guess . . . I just need some help sorting this all out. I mean, Bobby's like, *Internet strategy* and *social networking campaign*. I don't know anything about that stuff. I've got my Web site, shit like that, but all these people are writing me and asking me for interviews . . . What am I supposed to say?"

"Pete, listen to me very carefully." She took on that tone again—the Beth-in-charge tone. "I know you didn't go to China as some sort of career move. You went to right a wrong. That stands on its own. But you do want to get your career moving again, right?"

"Right."

"Well, this is your shot. If you blow it, it's going to be very hard to get another one. Do you understand?"

"Yeah."

"Now, if you want me to, I will handle it. I can take on your media strategy, your Internet and social networking strategy—everything. But you cannot fuck me over like last time."

Knew that one was still kicking around. "I won't."

"And fucking me over means running off with some groupie you fall in love with, or showing up drunk at events, or being insulting to an interviewer, or being late to meetings, or getting naked with the rabbi's niece. That, and everything like that. Got it?"

"That's humbling." Her expression didn't change. "Got it!"

"And once I start on this, you can't back out. You have to go all the way, or I'm not going to waste my time."

"All the way to where?"

"Let's turn that question around. Where do you want to go? Where does Pete Harrington end up?"

He never thought about ending up anywhere. "I thought ending up somewhere is what dead people do."

"No, Pete. It's what grown-ups do. Where do you see yourself in ten years?"

And strangely, maybe because he was working on the song about that house, he saw himself impossibly, so very impossibly, sitting by a fire with a son and a wife and outside all around just snow, and snow, and snow. Some life he'd never get a chance to live, that didn't make sense when you're sitting in an office on Wilshire Boulevard that has an Oompa Loompa costume in the reception. She was waiting for a real answer. "I don't know."

"For example, here's a scenario I could see for you. You record a new song, and people buy it. You go on tour, and people show up. You make enough money to live by who you are. And when it starts to subside—and someday it will—you have enough saved up to live decently and do what you want, and still make some money playing music."

"Not to be an ingrate, but it's kind of depressing when you put it like that."

Beth smiled back at him. "Pete, I can get you publicity. I can't get you eternal youth." She paused, as if they'd finished that subject. "So"—she put her hands together and asked with exaggerated naïveté—"how's that tour shaping up?"

"Okay, stop! You already talked to Bobby, didn't you?"

She gave a little shrug using only her eyebrows. "It's up to you, Pete. I don't need another client. I've got plenty of clients. I'm doing this because I want to help you. We're old friends; my kids love you. I want to see you be well."

It was amazing how good this woman was, so much better than he'd realized. He felt a fresh wave of regret at how he'd treated her all those years ago. It took him a few seconds to be able to respond. "Thanks, Beth."

"I'm glad to help. I'll have a memorandum of agreement drawn up, and you can sign it on the way out. I'll get you a contract later." She made a quick call to her assistant, then continued. "Let's deal with the most immediate things. First of all, do not answer any e-mails. Second, do not respond to requests for interviews. We do not confirm, deny, or explain. We let the video do the talking. Whatever you want to say, that video says it better."

"Okay."

"The idea now is to keep absolutely silent, because the more it builds on its own, the more people are going to want to talk to Pete Harrington, and there's nothing the media responds to more than inaccessibility." She shrugged. "Except maybe free food and booze. But right now, the less you say, the more valuable you get. When it's time to talk, we'll choose the venue and the message. Why talk to the *Los Angeles Times* when you can get paid thirty thousand dollars for appearing on *Good Morning America*?"

Nice! "Go on."

"If someone calls you or you get cornered somehow, tell them your legal counsel has asked you not to talk about it. That lets people know it wasn't faked, which is the main thing right now."

"Nothing fake about it, Beth. You know that. But I don't have legal counsel, except some bankruptcy guy."

"Fine. I'll have my attorney call you and tell you not to talk about it. Then you won't be lying."

"What if Peter Harrington really does sue me? He's probably got, like, a hundred lawyers on his payroll."

"You mean, what if you get sued for decking a guy who caused a hundred-billion-dollar meltdown? Pete!" She leaned forward and spoke with her eyes wide. "*Pray* he sues you!"

He hadn't seen Beth at work since she was a twenty-four-year-old girl from New Jersey. And, frankly, it was a little scary. She cared about him, though. He knew that, and he was glad to sign the agreement she wrote up. It looked like this was going to be an interesting ride.

Beth hit it like a freight train. Some tech guy from her office called him ten minutes after he got back home, and by noon all his e-mails were automatically forwarded to her office. The appropriate ones were being answered by those kids at her agency, expressing his thanks for their support, boilerplate shit like that. All speaking on his behalf, like he was too big a star to answer them himself. A little later they e-mailed him a PR questionnaire asking him all about his past career, and then about his new songs and what inspired them. Didn't everybody already know that stuff? They already knew he'd worked with Duffy, and they played up the DreamKrushers reunion angle a little bit. On the follow-up call, his new guy, James, laid it all out with a reedy, college-kid voice, talking about the new product.

"We need to rebrand Pete Harrington. We still want him to have that spontaneous energy that he's known for, but we want to mature him a little bit, so he's not just a kid who trashes hotel rooms."

"You mean he's worked his way up to trashing Wall Street dirtbags."

"Exactly! He's been around, he knows the score, he still loves good-looking women, but he's more than that. He's somebody who saw a wrong and righted it. He's an American hero."

American hero. He'd been talking to Beth, all right. Whatever, James.

A half hour later, he got a phone call. "Pete Harrington?" Some serious-sounding man with a faint southern accent. "This is Burke Ellis, of Norton, Ellis, and Weintraub. Beth Blackman asked me to call you . . ."

It was her lawyer, just like she'd promised. Beth was running this show now.

3

Red Dragon

✤

It wasn't until the meeting with Shenzhen Red Dragon that Peter Harrington realized that the little episode on the Bund wasn't going to stay secret. Until then, he had tried to pretend that as long as no one else knew about it, it hadn't really happened. For the first two days after the attack, he'd hidden out in his lair, concocting a detailed story of how his racquetball partner had hit him in the face on his backswing and doing his best to get out of the meeting that they'd been carefully orchestrating for nearly two months.

"I'm really not up to it, Kell."

"Get back in the saddle, my man! We've been going back and forth with these guys forever. They flew in from Hong Kong to meet you!"

"Come on! I'm just window dressing for this venture."

"Drop the fake modesty. These guys all know how to use the Internet and they all know you and your original investors walked away from Crossroads with an eight-hundred-percent return on investment. You're the rock star. I'm just another lawyer to them."

The phrase "rock star" struck him in an unpleasant way. "Kell—"

"Get down here! Come into the office a little early. I've got to tell you about the other night. Then we'll go meet them."

Harrington was looking in the mirror as he talked, examining his face. He had other business at the office: he wanted to check the Crossroads database and see if Pete Harrington was in it. "I'll see you at eleven." He took a painkiller and then held an ice pack against his nose and eyes. It brought the swelling down, and, with the purple fading, he could almost believe that he looked merely tired, rather than battered. He put on his suit and tie, and Ma drove him over to the office.

As he'd expected, Kell was highly interested in his "accident." Peter had prepped him by telling him the story over the phone the day before, but when he came in, his partner was still shocked at his face.

"A squash racket did that?"

"A titanium squash racket. Titanium. That's the stuff they make missiles out of." Kell raised his eyebrows. "Anyway, you can see I wasn't bullshitting when I missed the meeting yesterday. How did it go?"

"Very well. David Lau sends his regards."

Lau was the Chinese point man in their new venture. Kell's vision was to take advantage of financially desperate American states and municipalities by buying up public turnpikes, bridges, and utilities using Chinese capital. These investments would lumber along generating six or seven percent profit each year, but owning a utility wasn't the real play. The real play was in the bonds that could be issued. With each bond sale they would buy more infrastructure, and with more infrastructure they could issue new bonds, gobbling their way across the United States from horizon to glorious horizon, taking a small percentage of each transaction.

Kell spent a few minutes going over the Shenzhen Red Dragon Group and strategizing about where their hundreds of millions of capital best fit. Whatever Kell's off-hours habits, the lawyer was always completely decorous about money. His short stature and firm handshake seemed to anchor a prospective partner as securely as a chain attached to an immovable boulder. Beyond that, he radiated the sort of underdog street smarts that the self-made millionaires of China could relate to. He was the state-school guy who'd never gotten rid of the chip on his shoulder and never joined the club. His financial plays were devious and complex, because he liked complicated games and because he liked the idea of outwitting his "betters" from Wharton and Harvard Law. Kell was the impetus behind this venture. Aside from some capital he'd invested, Peter's part on these deals was primarily decorative: his presence lent a touch of celebrity to the fine office and the well-designed bilingual prospectus. Whatever the undertones of his reputation, Peter Harrington was a man who had made eight hundred million dollars in a very short time, and that was one pedestal that no amount of bad press could knock him off of. Now Kell sat back in his chair and rubbed his chin.

"Where'd you take off to the other night?"

Harrington answered indirectly. "I didn't think you would miss me."

"I always miss you, buddy!" He shook off the phony sanctimony. "Seriously, we ended up in some karaoke room and I looked up and there was Paul horizontal with his girl, and then this waiter knocks on the door and shows up with about twenty plates of food—"

"Twenty? Who ordered that many plates?"

"Nobody. So Angelina and the other girl are fighting with the waiter, trying to make him understand he has the wrong order. But they're totally wasted, and in the middle of it Paul's girl decides to get sick all over his shoes and then the manager comes in . . ." He shook his head. "Long story short, they threw us out. But it gets worse. After the girl throws up on his shoes, Paul loses interest in her and starts getting depressed. Why this, why that: what an idiot he'd been—"

"What's up with Paul, anyway?"

Kell looked at him meaningfully. "Goldman Sachs? Are you kidding?"

"I heard a few rumblings."

"Rumblings? They've already indicted six people from the Special Purpose

Vehicles Department. He told me he showed up at work two weeks ago and they were hauling out his computer in a box marked EVIDENCE."

"That's a bad sign."

"You think so? And this isn't just the SEC; it's the IRS. The fucking IRS! So it's not like you've got a bunch of guys building their résumé. The IRS is a dead-end career track, and they're highly unimaginative about the way they look at numbers."

"Is he guilty of something?"

Kell shrugged. "Who's innocent? But that's irrelevant. They've got to feed somebody to the mob and it isn't going to be the CEO. So Paul's on the chopping block."

Peter considered it. There'd been a few investigations since the collapse, but the government always went after them clumsily, their understaffed enforcement departments issuing a string of heroic press releases at the out-set and then bogging down in a swamp of motions and documents. Most of what he and Kell had done had taken place in areas where the law was vague or had been eliminated by lobbyists. He liked to joke that there was only one real crime on Wall Street: the crime of being obvious.

Losers like Paul Gutterman, though, who plodded along on a lower plane, were much easier targets, and they could be sacrificed to protect the corporation, like a lizard shedding its tail to escape.

"So what's he doing here?"

"I don't know. Maybe he wanted to get out before they confiscated his passport."

"Is it that bad?"

"Oh, yeah!"

"Why does he come running to you?"

Kell cast his glance away to the side. "Between us?" He waited until Peter nodded. "He helped me out with information once in a while."

It was common: some hint of large movements about to happen, or a critical nod, like the microgesture in a poker game that indicated what cards they might be holding. Those sorts of relationships happened all the time. Peter himself had had many of them. They kept a person on top of the game, but they also tended to stray into the illegal. "Is there any chance of you catching what Paul's got?"

"No," Kell said contemptuously. "They already went over me with a microscope and they couldn't get anything. Believe me, they would have loved to knock me down a peg. I don't do 'humble' very well."

"I've noticed."

They both laughed. "Seriously, where'd you go with Carol—"

"Camille."

"*Camille,* the other night."

"We'll get to that. Paul's flown all the way to Shanghai to look you up. What's he asking for?"

"He wants to be in on something."

"To accrue in value while he's in jail?"

Kell shrugged, and Peter went on. "So that's the favor he's calling in: you put him in on something; he'll keep quiet in front of the grand jury."

The bull-like lawyer seemed to wince almost imperceptibly; then he sputtered out a warm but discomforting laugh. "You are a cold SOB when you get down to it, aren't you?"

"Well, am I right?"

"Maybe on some level there's a grain of truth, but it's not all like that."

"What part isn't like that?"

"Look . . ." Beneath his success, Kell had the underdog's comprehension of disappointment and failure. "Say you're Paul. You're a modest guy. You've spent your life as a midlevel trader, doing what they told you and filling in the blanks that you knew they wanted filled in. You don't get to take the corporate jet to the Caymans or the thousand-dollar lunch at Le Bernardin. You're an underling, even though nobody comes out and says it. But when the shit hits the fan, you go down like an underling, with the CEO throwing his hands in the air and saying, *Oh my, how did that happen?* You've got one of my colleagues billing you seven hundred dollars an hour, and if your savings hold out long enough, he'll get you a guilty plea and a suspended sentence. And that's your life: you thought you'd scrape together a cottage in the Hamptons, not too far from the water, where you and your wife could bicycle down and watch the sunset, and instead you've got no wife, no money, and no career, and the only sunset you're seeing is your own life going over the horizon."

At that moment Harrington felt his phone vibrating. He took it out and recognized the Long Island area code. It was Paul Gutterman. "You gave him my number?"

"You two are old friends, aren't you?"

The phone kept buzzing, each cycle a fresh accusation. Harrington was relieved when it went to voice mail. "So, what are you doing for him?"

"The Akron sewer system. I'm giving him a small piece as part of a Chinese name I'm incorporating. Technically, he should declare it, but it's very hard to find if he doesn't. He's a footnote to a footnote to an addendum. And besides, there's nothing illegal about it." Kell shrugged. "I feel sorry for the guy. He's lost everything." With that, the lawyer changed the subject. "So what about this Camille woman. Who is she?"

"She's my tutor."

"No shit! And she took you to bed on your first night out? That's a breach of protocol."

"I didn't say she took me to bed."

"Get off it, Peter. You were running after her like a puppy."

Harrington laughed, shaking his head.

"And Nadia's cool with this?"

"Well . . . I haven't really worked that part out yet."

Kell laughed. "This is going to be entertaining. What's she like?"

"Interesting. She lives in a garden."

"Like a gnome?"

"No, a real garden. One of those antique ones, with houses and ponds and miniature trees."

"How'd she swing that?"

"She's some kind of special tour guide. As I said, she's interesting. There was a party there with artists and art dealers. Actually, we did some Ecstasy. I haven't done that in about ten years."

"Ecstasy, eh? And she had it?"

Harrington nodded. "I'm not really sure what to make of her."

"Same as the rest: you're potential rich-husband material, and it's just a matter of how she plays you. They've all got their styles, and the most interesting ones give you the most interesting ride."

"Yes, I know: in your world every couple is really just a successful financial arrangement."

"C'mon, don't give me the chump act. You've got, what, eight hundred million in the bank? For her, you're like a giant gold ingot with arms, legs, and a dick sticking out of it."

Harrington was irritated to hear Kell dragging the magical experience of the other night down to his own level. "For a man who's so sentimental about his business relationships, you're pretty damned businesslike about sentimental ones."

Kell laughed and clapped him on the shoulder. "I'm just giving you a hard time, buddy. Have fun. Fall in love with the pretty Chinese girl. I'll be the best man at your wedding."

Harrington turned to him as an afterthought. "You know, I'd like to poke through the old Crossroads database. You've got the most recent one here at the office."

Kell instantly became curious. "What for?"

"Oh, I just wanted to check out a few investors, see how much they were in for when it blew up."

"We're not feeling remorseful, are we?"

"No. There's a couple of small investors—distant family, that sort of thing. I've been thinking about, you know, maybe make them whole again. I'm talking about a few hundred thousand dollars. It's not a lot of money, and it will get some of my relatives off my back."

The lawyer shrugged. "It's your money."

Kell led him into the spare office and logged him in to the database. "Go crazy on it. We've got to take off in twenty minutes."

It took him a couple of tries to find Pete Harrington. The singer had invested late in the game, after he himself had sold his share. It was under the name of Jason Kiriakis Financial Services, probably his financial advisor, and the buy-in had been nearly eight million dollars. Now worth about a twentieth of that.

So that's what it had been about: money. Somebody had given him shitty advice on how to make an easy buck in the bond markets, and he'd bet wrong. Same old hypocrite bullshit! They always wanted to make a killing, and when the game went against them, they wanted to dump the blame on someone else. He felt like telling him, *Hey, idiot, I wasn't even in Crossroads when it tanked! I had nothing to do with your financial problems!* Just like all the assholes in New York. Suddenly, *they* were victims, even though the real losers had been the bank, or the pension fund, or the client, or the government, while they themselves got out with their fortunes intact, thank you. Middle-aged crybabies in Brooks Brothers diapers, tattling to the press. He would get to the bottom of this, very quietly and very privately, with no whining, and he'd deal with it.

Kell knocked on the door; then cracked it open. "It's time."

The restaurant had given them a woody, rice-screened private room and seated the head of the Red Dragon group facing the door, in the position of honor. The two men from Shenzhen spoke perfect English. They were worldly Hong Kong capitalists who had raised office buildings all over China and were looking to diversify their holdings. Mr. Wu and Mr. Lam. Harrington saw a look pass between two of the men when he came into the room. He'd seen it before. Yes, he was *that* Peter Harrington.

They began with the usual talk. One of the Hong Kong men had graduated from Oxford and the London School of Economics. The other was trained as a civil engineer and went back and forth between Hong Kong and Mumbai consulting on infrastructure projects. Both had spent lots of time in the United States and professed their admiration for the country and its people. "So we feel this project might be a good fit for us."

Kell warmed to this. "Your expertise in infrastructure would be a great asset."

The Chinese men had sat at tables like this from Hamburg to Dubai, but for all their poise, they seemed strangely ill at ease with him, preferring to direct their questions about regulatory law and utility rates to Kell. When Harrington said something, they would look at him uncomfortably and then quickly shift their attention back to his partner. Maybe it was his own paranoia, but they seemed to be staring at his broken nose. The meeting was floundering: it was polite enough, with all the questions and answers indicative of an incipient partnership, but the real reason for the lunch was to forge the personal bond necessary to business in China, and in that respect it was going badly.

The food came, and the conversation turned to family and hobbies as they began to eat. Mr. Lam, it turned out, played badminton. He'd even competed in the Olympics.

"I'm impressed!" Kell said.

"But that was more than thirty years ago," Lam returned modestly. "Now my son beats me!" He motioned to his partner. "Mr. Wu likes to ski. He is a fanatic."

Harrington sensed an opening at last. "I live for skiing! A few years ago, I took the entire winter off and skied at Aspen every day. I got in a hundred twenty-six days!"

Wu smiled broadly. "I am jealous! In my best winter I only skied fifty-four days!"

"Really! Where?"

They began to compare resorts. Mr. Wu had skied in Switzerland and the French Alps, also in Harbin, though he made a face in answer to Harrington's query about the Chinese areas. They both liked Gstaad. Harrington talked about the resorts in Utah and Colorado and the quality of the snow.

"I would love to ski in America," the Hong Kong man said eagerly.

"Did you ever do any backcountry skiing?"

Mr. Wu made a face. "I'm too old to go walking up a mountain! That's for young people, like you! But isn't it dangerous? With avalanches?"

"No!" Harrington overplayed his expertise a bit. He'd only gone backcountry skiing three times. "If you're careful, you've got an excellent chance of *not* dying in an avalanche."

Kell piped up. "The only thing dangerous for him is squash."

Mr. Wu didn't understand.

Harrington was surprised his partner had gone there, but he had no choice but to follow his lead. "This bruise," he said, pointing at his nose, smiling. The lie felt almost completely natural, and he was relieved to be able to get the whole matter of his swollen face behind him. "I was playing squash and my opponent accidentally hit me in the face on his backswing."

The effect of the anecdote was immediate. The two Hong Kong men visibly stiffened. Mr. Wu smiled uncomfortably. "Yes," he said, "that is un-fortunate."

Harrington flailed at it, knowing somehow that he was making a mis-take even as the words left his mouth. "It's embarrassing, because people always assume it's something far more interesting than that."

Wu gave him a strange, bulging-eyed nod, as if he were holding his breath, and both Chinese men turned to eating again, throwing the table into a paralyzed silence. With Kell's help, the conversation resumed, though in a stilted and slightly formal way. The lunch dragged on awkwardly for another twenty minutes. Then the two Chinese men excused themselves with a promise to do more analysis on the venture. Kell watched them go, then turned back to his partner. "What the hell happened there?"

"You had to bring up my nose! Just for laughs!"

"You don't think they were wondering? They were looking at you cross-eyed from the second they walked in. What the hell's going on?"

"I told you I did *not* want to come to this—"

"*That's not your choice!* You're goddamned Peter Harrington, the big, bad, famous wolf! They want to look you in the eye and know they're part of your pack and not one of the sheep!"

"Maybe I'm tired of being Peter Harrington! Did you ever think of that?"

Kell regarded him silently for a moment. "Is there something I need to know, Peter?"

"Yes! Know that I'm not coming to any more meetings this week!" Harrington stood up. "Next week, I'm available for whatever dog-and-pony show you want to stage."

As he crawled through traffic back to his house, he wondered if the Hong Kong men had known all along. It almost seemed that way. That would explain their reaction when he'd told them the squash story. No one wanted to invest two hundred million dollars with someone who lied to them in the first hour of their acquaintance. But how would they have found out? Even if someone had posted cell-phone videos of an assault on the street, how would they have known who he was and gotten word to the two men so quickly? He was seized by the nonsensical notion that somehow Gutterman had seen it, and with that he imagined something even more horrible: that Conrad, his son, would see it, too. Good God!

When he got back to his house, he frantically searched himself on the Internet. It was the usual stuff, with his own name and the musician's battling for the top rankings. Just like always. He felt a lessening of the panic that had been stealing up on him, and the reprieve spurred him to write an e-mail to Conrad. He tried to write his son every couple of weeks, but within a few sentences his efforts always ended up the same way: if he told about his life in Shanghai, it would remind his son that he'd abandoned him. If he asked about school, it would come off as an accusation. He didn't dare ask Conrad about his health or invite him to come visit. In the end, all he had was another stilted, unsent draft, saved along with a half dozen just like it.

The call came from Kell the next morning. He was surprised at Kell's tone: dry and demanding. "I think you'd better come down here."

"What's up?"

"I think you know what's up."

He responded in kind. "Actually, I don't. Why don't you tell me?"

"This is a face-to-face-type conversation. Just meet me here at the office."

"I have an appointment with my trainer at nine."

Kell sounded urgent, almost angry. "Cancel it!"

He showered and shaved. The swelling was almost completely gone now: there was only a slight puffiness and a shadow under both his eyes. At least that part of the experience was behind him. Yes, he'd been attacked, and he'd been shaken up by it, but he hadn't been seriously hurt, and it really hadn't changed anything. He'd rather just forget about it.

He wondered if the meeting had to do with Gutterman. Gutterman must have asked for more, or wanted some other sort of perk to buy his silence. Or maybe the investigators had already uncovered the link between Gutterman and Kell, and he was trying to figure out how to respond.

The traffic was parked, so Ma dropped him off at the station and he battled through the morning crowds, cheerful that his face was healing. Maybe he'd get together with Camille.

Kell greeted him soberly and asked his secretary to hold his calls.

"So," Kell began when they were alone. He didn't even give Harrington a chance to take a seat. "I think I figured out the problem with Red Dragon yesterday. Sit down and watch this."

The conference room had a large flat-screen monitor that was connected to Kell's desk computer. They used it for making presentations. Harrington sat down as the screen came alive with the operating system, to be immediately replaced by a Chinese Web site with a video embedded within. He recognized the architecture as that of the Bund. In the center of the picture was a man in a leather jacket with long blond hair, viewed from the rear. He started to get a sick feeling. Kell set it in motion.

The man was walking along the Bund, with the camera slightly behind him and then moving up to the side. It was definitely Pete Harrington, striding along and staring straight ahead with a purposeful air. If he'd suddenly turned to the camera and started singing, it could have been a music video from fifteen years ago. The cameraman said words that sounded like "Pete Harrington" in a slurred English, then muttered something in Chinese. A platoon of Chinese ideograms appeared at the bottom of the photo, then faded out.

Kell translated: "That says, 'American musician Pete Harrington.'" The financier started to speak, but Kell raised his hand. "Keep watching. It gets better."

He knew what he was going to see. The rock star walked on as the camera's point of view slipped up in front of him, then to his side again, then behind him, filming all the while. The musician seemed to spot something, and his step wavered; then he stopped for a few seconds before continuing on at a slightly slower pace. Now a little knot of three men became visible in patches between other pedestrians. A second crowd of Chinese characters appeared on the screen, and they too disappeared.

"That said, " 'American financial boss Peter Harrington.' " To his horror, he saw himself fill the frame, looking at Harrington joyfully, extending his hand, saying, audibly, "I know who you are! I really like your music!"

Harrington felt shame at the words, that Gutterman had been proved right about his Pete Harrington obsession, but he couldn't look away. Just as he'd remembered it, the musician growled, "Yeah, well . . . You're a fucking dirtbag!" More characters appeared on the screen, translating the dialogue.

The next part was excruciating. His attacker stepped forward and hit him with a blow that was industrial in its directness and efficiency. Even on the video, with the traffic noise and the voices all around, he thought he could hear the impact, like a wet slapping sound. His head rocked back, and he took several drunken steps to his rear before sitting down heavily on the sidewalk, clutching his nose. Harrington was kicking him. There were the fragments of Ernie and Mr. Ma's legs in the left side of the frame, and then his attacker was walking away, with one last pan toward where he lay on his back, rolling to his side and sitting up as blood poured from his nose. And then Pete Harrington's back, disappearing into the crowd.

One last Chinese ideogram filled the screen as it faded to black, and Kell's voice was flat as he translated it: "Justice."

Harrington sat there without speaking, overcome with self-revulsion. Kell picked up the silence.

"I put in a call to Guardian Services this morning. They're the people in Palo Alto who do our online reputation management. I asked them to see if something was out there, and they picked this up in a search of your name in Chinese. It was posted on a Chinese Web site, and on that site it's only searchable in pinyin, which is how I imagine our friends from Red Dragon found it. There's another one out there, too, from a different angle. Do you want to see it?"

Harrington didn't answer, and Kell went on, his voice iced with a disagreeable irony. "So you can imagine why our guests yesterday were feeling just a wee bit ill at ease, and why they found your story about the squash accident so very, very reassuring."

Harrington said in a low voice, "I told you I didn't want to go to that meeting!"

"You told me shit!" his partner shot back. "How could you blindside me with this? I'm your partner! And I'm supposed to be your friend!"

"I'm sorry! It was embarrassing."

"You're goddamned right it was embarrassing! Four of us sitting at a table, and I'm the only one who has no idea that you've just gotten your ass kicked by a washed-up rock star! What does that say about us?"

"Oh. I see: you're the real victim here."

"I *am* a victim here! Couldn't you at least have thrown up a block or tried to hit him back? You look like a complete jackass!" Kell caught himself, bowed his head with closed eyes. "I'm sorry," he said, opening them. "That was out of line. Goddamned Gutterman is driving me crazy. You're the victim, and you were embarrassed, and you figured it would all blow over in a couple of days. I get that. It's everything else I don't get. First of all, why him?"

"He was holding eight million dollars in Crossroads when it collapsed. I think he decided to get revenge."

"Revenge? Are you kidding me? How did he find you?"

"I don't know. I thought I was keeping a low profile, but obviously I can be found."

"So this was premeditated."

"I have no idea. From that video it looked like he spotted me on the street and went straight for me."

"I don't buy that. Who's the old guy standing next to you at the beginning?"

"Ernie? I met him at the Bar Rouge, remember? I invited him to lunch."

"Maybe he's the one who set you up."

"No. Ernie tried to stop him, but his ankle gave out and he got in Ma's way."

"So he tried to stop him, but the only guy he stopped was your bodyguard."

"Come on: he's an old man!"

"What's he to you? Why'd you ask him to lunch?"

"Because he's interesting! Okay? He was in the OSS in the Second World War, and he was in Shanghai from 1946 to '49. He has a lot of stories to tell, and I wanted to hear those stories. Is that wrong? Does everything have to be about money or available women?"

"You're implying that all I care about is money and women?"

"Have we talked about anything else in the last three months?"

The lawyer nodded his head evenly. "Fair enough."

"I'm definitely suing."

Kell answered calmly but decisively. "No. You won't."

"Why not?"

"You have no venue. The Chinese legal system will have zero interest in trying to extradite a foreign national from the United States for a fistfight, and any economic damage you suffer would be either in China or in the Caymans, where Metropolitan Partners is incorporated. There's no venue."

"What about as a human rights violation? People sue in U.S. courts for that, don't they?"

"Peter Harrington, multimillionaire, suing for a human rights violation? You really want to whack that tar baby? This video's already got six thousand views in China. It'll go to six million the day after you file suit. Metropolitan Partners doesn't need that kind of publicity."

"Can't Guardian do something about it?"

"I asked them that. They can keep it off YouTube—that's easy—but there's a million smaller sites out there with lower standards. There's no copyright violation here. You could try some sort of legal full-court press and harass anyone who posts it, but that's playing Whac-a-Mole. If you're not a major movie studio, that's going to get tiring. Another strategy is to try to bury the links, but that takes time, and if it goes too big, you can't control it. I set up an eleven o'clock conference with Guardian so you can get it straight from them." Kell hesitated and seemed about to broach a new topic, but stopped himself. "Let's just see where it goes. We'll see what Guardian can do. Maybe the whole thing will die down."

The next day, it went viral.

4

Market Forces

‡

For Peter Harrington, watching the transformation of the video from an isolated Chinese blog into a worldwide cage match was deeply disheartening. In three days, his beating had been scattered like stars across the online universe. The posts had titles like "The Most Satisfying Video on the Net" and "Pete Harrington, You're My Hero!" In weak moments, he would make the mistake of reading the commentary. "Did u see luk on b1tch's face! Loco good!!!" or "Kick him again, Pete! He's still moving!" There'd been an outpouring of hatred a year ago when the news of the fund's demise had first come out, but he'd developed a thick layer of cynicism about the complainers, had even come to revel in his bad-guy image. Now, though, it was infinitely more personal. The comments were uglier, more visceral, coming not from financial professionals sniffing about their losses or leftists weeping about the cruel world, but rather from a howling mob of commoners, who cheered against him in the online arena in which the rock star defeated him again and again and again. Harrington saw his own astonished delight as the singer came into view, then the confusion, the pain, the blood pouring from his nose, the cowering as he lay on the ground, the look of defeat. He'd been called many things in the wake of the Crossroads collapse, most of them ugly, but he'd never been called "loser."

He'd hired private investigators to look into the attack, and their report had added an even deeper strata of humiliation to the event. The people from Kroll International had come over the day after the incident, while his nose was still swollen: a Chinese man and an American, both in their forties. He admired their ability to show absolutely no reaction to his puffy features. The American asked most of the questions with a cordial and vaguely sympathetic manner. He asked about Ma and about the security regimen he followed and arranged to interview Ma in private. He asked about Ernie and the events leading up to the assault. He kept returning to the subject of Ernie.

"Did you ever see a passport or credit card with his name on it?"

Harrington felt stupid. "No."

"Could he have been in his seventies? Maybe an old-looking sixty-eight or sixty-nine? Because . . . you said he took down your bodyguard."

"I said he *fell into* my bodyguard. I didn't say he took him down."

The two men looked at each other; then the American one continued. "Give us a few days, Mr. Harrington."

They were at his house again in twenty-four hours. The rock star had been easy to trace. He had entered the country two days before the attack and left two hours afterward. They still weren't sure who Ernie was, other than a few references on the Internet and the address in Iowa. "However, we reached the family of the Ernie Sivertsen shown in that old Merrill's Marauders unit photo. He died in 2002."

The financier nodded, feeling a tremor of dread.

"We were able to pull the passenger list of Pete Harrington's flight to China, and there is one passenger on the plane that interested us. His name is Charles Pico. He fits the age range: he's eighty-six. He has a Service record, but he was honorably discharged in 1945 and we don't have anything on him after that. We asked around. There was a Charlie Pico who has an extensive background in security, and evidently did quite a bit of contract work for the CIA over the years, although we're still trying to confirm that.

His last known address was in Los Angeles. But the friend I talked to thought he was dead." He reached into a folder and pulled out a black-and-white photo. "Do any of these faces look familiar?"

In the antiquated-looking image, five men lounged in front of a wall of high leafy stalks. Sugarcane. Three of the men had dark hair and beards and were in military fatigues. One of the other men had a handsome face that was vaguely familiar. The fifth was Ernie, with dark hair that needed cutting and a pistol strapped to his hip. He wore a loose white shirt and khaki pants tucked into boots. He was no longer hunched or foggy-eyed. He looked fiercely alive, and he was smiling.

"Well, gentleman . . ." Harrington finally said, "you can tell your friend that Charlie Pico's not dead. Who are these other people?"

The Kroll operative leaned forward and slowly indicated each one with his finger: "This is Raúl Castro . . . This is Che Guevara . . . And this is Errol Flynn. It was taken in Cuba about 1958. Evidently the CIA was secretly running guns to Castro, and Mr. Pico was part of the operation."

In the silence that followed Harrington felt himself sinking into an even deeper sense of despair. Charlie Pico, he realized, was real. He truly was the living legend, a man he would have wanted to befriend and whose admiration he would have liked to have. Instead, Charlie Pico had viewed him as just another despicable mark.

He said softly, "So you think they were working together."

"This is what we think happened: Pete Harrington hired Charles Pico to help him set you up. Pico approached you the night before, played on your goodwill, and then told your attacker where you would be the next day. Then he disabled your bodyguard so that your assailant could get a clear shot at you and escape, though in those cases the bodyguard usually stays with the client in case of a second attacker. That's something a man of his experience would have known."

Harrington nodded, feeling sick.

The Kroll men went on. "The next thing we looked at is the video, which corroborates our theory to some degree. There was one principal video, the one with the Chinese subtitles, and that was actually edited from two videos taken from two different angles, which we'll call Video A and Video B. These are the three most prominent videos. They're unusually high-resolution for cell phone videos, though it's entirely possible they were taken by passersby that happened to recognize Pete Harrington. He does have some notoriety here in China, so it's not implausible. How they identified you is another question, because your face isn't immediately recognizable, at least in China. What's also interesting is that neither video shows the old man. You could almost think that the people shooting it intentionally kept him out of the frame. In the three other videos that have surfaced, the quality is much lower and you see more of Charlie Pico and the bodyguard."

"Okay."

"So then we ask who took them, who posted them, and how they spread. We couldn't really answer those questions. This isn't a criminal investigation, and without cooperation from the Chinese justice system, we can't access the metadata we need to determine those things. There was an aggressive linking effort in the first few days that we tracked, but it's a pretty sensational topic involving two well-known people, so it's not surprising that it spread quickly. There are no repeats of user names on different sites or user accounts that were set up an hour before the post. Those are the kinds of things that indicate an organized campaign. This appears to be a spontaneous event." The agent shrugged apologetically, but Peter imagined he saw a trace of a smirk slither across his features. "People are interested in you, Mr. Harrington."

The Kroll briefing, coming on the heels of the humiliating business meetings with Kell and Shenzhen Red Dragon, sent Peter Harrington into a deep depression. He muddled around his house, too depressed to face Camille, until, like a bubble rising from the depths, in the space of a few hours, his depression swelled into outrage. Did Pete Harrington think some legal loophole would protect him? That he could hit him and just walk away? Within twelve hours of the second meeting with Kroll, Peter Harrington was staring at the vice president of Guardian Services blown up to life-size on his flat-screen TV. He looked like he was about twenty-five years old. They'd moved fast: Harrington was an A-list client with a lot of money to spend, and he was angry.

Guardian had already developed a two-pronged strategy, the man said. Part of it was defensive: burying the links. They would help Harrington set up a scholarship fund: something on the order of about ten million dollars would be enough to get traction. They'd create a Web site and staff the foundation with a few employees who would set about giving away scholarships and grants to the needy. This would be touted across the Web in a dense thicket of Internet links and announcements. They'd work with a press agent to get media coverage. It wouldn't make the bad links disappear, but they would counterweight them with pictures of happy kids with schoolbooks. Or they could set up an environmental fund: it didn't matter which. Meanwhile, they would go after Pete Harrington's reputation with an ice pick. "He's definitely got a history," the Guardian man said. "Paternity suits, assault charges, critics trashing his music. And that's just a ten-minute Internet search. We'll paint a picture of a washed-up rock star who assaults you in a desperate, pathetic attempt to get people to pay attention to him. We'll hit Pete Harrington with that truth from a thousand directions, and we'll hit him over and over and over. Roboposts on message boards, blog commentary, press releases, a social-media campaign. We will make him cringe every time he turns on his computer. I guarantee you: he will come out of this looking like a loser. We can put five people on it, starting whenever you say the word."

Revenge was a petty motivation, but in the absence of anything more noble, it lifted his spirits. He was Peter Harrington, the man who had amassed hundreds of millions of dollars in five short years. Dispensing with a has-been like Pete Harrington would be nothing for him. Aside from his own feelings, though, Peter Harrington found he had a bigger problem with the video: it made the world remember who he was. Within a week of the attack, the whole universe seemed to know that he lived in Shanghai and was partners with Kell McPherson in a business dedicated to privatizing American public infrastructure and putting it into the hands of Chinese investors. The hate mail began to flood in. The volume became so large that Kell had to hire Guardian to screen the messages, and now, when a search was done on Metropolitan Partners, it immediately turned up page after page of scorching hate posts and videos of Peter Harrington being knocked to the ground. Even some of the financial papers discovered a sense of irony, reporting on the attempt to buy up assets by some of the same people that had helped crash the economy in the first place. In America, a public television network was putting together a sensationalized "exposé" about their attempts to acquire the Akron sewer system and the Pennsylvania Turnpike with the working title "Return of the Predators."

A week after the video first surfaced, Kell called him into the Metropolitan office. The day had already had a brittle start. At ten that morning Nadia had announced from Beijing that she didn't want to see him anymore. The call had been expected, and he cut her off as she began her scripted explanation. "Let me know when you get back to Shanghai," he'd said brightly. "I'll send your things over to your apartment." He didn't really care: the night with Camille had brought home to him the emptiness of the relationship. Kell hadn't asked him to attend any more business meetings since the debacle with Shenzhen Red Dragon, and he hadn't seen his partner in several days, ample time to regret not being more honest with him. They shook hands, and Kell complimented him on the fact that his nose was back to normal, asked in a joking way how the Camille-Nadia balancing act was going. He received the answer with a philosophical toss of his shoulders. "Camille seems more interesting, anyway. And she can order for you at restaurants."

"Thanks for your support. What are we doing here?"

"Yeah." The lawyer glanced at the carpet, then up again. "Peter, how badly do you need this?"

"What are you referring to?"

"Metropolitan Partners, the venture—the whole plan for monetizing infrastructure."

"Is there an issue?"

Kell seemed uncomfortable. "To be honest . . . lately, there has been something of an issue—"

"You mean you want me out?"

His partner smiled at him. "That's one thing I've always admired about you: you cut through the bullshit. The answer is: No. *I* don't want you out. But, unfortunately, other people do." He went down the list of limited partners who had either dropped out or were beginning to reconsider. "I talked to David Lau about this for three hours, and you've got to understand: this is coming from him, not from me. This video that's out there: it's a problem. Not to rub salt in the wound, but you lost face. In China, that's a big deal. Bigger than just money. Not only that, it makes Crossroads controversial again. Not that it wasn't a very successful fund in its time, but there's a sense that it damaged people and that you're responsible—"

"But I'm not responsible."

"Yeah, I know: it was market forces. Who could foresee that those mortgages would collapse? Besides us, of course. Which is why we shorted the hell out of it!" He laughed.

"Everybody hedges!"

"Peter!" He motioned toward his own pinstripe-suited body, smiling. "You're talking to your partner here, not the SEC. I remember those conversations. We both knew the backing on those bonds was shaky and that a certain percentage of them were going to fail."

"We knew there was *risk*—"

"No, Peter: we knew they would fail. You knew it better than anyone, because you put them together. That's why you sold out, and that's why we shorted them. Period. Don't get me wrong! It was a brilliant play!"

"But that brilliance is no longer a selling point for Metropolitan Partners."

Kell lost his levity. "Right now, you're poison. It's all out there in everybody's face, and the only way we can save this project is by reincorporating under a new name that doesn't have yours attached to it. I have to be able to go to the remaining limited partners and tell them you're no longer an active partner with the company. Which is not to say that in a year, when you've cooled off a little, you couldn't quietly get back in."

"Great! Maybe Paul Gutterman and I could be footnotes on the same project."

"You've got a talent for putting things in the most negative way possible, you know that?" He added, more softly, "Actually, I thought about it, and you ought to consider incorporating something with Paul. I could help you, and that would solve a couple of problems at once."

"Christ! Did you really just say that?" The lawyer didn't answer. "So let me get this straight: it's not really about Crossroads, because that information was already out there. It's not that I allegedly conned investors for hundreds of millions of dollars. It's because I was ambushed by a has-been rock star. Because I lost face."

Kell answered evenly. "This is Asia. Face is very important."

"So if I'd blocked his punch, or hit him back, or if Ma had stopped him, none of this would be happening!"

Kell thought about it, then raised his eyebrows. "Probably not." He shrugged. "If you'd decked him, the phone would be ringing off the hook."

"This is fucking unbelievable!" Unbelievable though it might be, he knew that Kell's points were indisputable. Harrington stood up and went over to the window to look out onto the Shanghai skyline across the river from them. The Metropolitan office was an expensive one, and it afforded an excellent view of the Bund. He could see perfectly the spot where Pete Harrington had accosted him. "How badly do I need this?" He let loose a long stream of tired air. "Not badly. Not at all, really. It's not like I need more money. I was doing this because, well . . ." He turned to his partner. "Why the hell was I doing this?"

They looked at each other.

Kell finally said, "If you can't answer that question, maybe you should be doing something else." Harrington didn't answer, so his friend continued. "C'mon! You never had your heart in this! You were going through the motions. Why don't you just relax until this is all sorted out. I'll sell the investors. We'll discreetly work you back in down the line. You can concentrate on Camille. Take her to Europe or something!"

"I thought you said Camille was a gold digger."

"What do I know? I've been married three times in fifteen years! You want to take relationship advice from me? Here's my advice: follow your heart."

"As long as I follow it somewhere far away, right?"

"Buddy! It's not happening as long as you're on the prospectus! Let me carry things forward and you can jump back in when all this dies down. I promise you. And remember what I said about Paul."

Harrington stopped and became silent for ten seconds. He was thinking of the mocking, desperate Paul Gutterman, the loser: his prospective partner. An ugly possibility stretched across his thoughts: maybe Paul Gutterman had been his other life all along. "You know what, Kell? Just cash me out for my part of the capitalization. I'm out. Completely."

Kell opened his mouth. "Peter . . . That's forty million dollars. Don't you want—"

"Just do it, Kell!"

"Okay!"

There was an uncomfortable moment. Kell's voice changed to one without bombast or guile. "I'm really sorry about this, Peter."

He looked at the man he'd considered one of his closest friends for the last five years. "I know, Kell. You're as sorry as you ever can be."

"Look at the big picture: you've had a pretty impressive run. Eight hundred million dollars. When it's all said and done, you crushed it."

"Yes, Kell." He walked over to the desk and picked up his leather portfolio. "Except it's not all said and done."

He stepped out into the waiting room and came up short. Sitting on the couch was Gutterman, his jacket slung over his arm and a look of surprise on his face. He came to his feet as his face took on a foxy grin. "It's the rock star!"

Harrington knew immediately that Gutterman had seen the video. "Hello, Paul," he said stiffly, and he stepped around him.

"Peter!"

He turned to face him and saw Gutterman's expression widen into a smile of complete triumph. "Next time you make a movie, hire a stunt double. I mean, a man with your money . . ."

"Did you spend a long time thinking that up, Paul? I can't wait to see what you'll come up with after a couple of years in a jail cell."

Gutterman seemed to collapse slightly, and then a raw, painful anger burst forth across his features. "You got just what you deserved!" he hissed. "The whole world's going to laugh at you. Especially your wife and son! Who you *abandoned*!"

The curse fell over Harrington with a force more devastating than Pete Harrington's blow to his face, and he felt himself flushing. He stood dumbly trying to mount some reply, knowing that he had none and that everything Paul Gutterman had said from the moment he came to Shanghai was true. After years of rivalry and without even trying, Gutterman had finally vanquished him.

5

The Dream of the Red Chamber

⁜

Mei Lin loved the garden. Even coming in late at night, alone, with little animals rustling in the shrubs and tiny bamboo groves, when other people might fear ghosts as they walked past the antique furniture and the narrow pitch-black hallways, she felt that she was in her home. She had been living here nearly three years, since Mr. Xin, at the Ministry of Culture, had seen fit to give her the caretaker's job. Before her there had been an old woman, an elderly aunt of the previous Minister of Culture in Shanghai, who had persisted into Mr. Xin's term. Then inquiries were made, and the old woman was given twenty thousand yuan and a train ticket back to Wuxi, where she would live with her sister. No one was entitled to swim in the dream life forever. Even her own stay here was only temporary. One day someone else's niece or mistress or brother-in-law would be living in this cloud of branches and stones and white plaster. That was how things were down here in the Red Dust.

There were several real caretakers, of course—some carpenters and two old gardeners—but they came in the morning and left in the evening. Some-times she joined them for tea in one of the empty old family buildings, where they had set up a hot-water maker and a wooden table. If they had any suspicions about how she had gotten her place there, they didn't voice them, and she didn't care anyway. For now, it felt as if she'd always been here. That was how things were in the Red Dust, too.

She picked up her *pipa* and began to strum it. She was to play music that afternoon. A trade delegation from Europe was coming for a private banquet, and she was to entertain them with traditional music and show them the garden. She was expected to eat with them afterward, though they were usually boring, asking her the same questions every time. They were typically politicians or bureaucrats who had managed to get themselves a trip to Shanghai at the expense of their citizens. So tonight she would play and join them for twenty minutes and then leave.

Her little pink phone chirped with Peter Harrington's ringtone, and she decided to answer it. After their night out, he had canceled his next two lessons, and she hadn't seen him in nearly a week. He had said that he'd had an accident playing squash and wanted to recuperate.

"Hello, Camille. It's Peter."

"Peter! How good to hear your voice. How is your injury?"

"Oh! Much better, thanks."

"So we will have our usual lesson on Friday?"

"That would be great. I . . . I wanted to thank you for bringing me to that party, and the garden, and . . . everything else."

"It's my pleasure, Peter."

"I've been, *um,* trying to process everything."

"Process what?"

He sounded discouraged. "Well, you know. The other night."

She smiled into the phone but didn't answer. To process things, he had said. It was a bit funny. He really meant, to decide if he might change women—perhaps break with the lovely Nadia. That was what processing was to him. For her, no processing was necessary. Maybe she would only be his tutor. Maybe they would get married. She had no plan.

Now he sounded uncertain. "Yes, so, we're on for Friday. Great. Actually, though, I wondered if you might have some time tonight. There's some things on my mind, and I thought you would be a good person to talk to."

She knew that he had reason to sound as he did. A few days after he'd canceled because of his "squash accident," her friend Wen, who owned the Phoenix Gallery, had called her about the video and sent her a link. It had been shocking. Peter had seemed so innocent when the man walked up to him. And then, on the ground, he had looked so hurt and childish. So defeated. She felt sorry for him. Within a few days, there were already several blogs up explaining the situation. None of them were kind to Peter Harrington.

So perhaps she should be kind. "I have an idea, Peter. I want to take you someplace. A surprising place. Would that be acceptable?"

She could feel his relief through her telephone. "That would be wonderful!" He sounded so grateful.

She texted him her address, then slipped the phone back into her purse. She liked Peter Harrington. He wasn't crude, like some of the businessmen she knew, or like his friend Kell. He was not one of those who had settled into a deep, boring sense of satisfaction with themselves and the world as they had made it. She had seen so many of those, especially Chinese men, who assumed that they could buy her for the price of a flat and expensive perfumes and that she was desperate to marry a rich man, even if he were much older than her and not handsome. With one look, they thought they knew her family and her prospects. They measured her, and she laughed at them.

The funny thing about the businessmen was that they all imagined themselves as heroes. All of their exploits and their great accomplishments, and what did they really achieve? Han Shan, the poet of Cold Mountain, would have made jokes about them. He would have found Peter Harrington silly, not admirable. Han Shan had lived penniless in the mountains, sleeping on the bare floors of caves, eating roots and wild greens or a bit of rice he bought with whatever coins he could beg. The clouds were his pillow; the earth was his bed. He scrawled poems on doorways and rock faces without ever signing his name, and a thousand years later people were still reading them. He lay in the Red Dust and dreamed in heaven, but he knew that heaven wasn't something he could ever make.

Her phone rang again, and this time it was the Dutch businessman that she taught Monday, Wednesday, and Friday. He worked for an electronics company, a very tall and bulky man with glasses, nondescript, as if he'd been stamped out on an assembly line in Changzhou. A nice man, but she had to be careful not to encourage him. He had divorced his wife, and he could only too easily imagine that the young Chinese woman would simply love to return to Holland with him. Though he would probably buy a painting. She would take him to the galleries at Moganshan 50, show him the work of Xu Ruoshi and others. Make her commission. She put the phone back in her bag, and it went silent.

She sat back against the lattice railing along the pond as she brushed the strings of the *pipa*. There was a passage in a new song she was learning, a part where the instrument went silent and she had to continue telling the story in a high falsetto voice that rose and dipped like a swallow. *In the high mountains, the winter snows fall without end. Falling, falling, in the pass that has no name. The memory of my youthful love. Without a name.*

One of the old gardeners had been waiting just out of reach for her to finish and now came scuffling along the path with a rake and a hooked knife. "Better without a name, Miss Mei! Then your husband cannot get jealous later!" She chided him on his grandfatherly advice and told him that the goldfish were complaining because they hadn't been fed.

Actually, Peter Harrington would be a good choice. She liked him. He was kind, and very clever, for a foreigner, with that clumsy way they had of being clever. She could love him, in a practical way. Enough to say, *You are my husband, and we are on this journey together.*

Of course, he would tire of Shanghai one day and want to return to the United States. Or maybe they would live in Europe and go skiing in the Alps. They would have a big house, and he would want her to have babies. Little Chinese babies with American eyes, or little American babies with Chinese eyes. In five years he would be bald on the top of his head, and he would probably be plump. If she married Peter, it would be like that: steady, easy, with everything in reach.

She could not be too familiar with him yet; men like Peter needed to win prizes. But she had enjoyed astonishing him. She could practically feel his heart beating when they had stood in the cave. She had made him understand that in the garden, everything was a metaphor. The cave was actually the deepest darkness; the bamboo grove was really a grove in your imagination. Everything contained another secret waiting to be unlocked, because when you were standing in a little courtyard, it was also a clearing in a forest, and a place in an ancient folktale, and the moment when a Qing official had hugged his daughter two hundred years ago, and a colored bead on the string of one's own unlikely life. You yourself were just floating through those worlds, completely free, as you always were but so often forgot. And that was far more important than winning a prize. It was the prize that one received without winning.

She had known this about gardens from a very young age. She'd grown up in a cold, dark flat in Suzhou, a city famous for its ancient gardens. Her father made costumes for the Chinese opera. Her mother played *Pingtan,* the traditional folk music of the area, and performed several times each week in teahouses or hotels, dressed in ancient-style robes. She often played in the gardens, her hair swept up onto combs in the manner of the Song Dynasty or the Ming. She was so elegant, and the clusters of tourists from Taiwan or Hong Kong seemed so ordinary. Mei Lin would go and watch from the back as her mother strummed the *pipa,* and then she would go and explore the garden and sneak into the empty houses, imagining the lives that had transpired there, filling in the details with passages that her mother had read to her from *The Dream of the Red Chamber.* She could almost see the servants and the in-laws, the spoiled children and the domineering grandmother who stealthily destroyed so many of the lives around her. When she played the few songs her mother had taught her, sitting on a balustrade beside the black-green pool of fish, she felt, even then, that she wasn't simply herself, but different shades of many people: a maid pining for her missing love, a loyal wife, a courtesan. She was all of those things.

She felt as if she lived her entire childhood in those gardens, the Humble Administrator's Garden, the Master of the Nets Garden, the Lion Grove Garden, the Garden of Lingering. As enchanting as the gardens were, though, the idea of Shanghai came into her life with an allure that was more immediate and noisy than the softly echoing *pipa* of the past. Suzhou had a reputation from ancient times for tall, pretty women, but as she got older, those far-off women that her mother personified seemed bland compared with the girls from Shanghai who made school trips to the gardens. No lingering of Song *dai* tradition about them. They wore their hair in waves and streaks, in unusual colors or even bright blond, instead of the long, straight black hair of the Suzhou girls. Their clothes were more daring, too. Even the way they talked, with that hissing *s* of the Shanghai dialect, slightly snakelike and jaded, had impressed her. From a young age, she'd known that there was something in Shanghai, something she couldn't quite imagine, that cast its dark luster onto all Shanghai's inhabitants, and she wanted to get close and bask in its wicked light.

When she turned twelve she asked her father if she could study in an English institute. There were all manner of English institutes in Suzhou: the nicer ones for the more privileged children, with their videos and their computers and their young foreign students in blue jeans who didn't speak Chinese, all the way down to the rough ones in the townships that the children of peasants and factory workers attended, with just a few posters on a bare plaster wall and a teacher who barely seemed to know English herself. She'd gone to a cheap one: they had five computers, but no glamorous Americans or Australians on the staff. She hadn't hidden her disappointment from her parents: surely an institute should have at least one foreigner! Her mother had seemed ashamed for some reason, and her father had just said woodenly, *That is your school.* Her grandmother had been the only one to react: *You silly girl! Do you think your father has money to spend on your selfishness? With your mother needing all those medicines!* She still felt sorrow when she remembered it. She hadn't even known her mother was sick.

At the institute, though, life was magnificent. She had a talent for language, and within a year she had won a scholarship to one of the best institutes in Suzhou. The New York Language Institute had a nice waiting room, with couches and a hot-water dispenser. It prided itself on being the most current institute, claiming to educate its pupils in culture as well as language. At this school, every class was taught by a foreigner, usually an American or Canadian of about twenty-five years who seemed to have, by Chinese standards, very little direction in their lives. If they were Chinese, they would be regarded as drifters, incipient failures, but as foreigners they still seemed high-class, and a good deal less ugly than when she was a young girl. Everyone knew that at any time they could go back to their countries and easily become rich. Some of the older students flirted with them, and more, because they knew that if one managed to strike up a relationship, to even get married, then they, too, could go away to the easy life, and make money, and come and go to China and the rest of the world as they pleased. The families of those girls were lucky, as the good fortune of America nearly always washed all who were around them.

She decided to try one out when she was only sixteen. He was a fleshy, slightly awkward foreigner named Thomas, with brown hair and a shy manner. She sensed he was someone attainable. He was soft-spoken and a bit withdrawn: she felt like the elder even though he was ten years her senior. Chinese girls were taught to be submissive: when the older girls gossiped about it, they always said that that was the quality that foreign men especially liked about Chinese girls, because their own women were so strident and large, with their big shoulders and hips. Chinese women, like herself, were more delicate, and in getting Thomas's interest she was as sweet and humble as the fresh jasmine blossom she sometimes wore around her neck as perfume. She asked him questions about idiomatic American expressions. She flirted and she retreated. She put herself in his presence and then pretended that she was very busy. He had finally, clumsily, clutched her to him, and she'd had to fight down the panic of the sudden intimacy. They'd kissed in his office, he'd rubbed her breasts, and though it wasn't so pleasant in itself, the triumph of knowing that she'd been able to get this far with him was exciting. She made what she thought were the appropriate sounds, sounds people made in movies, and she reached down and put her hand into his pants, because that's what some of the girls said was the thing to do. When her hand had suddenly gotten gooey, she gave an involuntary little cry of surprise, and he'd laughed, then given her some tissues to clean up. As soon as she'd gotten free she rushed to the bathroom and washed her hands for a long time, then came out faintly ashamed. Later she'd gone over to where he lived, a sparse, slightly shabby three-room flat he shared with another teacher, and they'd ended up having sex in his bare-walled room. It was strange because he was a foreigner and much older than her. Strange because it was her first time. What had really shocked her, though, was the bareness of the apartment, the sense of shabbiness, so different from what she expected a foreigner's apartment to look like. Where were the bookcases and the movie posters? By the time she left, she was already wondering what she was getting from this whole thing. And within a week it had ended, Thomas pretending to break it off with a gallant and overly formal speech about her age and his responsibilities as a teacher. The next semester he was gone, and, without him around to remind her of how awkward it had all been, she could revel in her first seduction of a foreigner. She was a worldly woman now. Next time, she would set her sights higher.

By seventeen, she had slept with two other men, and if she had been a traditional Suzhou girl, she might have worried about the loss of her purity. But in the eyes of her parents, she was still as pure as they had created her. And in the eyes of the imaginary Shanghai woman that she hoped to become, she was far too pure altogether. The vice director of the culture institute began to get her work playing the *pipa* for foreigners, as her mother had, and giving tours in her excellent English. She would dress in her mother's fine, embroidered robes and make a fortune in tips. She began to save her money for the move to Shanghai.

Things had begun to go better for her father; he was getting work providing costumes for the big dynastic dramas that had become popular in the movies and on television. He would travel to Shanghai and Beijing to meet clients. Her mother, though, became ever less mobile. They could do little to arrest her disease, and the drugs they gave her bloated her body, even as her muscles became less responsive. Her face had lost its beauty and become wide and slack, and her limbs, always so graceful, became leaden. Where it had first been difficult for her mother to walk, it now became difficult to breathe, and Mei Lin spent agonizing weeks with her as she struggled. In the end, she was content simply to sit there for hours practicing the *pipa* as her mother silently watched her.

She was almost happy when her mother passed away. Her mother was free now, and she herself was no longer weighed down with the fear of her mother's death. She had long ago stopped asking why her mother had to die at the age of forty-one, why she turned from a butterfly into a slug. Here in the Red Dust, that was simply how things went.

That fall she was admitted to the Suzhou Uni to study classical performing arts. She continued her *pipa* and began learning the *guzheng,* the giant zither, and the *erhu,* the two-stringed violin. She studied Costume and mastered the elaborate hairstyles of the Qing, the Ming, and the Song. She realized at last that that was what she was preparing to become: a Song Dynasty courtesan, elegant and clever and worldly.

After a year, she became bored with the Uni and moved to Shanghai. Not to a luxurious hotel filled with foreigners, but into a worn one-bedroom flat with narrow gray hallways and cold, drippy plumbing. The city felt infinite and impersonal, as if she was staring up at the underside of a massive floating object. She was another girl in the streets, passing other girls like herself every minute, some prettier, some better-dressed, some obviously privileged and already on track to succeed. It didn't matter. At last she was in Shanghai, and she could still sense the connection between herself and that other woman of her imagination who dipped into the furor of the city like a swallow and glided out again, gracefully and nimbly. That Shanghai woman.

Her father found her a job with a television producer that he often worked with, Mr. Zhang, and her job was to help on the shoots and do the English translations for the videos. She liked Mr. Zhang. He was a slight man about her father's age who wore a brown leather jacket and treated her as a daughter, rather than with other overtones. Mr. Zhang produced videos for Chinese companies, and she went on many tiresome shoots of electronics factories and offices. These outings always involved a long lunch, often with some of the executives of the factory to discuss the message they hoped to convey. It was during one of these banquets that she met the director of the East China Domestic Electronics and Tools Corporation. He was about Mr. Zhang's age, had a slack, fleshy face with large pouchy lips. He treated her with a mildly paternal indulgence, inquiring about where she was from and why she had come to Shanghai. She was surprised when Mr. Zhang told her that the man wanted to invite her to dinner. Her boss looked uncomfortable but asked her to go, since the director was an important client of his.

The director ordered the most expensive dish at a very expensive restaurant. It was the top grade of shark-fin soup: she could live for a month on the cost of two small bowls. Along with that, he ordered at least a dozen more plates, like lobster and hairy crab and a special Japanese beef, so that of the last eight dishes she could only take a single bite each, then leave the rest to grow cold. And meanwhile, he talked. He talked about his business dealings and his trips to Germany and Thailand. He had gone to Rome, he said, and he showed a picture on his cell phone of himself standing at the Colosseum. Had she been to the exterior? She should go—the foreigners loved pretty Chinese girls. He asked about her family and her schooling. He didn't realize that she did English translations. Maybe she could give him English lessons . . .

She knew that it wasn't English he wanted lessons in. She debated what to say. He was a tiresome man, but he was also an important client for Mr. Zhang. She gave him a bright smile. She would be happy to teach him! She could come to his office three times per week, and she would only charge the equivalent of one bowl of top-grade shark-fin soup.

From this man, she learned how to be a tutor. Not simply a tutor, but a tutor of wealthy older men who hoped, by paying her, to possess her. Sometimes they didn't even want to keep up the appearance of a lesson: they just wanted to talk about their business or their wives or their longing for something that kept escaping them. They were men who owned factories and

had relationships with high officials. They would give her expensive perfumes, bring her shopping, take her to costly clubs and restaurants to meet
their business friends. They always introduced her as a tutor but let their
friends think that she was their mistress. They invented nicknames for her,
always circling closer, letting her feel that their golden fortunes were within
her reach. The trick, she realized, was to not care about their money. When
you became attached to what they could buy you, they could control you
with that attachment. If you didn't care, you were free.

In time, she began to meet foreigners. She found them much easier to
manage, since they were already slightly off-balance in Shanghai. Sometimes they simply wanted to learn Chinese. There were young businessmen
who would still go after her, and once or twice she had slept with them, but
always with no concern for the future, and it was they who ended up wanting to be attached.

Peter Harrington was a bit like all these men, but he was also different.
How much alike and how different was still to be seen. Today he would
reveal what had happened to him on the Bund, or else he would try to
maintain the silly face of the rich, strong man who is always clever and can
never be beaten. Today she would find out who he really was.

When he arrived, she came out to the curb and locked the garden door
behind her. He seemed disappointed when she didn't invite him inside the
garden, but he greeted her with a light kiss on the cheek and held her just a
moment longer than normal. She could sense an awkwardness about him.
At first glance he had nothing wrong with him, only a very slight roundness
at the top of his nose, which might have been there before. There were other
signs, though.

"Where is Mr. Ma?"

He hesitated. "It was time for a change," he said. "This is Mr. Hu." He
ushered her into the car and got in on the other side. "I'm dying to know
where you're taking me."

"A place you would never guess. Now I must talk with Mr. Hu." She explained the situation to Mr. Hu in Chinese, and he smiled, charmed by her.
Peter didn't understand a word of it.

"What did you tell him?" he asked.

"You must study your Chinese harder, Peter. You will find out when we arrive."

The twilight had come down, and the rush-hour traffic was wall-like, choking, impossible, as always. Peter asked about her week, and she laughed. "You know my life: very boring. I played two concerts. I taught my clients."

"Yes, I know how boring your life is, Camille. Living in a Chinese garden, going to elegant parties with artists and gallery owners."

"You're right," she answered. "Perhaps not a hundred-percent boring. Maybe only eighty percent."

"Well, I hope you don't consider me part of that eighty percent."

Peter brought up the matter of Xu Ruoshi, the artist from the other night, and his photograph. "I love that photo. Do you think I should buy it?"

Wen was pushing her hard to get Peter to buy it, at three times the price she had been asking two weeks ago. She'd even promised her a larger commission, because a big sale to a foreigner would elevate the price of Xu Ruoshi's other works when they came up for auction next month. The money was inconsequential to Peter, but still, at three times the price, it wasn't fair. "It is a very strange and beautiful piece," she said. "And Xu Ruoshi is a rising artist. He is getting attention in New York now. Do you know what price she has put on it?"

"No. Maybe you can help me with that."

She nodded without committing to anything. She needed to consider this.

It took them a half hour to reach their destination. Peter never mentioned what had happened, but she could feel it between them. When they pulled in sight of the huge building, he laughed. "You're kidding me!"

"You said you like to ski!"

The driver stopped before a huge blue and white building. On its side it said, "Yinqixing Indoor Skiing Site."

"I've heard of this place," Harrington said, "but I always thought it was too ridiculous to exist."

"Not at all! Now you can show me what a great skier you are."

The building was divided in two, lengthwise, one side a strange fantasy and the other an even stranger fantasy. The outer strip, running alongside the ski hill, was where skis and snowboards were rented. The theme was alpine, with huge blow-up photographs of Europeans slashing down steep fields of snow. There was a ski shop and a "mountainside" restaurant that looked out over the huge refrigerated room where people skied. The slope itself was gentle, over a thousand feet long and covered with a foot of "snow" that seemed more like shaved ice. It was covered with young Chinese people in rented parkas falling their way down the hill and taking a long rubber moving sidewalk back to the top. She had come here to take lessons before she had allowed one of her tutoring clients to bring her skiing.

"Can you ski?" he asked her.

"I am an expert skier."

He rented them skis, boots, and parkas, and they took the escalator and stepped onto the top of the slope that ran down the massive, cold room. She could tell that he thought the entire place was very funny. All around them Chinese people were skiing badly and falling with little shrieks. A few more accomplished athletes descended with expressions of bored superiority.

They stood at the top, putting their hands through the loops on the poles.

"So you really know how to ski?" he asked her. "How did you learn?"

"I have skied in Heilongjiang some years ago, and in the Alps."

She could see the questions on his face. Skiing was an expensive sport, and so was a ticket to Europe.

"Who did you go with?"

"I went with a friend," she answered blandly, then smiled and pushed off. She went down the hill in quick, graceful turns, as she'd been taught, as regular as the teeth of a zipper. He chased along beside her. "Really! The Alps! Why didn't you mention that the other night?"

"Oh! I am sorry, Peter." She smiled at him. "I was enjoying *your* story about skiing. My stories are quite boring."

He laughed as he rode along beside her. He turned around and skied

backward for a while, facing her, then turned frontward again. He did seem
to ski well, but he had nowhere to go on this long, flat hill. They did a few
more runs and then the joke was worn out.

It seemed to spread into his mood. He became more silent, mentioning
that he missed skiing, and by the time they'd gotten to the restaurant, he
seemed slightly remote, burying himself in the menu. He'd chosen a Swiss
restaurant in the International Quarter to have fondue, suggesting it to be
funny, just as she had taken him to the silly indoor ski slope. The restaurant
had that same tinge of falseness, with its rough, dark beams and alpenhorns
mounted on the walls.

At last she prompted him. "You look sad."

"That skiing got me stirred up. I haven't been skiing since Crossroads
crashed."

"And that made you sad?"

"It made me think of an experience I had in Aspen. It was that last winter, the one I told you about. A man I met. It was very strange. I still think
about it."

From his expression she realized that he wasn't just telling an offhand
story to amuse her, but that he had been considering it since they had left
the ski hill.

"I met him on the lift: he was probably in his forties, and he looked a bit
ragged. He had duct tape around the cuffs of his ski pants and this grimy
red rain jacket—pretty worn stuff. Except he had really expensive skis,
brand-new Rossignols, the best they make, with high-end boots and bindings: probably a two-thousand-dollar setup, and I knew that because they
were the same as mine. It was incongruous.

"So we start talking about the skis, and then about him. He was from
Alaska, and I asked him what he did there, and he said he ran a hardware
store and did some construction on the side. And I thought, well, that's too
bad, because, of course, I'd just made a lot of money and I thought I was
pretty hot stuff, and he was just some guy who ran a hardware store. But it
turned out that he was in Colorado because his son had just competed in a
Big Mountain snowboarding competition. He'd come in fourth, and I

thought that was cool, because even if he's fourth, it means he's an incredible snowboarder. And I congratulated him, and he said, 'Oh, he doesn't listen to me! I'm his dad, so by definition I don't know anything.' Evidently the kid who won was his son's best friend, and they'd been neck and neck since middle school."

"And you have a son, also."

Here Peter looked down at the table before continuing. "Yeah, but, he doesn't snowboard." He seemed to shake himself. "So we're talking as we're going up the lift. He's very low-key, not superchatty but friendly in his own way. I asked him about Alaska, and we talked about bears and salmon and that sort of thing. He lives on a mountain, and in the winter they close his street and it becomes the neighborhood sledding hill, so all the kids go and sled in front of his house. It sounded really nice. They have a ski area, and sometimes he does some heli-ski guiding because he's friends with the owner, and I'm thinking, this guy is actually pretty cool. I mean, you have to be pretty dialed in to be a heli-guide, because people's lives depend on you. So we get to the top, and I invite him to do a run, which is sort of a breach of protocol, but, you know, what the heck? And he says okay, he'll follow my line."

Peter's language was changing now, to that of a different Peter.

"So I head down through the first, open part of the slope, fairly steep, you know, black diamond, and I'm swerving around the drops and absorbing the rollers with my knees, keeping it on the ground but trying to go as fast as I can, because I'm assuming this guy can ski, and, you know, I don't want him to think I'm a moron. So I get to the edge of the trees and stop, and I turn around. And he's this small black and red figure at the top of the slope. And he pushes off. And I think, *holy shit!*"

She laughed.

"I mean, seriously: he turned twice, and just from those two turns I could see that there was something really different about this guy. And then he faces straight down the slope and starts accelerating. Places where I swerved to avoid a ten-foot cliff, he'd go straight over it, and land it like nothing, and keep speeding up, and then hit the next one even faster. And I'm standing on the edge of this fairly tight stand of aspens, expecting him to stop, and instead he barely slows down, I just hear this swoosh of snow and he blows past me, right into the trees, and he starts weaving through them like a freaking cruise missile! I swear . . . I have *never* seen anything like it, and I've seen some amazing skiers: ski racers, ski instructors, people who skied in the Olympics. Never!

"So I pick my way through the trees, and I see him waiting down below me. And there's this one three-foot drop, and I think, well, I've got to bust something out here. I mean, he's been hitting ten-foot drops and making it look easy. So I hit it with a little speed, and right as I get airborne I freeze up, as I always do, and when I land I bury my tips and go somersaulting down the slope about fifteen feet and both my skis come off, and my goggles get filled with snow, my ears are filled with snow, and there he is, waiting for me, and he says, 'Looks like you're having some trouble with the drops.'

"And I wipe the snow out of eyes, and I say, 'You noticed! I always freeze up.'

"And then he says, and I remember this clearly, 'That's because you're being two people. One of you is trying to land it, and the other one's looking at you from the outside. You can't be looking at your life from the outside. You want to land the drops, you've got to be all the way in it.'

"So he points to this roll-over about a hundred feet further down, and he says, 'I hit that one a couple of days ago—it's about five feet. I'll go first and post up down below. Then you hit it, and this time focus completely on tucking and expanding. You ski like somebody who's had lessons, so I figure you know already. But this time, just focus on what you're doing. Nothing else.'

"And then he takes off, hits it—and he's gone. I wait a few seconds, and I hear him calling something, but I can't make out what, and I think, Okay. This is it. This is the moment. If I'm ever going to do this, it's now.

"So I head down, do a couple of hard turns to check my speed, then get about seven feet about the edge and straighten my skis out for the takeoff, and then, boom, I'm in it. Except, it wasn't five feet! It was, like, an *abyss,* and I'd just *launched* it! And this is the point where I'd usually panic, but this time, the fear sort of flickered across my mind, and then it was gone. And everything suddenly slowed down. I was just floating there in this silence. And I thought: Cool! I have all the time in the world. I'm moving so slowly. This is so easy. And I floated there awhile, and when I got close to the ground, I started expanding. And as soon as my skis touched the snow, everything sped up into fast motion again." His face had a look of astonishment. "And it was just . . . immaculate! The most perfect two seconds of my life. I have to say that I have never felt better. When I got to the bottom his comment was, 'You know, I was wrong about that one. It's more like ten or twelve feet. I was trying to warn you.' And then he says, 'But you landed it.'"

And I was thinking, *Yes*, you're god damn right! I freaking slowed down time and I *landed* it! I told him what had happened, how amazing it was about that moment just going on and on, and his only comment was 'Yeah. It does that.'"

Peter laughed at the memory. "Like, 'Yeah, transcendent moments happen to me all the time!'"

"So we skied back down to the lift, and then he had to go meet his son. Of course, I knew better than to try to keep up with them. So we shake hands, and he looks me in the eye and he says, 'You impressed me up there.' Then he told me his name was Harry, and if I ever got to Juneau, he managed the True Value hardware store there. He said, 'I'm easy to find. Just go to the downtown True Value and ask for Harry. Come in the winter. We'll do some runs.'"

Peter paused and collected his thoughts. "And you know, Camille . . . I had just cashed out for three hundred million dollars. I'd been profiled in *The Wall Street Journal* and *The New York Times*. And it didn't matter. What mattered was that I'd landed the biggest drop of my life and that I'd . . . had this incredible moment. All because of this guy that runs a hardware store in Juneau, Alaska. And it was all so . . . mysterious. You know? His whole life was this mystery that I'll never get to the bottom of.

"And all that day I kept thinking of what it would be like to be that man, to be fortysomething or fifty and ski like that, with that freedom, and have children you were proud of and who looked up to you, to run a hardware store, and just not really care about all of the things that were so important to me—status and keeping score and being a player. And that really stayed with me. I still find myself reconstructing this guy's life from whatever pieces I can scrape together. The way people do, you know: a log cabin with a cast-iron stove that I probably saw in a movie. Some mountains from . . . I don't know, probably a photo in a magazine. A blond wife in some sort of 1950s snowflake sweater. His son, who probably looks like him, a daughter who looks like his wife. The whole thing, just like you would picture it. The snow. The fire. The house."

Something inside of Peter seemed to move, and he gave a deep sigh. His voice changed from wonder to profound sadness. "My son tried to commit suicide a few months ago. He's thirteen."

She involuntarily raised her hand to her mouth. "I'm so sorry."

Peter went on. "He's okay now. He went through rehab." His tone was flat and injured. "I went to New York to see him, and after an hour he told me to go back to China. That he wasn't a tourist attraction. He's extremely angry at me. And he's not the only one." He stopped and cleared his throat. "Something happened to me last week."

She was relieved he had finally brought it up. "You were attacked on the Bund."

"You know about that?"

She shrugged sadly. "I have known about it since several days ago," she said. "A friend sent me a link. I'm very sorry."

"So you knew already. I must look like a complete ass."

"You look like a man who is embarrassed. That's normal."

The fondue pot came with its bubbling white contents, along with cubes of bread and pickles. He paused from their conversation to taste the wine and to dip the first cube of bread. She followed his example.

He sighed. "It is embarrassing. It's been a really hellish week." He told her the whole fantastic story, describing how the old man had pretended to be his friend and then led him to a place where he could be attacked, and how it was even possible that the singer had somehow arranged the videos simply to embarrass him and to make himself look like a hero. "And he succeeded. You can't imagine how it feels to know that there's millions of people watching you get punched in the face and cheering."

"That's terrible," Camille said softly.

"And it doesn't end there. It's ruined our business. Kell and I had to dissolve our whole corporation and have him reconstitute it without me. I'm too much of a liability. I lost face, as they say here."

She nodded sympathetically and reached across the table to put her hand on top of his and squeezed it. "That's just face, Peter. It's only appearance."

"But if you lost face, publicly, in front of millions of people, you would feel bad, right?"

"Yes. But I would be stupid to feel bad."

"But you *would* feel bad!" he insisted. "No matter how much you told yourself not to. And in this case there've been real consequences with my business, my loss of an investment opportunity, physical pain—all of those things!"

She withdrew her hand and picked up her wineglass.

"So, naturally, I'm not going to just lay down and die on this."

"What will you do?" she asked, looking at the piece of bread on her skewer.

"I'm going to punish him." He sounded cold and arrogant. "I have a PR firm that specializes in dealing with exactly this sort of problem and they will crush him like an egg." He told her how they worked, how they could destroy Pete Harrington's image forever. Now Peter's face had become almost red. "He's not getting away with this! He thinks he can just walk up to me and assault me with no provocation whatsoever then use it to relaunch his career? That's bullshit! It's twisted! I'm not going to take that from some two-bit has-been rock star!" He noticed her reaction, and he leaned back in his chair. "I'm sorry. I get a little bit overwrought." He sipped at his water, calming himself. "So. What do you think?"

She was quiet for enough time to dip a piece of bread into the cheese and drink a few sips of wine. She reached over and squeezed his hand again. "Do nothing," she said.

"Why?" He looked puzzled and irritated.

This was the moment to be unattached. She looked directly at him. "Because you deserved it."

He pulled his hand away. "What?"

She smiled. It was really rather simple. "Of course you deserved it!"

He shook his head, stunned. "How can you say that? Everything I did was legal, and it was done in good faith. Every investment—"

"You made *so much* money, Peter!" He didn't like being interrupted, but she went on anyway. "And you got to keep that money. That's good! You were trying to find your other life. But people like Pete Harrington—they lost money. Maybe for him, a lot of money. For *your* other life. Your life swallowed his. So, yes, he has a right to hit you."

"I can't believe this! You're basically saying you agree with all those people who've been posting hate messages all over the Internet about me? You're saying they're right?"

"They are right to be angry! Of course! And when you accept that, I think you will be much happier."

"You think I'll be happier?" He struck his forehead with his palm, chuckling bitterly. "This is crazy!"

"Is it really crazy, Peter? How happy are you now?"

"How happy am I now?"

"Yes. At this moment."

The question stopped him completely. "Well . . ." He lifted his shoulders and tossed his hands to the sides as if he'd forgotten where they belonged. She saw his throat move up and down as he forced a smile to the surface. "Not so very happy, to be honest with you." He brushed his eye with the back of his hand, beaming at her at the same time as he looked deeply sad. "It's confusing, actually. Fairly confusing. I'm supposed to be very successful." His voice became thin. "I mean, as people measure success. I've got a ton of money. I've got a son that I love, though I guess really, I'm not much help to him. I've got great friends all over the world—not so much in

Shanghai, but in other places. I have everything. What else could I wish for?" He laughed, and it made his teary eyes overflow. He wiped it with the napkin. Other diners were staring at him, but he didn't care. "This is so crazy! *Happy!*"

She let him sit with his thoughts for a time. Neither of them were touching the fondue. She poured them both a bit more wine and waited for him to begin again.

"I have no real reason to be here now," he finally offered.

"You never had a reason."

He looked down toward the table, then back up at her. "You could tell?" She didn't answer him, so he answered himself. "I thought China would be a change from New York, but the whole thing with Metropolitan Partners was more of the same. Or worse. I mean, look at me: I'm incorporated in the Isle of Man. My official home is a post office box in Bermuda. I pay nothing in taxes, and my most recent business venture is based on taking advantage of distressed public infrastructure. No wonder people hate me. *I* hate me! I'm a bored, selfish rich man of a type that's existed throughout history. The only dignity I have left is trying not to tell myself I'm anything other than that." He opened his fingers in a gesture of helplessness and sat back in his chairs to wait for her reaction.

"That is all true," she said at last. "But you take it too seriously."

He looked at her, surprised. "I'm sorry; I'm in the middle of a major life crisis, and you feel I'm taking it too seriously?"

"Far too seriously, Peter!" She could see he was becoming quite annoyed. It made her laugh. "It's so simple! You keep looking for the Other Life. But your own life *is* the other life."

He opened his mouth to throw back a sharp answer, but he held it back, then stared down at the table with his lips half-apart. He smiled and looked back at her. "I'm trying to understand what the hell you just said."

"Peter! Look around! This is what the Other Life looks like. Close your eyes and listen. Right now!" She watched him shut his eyes and listen to the clattering and clinking and bits of conversation. She leaned toward him as if she was telling him a secret. "This is how it really sounds!"

He opened his eyes and looked around the restaurant and at her. He gave a single dry laugh. "I'm sorry, Camille. I'm just not getting it."

"It's okay. You can think about it if you like." She leaned back again. She was suspicious of long talks about philosophy. They always turned back on themselves and lost their real meaning. "And something else on another subject: that picture, by Xu Ruoshi? It is too expensive. Offer half of what she asks. Then pay a bit more. Diana made the price three times higher after Xu Ruoshi won that prize. But don't tell her I warned you, or it will create problems for me."

He considered it, knowing what it meant that she had told him. "Thank you, Camille." For the first time that night he actually seemed happy. They each ate a few pieces of bread dipped in cheese, and talked about the food in Switzerland. They speculated that this restaurant must have an exact fake-Chinese counterpart somewhere in Geneva or Bern, where people were looking at outdated Chinese clothing and musical instruments and imagining a China that no longer existed. For a little while they were simply two people out for the evening, though she knew that everything had not simply gone away with a few pronouncements. At last he let the conversation go silent so he could speak.

"So, Camille, what would you do if you were me? Seeing as I have no purpose in Shanghai."

"I thought of that. If I were you, I would go to Cold Mountain for a while. Look for Han Shan."

"Who's Han Shan?"

"The sage of Cold Mountain. I told you about him last week. That poem. *The mountain is massive. The mountain is mist.*" Peter didn't understand anything. "In the Tang Dynasty. More than twelve hundred years ago. No one knows if he was a real person: all we have are poems." She told him about Han Shan and his poems about the mountain and the high paths and the mist. How the legend said that he had gone finally into a cave and closed it up behind him.

"I give you credit for one thing, Camille. You're not a slave to linear thought." She merely indulged him with a smile. "Let me make sure I've got this right: I'm a global laughingstock who's been physically assaulted, dumped by his girlfriend, and kicked out of his own business, and you think I should go and look for a legendary poet who's been dead for twelve hundred years? *That* should be my next move."

"Do you have a better idea?"

He pressed his lips tightly together and looked down at the tablecloth. He considered it for quite a while, and she could see different expressions going across his face. Finally he turned back to her. "Where is Cold Mountain?"

6

The Elephant Hunt

❖

The chorus of Pete Harrington's newly rediscovered fame didn't start going out of tune until a few weeks after he'd gotten back. He'd been putting together a touring band, auditioning players with Duffy and seeing how things felt. They were doing well fleshing out the songs he'd written with Duffy, but he hadn't come up with anything new since Shanghai. Strangely, he felt dry again.

The days of going to the Rainbow to write, or even pretending to write, were over. People recognized him everywhere, and though it had been fun to have that back the first week or two, he gotten pretty sick of fending off the same questions over and over again. People wanted his autograph, or to know how he'd felt, or to congratulate him, or to shake the hand that had punched Peter Harrington in the face. The babes were back, too, or rather, the babes had gotten younger. But it wasn't like being twenty. The game felt old.

He was spending a lot of time in front of his computer. Before Shanghai he never ego surfed because there was nothing new anymore, just the same stale pages and outdated hero worship going back twenty years. Now, though, everyone was talking about him. Entertainment and celebrity sites, people who'd lost money in Crossroads, sites that specialized in fight videos, fan sites, political sites, social media pages, blogs of every stripe. It had even spawned sites of its own. He turned up one called BitchSlapBankster .com that featured his videos and a list of banksters still in need of bitchslapping, complete with their pictures and addresses. The comment board was a sinkhole of ugliness, the hatred slopping over to Republicans, Democrats, Jews, Chinese, traitors who didn't carry a copy of the U.S. Constitution in their pocket, even to Pete Harrington himself: *If a d1ck head like Pete Harrington can do it, anyone can!* Or, *This video makes me laugh. 2 f@ggots getting it on!* These were the people he was trying impress? He registered under a phony name and wrote, *You r all just fat shyts in undershirts writing comments and jerking off to porn. You wouldn't have the guts. F&ck U Pete Harrington.* Let 'em figure that one out.

He tried to imagine what Charlie would say about this. Charlie didn't worry about his online reputation, or downloads, or what people thought of him. He was beyond reputation. It had been simpler back in his day: you just do hero shit and nobody ever knows except your buddies, or the president, or some guy back at CIA headquarters who calls you into his office and says something like "Well done, Pico. You saved the Free World." He missed the old man. Charlie'd pulled him into a universe where you put your fear aside and did it, period, because that's who you were. He didn't have Charlie by his side anymore, though, and he wasn't sure what new universe he'd ended up in. The universe of *2 f@ggots getting it on!*

A music video of "Kickin' It with The Man" had showed up. It was footage from the "Chinese Justice" video mixed with other footage of Shanghai, and then some cuts of him singing a sort of demo video of "Kickin' It" that they'd put out, all lifted from the Net and spliced together with his new song so it cut to the beat. Not professionally produced, but witty and cool, a good mix of angry footage with lighter stuff—street scenes of Shanghai and clips taken from commercials for insurance companies and banks. Foreclosure-sale signs and shots of people with all their belongings out on the front lawn. Always cutting back to him singing "Kickin' It" and the banker going down to the pavement over and over again. It looked almost too good to have been produced by an amateur, but there were all sorts of obsessives out there these days, and they all seemed to have access to a laptop and editing software. His favorite version of the song used LEGOs: his square-bodied styrene persona kicking the crap out of a plastic guy with a top hat and tuxedo. It had two million views.

He noticed a mention in one of the trade papers about the songs he and Duffy had written. DREAMKRUSHERS DUO BACK IN THE GAME. "Riding high on interest in their new Internet-driven hit, 'Kickin' It with The Man,' '90s troubadours Pete Harrington and Duffy Scofield are going into the studio to record new material for an upcoming tour." It had been years since he'd seen his name in *Variety,* and he knew things didn't just appear in *Variety* by themselves. Beth was on it.

The weird thing was, he didn't have too much interest in "Kickin' It" anymore. Let's face it: he'd already kicked it. Instead, he kept thinking about that house outside Wilksbury, and that song that he'd never gotten right. He couldn't put his finger on what it was about. A small house in a small town. Guys in plaid shirts sitting with a cup of coffee talking over shit that had happened twenty years ago. It was like . . . everything that got away: the girl who got away, the friend who got away, the years that got away, his grandfather. It all got away, eventually, and there was something beautiful about that, too: everything perfectly in place at the same time that it was disappearing. That's what he wanted to write about, but he didn't have a tune and he didn't have a first line and the song was all one big nameless beautiful thing that hung over him then disappeared into the mist whenever he tried to nail it down. When the mist cleared, all he saw was himself as a plastic mini-figure, punching a fan in the face over and over again.

The bullshit started to crop up about two weeks after "Kickin' It" hit number 4 on the charts. Not that Peter Harrington, financial swindler, had a lot of defenders out there. Most people took it as exactly what it had been: a pissed-off victim finally laying some fucking Truth on someone who mistakenly thought he had all the truth he needed. Ninety-eight percent of the

comments were happy as shit, but there were always a few droolers and
know-it-alls ready to down you for one thing or another. Anonymously, of
course. The first scattering of theories claimed that the Pete Harrington in
the beat-down video was a look-alike, or that the banker was an actor. They
cited the "fact" that the victim did nothing to defend himself, and they
compared the finely tuned right cross of the "Pete Harrington" in the video
with the clumsy Pete Harrington that had flute-whipped the bassist of
Uncle Sam's Erection three years before. To these buttheads, there was one
ultimate proof that the whole thing was a publicity stunt: it had gotten
publicity.

After the conspiracy nut-jobs came the computer geeks, Silicon Valley
eggheads teaming up with some Chinese tech know-it-all to track the spread
of the videos. Like, excuse me, guys, but shouldn't you be hacking into
X-rated Web sites and stealing porn or something? They were talking about
ISPs and diffusion velocity. They pulled apart all the videos and matched
them shot for shot, claiming that some had been spliced together from multiple cameras or that the quality of the cameras was too good not to have
been staged. Even though he knew the chatter was bullshit, he couldn't help
reading the questions. Such as: the release of the video in Shanghai had happened only three hours after the event, and had appeared with titles a few
hours later. How had the financier been identified so quickly? Such as: the
link had first been posted at ConnedbyCrossroads.com by a user who had
registered only six weeks earlier and had never posted before that. The verdict of the geeks: it was a professional job, from beginning to end. A publicity stunt.

It took some serious iron will to keep from climbing into the Internet
arena and busting out some raw language on them, but he held true to
Beth's rules. He never confirmed, denied, or explained. Still, it made him
start to turn it all over in his mind. He'd had at least a dozen passersby
filming him when he walked up to Peter Harrington. Could there have
been some ringers in there? And what about when he'd gotten back: Bobby
had asked him if he'd gotten good footage, then played it off like he'd asked
whether he'd kicked the banker. *Footage.* An unusual choice of words, and

Bobby was no poet. Could Bobby have set it up from L.A.? Did he have
those kinds of connections? Or Beth? If they did, how'd they pull it off
without Charlie finding out? They'd have needed some cameramen in China
following him and Charlie all the way to the setup, and Charlie'd had a
lifetime of experience spotting tails. Charlie probably would have led him
into a dark alley and then slammed him up against the wall, old-school, to
make him talk.

But the only one who got ambushed was him. It was some enterprising
camera crew from *Entertainment Today.* Not the second string here, not a
Web site, but Frankie Lang himself, probably trying to show that he could
have been a real journalist if he hadn't gone "lite." He'd showed up at their
studio right on time with a few free CDs to sprinkle to the crew. It was supposed to be about his new album, talking about the songs and the inspiration behind them, touching very lightly on the whole thing in Shanghai,
but instead Frankie did the classic: asked him some easy questions, gave
him some strokes, got his trust, then stuck the knife in.

"You know, Pete, speaking of Shanghai, there's been some controversy
out there . . ." Frankie started spewing out some jibber jabber about videos
and postings and various other crap that he couldn't really follow because
this other little voice was saying, *Wow, I'm getting ambushed by Frankie Lang,
the fucking royal flush of fake journalism! And he's just talking shit he read on the
Internet! As if he knows anything at all about Charlie or push-ups or walking up to
that guy with his bodyguard while the whole world is pointing their cell phones at
you . . . Where the fuck did this guy—?*

He realized Frankie's mouth had stopped moving and that the last words
he'd heard were "What's the real story, Pete?"

He was supposed to say something now, with Frankie looking at him like
he was some sort of boss investigator. "The real story? Here's the real story:
I was there fucking standing up, while you were here pimping for sex lubricants and cut-rate car insurance. Is that real enough for you?"

He stopped suddenly and held up his hand, smiling. "Whoa! Hold on.
Cut! Cut!" This definitely violated the "being insulting to an interviewer"
part of his agreement with Beth. "Hey, I'm sorry, Frankie. Cut that. I

didn't mean it. You're just doing your job. Ask me again and I'll answer the question."

The interviewer smiled and asked him the same question again.

"Frankie, I was there, on the ground, face-to-face with the beast. There were at least a dozen Chinese people taking videos, just like if I go walking down Sunset Boulevard someone might whip out their cell phone and take a video. I have no idea who they are and no control over what they do with their footage. But I *can* tell you, a hundred-percent sure, that there was nothing staged or phony about what you saw on that video." He nodded. Very professional. Even Beth would have to admit that. "How's that?"

"So you admit that someone might have purposely spread it."

He looked at him. "What is this, man? A fucking witch hunt?"

He was still steaming when Bobby called him to check on the new band and brief him on the latest good news. It was all good news from Bobby these days. Every time he called there was a new gig or a fresh deal. It was like the old days. So he let about ten minutes go by with Bobby telling him about the new date he'd scheduled in Seattle and how the gig in Anchorage had sold out and they'd added another night. No longer necessary to pump him up with BS about Anchorage being the new Seattle. Even better—and here Bobby practically made him hold his breath—the leading late-night comedy show in the country, with an audience of sixteen million people squarely in his demographic, was talking to Beth about bringing him on as a musical guest.

"That's huge, Pete! It means you're back!"

And that was all very cool, but it didn't erase this other question, this silly, stupid crap about the Shanghai thing being a publicity stunt . . . "Listen, Bobby, things got a little rocky at my interview today." He told him what had happened.

"You called him a pimp? On camera?" Bobby considered it a second, then changed gears. "Here's what's real, Pete: You went out alone, with your spear, and you brought down the elephant. Now all the little villagers that didn't have the guts to go after the elephant themselves are gathering around to snatch their little pieces and tell you how you could have done it better. You're the one who knows what really went down in Shanghai. Why would you pay attention to a bunch of chattering monkeys?"

He liked hearing it, but it didn't answer his question. "Bobby. You remember when I got back from Shanghai and you asked me if I'd gotten any *footage?*"

There was a silence on the line. "Not really. That was a long time ago. Are you sure I said footage?"

"You said *footage,* and then you said that you meant, Had I kicked him?" Bobby didn't answer. "I just think that's a strange word to use."

"Pete, I don't know what I said. And you were pretty wiped out, as I recall."

"Just give me a yes-or-no answer, Bobby. Did you have those videos made?"

Bobby was quiet again. Pete could tell that, in his mind, Bobby was jumping through the elaborate qualifications that would make "no" a truthful answer. Like, *No, I hired someone else, and* they *had them made.* Or, *No, I just arranged for some raw footage, not actual . . . Video!* "No . . . ," he said slowly.

The trap was closing now. "Does that mean, *No,* or does that mean, *No, not exactly, but kind of.*'"

There was a long silence. "Honestly . . . I'd have to say it's the second answer." Bobby was struggling now, almost pleading. "Don't go down this road, Pete."

"What road is that, Bobby?"

"Pete! Look—you found this guy. You trained yourself. You got straight in his face, and you served him a steaming-hot helping of *fuck you!* compliments of the little people. There is no part of that that is not hero shit."

He wasn't distracted by Bobby using his own terms. "So you're not denying it?"

"Denying what?"

"C'mon, Bobby!"

"I'm not denying it and I'm not confirming it. I'm saying, it doesn't matter. Let it drop, Pete."

"Let it drop? Am I a fucking golden retriever?"

"Pete, slow down—"

"Fuck you, Bobby! I am not going to be part of this!"

"You need to talk to Beth—"

"*Beth?* Did Beth do this?"

"I'm just going to back off a little bit because Beth's really the person—"

"No, Bobby! You are not dumping all this on Beth. We're fucking dealing with it! Tonight! You, me, and Beth. In two hours. Set it up!"

"Pete—"

He was shouting now. "Set it up!"

7

Jersey Girl

⁓

It had taken some time, but when Beth Blackman finally learned to recognize that life progressed in circles and spirals, and that moving backward was the same as moving forward, she was able to view her status as Pete Harrington's ex-wife as a privilege. Before that, she just wanted to slap his silly face and rip out his little gold earrings one by one.

Pete had been one of her first big clients when she came out to Los Angeles from the East Coast, a Jersey girl with a reputation for brilliant solutions and the ability to keep a supercomputer's worth of detail live and crackling in her brain. Her father had warned her to keep her head screwed on straight, but she was twenty-four at the time and he was a real rock star and it was the first time she'd been thrown full force into that world of people who were richer, more famous, and better looking than her. Just the fact that he would want to sleep with her was a pretty big deal. Not that she was ugly. She'd never have one of those chic, slim woman's bodies with big breasts: she didn't have the genetics, and even if she had the work done, she would still be just over five feet tall, and she'd still have real hips and thighs. She liked her body, thought of it as a wonderful, useful body, even if she didn't look like a mink, or a lynx or a fox, or a sorceress, or a porn star, or a

Catholic-school girl, or any of the other women that constantly made themselves available to Pete Harrington and his band. But for some reason, Pete
wanted her, and that in itself was a powerful drug. As long as she could see
him as a client she enjoyed a certain immunity, but when that slipped,
when they went to his ranch in Montana for a few days, allegedly as friends,
and she ate mushrooms for the first time and sat for hours next to a stream
with him saying almost nothing, her construct collapsed, and she went soaring into his blue eyes and his famous strong chin. He was an artist, an
angel, a rebel: all the crap that she spent eleven hours a day perpetuating
instantly became true. But now, she was inside it.

Their union lasted exactly twenty-two days. She liked to tell people that,
as with many other marriages, the first third had been blissful—it was the
second two weeks that were the problem. In that time he cheated on her
with three different women, and she finalized the matter by beating a raw,
gray dent into his locked bedroom door with a cast-iron skillet, a cliché
that, incredibly, they both joked about all these years later. She'd ended up
with no job and a ruined professional image, forced to start her own agency
and make do with up-and-comers who hoped to parlay a scandal or a bit
part in a movie into marketable notoriety. And those were her good clients:
her bad ones didn't even have the scandal. She had to create their fame from
scratch, a challenge that honed her publicity skills to a frightening acuity.

For a few years, she hated the man. The sight of him at occasional industry events reduced her to a caldera of anger and shame, no matter how hard
he tried to make it up to her. She secretly relished the first missteps in his
career. As her agency took off, though, their relationship progressed to
guarded nods and brief, brittle conversations. She could sense his regret, and
if at first she had reveled in it, a time came when she began to feel sorry for
him. In his often-goofy way, he was trying to get her forgiveness, and four
years later, attending an awards ceremony, she spotted him making straight
for her with a pleasant-looking, dark-suited man with horn-rim glasses.
Great, she thought, *he's going to do some weird trophy dance over me.* She said a
nervous hello and he introduced the man: a literary agent Bobby had pitched
Pete's life story to. Pete kissed her on the cheek, then spoke to him with

fierce and urgent sincerity: "Ira, Beth is my ex-wife. I messed up and she booted my silly ass out of her life. This woman is more than a queen: she's a fucking *lioness,* and I was too stupid to realize that." He finished his strange apology, or introduction, or whatever it was, and they all stood silently for a few seconds, uncertain where to go after that testimonial. He clapped them both on the shoulder. "Now, you kids get to know each other!"

It was Pete being most himself: intuitive, impulsive, ridiculous, and weirdly brilliant. Ira proposed six months later, and she got him a job as a book agent at the L.A. headquarters of Creative Artists Agency. They invited Pete to the wedding, though she asked him not to make a toast, and he became a casual dinner guest and family friend over the years. She built her company into one of the most powerful boutique publicity agencies in the business, and with the help of a nanny, a cook, a housekeeper, a pool boy, and a gardener, she and Ira raised their two children, who loved the musician like a big brother. Pete performed briefly at her son's bar mitzvah party, though most of the kids didn't know who he was.

She liked having Pete on the periphery of her world. In a quietly mystical way, she had come to recognize that whatever disaster he'd unleashed in her life had changed its course for the better, and he remained a sort of cosmic clown for her, silly and self-involved but, with his innocence and his childish optimism, somehow able to defy the ponderous forces that ultimately pulled so many others to earth.

Which is why, when Bobby had called her that night and told her Pete was going off the deep end, she'd hurried over. Of course she'd tried to talk him out of his "epic" revenge plan, knowing all the time that asking Pete to listen to reason simply goaded him on to further insanity. After he screamed "fuck you!" and slammed the door to his bedroom, she sat there with Bobby trying to figure out what they could do for him.

Pete had had a great run: four or five years as major act fronting the DreamKrushers, then a successful solo album that reached number 4 on the pop chart, and then a Greatest Hits compilation and a couple of solo releases that had done decently just by selling to his fan base. So, ten years of success, and after that he could have retired gracefully and produced other artists, kept his hand in, stayed current enough to slip in a hit later on, like Robert Plant or John Fogerty did years after their bands had split up. He had a certain second-tier "classic rock" status he could have parlayed.

But that wasn't Pete. He'd kept flogging it long after it had gotten sad. First with the New DreamKrushers, then, after the lawsuit over the name DreamKrushers, with a fairly desperate succession of styles: ska, reggae, techno. Finally that rap album, so brutally bad that the late-night television shows ran the unaltered promotional video as parody. And now she and Bobby were sitting silently in Pete's soon-to-be-foreclosed-on house with his last "fuck you!" hanging in the air.

"What are we going to do?" she asked Bobby.

The manager tossed his head to the side. "We'll pay Lev to get his financial shit in order, get a bankruptcy lawyer, hire someone to sell his stuff and move him into a new place. After that? Try and get him back into rehab."

"What about this tour?"

Bobby grimaced. "I'm not sure the word 'tour' applies here, Beth. We've got a confirmed gig in Elko, Nevada, some interest at Harrah's in Reno, and a probable date in Anchorage, Alaska. That's it."

She wondered how hard Bobby was pushing that tour, but, at the same time, she knew firsthand the dispiriting sensation of whipping a dead horse. Pete had heard the noise, and the noise had been deafening. But now the noise was gone. The arena was empty. "So there's nothing you can do?"

Bobby pronounced his verdict with weary professionalism. "It's over, Beth."

She sat with the depressing news, trying to imagine Pete pulling himself together, but not really believing it. She knew where he was headed, and it wasn't a pretty place: another drunken, drug-addled Peter Pan with dyed hair and wrinkles flunking out of rehab that some desperate family member had paid for. Pete was almost there already. He probably knew it himself, and that's why he'd tried to throw this absurd hero scheme up between himself and the inevitable.

"He's right, you know," Bobby said at last. "About wanting to beat that guy down. The fucker deserves it. If Pete ever really does that, I definitely want to see the video."

"Yeah," she said absently. She heard the words and let them pass, and then circled back around and heard the words again, but suddenly they were different. She saw the image of that video in her mind, and then that image multiplied and opened suddenly into a myriad of images that went shooting in a hundred directions, so that in the space of five seconds it lay clear in front of her like fireworks dazzling and disappearing in the sky. What had Pete said? *I'm going to beat this guy down . . . and the whole world's going to stand up and cheer!* "Oh my God!"

"What is it?"

"He's right!" She laughed softly, then shook her head. "He's right! Bankers are as popular as dogshit on a dinner plate, and they're completely untouchable. Right?" She laughed again, excited. "Listen! Say Pete goes and clocks this guy. And, Bobby, that in itself would make him a national hero. But hey! Somebody got it on a cell phone! Hey, it's on YouTube! Hey! It turns out there's a video, and it's all over the Internet! Wow! Some fan takes the footage and turns it into a music video of Pete's new song, and it goes viral! And then the gods really smile on us and the victim presses charges! This is a guy who ripped off . . . how many people? And Pete's on the front of every tabloid in the country for decking him in broad daylight? Bobby, you can call it 'epic' or 'hero shit' or 'assault,' or whatever, but tracking down a widely hated financial operator and punching him in the face is what we in the business call a 'publicizable moment.' And that, my friend, is golden!"

Bobby had perked up. "You're a very bad woman, Beth."

"This is it, Bobby! Pete decks this guy, and he's living out the fantasies of three hundred million people! And not just screwing groupies and trashing hotel rooms, but knocking the crap out of an elite criminal who ripped his victims off and then laughed at them. Pete was right: this *is* epic-heroic! If he does this, I can make it huge! I can get him *Late Night.* I can get him radio station breaks. I can get him a million places he probably couldn't touch even in his best days! He *will* be an American hero! And that, Bobby, is when you take him on tour!"

Bobby nodded, excited. "He played me a few lines of his song! It actually sounds pretty good!"

She wasn't listening to him—she was seeing. Get him to the right parties, red-carpet him at some awards shows, a few stunt dates . . . Maybe a slightly older actress, someone that still had some juice and maybe had just ended a stable relationship and could use some "bad boy" credibility to show she was back in the mix. He could be Mr. Wrong. Or maybe an up-and-coming starlet, someone sexy. Or both. At the same time. You'd want him on the big gossip blogs, and you'd want to get him ambushed by a camera crew someplace hip, like the front row at a Lakers game or announcing an MMA cage fight. He could catch a second wave, get the old songs on some younger iPods, placement in a hot video game, and, with a little luck and the right backing, get one of his new songs into heavy rotation. Down the line, they could start pitching reality shows.

Of course, there were certain things Pete was and wasn't capable of. Punching the banker out: he could do that. He was reckless enough. Writing songs and performing: it hadn't really happened in a while, but she still had faith that he could reach deep down one more time and pull out whatever had made him successful before.

But Pete would never do this as a publicity stunt. As a messianic quest, no problem, but as a self-serving ploy to jump-start his stalled career—he'd never agree to do it, and even if he agreed, he'd never be able to cover it up. Pete didn't know how to lie. And while the story of a man looking for justice was powerful, the story of a man looking for free media coverage was one of the most tawdry narratives around. The slightest hint of that and the world would revile him as quickly as it had lifted him up. He'd be a laughingstock, and she'd be responsible.

So that other part—getting the video footage, managing the media exposure, initiating a long-term career strategy that built on his past, above all, keeping the whole thing secret—that would have to fall to her and Bobby, and Pete could never know.

Which was why when Bobby showed up at her office without an appointment and asked to see her right away, she'd felt a deep uneasiness.

"We've got problems."

"What do you mean?"

"Today Pete asked me if we were behind those videos. Frankie Lang interviewed him this morning and accused him of setting the whole thing up as a publicity stunt. Pete wasn't cool about it."

"I told Pete to ignore those questions."

"Why didn't you send a minder with him?"

"Frankie Lang does fluff! He was supposed to talk up the new songs and the tour. How bad is it? What'd Pete tell them?"

"I think the phrase 'fucking witch hunt' came up. But that was probably *after* Pete accused him of being a huckster for sexual lubricants."

She raised her eyebrows. "I'll call Frankie and try to get the whole thing pulled. What got Pete thinking about this? Could Charlie have tipped him off somehow?"

"I highly doubt Charlie would have said anything. In fact, if someone does find out, I suggest we hire Charlie to kill them."

Beth rolled her eyes. "I love Charlie, too, but we've still got a problem. What made Pete think we were behind this?"

"He's been seeing this crap on the Internet and I guess he started to wonder. Also"—Bobby looked down—"when he first got back, I accidentally asked him if he'd gotten any footage. I tried to play it off, but he keeps coming back to that."

She gave a long sigh. People made mistakes. It didn't matter now. "So what was the upshot of your conversation today? Did you tell him?"

"That depends. Do you mean literally?"

"Bobby—!"

"I didn't *not* tell him." Bobby could see she wasn't happy with the answer, but he pressed on. "He wants to meet with both of us, tonight."

"So this is it." She leaned back in her chair. The screen saver on her computer had come on and a picture of her and Ira and their two children in Saint Barth's was floating across the screen. Damn! This wasn't just about telling Pete. The first problem was that she'd have to tell Ira. "If this gets out, Pete's finished. Forever."

"It's not going to make us look too good either."

"Yes, but it will *destroy* Pete. In every way you can destroy a person in this town, except death. And the ironic thing will be that he's the one who's actually innocent." She closed her eyes to shut out the world, then opened them again. "I should have left him alone."

"No. We both knew where that went. You tried to help him, Beth. We both did. That's not wrong."

"Be that as it may, I can't keep lying to him. And if I don't lie to him, he won't be able to keep lying to everybody else."

"We'll just tell Pete to say 'no comment' whenever it comes up."

"Yeah, Pete's always exercised a lot of restraint. Like in China, when he made that announcement about Tiananmen Square."

"We took that one all the way to the bank!"

"Hear me, Bobby: this one doesn't end at the bank!"

"So what do you want to tell him?" Bobby asked.

"The truth. I don't see what else we can tell him. It's up to him now. He's going to have to stick to his lines. And that's something he's never been very good at."

Bobby looked pretty down, in a genuine way, not in the usual *I guess I'd better look sad about this* way. "Let's do this, Bobby: let's all meet at my house after dinner. Ira can be there: he's a stabilizing influence on Pete. I haven't told him anything, but I'll talk with him this afternoon. Call Pete and tell him seven thirty."

Bobby stood up, holding his porkpie hat. "We're doing our best, Beth."

"God, I hope so."

Bobby left, and she stayed at her desk, staring absently at the computer. It all depended on Pete now. He'd have to decide.

The screen saver filled her monitor with another photo, and at this moment, with the whole complicated problem with Pete that she had created hanging over her, the simplicity of the image sent a pang through her.

It was of a small stone house with a peaked wooden roof. There were icicles hanging from the eaves and behind it the sky was full of clouds that glowed on the screen as if with some secret meaning. Beth remembered the sound of the goats that she never saw, and the possessions of the family all neatly in their places, and the stairway that disappeared into the upper floor. The picture showed all of that without showing any of it, while out-side the frame, in a photograph visible only in Beth's memory, the Swiss woman was standing and staring expectantly at the mountains as the snow blew in. In all these years, Beth Blackman had never stopped wondering what that woman was waiting for.

8

Blue Winter Light

⁜

When she woke up the blue winter light hung like enamel inlays in the gray walls of the house. The comforter had slipped off her shoulder, and the cool touch of the night reminded her that the house was cold. Her husband lay there, partly awake, unsettled by the fresh snow that had fallen outside, the way he always was on mornings like this. She reached for her robe and pulled down the soft mass of darkness from the wall, fit her feet into the fuzzy charcoal islands on the floor beside her bed, and closed the door behind her. The wooden stairway creaked with her footsteps, like ice on a frozen lake.

She loved this time of morning in the winter. The rooms of the house were boxes of shadow, and in each box was the twilight version of all the things in her life: her son's snowboard, her daughter's sweater flung over the couch, the woodstove, her husband's boots. These were all her things, her possessions, and she felt as close to them as she did her own body. A wonderful body made of other people's lives.

In the meager light from the window she could make out the neat basket of kindling. She knelt in front of the open door of the stove and began stacking the rectangular sticks across two larger pieces. He had a knack for sizing the wood. He could split a cord in two hours and come out with three perfect sizes for fire, plus the big knotty chunks that you threw on top once things were really going.

She crumpled up a piece of newspaper and pushed it underneath, then struck a wooden match and touched it to the paper. The flame was intensely orange in the slate-colored light, like sunrise. And she was its servant.

She leaned back on her haunches and watched the lines of embers grow along the edges of the kindling. The tin sheeting of the stovepipe began to tick. This moment of the day, just when the fire was catching with its soft catlike purr—this was the moment when she had everything. Her children were asleep upstairs, her husband was in their bed, and she had all of them safe and close.

The fire had caught enough now that she could leave it and go into the kitchen. Still in the dark, she flipped the switch on the coffeemaker and it glowed red. Then she went to the back door and dug the cast-iron Dutch oven out of the snow and brought it inside. It was chicken and dumplings, still uncooked and frozen solid overnight. When she left she would put it on the stove and turn the heat on low so that it would be ready for Saturday dinner.

The window had started to turn light blue, and she could see that it had stopped snowing. The porch railing had a sharp pyramid of snow running along it, and the cars outside had been turned into pillows. For the last three days it had come down almost constantly, day and night, in a way that felt dreamlike and eternal. It covered all the details of the world, transformed all of the hard things into distant suggestions of a tree stump or an abandoned shovel. She could walk out the front door and step into her skis and go for hours in the woods, stride after stride. Up high, it would be dangerous: they'd be trying to knock down the avalanches over the main road with a howitzer. Here, though, it was perfect. All footsteps were gone. The world had been rewritten.

Her husband's weight creaked across the ceiling to the bathroom; then she heard the soft clunk of the toilet seat. He didn't need to be up for another hour, but on these kinds of mornings it seemed like the snow itself woke him up, the sound of it, or the smell of it. He'd roll around in the bed from his back to his side, like he was rolling around in a drift, and then he'd wake up in one of those moods where he was distant and in his own thoughts.

She opened the glass door of the woodstove and placed some larger pieces of wood on top, about the thickness of her wrist, then closed it. She'd built thousands of fires over the years, and every one of them was fascinating. This was the most primitive form of chemistry, a form every caveman or -woman had understood from the beginning, not as the process of oxidation giving off heat, but, more deeply, as a sure sign of all that was divine in this physical world, hiding within wood. It warmed you; it danced for you. A god that made fire had to be a god that loved humanity.

The coffeemaker was starting to gurgle. If her husband got up, she would make him some oatmeal or bacon and eggs, eat breakfast with him before she ran out.

A magazine was lying next to the stove, and she could see it in the light coming from the windows. She still had a subscription to *The New Yorker* that her husband renewed every Christmas. The last vestige of her old life. The page was open to a perfume ad. An Asian model getting out of a car someplace expensive. Someplace far away.

She'd had a bottle of that perfume once, or rather, a vial. Her son had gotten it for her at one of the tourist shops downtown for her birthday, a little tiny sample that they'd probably given to him: he was only ten. And when they went out to dinner that night, just she and her husband, they'd gone to the Gold Room at the Baranof Hotel and he'd looked so handsome in his sport jacket, and she'd been wearing a black dress and the pearls her mother had given her, and for a minute there, with the candles and the waiters in tuxedoes and the shining metal serving platters with their mirrored tops, she'd felt like they were elegant.

She heard the creaking moving across the ceiling, then his footsteps coming down the stairs. The coffee was ready and the warmth was starting to pour off the front of the stove. His feet appeared, then his legs. It was happening. Their day together was beginning.

9

Zombie Apocalypse

✤

Pete Harrington pulled his Volkswagen shitbox in between Beth's maroon-colored Jaguar and the huge black SUV that looked like the kind of government vehicle that always got nuked by some dude with an RPG in action movies. And nuking shit with an RPG was definitely the theme for tonight, a theme that came on even stronger when he saw Bobby's 1961 Cadillac convertible parked across the driveway. He already had a plan. He was taking no bullshit and no prisoners. He was going to find out everything: who'd shadowed them in China, how they'd set it up, and why it had all been done behind his back. And then he was going to tell Charlie about it.

He crunched across the gravel and knocked extra loudly on the door, just to let them know he was pissed. The bullshit was over. No small talk, no cocktails. When that door opened, it was Go time.

He raised his fist again and brought it down hard on the wood. *Knock knock, I'm pissed!* Before he could finish the third knock, the locks clicked and the big wooden door swung open. A small teenage boy was standing in the entry. Dylan.

"Uncle Pete!"

" 'Ssup, Dylan!"

The boy reached up and they bumped knuckles. Dylan took after his mother: he was small by nature, like her, and along with that he hadn't hit puberty yet. He looked like a twelve-year-old, though he was nearly fifteen. His voice hadn't changed and his face was still smooth and childish. Pete had known him since he was a baby.

Pete put his hands on both of the skinny shoulders and squeezed him. "When are you coming over to hang out, my man? I got the new City of the Dead and I dominate!"

"What's your favorite weapon?" the boy asked.

"Shottie, hands down."

Dylan shook his head. "Meat cleaver: you never have to reload."

"Seriously?"

The boy pointed to himself. "Level eighteen!"

"*Fuck!*" the musician said in admiration, then put his hand over his mouth and looked to the sides to see if anyone had heard. "I mean, *impressive!* I keep getting swarmed in the hallway at level six."

"You need to go to the garage and get the can of gasoline." The boy was about to tell him how to incinerate the swarm of zombies on level 6 when his mother appeared. "Pete! Welcome!"

"Hey, Beth." He bent down and pecked her cheek. He remembered he was supposed to be angry, but he couldn't get it straight with Dylan standing there.

"Hey," Dylan piped up. "I saw you in that video. You fucked that guy up!"

"Dylan!" Beth said sharply. "Is that language really necessary?"

"You know what's necessary, Mom? *Oxygen.*"

Beth rolled her eyes at Pete, and he remembered her mentioning they'd been having trouble with him lately.

"Your mom's right, Dylan. Language."

"You *soooo* smoked that guy!"

Beth was watching him, which meant he'd better wheel out some boilerplate role-model shit. "Well . . . I did smoke his silly ass. But, you know, violence isn't really the way to solve problems."

"Who cares about solving problems? That was awesome! And he deserved it, didn't he?"

"He did, but, uh . . ."—he pulled another one off the message boards—"a person shouldn't take it on themselves to be judge, jury, and executioner. Society can't work like that."

The boy was at a loss, and Beth picked it up. "Dylan, I have to talk with Uncle Pete about some things in the den."

"Text me when you're done," her son told him. "I'll show you how to deal with the swarm on level six."

"It's on!"

He followed Beth down the long hallway. "I'm really pissed at you, Beth, but how's Dylan doing?"

She sighed. "His grades are cratering and he's got some new friends that I do not like at all. I just wish he'd hit puberty already. He's very depressed about his size. The kids at school call him 'shrimpie.'"

Pete felt a flash of anger. "Punks! I'm sorry to hear that." He thought for a moment. "Maybe he could come over and hang out at my house once in a while, sit in on rehearsals and stuff. You know, the rock star thing. It might give his ego a boost. We can play some video games. Have a boys' night out."

They'd reached the den, and she opened the doors. It was a big, low, dim room with dark furniture and a soft carpet. Bobby was sitting in an armchair and Ira was perched on the couch with a manuscript next to him. He looked up.

"Pete!"

"Hey, Ira." Had Ira been in on this, too? He clenched up inside at the thought, then he remembered his resolve: No prisoners. No bullshit.

Pete took a leather armchair, and Beth sat down next to her husband. There was a little pause as they waited for someone to start talking.

"We might as well get right into this, Pete," Beth started. "Bobby and I arranged for videos to be taken in Shanghai and for them to be leaked onto the Internet."

Shit. So it was true. It was true! "Both videos? The one with the Chinese subtitles, too?"

"Yes."

"Okay." He nodded. "What about the music video that mixes clips from the fight with performance footage and advertising stuff? The supposed Fan video."

"That was us, too."

"Then . . ." He threw his hands into the air. "This whole thing was fake!"

"Millions of views isn't fake," Bobby said. "That's real. All we did was get it started."

"No! All you did was take my life and turn it into a giant lie. Thanks!"

"Hold it," Beth said in her handling-it voice. "Before we go there, let's look at where you were when all this started. Okay? Your career was at a standstill and you hadn't written a new song in years. You had no tour, no band, and you'd lost pretty much all your money in the Crossroads scheme. Do you remember that? Because I remember it well."

He looked at the ceiling. Fucking *Beth*! "Conceded."

She continued. "Okay, so three months ago, I was sitting with my family eating dinner, and Bobby called me. He told me you'd lost all your money and you were in a very bad way and he didn't know how to handle it. He was afraid something awful was going to happen. Right, Bobby?"

"Right."

"Naturally, I dropped everything and rushed over to your house. And from my point of view, Pete, this is where the story really begins. Because the one thing that you articulated in those very confused hours, which included screaming 'fuck you!' at me and firing me as your ex-wife, was that you were going to find this Peter Harrington, punch him in the face, and write a song about it. Would you say that's an accurate rendition of events?"

He spread his arms to the sides. "Conceded!" He felt like he was being set up again, that Beth was putting everything in place just the way she wanted it and he'd have no alternative but to admit that she was right. "But—"

"Hold on! Let me just tell my side; then I'll listen patiently to your side. You said you wanted to touch the untouchable, and that that was what you needed to do to save yourself. Right?"

"To get justice, yes. Not to turn it into a public-relations event."

"I know that. Bobby knew it, too. But what does 'saving yourself' mean, Pete? I mean, *really*? Because you can touch the untouchable, or get justice, or payback or whatever you want to call it, but eventually you're going to get back home. And if you're still broke and your career is still going nowhere, have you really saved yourself?"

Bobby leaned forward. "It's like they say, Pete: if a tree falls in a forest and nobody hears it . . ." Bobby shrugged, as if he'd just laid down some ancient wisdom without even remembering the rest of the saying.

"*I* hear it. That's what matters."

"You hear it." Beth went on. "But how well are you going to hear it six months later, when you've got six new songs and nobody could care less."

Bobby picked it up again. "Pete, we did some great stuff and had some big wins, but the last five years, frankly, sucked. I'd make calls for Pete Harrington and nobody would call me back. I'd try to book dates, and the only places interested were crap venues that paid bullshit. Which didn't matter, because, to be brutally honest, I was afraid to book them for a client that hadn't written a song in five years and was too wasted to put together a band. I didn't want to end up with a bunch of nonperformance lawsuits like we did four years ago. Now, managers are kissing my ass to try to get their bands a gig opening for you. And that's all because of Beth."

What could he answer to that? Bobby was telling it true. "Conceded," he said softly.

"Pete," Beth continued, "there's a certain kind of rock star you don't want to be, and I see them all the time: guys trying to reboot their careers from nothing, or living on the vapors, looking over their shoulder hoping somebody will recognize them. They die a little every time some up-and-coming artist gets a paragraph in *Rolling Stone* because it used to be them, and it never will be again. They're bitter, sad, lost alcoholics. I didn't want to see you become one of them. That's why Bobby and I stepped in. Now you've got six new songs and your first hit in fifteen years. Millions of people want to know about you and your music: all kinds of people, not just your old demographic."

He hated seeing himself painted that way, like everything he did depended on them. "Yeah, but I wrote those six songs *before* I went to Shanghai. When I was still nothing, by your standards."

"Not nothing, Pete. You were still you. You were the guy that was willing to fly to Shanghai and punch that asshole in the face, which he richly deserved. That stands on its own."

"But you were manipulating me the whole time!"

"No!" Beth answered. "We were *facilitating* you. It was your idea and your determination that made it all happen."

He was confused. He'd come here tonight to get something straight, but he wasn't sure what it was anymore. "What about Charlie? Did he know?"

Bobby spoke. "Charlie knew everything, Pete. He arranged the videos. He got them shot and posted in China through his contacts there. He set it all up."

Pete didn't say anything. Charlie, too. He'd probably had people in the crowd of fans, or standing around on the Bund like tourists. Maybe that Chinese girl he'd met, too. Maybe it was all Charlie, even the part when he wanted to back out but went through with it anyway, for Charlie's sake. Maybe that was just Charlie playing him, again. He shook his head and let out a long breath that he hadn't realized he was holding. "Well, you got me on that one," he said quietly. "You got me."

Ira cleared his throat. Even though he'd been in Hollywood for a long time, he was still a book dude from New York, which set him apart. "Pete, I just heard about this a couple of hours ago, so I'm looking at it from the outside."

That was a relief. "Well, I'm glad there's at least one person who wasn't in on the joke."

"I admit: it's not a perfect way for things to happen. In fact, it's pretty damned weird. But I think Beth and Bobby were just trying to help you in the only way they could."

"Ira, they lied to me! I mean, you're a moral person: don't you see that's wrong?"

"Yes, it's wrong. They weren't honest. But they couldn't be. If they had been, then millions of people who've gotten a little bit of joy or a little feeling of justice from what you did never would have heard anything about it. There was nothing phony about what happened in Shanghai."

"I know that, Ira! I was proud of what I did! I thought I did something good. Something pure. For myself. Now all I think is, I got played! Again! Like I always do! And I'm supposed to spend the rest of my life lying about it! All these people are accusing me of a publicity stunt—I just want to say, Yeah, you're right! You're fucking right! It *was* all a publicity stunt! That's what I want to tell them."

Bobby actually came to his feet. "Pete, hold on! Just hold on! You need to get this straight! You're going on tour in one week. It's fully booked; we're adding extra dates. You're making six thousand dollars a day just in downloads. You can't fuck yourself over like that! You're mad at me? Fire me! But for God's sake, Pete, please don't piss this all away. You did something for people that they could never do for themselves, and they love you for it. They love you like a hero! But they love you because you're real, and they will hate you even harder if they think you're fake. They will turn on you like piranhas. Take a minute and imagine what that's going to feel like!"

Beth took up where Bobby left off. "You have all the power here, Pete. All you have to do is say *one* word in *one* interview, and it will all come crashing down. Within days. And all your effort to find that prick and strike a blow for the little guy will be completely undone. Your career will be over, and that will be permanent. That will be the rest of your life." Her voice caught. "Everybody in this room loves you, Pete. You're the only one we know who's crazy enough and brave enough and just . . . completely unreasonable enough to do what you did. You touched the untouchable. You really did. Please don't make it all look like a sham. Because it wasn't one."

He sat there hunched over and staring at his shoes. There was nothing he could say that they wouldn't have a perfectly good answer for. "You all see me as just a silly guy who sings okay and who'll act crazy enough to sell a few tickets. And you know something? Finally, I see myself that way, too. Thanks for making it all clear." He stood up to go. "Ask Charlie to call me, please."

"I'll do that tonight." Beth stood up. "Pete—"

He held up his hand. "Forget it, Beth. I can find my way out. I'd rather go out alone, if that's okay. Just respect me in that, at least."

"We'll talk tomorrow," she said.

"Sure, whatever. I'm still in. I'll shut up like a good boy." He opened the door of the den and hesitated. "You know the most demoralizing thing about all this, Beth? The most depressing thing? It's that I know you're right. Without you and Bobby, I'm just another over-the-hill rock star with a bunch of new songs that nobody wants to hear. I'm a nobody."

He went out and closed the door behind him. When he turned, Dylan was sitting there, watching, listening. He'd been waiting to show him how to advance in City of the Dead.

"Hey, Dylan."

The boy got up from the chair and stood in front of him. "What's wrong?"

Pete looked down at him. Dylan's eyes were at the level of his chest, gazing upward to his own. He wanted to get on his knees and talk to him, the way he'd used to, but Dylan was too old for that now. He patted his shoulder awkwardly instead. "Sometimes, my man . . ." He trailed off. He couldn't think of anything to say, didn't have some stale bromide he'd pulled down off an Internet commentary board. He looked down at the little person wanting so badly to grow, to be taken seriously, to be in control. All that impatience and unhappiness swirling there in that little face. "I'm really sad right now, Dylan. I'm forty-five years old and I don't understand life at all."

"Neither do I," the boy said, and he gave a beleaguered little smile. "But at least I can get you past level six."

Pete started laughing; then he felt his vision blurring. "Level six, eh? That's a start." He wanted to reach down and hug that last vestige of childhood but he knew it would make Dylan feel awkward, so he just stood there beaming at him for a few moments. At last he clapped his hand on the boy's upper arm. "Do your homework, man. 'Cause this weekend, you and me, we're fuckin' some zombies *up*!" He walked down the hallway, threw back, "I'll have my people set it up with your people."

"Got it!"

"That's your mom and dad, in case you were wondering."

"I know that!"

"Tell your sister I said hello."

"Okay!"

He unlatched the door and stepped outside, then put his face to the opening. "I love you, Dylan."

The voice came back to him. "I love you, too, Pete!"

He closed the door and started along the footlights that led to the driveway. The lawn was green in the little pools of footlight and black beyond that, and he walked along from pool to pool listening to his soles scuff on the brick pathway. He was going to be asked about Shanghai in e-mails and in interviews, forever. His mother was going to ask about it, and so would his sisters. Even Dylan would ask him one day if it was real, and he'd have to go on lying. He felt a mixture of sadness and confusion and grief and, somewhere in there, the warmth of Dylan's consolation. And maybe it was supposed to be like that, that mix of all those opposite things at once, that you were supposed to just let wash over you without trying to identify and name each one. He gave up trying to figure any of it out and just let it play across his mind. His phone buzzed, but he ignored it.

When he got home, he checked his voice mail on the call he hadn't answered. Charlie had left a message, and, as pissed as he was at him, he couldn't help feeling a flush of affection when he heard the old man's voice. "Pete! If you're not sore, I'd like you to meet someone."

10

Super-Hot Mystery Babe

✢

Pete guessed the heat was off. Beth's lawyer had already said there was no real legal threat, and whatever other revenge Peter Harrington might be planning didn't seem to be happening. No nasty letters. No smear campaign. It seemed like the guy had just decided to drop it. Charlie named a coffee shop up on Melrose and said twelve noon would be the best time. It surprised Pete that he didn't specify Canter's Deli, their usual place. When he got there, Charlie was sitting in a booth at the back of the room, facing the door. He pulled himself carefully to his feet as Pete came in and watched the singer cross the restaurant, a serious look on his face. He put his hand out to shake, then motioned toward the booth. "Your ex called. I figured it was time we talked."

"Thanks." Pete slid onto the plastic cushion, acutely aware that his back was to the door. Charlie could have somebody slip in with a silenced .25 and put a slug into his skull. The old man seemed a little sinister now, and, at the same time, there was a crap-load of stuff he was itching to talk over with him. They'd never done the kind of postgame commentary where you talk shit about the touchdowns you scored and all the mistakes the boneheads on the other side made. He wasn't sure where to start. There were three menus on the table, and he picked one up and looked it over without saying anything. Let Charlie make the first move.

"Are you sore at me?" Charlie finally asked.

"Why would I be sore at you?"

"C'mon, Pete! We went over there and we got the job done. That's something to be happy about."

"You lied to me, Charlie."

He gave a soft sigh. "I did what I was hired to do—"

"Yeah, I understand that. Your job was to lie to me. That whole time, when I thought I was doing some hero shit and striking a blow for the good guys, that whole time I was just somebody being *managed*."

Charlie didn't get excited. "Do you wish you'd known? Because my guess is, to your credit, we'd have flown back from Shanghai right away. And I say to your credit because I know you're not a phony. You've got integrity. You'd never do something so calculating and self-interested. Instead, you'd have spent the rest of your life sinking into some long, pathetic, drunken retirement, wishing you'd taken that one shot when you had the chance."

"You're right, Charlie! Okay? That's been explained to me six thousand times already. I'm all out of logical resistance. But somehow, I just wish it had been real."

"Pete, it was real!" Charlie got a strange expression on his face, almost a smile. "You think it's not real, but it's a bigger real. That's what I wanted to show you today."

"What do you mean?"

"You'll find out. But let me say this: I'm sorry I wasn't straight with you. This job was on a need-to-know basis for all the obvious reasons, and I'm sorry I couldn't be completely honest. I thought I was looking out for your best interests." Charlie cleared his throat. "Also, I never got a chance to tell you how much you impressed me. I've seen a lot of trained intelligence professionals who would have had trouble pulling that off the way you did, first time out."

"Thanks, Charlie. But now I've got to lie about it the rest of my life. How do I manage that?"

"You just tell your part of it," the old man said mildly. "You had a gripe, you went to Shanghai, and you set Peter Harrington straight. You don't know anything about anything else. After a while, people will quit asking. They always do."

"Great. That's kind of depressing all by itself."

"Do you forgive me?"

He looked at the deep wrinkles in Charlie's old face and the misty eyes. Yeah, he was a deceptive, manipulative old man, but there was something there that was true. "Charlie, man, how could I be mad at you? I'm not capable of staying mad at anyone. It's a fucking character flaw. And you know something? By the time we went to Shanghai, I wasn't even pissed at that guy anymore. I only hit him at the end because I didn't want to fail on you." He lit up at the memory. "Especially after you took down the bodyguard. Dude, you played him like the two of clubs!"

Charlie grinned. "Aawww! That was easy. You should have seen it: he kept apologizing all the way to the hospital."

"Were you hurt?"

"No. But I didn't want them to know that."

Pete saw Charlie's gaze shift past his shoulder, then his face took on an expression he hadn't seen on him before: a rapt and delighted smile that filled his eyes. Charlie began to slide out of the booth, still looking toward the door, and Pete turned around.

There was an old woman coming toward them across the restaurant. She must have been eighty, slightly bent at the shoulders, wearing a powder-blue cashmere sweater over a pale pink blouse, her white hair twisted into thick braids that were wrapped gracefully around the top of her head, Heidi-style.

"Pete, I'd like you to meet an old friend of mine. Anna Maier."

"Anna Goldstein," she corrected, raising her hand toward Pete. "It's a pleasure."

"With all due respect for Mr. Goldstein," Charlie said, "she was Maier when we met. Old habits die hard."

Charlie had the kind of lift in his voice that Pete's grandfather would have called "chipper," a word he'd never used before but that fit perfectly here. Pete grasped her hand, which was small and dry and delicate, and mumbled something polite. He took in her powdered face, with the lipstick and rouge she'd applied, the snowy cables of hair held perfectly in place with bobby pins, the pearls. She'd made an effort to look pretty, and she *was* pretty! Charlie was *beaming*! It was really happening here!

They all sat down, with Pete and Charlie facing Anna. She had rich brown eyes. "This is very exciting for me," she said, pleasantly. "I don't get to meet many famous people."

"Hey! You're the star at this table. I'm just hoping some paparazzi ambushes us: *Pete Harrington Seen with Super-Hot Mystery Babe!* My buzz will skyrocket!"

She laughed and looked at Charlie, who shook his head at her. "I told you!"

"So how do you two know each other?" Pete asked.

"We met in Shanghai after the war," the woman explained. "Then we didn't see each other for sixty-four years."

"Which is a long time to wait for a second date," Charlie threw in.

Shanghai . . . Pete looked at one, and then at the other. He could tell he was riding the surface of a very deep swell.

The waitress came over and they hurriedly scanned the menus. He put on his Gucci reading glasses.

"What are you having?" Charlie asked him. "They've got a pretty good clubhouse sandwich here."

Pete started to order it, then stopped and looked at the old man. "Forget it! You're just trying to see if you can get me to order the clubhouse! I am so on to you." Charlie started laughing as Pete turned to the waitress. "I'll have the bacon cheeseburger, thank you." Then, "Beware, Anna. This man *will* play you!"

"Thank you, Mr. Harrington, but I think I can handle Charlie." They finished ordering, and she stood up. "Excuse me, gentlemen. I'll be right back."

Pete watched her walk away, unable to keep himself from checking out her shape. This was how Charlie saw her, how he'd seen her sixty-four years ago. Pete slid into her side of the booth, then leaned across the table. "So . . . Charlie . . . What's up, my man?" Charlie grinned back at him. "This is, like, some Shanghai situation. I thought it was the waitress at Canter's!"

"You never have been too quick on the uptake when it comes to women."

He opened his mouth wide. "Whoa! No! You *cannot* groin kick me about women!"

"Your ex? She's a piece of work."

"Beth is a fucking *Charlie,* Charlie! No! Beth's the person Charlie reports to, which is even more badass. Besides, that was a learning experience. Let's talk about you. And Anna. *Anna!* And, by the way, I heard you call her 'Maier,' trying to remind her how single she is. Believe me, you will never come up with a play that I haven't already thought of"—he raised his eyebrows—"*or tried.*" He shrugged. "Successfully or unsuccessfully."

"Yeah, yeah."

"Seriously, brief me on the Anna situation."

"Well, you remember I told you I had some loose ends to tie up in Shanghai." And with that the old man teed off on the whole incredible story, with the Jewish refugee and the ex-Nazi and the shifty black-market dude and that whole lost city that Pete wished he'd known to ask him about when they were there. He heard the entire story then he just sat back. "*Wow!* You actually shanked him? That's fucking *intense!* How did you find Anna again?"

"After you left, I went to the Shanghai Jewish Refugees Museum and checked their records. She was here the whole time! Right under my nose. I just never made the effort."

"Why not?"

He tilted his head. "Oh, Pete. I'd had a whole life. I thought it wasn't important anymore. When I found out your job was in Shanghai, it got me thinking." He leaned in, astonishment in his voice. "Sixty-four years, Pete! It's a miracle." He leaned back, nodding his head. "And this has all happened because of you and your crazy idea about getting even with Peter Harrington. You know, I went back there to prove to myself that I still had it, but what I found out was, it didn't matter. I already had it. I always had it."

"What do you mean?"

But then Charlie's gaze shifted and his face lit up again, and Pete knew that Anna had come back.

They had a long, relaxed lunch, talking about his upcoming tour and the music business and the events of the long years that had gone by since they had met. After a while it was time for Pete to go back to preparing for his departure.

Charlie stood up. "It's good to see you, my friend. When are you getting back to Los Angeles?"

"Two months. Three months. Not sure. They keep adding dates. But I'll call you. I still want you to teach me that Chin Chin stuff."

"Chin-na. You want to learn it?"

"Yeah."

"You know what kind of teacher I am."

"I know, dude: a crazy one! Let's do it!"

"Good!" Charlie clapped him on the shoulder, his old eyes gleaming. "I'm retired now, you know."

"You are? Why?"

"I don't need it anymore!" Charlie stood there silently with his hand on Pete's arm, as if he couldn't quite figure out exactly what words to hang on his thought. Finally he spoke in a voice so soft that only Pete could hear: "You already have it. Remember that."

Pete nodded, not knowing how else to answer. He threw a fifty-dollar bill onto the table. "It's my treat, kids. Anna, it's been a pleasure. I hope I'll see you again before too long, and in the meantime, take my advice: if paparazzi get in your face and you have to deck one, try not to break the camera, because they charge you extra for that in court."

She smiled a sweet old-lady smile. "I'll certainly remember that."

He turned back and looked at them before he left. They were leaning slightly forward over the table, chatting like any two very old people that he might see in any restaurant, people that had survived the war, the one-sided unwinnable war where everything was taken away—mothers, wives, children, friends—and nevertheless they were smiling, laughing; they were reaching for the sugar or the cream. There was something noble about that, that you could be so very old and still be open to the magic, not some marquee, reality-show version but something more hidden, quieter, more resonant. He wanted to write about it, and since it was about old people it should theoretically be a sad song, but what he really wanted was something miraculous, something awesome and moving and magical, that told everything about Shanghai and time and lost years and the things that were right in front of you if you just knew how to recognize them. But he knew he'd never find a name for it, and he had no idea how it should sound.

He stepped out into the relentless sunshine of Los Angeles. The street felt parched and arid. He'd leased a BMW and it was parked a block away. People recognized him as he walked, but he returned their greetings with an empty nod and didn't break pace. He had a song at number 4 on the pop charts and a string of sold-out tour dates, but he felt empty and alone. No wife, no girlfriend he'd been loyal to for more than a year, no kids of his own to give advice to. Even his music felt empty right now, like it had been written by another person, and that person would shortly be on tour, performing, while he looked on from the outside.

11

Alaska Coastal Airlines

✛

The strange thing was, Pete Harrington wasn't supposed to be in Juneau at all. It was a mistake; he was headed somewhere else and instead ended up pinned between the sea and the ice fields in some end-of-the-world town. He and the band were on their way to the concert in Anchorage, a place they'd played years ago, before they got big. They'd left Seattle at some ridiculous hour of the morning and he'd listened in the dark as the pilot announced places he'd never heard of: Prince Rupert, Ketchikan, Sitka. Just past Sitka, strange sounds started coming from one of the engines, and the flight attendants nervously picked up the drinks. A few minutes later they were plunging out of the clouds toward the steep, ragged mountains of the coast. Snow began whipping past his window, curving off into the dim morning.

From above, it was a hostile-looking place. The mountains were sharp and steep at their tops, dropping down in thick black forest all the way to the ocean. Shreds of cloud were trapped across some of the ridges, and the scene looked like twilight, even though it was seven in the morning. There were long white glaciers creeping out of a vast ice field behind the town, crawling toward the dark sea. It was a world of white and black and gray.

The plane banked so steeply that it threw him to the side of his seat; then the engines roared louder than he'd ever heard before. They swooped down, and there was a bump and a loud bang, then another bump, and then they were rolling down the runway with the flaps up and that forward lean of deceleration. A cheer went up, and then a round of applause, and then the pilot came on and welcomed everyone to Juneau. Alaska Airlines personnel would be waiting to arrange their connecting flights at the ticket counter.

The upshot was that they weren't going anywhere. The planes weren't landing because of the snow, so there were no planes to take anyone onward. They might get out the next day. It depended on the weather. Bobby booked them a hotel in the city's center.

He stepped outside. The air was cold and fresh. Nothing was flat except some marshes and the narrow strip of ocean bounded on the far side by a giant island. In every direction, the mountains rose abruptly out of the water, and they were covered with snow-crusted trees that gave way to perfect white heights. On the land side, a blue-white glacier rose out of a gap in the wall of peaks and climbed to the horizon.

They couldn't all fit into one taxi, so he sent the band ahead in the first van and said he'd wait. Duffy offered to hang with him, but he wanted to be alone, anyway. The first round of taxis had already left, and he stood there shivering for fifteen minutes in a baseball jacket until another taxi arrived.

The driver was a heavyset man with dark skin and wide cheekbones who didn't recognize him. At first Pete thought he was Japanese, and then he noticed the tribal insignia on the man's ball cap—some sort of stylized whale—and the TLINGIT POWER bumper sticker. The driver asked him if he was on the flight to Anchorage that got forced down. "Lucky you guys could land," he said. "Nobody's gotten in or out for the last two days 'cause of the snow." The snow was piled up in huge berms everywhere he looked. The parking lot had a mound twenty feet high, and along the short highway giant plows were hustling here and there, grinding their blades.

By the time he reached the hotel, it was eight in the morning, but there was no visible sun and the landscape was still dim. The hotel room was the same kind of anonymous place he was used to, distinguished only by the totemic artwork and the window filled with the faint outlines of ocean and mountains. He was hungry, and he asked the desk clerk for a good place to eat. She was Indian, too, he guessed, around his age, heavy, no-nonsense. She looked sleepy, like she was finishing up the night shift. She didn't recognize him, though she must have suspected he was someone be-cause she'd seen the rest of the band. Maybe in this town, everybody was someone.

She recommended a restaurant across the street and he ordered coffee with bacon and eggs; then he canceled the bacon and ordered oatmeal, like, *Yeah, healthy choices.* He looked out the window at the wintry sea and the black-green mountains that rose out of it. The waitress was a young woman with a pierced nose, kind of that Seattle/Portland vibe but rougher. No makeup, no color in her hair. She was pretty, in a careless way, a way some-one who had grown up in this town would home in on and fall into com-pletely, and he had a strange urge to say, *Hey, I'm Pete Harrington and my plane broke down on the way to Anchorage,* but he wasn't sure why he would say it and what he would ask her for. A couple of older men were sitting at a booth with a pot of coffee between them, talking something over in serious tones. One had on blue coveralls that said ALASKA COASTAL AIRLINES and his name in a little oval on the front, and the other was dressed in the kind of plaid shirt his grandfather used to wear, as if Gramps had somehow got-ten here, to this little town.

The waitress brought him his bowl of oatmeal and his coffee and gave him a smile that made him look at her again, thinking *maybe . . .* He started to flash on the possibilities, but he stopped himself. She was way too young for him. He was forty-five years old, and if all the pieces were going to sud-denly fall into place, the way they had for Charlie, a twenty-year-old prob-ably wasn't going to be one of them.

Something about that thought put him at ease. He ate his breakfast and left ten dollars on the table and went out onto the street. The sky had got-ten light and the place suddenly seemed mysterious and beckoning. He had the distinct feeling that somewhere in this town, somewhere in those clusters of little wooden houses perched above on the side of the mountain, there were possibilities so unlikely and gorgeous that even though he couldn't admit to hoping for them, he couldn't let them go. He no longer cared about the next flight to Anchorage, where Pete Harrington was scheduled to play. He was where he was, in this little town on the coast of Alaska, which he'd never foreseen but that felt entirely familiar. It wasn't like the "Vanity Fair" song he'd written at all. It was more like the song he'd never been able to write, the one about the house, and his grandfather, and the girl, and the light in the window. As ludicrous as it was, he had the strange conviction that he could stay here his whole life and be happy.

He started to walk up the hill. He went two blocks, past a health food store and a barbershop and a bank, then turned toward the mountain and kept going. It must have snowed like crazy the night before because the snow was nearly a foot deep and still untracked in the early morning. He could feel it filtering in at the ankles of his tennis shoes, but he didn't care. It had been so long since he'd walked in snow like this. So long. Probably since he'd been a kid. He and Cody, sledding.

There were only houses now, neat little dwellings, each in their own lot, with bags of salt and snow shovels leaning up against their porch railings. The street ended here and became a stairway that continued up the mountain. He walked to the bottom of it and looked at the long succession of metal treads that climbed higher and higher through a tunnel of overhanging branches. He couldn't make out what was at the top. Far away he heard a voice call out, then a child's voice answer back, and then a door shut. He held perfectly still. The whole world seemed to vibrate around him.

He felt himself disappearing. He didn't have to be Pete Harrington anymore; he could be nobody. Just some guy who lived here near his old friends, and had known their kids since they were babies, and had his own kids. Somewhere in this town was his house, coming awake in the early morning with a cup of coffee percolating. It was dawn of that day, that one single day that contained his entire life stretching out before and behind it, the only day, always, beginning.

VI

✦

The
Unnamed
Line in the
Distant North

✦

The snow came down whispering, ceaselessly whispering in Harry Harrington's ear, in a cold, insinuating voice that made him go quietly, secretly insane.

It had started three days ago, a heavy, wet, ten-inch dump that had loaded down the slopes and sagged longingly toward the valleys. It rained after that, saturating the snow at the lower elevations and then cooling down and freezing as hard and smooth as porcelain. The avalanche center reported the hazard as "moderate."

Then it started snowing again, fine snow shaken out of a hard silver sky at temperatures near zero, and Harry watched helplessly as the tiny flakes fell around him, flakes so light he could scatter them with his breath. It leveled up at sixteen inches, crouching on the shoulders of the mountains and hissing down the steeper slopes in little unseen sloughs. The avalanche center reported the hazard as "high."

The following day, Friday, the sky went dark and fretful with the heaviest snow of the year, lashing two feet onto the mountains in less than twenty-four hours. Strong winds moved it across ridges and left it hanging on the lee sides in massive slabs. Cornices hung above steep mountain slopes like the crest of three-thousand-foot waves. Millions of tons of snow settled and stretched and fissured at invisible stress points. The avalanche center raised the hazard level to "extreme."

"Dude, we're naming No Name today."

Jarrod Harrington felt a tiny thrill go through his stomach like a guitar riff, but he took his time, then spoke into the phone in a low, monotonous rumble. "Who else is in?"

"You and me. Brandon, Lucas, TJ. The boys!" Jimmie kept up in that promoter's voice of his. "C'mon J, how often do we get to ride together? I'm out of here tomorrow."

He peered out the window at the delicate ridge of snow balanced ten inches high on the railing of the back deck. "The avalanche hazard's gotta be ridiculous."

"Not in the steeps. Anything that could slide already has. It's self-controlling."

Self-controlling. Jimmie was resourceful in coming up with crap like that. "Lucas said he's in?"

There was a slight hesitation, then Jimmie said lightly, "Lucas's in. I just need to talk to him." His voice suddenly lost its wheedling tone and became matter-of-fact. "No Name's never going to be better, J. You want to ride immortal, you gotta live with some risk."

He'd heard Jimmie spout crap like that a hundred times over the years, and little alarms went off whenever his friend started working him. But the truth was, Jimmie *did* ride immortal. He'd won a half-dozen big-mountain competitions and had a sponsor that kept him in gear and spending money and sent him to South America in the summer to ride on. He could read about him in *Transworld* getting heli-bumps in Haines or partying at some-body's secret Bugaboos hideaway. "Lemme think it over."

Harry Harrington's only son hung up the phone and looked out the window. From the kitchen table he could see across the water to where the clouds were swarming over the tops of the mountains. Jimmie was full of shit about it being self-controlling. The avalanche hazard would be insane. But for all his bullshit, Jimmie was right about one thing: they'd never have better conditions for dropping No Name. And whoever dropped it, named it.

Jarrod lived with his parents in an old wooden miner's house perched in the part of town where the streets sliced up the side of the mountain so steeply that they had to be closed in winter. His great grandfather had built it in 1932, a little house with three tiny bedrooms and a potbellied stove. With its steeply peaked roof and its deep eaves it looked a bit like a gingerbread house, just like the other houses on the street. He supposed that it might be his someday, or his sister's, but he didn't care much. He had bigger destinies in mind.

His gear was hanging in the corner by the hot woodstove: huge black boots, waterproof pants, and a baggy snow jacket. He thumped down to the basement and came back with his board, a cherry-red big-mountain splitboard from Canada that stretched a foot longer than anyone else's and was made exclusively for going at high speeds in deep, untouched powder. An expensive and fairly exotic piece of equipment, it split apart into two skis for the ascent, then fitted together into a snowboard again for the ride down. A high school graduation present from his father, which, like most things from his father, came without a lot of words.

Jarrod loved the splitboard. It matched his tall, thin body and looked competent and slightly dangerous, like an electric guitar in a stadium, except his stadium was an amphitheater of snow and wind. The board was his battle-ax and his shield. He was invincible when he strapped it on, could drop any cliff and straight-line down even the steepest pitches, pull out into a turn, and feel the powder explode up into his face. He could fly off a little knoll and land it sixty feet away, then keep on going, like it just didn't matter. And that was the essential thing about life, among the wondering about what work he'd do someday or if he'd finish college: that at bottom it just didn't matter. If you could go fast enough, and fly far enough, you were free.

He laid the board on the floor and began tightening some screws in the bindings. So there was some avalanche hazard. Sure. There was always hazard. But the boys would all be there, and just that fact meant it would turn out okay. No matter what kind of crazy shit they'd taken on over the years—jumping off the bridge, driving shit-faced, free-climbing the cliffs above the glacier—it always turned out okay, while the bad stuff happened to other people. Besides, the hazard was on the slopes, while they'd mostly be in the woods and then on the ridge until they got to No Name. And Jimmie was probably right; the steeps usually were self-controlling, and No Name was the steepest thing around.

Then his little game ended and he thought of No Name itself, and the avalanche talk just felt like a cover for his own fears. No Name was the real player here. From some angles the chute looked doable, but from others it didn't, except if there was a lot of snow. The only way to know for sure was just to drop in, and then you'd know. No Name was the blank stare; it was sudden death—and, as he thought about it, either of those would be good names for it if he managed to be the first to drop it. Or maybe he'd name it Jarrod Harrington Dropped This Chute and Nobody Else Had the Balls. That would look good in *Transworld Snowboarding*.

He'd had a few photos in there already. When Jimmie won his first competitions, Brandon's pictures of him started showing up in *Plank* and *Transworld*, and then he'd been able to start selling shots of the others, too. Images of them getting insane air or launching off of snow-covered trees into the sick blue void, accompanied by their names and the words "in Juneau, Alaska." The ski lodge displayed the pictures in a glass case, and everybody in town who rode looked up to them. Him, Jimmie, TJ, Lucas. They were the local boys—this generation's big dogs.

There was another generation of big dogs, though. The last generation. Now they were carpenters and contractors, worked in the city assessor's office. Nursing ruined knees and paunches, they skied hard, but not as hard as they used to, and mostly on weekends. Twenty years ago they'd been the ones getting dropped off in scary places in the ice fields, making first descents on gear that had seemed exotic and hypermodern at the time but were now antiques, yesteryear's thousand-dollar boards seen only in some anachronistic corner of the used ski swap with a $1 price tag on them. Peter

"Harry" Harrington was the biggest of those old dogs, walked now into his kitchen and glanced at his son adjusting the bindings on the big red board.

Harry Harrington was long and lean-faced, like his son, but heavier at the shoulders and wider in the middle. His sandy hair was dulling to gray on the sides. His picture was under the glass at the ski area, too, though the colors had yellowed a bit.

He was a quiet, intense man who rarely raised his low voice but radiated a calm authority. Even Jarrod's friends admired him. They'd all watched the few ancient videos of him posted on the Web. They joked about the funky ski outfits and ridiculously long grand-slalom skis, but he did things on those skis that were hard to do now on the fat new gear that made everything three times easier. He'd still go ripping through the ski area, moving with an almost frightening speed, dropping eight-footers without slowing down and blowing through the trees like a freight train. Even the Boys went silent when he whipped past. *Dude,* they might say, *your dad can ski!* They'd all seen the old photos and heard the stories: how he'd dropped a hundred-foot cliff in Utah and how he'd skied a line in a competition that the guy after him had been killed trying to follow. But stuff that had happened twenty years ago seemed archaic, like that old gear. And the world champions of before would just be pretty good skiers now. Wouldn't they?

"I'm making some oatmeal," the father said. "You want some?"

"I'm good. Here in the twenty-first century people eat breakfast cereal."

"You think it's old-fashioned. It's not old-fashioned. Oatmeal kicks ass all day long."

"I'm good, Dad."

He put some extra in the pot anyway. Sometimes the boy said no, then ate some after all. Butter, brown sugar, raisins: it was like sliding a nuclear fuel rod into your stomach.

He walked over to the board to check out the bindings. "Hey!" he said. "How about I go skiing today and you go in to work for me?"

"Old guys are supposed to work. It's the way of the world."

"Where are you going?"

"We're not sure yet. We might end up setting up a jump on the back side of the ridge and practice spins, I'm getting my ten-eighty dialed in."

It was a fairly transparent misdirection; the splitboard was completely unsuited to those kinds of tricks. It was his son's way of telling him something was up. "Where else might you go?"

The boy answered with an irritable groan, then reluctantly offered, "We're thinking about going out to the Wedding Bowl. There's a chute there we've been wanting to hit."

The Wedding Bowl was a huge hollow in a mountain that took two or three hours by snowshoe or ski to reach. Its upper rims were sheer cliffs, split by fissures that had eroded over the millennia into near-vertical chutes that could be skied when they were full of snow. Some were wide enough to make an easy side-to-side descent. Others narrowed to three feet, where the only option was to point it down between the jagged rock walls and try not to panic until it widened out again.

Harry had skied most of them as a teenager, but now the kids used different names: Shit for Brains, Cropley Extreme . . . "Which one were you thinking about?"

"We just call it No Name. No one's ever done it before."

The older man nodded slowly. He had a nearly photographic memory for difficult runs, but even without a description, he knew which chute they were talking about. It hadn't had a name in his day either. They'd called it That Other Chute.

"Second to last one out on the east side, right? It's narrow at the top, cuts left around some boulders, then seems to cliff out at a narrow gorge so you have to line it up perfectly, drop about twelve feet straight down through the throat, and land it without turning your skis. Then there's a second cliff, maybe thirty feet, with a good landing zone."

Jarrod raised his eyebrows, impressed. "That's it."

"Except you can't really get a good look at it. Unless you got a helicopter."

"No," his son said.

Harry remembered it clearly. The closest he'd gotten was to stand up at the top of it for a half hour one day. His buddies had been silent on that one:

no cheering, no jokes. Not even impatience. He stood there, and then the clouds started to move down, and the light got flat, and it started snowing hard, and someone said they could get whited out pretty easily. He finally did the next chute over, and they'd skied home without much talk. He'd always felt he could have done it if he'd taken that first step, but there was no payday in it; just a nasty, dangerous little chute that maybe forty people in the world knew about.

He shook the memory off. "This one of Jimmie's ideas?" he asked.

"Sort of," his son muttered. "And mine, too."

"Have you thought about the avalanche hazard?"

"Jimmie says it's self-controlling."

He swung his head back and forth, irritated. "Let me tell you something about Jimmie: he's the kind of friend who'll get you killed. It's all fun and it's all cool and *rah rah, let's go for it, boys,* and then somebody's lying there with a broken femur and all Jimmie can do is say, 'Oops! Sorry, dude!' I've seen plenty of guys like Jimmie. Who else is in on this?"

Jarrod looked to the side and frowned, reciting the usual crew. They'd all been on boards since they were toddlers. TJ, a wiry little ski-racer whose father had been Jarrod's dentist, and Brandon, a Filipino kid who had started selling his pictures to magazines. Lucas, a low-key, polite boy who said little but had taken a wilderness EMT course and would be the one with the radios and the first-aid kit. If Lucas was with them, there'd probably be a degree of good sense exercised.

And then there was Jimmie, a reckless half-wit who'd already been busted for drunk driving and was the one kid in Jarrod's little gang that Harry had never liked. He was slick even in grade school, always in the middle of the problem and always with a good excuse for why it was someone else's fault. He could ride, though: he'd won a bunch of big-mountain competitions and had been in some movies pulling double corks off sixty-foot cliffs: stuff they hadn't even invented back in Harry's day. He'd shown up on the cover of a magazine last year going huge in Valdez, and that seemed to cement his position as leader of the pack whenever he was in town. With Jimmie there calling the shots any jackass stunt was possible.

"Yeah," he looked to the side before he spoke, gathered himself. "I wouldn't go out there today. The lee side of the ridges are going to be wind-loaded, and there's still that layer of glazed snow that all this lighter stuff is sitting on. Wait a few days for the snow to consolidate, then hit No Name, or whatever it is."

"We'll all have avalanche gear."

"Does that include a backhoe? Because if I was buried under ten feet of snow I'm not sure I'd want to bet my life on how fast Jimmie could dig me out with his little aluminum shovel."

His son hesitated before trying to negotiate. "How about, we go check it out, and if it's too unstable, we'll come back."

"After a two-hour climb you're just going to turn around again? I don't give Jimmie credit for that much brains."

"We're not talking about Jimmie; we're talking about me!"

He backed off. A little too vehement there. A little too Dad. He brightened up. "Why don't you guys ride in-bounds today? The powder's going to be awesome. Or go set up jumps on the backside of the Ridge, like you were talking about."

"We've been up there a thousand times. Nobody's ever dropped No Name."

"Yeah, well . . ." His son was glaring at him. He was nineteen now, barely stopping in at the house to sleep. He didn't have too many direct orders left. He said flatly, "You're not dropping it today."

Jarrod went back to his board without answering, and his father took that as acquiescence. He was a sensible kid.

The oatmeal was bubbling now, and he went over to the stove and slid it off the burner. "I made a little extra, if you want—"

"I said I'm good!"

"Hey!" He quieted his voice again and said, "You're going skiing. I'm going to swing a hammer all day. On a Saturday." He mixed in some raisins and walnuts, then added some more butter, just in case. Maybe he'd go up in the afternoon and do a few runs, if he finished up in time. He always told himself that.

He looked at his watch. "Shit! I'm late!" He put on a jacket and a hat and brought the bowl of oatmeal with him. When he stepped out the door, his foot sank into ten inches of new powder. Light snow. God's-grace kind of snow, covering up the dog shit and the litter and making the world fresh and perfect. He stopped there, paralyzed, as an agonizing remorse swept over him. In that moment his whole life felt useless and defeated. He should be up there, where it was white, angelic. Instead, he was going in to work.

He looked up into the woods behind his house. The forest floor was covered under the lumpy cushion of fresh snow, leaving only the dark gray bark of the hemlocks rising out of it in columns. He could imagine coming down the mountain and doing a perfect tree run, cutting into his neighbor's backyard, and then popping off that little roller between the two houses, landing it in the street and spraying a big rooster tail right into the back of his truck. He'd done that before, a long time ago, when it was deep like this. Did it with Guy, flailed through waist-deep snow for an hour and a half just for a one-minute run, and Mother had met them at the door with a cup of cocoa in a blue-enameled tin cup. He remembered the metal hot against his lips. Must have been twelve. Didn't worry about avalanches back then.

He thought of the boy again, then turned back to the house and walked in as far as the entry to the living room, still carrying the bowl of steaming oats. Jarrod had gotten his short board out and was smoothing wax on it with the iron. The big board was leaning against the wall next to the basement door. His son kept smoothing the wax, silently, but Harry felt a wave of gratitude and affection for him. "Thanks, Jarrod. When conditions are better, you want to do that chute, I'll go with you. Maybe I'll do it myself."

Jarrod didn't answer, and Harry started again, "Hey, I said when conditions are better—"

His son cut him off. "I got it, Dad. Go eat your oatmeal."

He clenched his jaw and went out again. Across the street, his pickup was softened by a thick cake of snow. He'd grown up in this house, knew every board and shingle on this street the way he knew every pillow and turn on his favorite runs. The Caspersons had lived in that green house back when it had been white, then the Sundquists, who had the palsied kid, then the Heberts and that young couple who he never got to know. Now it was Rajiv and his family. He could do that with every house on Kennedy Street, like he was lazing down a not-particularly-difficult line whose gullies and drops descended through the last forty years. He was a local, not just to the town or this neighborhood, but to this southern block of Kennedy Street.

He brushed the snow off the windshield and the hood with wide, sweeping strokes. The flecks of white floated slowly away in the still air. He'd always said he'd never go to work on a Saturday if there was fresh powder. That in itself was a fallback from when he used to say he'd never go to work on a powder day, period. Punk kid talk. Now here he was. Put in five days at the hardware store, and now this. His brother-in-law was behind on the project, and he wanted to help out, and he damn sure needed the extra money after that stock-market mess. His father had been a partner in the hardware store, had taught him enough about the business to give a sense of inevitability to his life, no matter how long he tried to duck it on the meager circuit that had existed for extreme skiers back then.

Not that there had been anything glamorous about it. He remembered the hotel rooms with cheap wood paneling, the beater cars and the sponsors who were always nickel-and-diming him about gas receipts and bar tabs. In a great year, he earned five thousand dollars and spent the other six months working construction or fishing out of Bristol Bay. Not too much glory, either: nobody was famous except for the little cloud of notoriety that hovered among a small circle of skiers at each mountain, something you saw in the eyes of people helping with the event or sitting around a wooden table in some tavern at the end of the day. That was the nature of being the best in a sport nobody cared about, but it never occurred to him that he was missing anything. Other people had jobs, while he was paid to live in a world of pure motion that came rushing up in front of him and dropped away behind in a single, continual moment. A single moment that became a single day, that became a single winter of snow and velocity and fire. But now, years later, that moment was gone.

He wished his wife were around. She'd settle him down with something like, *That's what puts food on the table!* Or, *Don't worry, honey, there'll be more snow tomorrow.* But she wouldn't be home from the hospital for another hour. They were making her work half shifts on Saturdays, which they both hated, but with the staff cutbacks she had to fill in until they could get things back on course. Wasn't supposed to be like that. She was supposed to have seniority. But nobody had seniority under the new ownership, and all hands were on deck.

At forty-four, she was still a good-looking woman. A little more curvy, a little more weight settled down to her butt, but still a desirable woman, by any standards. At his age, he could appreciate someone more rounded. When he was young, he'd been looking for the hard bodies, the muscular women with no fat, and she'd been one of those. Straight blond hair, moved up from Colorado. Typical kind of Swedish blonde, right out of a magazine. But educated. Graduated college. Her father was an architect in Denver and didn't hide the fact that he thought she was marrying down. He could still remember meeting her at the Alaskan, when she'd been sitting around a table with a couple of her friends and a couple of his, and Dave had shouted, "Wreckage!" as he walked up to the table, then congratulated him on his win at Valdez. The kind of introduction a buddy gives you when he wants to make you look good. "Wreckage" was playing everywhere back then, when he was twenty-five. For a while he'd had that as a nickname, because his given name was Peter and because he skied so fast and wrecked so hard, on those rare occasions when he wrecked.

"What did you win?" she asked him when he sat down. Not much, he told her, because it wasn't much. Four hundred bucks and a beer mug. A couple of free rides in a helicopter. That was the prize for being the best in those days. That, and having a good opening line in the bars.

"I mean, what did you win *at*?"

He'd shrugged. "Put fifty guys up on a mountain and see who takes the most outrageous line down, give him marks for style, and if you're just a little crazier than the rest and all your arms and legs still work at the bottom, you win four hundred bucks and a beer mug."

But actually, the secret prize was much more than that. The secret prize was, you got the girl. The secret prize was, you could do it, and very few others could. The secret prize was something you couldn't explain. Glory, maybe. Not fame, because fame required a lot of people knowing, and they could know something silly or shallow; just the fact of a million people knowing it made it fame. But glory was what a few others knew or just you knew—that you had done something extraordinary and courageous and that fear hadn't stopped you. It was true. It was real.

So he'd gotten the girl. Charmed her, wowed her, bedded her, married her. Sat with her through two labors right in his own house, in the same bedroom where his father had been born. Fought about how to raise the kids: her always too soft, him too strict, but so far they'd turned out pretty good. Great kids that would be great people when they grew up. Yeah, that was the real prize, he guessed.

A song came on the radio, and the familiar voice turned the prize into vapor and whisked it away. Some song about Shanghai. It was a voice he associated with his "spin through Hollywood." He always called it that because naming it seemed to pin the whole thing in place and make it less painful. Back when he'd been competing, Pete Harrington had the life every young man wished he could live: with rock star money and rock star girls, while all he had was rocks and snow and the occasional girl. He'd met him that time at the end of all that talk about liquor endorsements and stunt-double roles, and for a few days it had looked like Pete Harrington was going to usher him into a bigger, shinier life. Then there was the accident, and his life had shrunk back down to something small and usual. What it was now.

He turned off the radio.

The snow was falling all around him. He was working today because his wife wasn't making the money she used to at the hospital. The city had sold it off to some big company, and if you didn't want to work on their terms they could darn sure find somebody from down south who would. That, and the fact that he'd lost most of their retirement chasing hot stock tips from the "pros" on Wall Street.

It still hurt him to remember those days. He'd thought he was so smart, and everybody else was so ordinary. Getting up at 4 A.M. for market opening back in New York, like he knew what he was doing. A couple of wins, then the first losses, then more losses. Always some new "disrupting" product or business model that was going to get all their savings back for him. And none of them did. Finally having to tell his wife. It was the only time he'd ever made her cry.

According to Riley, the electrician, it had all been rigged from the get-go. The whole thing had been planned out by ZOG—Zionist-occupied government. ZOG was the culprit. All those guys on Wall Street were Jews, and the bankers and the head of the Federal Reserve. Of course, Riley was full of shit about a hundred other things; no reason why he'd start getting it right on this one.

He needed a new drill bit, so he drove the four blocks to the hardware store. He got out of his truck and stood for a moment in the parking lot, looking up at Mount Juneau, whose two-thousand-foot cliffs rose behind the town. When he'd left the house, it had been visible, but now the thick snow clouds had come in and spirited it away within a white fog, like a magician's silk curtain.

Arnie saw him pull up and met him at the door. Arnie was his dad's old partner and owned half the business. At the age of eighty-nine Arnie still liked to come in and putter around, and Harry could understand that. Harry felt good in the old store; it was a place that implied that everything could be repaired. Whether it was marine epoxy or a timberlock-beam screw, somehow there was a way to put together anything that got broken, refurbish things that were worn out, and even if they didn't look shiny and new, they would still work.

Arnie was a little guy, partial to Pendleton wool shirts in red and black plaid, with the traces of a Norwegian accent from his Petersburg parents. He was a Viking skier of the old school, and even now you could see him up on the mountain on the best days in spring, slowly and carefully making his way down the groomed runs, stiff, a little bit hunched, but still skiing. He never wore a helmet. He'd survived Monte Cassino and the Battle of the Bulge, he said. He didn't think he had a hell of a lot left to fear from winter.

"Harry! Didn't expect to see you today! I thought for sure you'd be up skiing."

The remark went through him like a dagger. "I'm helping Jim out. He's behind on a job."

The old man looked up at what could be seen of the mountains. "Must be some job."

"I want to kill myself."

Arnie smiled. "Come on in, you poor bastard. Have a cup of courtesy coffee and a cookie."

He followed Arnie in through the front door. He needed a nine-sixteenths router bit, which Arnie got for him as he filled a Styrofoam cup with coffee and picked up one of the stale vanilla-crème cookies in the basket. There was a magazine on the counter and it was open to a perfume ad where a woman was sitting in what must have been some sort of fancy limousine, dressed in an evening dress that some guy's hand had hiked up to her thigh. She looked Chinese or Japanese.

Arnie had come shuffling back to the desk with the bit. "What do you think about that?" Arnie said.

He compared her in his mind to his wife. He spoke with a little more finality than he actually felt. "Think I'll stick with the one I've got. This one doesn't look like she's carried a lot of firewood."

"I don't think she's the firewood-carrying model."

Harry looked away from it and turned to the door again, lifting the light grabby walls of the Styrofoam cup to his lips. It was really dumping out there. Visibility would be low, but with all this snow, you could just ski by Braille, feeling your way down the slope, moving through the white above and the white below until you got to the trees. He was itching to try out those new reverse-camber fatties Rossignol had sent him. He still had a couple of fans there, older guys, who kept him on the free-skis list. Younger guys not too much, except occasionally he'd get some sort of e-mail from some kid who'd seen a clip somewhere or somebody wanting to interview him about the early days. Every once in a while he'd hear about them using an old clip of him in some sort of retrospective, calling him one of the legends of the sport, stuff like that. Not that any of that mattered: it was a Saturday, there was a foot of the kind of powder that refined your life to something simple and perfect again, and he was down here working. He looked out the glass door toward the mountains, thinking about it.

"Would it really kill you to take the day off?" the old man said behind him, also looking at the snow. "Call in sick."

"Jim needs the help," he said. He didn't want to say, *And we need the money.*

Arnie wrote the drill bit's code number on a clipboard and put the piece into a little paper bag. Harry remained standing at the counter, miserable, looking for the right words. "These perfect days," he finally said. "They just destroy me. They come and they go, and I always feel like I've got to grab onto them . . . And I never can."

The old man nodded gently. "I'll let you in on a little secret: there's a never-ending supply of perfection out there."

A couple of the guys were already waiting for him, warming their hands with steaming paper cups. One of them said something about skiing, and Harry forced a mute smile. They were working on a duplex built in the eighties. It was a rot job, his least favorite kind. Nothing constructive about a rot job. You followed it through the walls, cutting and replacing, and when you finally finished, it looked exactly the same as when you started. On top of that, the client usually complained about the cost, because they hadn't expected it to go so far. Like the whole country: who'd have thought the rot went so deep? Wall Street criminals sucking the life out of the place, politicians on the take, corporations running everything. It looked the same on the outside now, but after the collapse it never would be the same again. The curtain had been pulled away and people had seen how things really worked, and instead of revolting, they'd just shrugged and gone on like before. Him included. Said, *Okay, pick this carcass clean.*

The guys had the usual garbage on the radio: someone going off about illegal immigrants. Mexicans swarming over the border like rats. Matteo could hear it plain as day, but he didn't say anything, because this was what the crew always listened to. A stealth invasion of the United States. Everybody would have to learn Spanish or be arrested by the government. Harry looked over at Matteo, who was holding a piece of drywall with one hand and screwing it with the other. There was something inward and tense about him. Harry got up and changed the station.

"Hear about what happened with your cousin?"

Riley'd come in from the other room and was standing over him in his black horn-rim glasses, his little eyes swimming crazily behind the thick lenses.

"What cousin are you talking about?"

"Pete Harrington! Of the DreamKrushers! He hammered one of those Wall Street banksters. Just walked up to him on the street, and"—he pantomimed an overhand right—"BOOM! Right in the nose! Dropped him like the sack of shit he is!"

"Really?"

"Yeah! Check this out!" He pulled out his cell phone and began to look for the video.

Harry was still hoping to get a couple of hours of skiing in, if they could at least finish the drywall. "Maybe now's not the best time, Riley."

Riley ignored him, staring at his phone. "Get this: the bankster is also named Peter Harrington. He was that guy a few years ago, remember? Stole a shit-load of our money in some Wall Street rip-off."

"What sort of rip-off?"

Riley looked confused. "You know—Wall Street!"

Harry didn't respond, which didn't keep Riley from rolling right along. "So this guy's living in a twenty-million-dollar mansion in Shanghai. On *our money*! We bail 'em out; they go to Shanghai on our dime and live it up. And who do you think pulled the strings on that bailout? Huh?" Riley leaned down to him and said softly, "ZOG," then nodded his head secretively, knowingly. "Zionist-occupied goddamn government." The video had finally come up. "Check this out."

On the tiny screen of Riley's phone, Harry saw a blond-haired man walking down the street, shot from behind. The camera moved around him, and it was undeniably Pete Harrington, the same Pete Harrington he'd met years ago naked in a hot tub. He looked older now, the cheeks were softer, a bit less square and handsome, but definitely that same famous face. He watched him walk up to a slightly chunky man with a large forehead who held his hand out eagerly and said, "I really like your music!" Someone started a table saw in the other room, so he couldn't hear what the musician said in return, but the next event was unmistakable. Pete Harrington stepped forward and punched the man squarely in the nose, and the man staggered back and fell onto his butt, blood streaming down his face. On a human level, he felt sorry for the victim, who looked miserable on the ground. Riley was shouting over the undulating scream of the saw, ". . . bankster! Living in a twenty-million . . ."

Harry took the phone in his hands and played it again. This time, the banker's face looked craven and greedy, the embodiment of all the faceless financial scammers who had somehow taken his retirement savings and were gnawing away at the hospital and his insurance and the country itself.

He was sick of it all of a sudden. Sick of Riley's idiot conspiracy theories, sick of the conspiracies he knew existed but that he'd never discover. In Shanghai some guy with his name was living it up in a twenty-million-dollar mansion, and he was working on a Saturday when everywhere else but this rot-filled building was purified and sanctified with deep and perfect snow.

"I left something in my truck," he said, and he pushed the door open and stepped outside. He didn't really need anything in his truck; it was just that his sense of anguish was too great to be contained in the raw space of the rehab. He looked up at Mount Juneau, its frozen waterfalls bounding down along the rock surface. Higher up, it went white and blended in with the sky. Why couldn't he be up there? He heard a familiar voice say hello to him. He turned to see a medium-sized kid with brown hair and a hooded cotton sweatshirt that said ALASKA HELI-SKIING on it. It was Lucas. The responsible one.

"Lucas! What are you doing here? I thought you went with Jarrod and those guys."

Lucas glanced sideways. "No. They're going all the way up to the Wedding Bowl. I have to be at work at three."

"The Wedding Bowl? I told him not to go there!"

"So did I. It's gotta be loaded."

Harry swore quietly. *Fucking Jimmie!* He wanted to kick the crap out of him. "When did they leave?"

"About a half hour ago, I think."

"Jimmie talk him into this?"

Lucas was silent for a second, then offered, "Jimmie's kind of an idiot."

"Who else is with them?"

"I think TJ and Brandon went. There's a chute they want to drop out there." He shrugged. "I told them not to."

"I know that chute." He nodded. "Thanks, Lucas."

He took out his phone and dialed his son, but no one picked up. He was ducking him, or else they'd already headed out. In that case, there would be no reception until his son reached the top of the ridge. Harry Harrington stood there for a half minute looking up at the white streaks of avalanche chutes that had cut their way through the black-green apron of forest. He thought of the people he knew that had been killed in avalanches. Guy, down in Tahoe. Had his skull and spine crushed in a slab avalanche. Rick'd had it even worse down at Mount Baker. He'd been buried seven feet deep and suffocated while they were digging him out. Both of them young, both incredible skiers. It wasn't the mediocre skiers who died in the mountains. It was the ones that had to be there, that had to take a bold line.

Across the channel the trees were crusted all the way to the waterline. The parked cars were a couple of feet deep, disappearing into their winter burial. He thought of Jarrod up there, following Jimmie up to the ridge, then dropping onto that slope. He could call his wife, but he already knew what he had to do. He walked back into the building. The radio was back to that station, and the commentator was going off about gun rights and the government. Riley was cleaning out the hose to the sprayer, and he tapped him on the shoulder. "Something came up. I've got to go. If the boss man comes around, tell him it's an emergency."

Riley grinned at him. "Don't bullshit me. You're going skiing! I know you too well."

"Just tell him I had an emergency." He picked up his thermos and his tool belt and left. Riley'd finally gotten something right.

He climbed into his truck and started home through the narrow streets, block by block, hurrying to each stop sign and then slowing down a bit before rolling through. That idiot Jimmie! Always the troublemaker: getting them busted for pot so Jarrod lost his scholarship, and the time they'd broken the windows in another kid's car, supposedly a joke gone bad. He was reckless, which meant he could ride a little bit faster, go just a little bigger, and that kept his place as king shit of their little tribe. And when he got his stupid ass killed all his friends would sit around and drink beers and talk about how damn brave he was.

His wife was sitting at the kitchen table with her glasses on. He noticed again that she had a little rectangle of gray hair at the top of her scalp. She was trying to save money by spacing out her visits to the hairdresser.

"Hey!" she began pleasantly. "This is a nice surprise!" She noticed something right away. "What are you doing home?"

He glanced over at where his son's shorter, in-bounds board was resting. "Jarrod went up to the Wedding Bowl with Jimmie and his friends."

"Isn't that dangerous right now?"

He changed his demeanor. He didn't want to worry her. "It's not super-safe. I'm going to catch up with them and tell them to call it off."

"I thought you were working today."

"Not anymore."

He could see her getting alarmed. "Did you try to call him?"

They had a brief, sharp conversation about cell-phone reception and Jimmie and the fact that he'd told Jarrod not to go up there. Then he said, "I've got to get going."

"Shouldn't we call the state troopers or something? They could send a helicopter."

"They won't be flying in this weather." And even if they were, he thought, he'd be looking at a $2,100 bill. "I can catch them. They're only about fifteen or twenty minutes ahead of me, and they won't be in a hurry."

"I'll go with you."

Not just talking: she was faster than him on cross-country skis. "No use both of us going. I'll catch them."

She seemed about to argue with him some more; then she must have seen something in his face. "I'll pack you a sandwich and water while you get your stuff together."

He went down to the basement, where an orderly assortment of his entire outdoor life hung on the walls, lit by a single fluorescent bulb. One side of the basement had a chunk of gray bedrock sticking up out of the mountain through the floor, right next to the washer and dryer and the big basin sink. Nearly every other space was filled with tools or outdoor gear. Skis of every sort and length were fixed neatly to the walls, along with a coil of climbing rope, ice axes, crampons, snowshoes, fishing rods, yellow rubber rain gear, dark green rubber rain gear, breathable nylon rain gear, rubber boots, chest waders, flotation suits, insulated coveralls, and a small outboard motor. He picked out his backcountry skis and collapsible poles, then fished the climbing skins out of a nylon bag, testing the adhesive with his finger. Not much stickiness left, so he fixed them to his skis with loops of gray duct tape. He put new batteries in his avalanche beacon and packed his probe and shovel into a knapsack, along with a headlamp and a lighter. He hadn't used any of it for a couple of years. No need for a helmet: he wouldn't be on anything steep. His wife had made a peanut butter and jelly sandwich and filled a bottle with water. He put everything into the pack and told her the route he was taking to the Wedding Bowl. "I'll call you when I get up to the ridge." When he walked out the door, a little rush of excitement came over him. He'd shaken loose now. Everything had changed.

. . .

The drive to the trailhead took twenty minutes. The snow was fluttering down and melting on his windshield and his truck moved with a muffled crunching sound over the near-empty parking lot. He recognized Jimmie's parents' car tucked into a berm at the trailhead, alone, and his throat went tight with anger again. Nobody else would be stupid enough to go up on a day like this. There wasn't much snow on the windshield, at least. A good sign.

He took out his skis and snapped his feet into them. He'd taken his *randonnée* bindings, which let him ski up cross-country-style and then lock down, like alpine skis. They'd been the sexy new gear ten years ago, and he'd gotten a set for half price because he was Harry Harrington. They were relics now, but the damn things still worked as well as the day he'd gotten them, and that was good enough. The skis themselves were newer, only three years old, fat Coombas with a flat camber. Good skis that had made him 10 percent better the first time he clicked into them. More agile, better flotation, quicker turning. That was what new gear did. In the old days he'd competed with a set of 210 grand-slalom skis, made for carving hard, icy slopes at high speed, not for executing jump turns in deep powder. Like taking an Indy car to a dirt track. It was a little detail he never bothered mentioning to anyone, because he thought it would sound like boasting, but with these new skis he could actually ski better than he did twenty years ago, when he'd supposedly been in his prime.

The trail was packed with the boys' ski and splitboard tracks, pressed ten inches into the new snow. He was glad it was this deep, because breaking trail would slow them down. With the first few sliding paces, he couldn't keep from smiling. He was free now, whatever the reason. For the next few hours, at least, it didn't matter how far behind his brother-in-law was on the job or what stupid-ass ideas Riley was spouting. Things had gotten real simple all of a sudden. He'd almost forgotten what simple was like.

He pushed off into the forest, going at a fast pace, sliding one foot in front of the other along the track. After fifteen minutes sweat was dripping along his ribs, and he stripped down to a T-shirt and hat to keep from soaking his clothes. He moved through the dark hemlocks, an old-growth area where the standing trees towered overhead in five-foot-thick columns and the fallen ones formed massive barricades across the forest floor. The sky seemed distant, blocked out by the black branches and the pale green lichens that festooned them, and the woods formed a strange symphonic screen of grays and dark green and white. He hadn't been on this trail for fifteen years, and there was little familiar about it anymore, except the quiet. Occasionally a chunk of snow would slough off a branch and thump softly into the ground. A raven would call out in one of their many voices. Alone in that silence, things began to feel magical again. As he pushed his skis forward, one in front of the other, his job and money and everything else became part of a distant place, something flat and gray-colored, like a tiny little island on a map. What was real now was the immaculate purity of this world and the trail in front of him and his son up ahead. It was the only thing he'd done in a long time that felt like it deeply made sense. Not selling screws, or swinging a hammer. This was worth doing, far more worth doing than painting drywall. Put it on the list. Coming home from Europe to be with his dad when he was sick: worth doing. Getting married: worth doing. Dropping out of school to go on tour in 1990: worth doing—he'd kicked ass. That photo shoot, the one on the cover of *Ski* magazine with the caption "The Greatest Extreme Skier on the Planet." And then that movie part at Squaw Valley.

The surrounding woods seemed to disappear as he stared down at the white trail in front of him.

That hadn't been his fault. They hadn't done anything reckless or crazy. Nobody was hot-dogging. It was a movie shoot, just like other movie shoots. Along with the trip to Hollywood and the ski date with Pete Harrington, it felt like the logical flow among all the cliffs he'd dropped and spines he'd run and the hours he'd spent planting his poles just so and initiating his turns just so: the infinitesimal refinements in technique had enabled him to ski like no one else. It was just another shoot for a low-budget ski movie.

The producer had spotted the run the previous week, but it had been blowing hard the night before and he was worried that maybe parts of it had gotten scoured. Guy'd been along to help, just carry equipment and that sort of thing. They'd been ski-bumming together that winter. They decided that Guy would go down a nearby run with the same aspect and check it out, then radio back up to report on it.

When he thought of Guy he always imagined him skiing. Guy was fine-boned and on the short side, with sandy hair and a reedy voice, an amazing skier who could ski anything but wasn't interested in competing. Harry had always reckoned Guy a better skier than he was, but different. Guy was all about the pure line, the graceful line over cliffs and through trees, swooping and flying, like he was signing his name in cursive. He made it all look easy and beautiful, and Harry loved following him because his descents were always filled with unexpected detours and cuts that surprised him in a joyful way. It had been Guy's idea, when they were kids, to come down through the woods and hit that kicker right into the street in front of his house. When they started going into the backcountry, Guy was always the organizer, and the one who brought the first-aid kit, while he himself was always the one who broke the silence when they were standing at the top of an unknown run and someone asked, "Who's going first?"

But this time, Guy was going first. The run started in a wide field of snow at about a thirty-five-degree slope, which descended two hundred yards and then steepened into a series of rocky chutes with cliff drop-offs at the end of them. The landing zones were good, so he wasn't worried about the cliffs. They dug a snow pit to check the snow stability, and it looked okay, so Guy took off with a couple of brief, happy turns. Harry watched him go dancing down the slope, and then, sickeningly, the whole thing released.

It was a slab avalanche nearly three feet deep, with a crack that started just below Guy's feet and then worked its way in seconds across the entire slope. Guy heard the booming sound, because he glanced up, and when he saw it cutting loose behind him he tried to go diagonally to get out of its path. He'd done that before: they both had, but this time the whole slope disintegrated around him, liquefying into a white river that sucked him in and bore him down toward the chutes below. He saw Guy on his back, struggling to keep his head up, and then some of the bigger slabs obscured him. Slabs like refrigerators, like queen-sized beds, frozen to the hardness of concrete. He watched it with a sick feeling of helplessness, pushing his feelings aside and tracking Guy's fall line all the way into a gully that filled up and then partially emptied again. He heard the fellow next to him say something, but he just kept his eyes on where Guy had last been, and the area below it.

It was the only time in his life that he panicked. When the snow stopped moving, he didn't even turn on his beacon. "I saw where he went. I'm going down." He made a turn or two and then came to the crown, a three-foot drop onto the bed of the avalanche, and, without thinking, he popped over it. It was pure ice.

He turned sideways and jammed his ski edges into the surface, but he had too much speed and couldn't get any purchase. He hit a knob of rock and went tumbling over it onto the slick incline, landing on his back and sliding headfirst downhill at forty miles an hour, his poles clattering uselessly beside him. These were the days before helmets, and he sensed his head aiming straight for the icy boulders. He jammed the handle of one ski pole into the ice, and it created enough friction that his body spun around until he was sliding feetfirst. That saved his life. Seconds later, he slammed into the back end of the debris, and he felt his leg fold up and shatter beneath him.

So, no, he didn't make it to his appointment with Pete Harrington that afternoon. He was so doped up for the next two days that the meeting only existed as a sort of vague obligation, drowned in a haze of opiates into which floated doctors, nurses, his parents' faces, a few friends, and the softly lapping tide of grief and guilt about Guy. He was out for the rest of the season, and the next year he started taking seconds and thirds in the competitions, and he knew it was over. It wasn't that he'd lost any strength or skill, it was that every line he chose was the wrong line. The harder ones he skied too fearfully; the safer ones he skied too hard. It was over. All of it.

· · ·

He'd been on the trail for about forty minutes now without a rest. Not in the same shape he used to be, but Jarrod's life was on the line, and he knew if he kept up this pace, he'd catch them. He could read that from the trampled places where they'd stopped to rest. Jimmie liked his cigarettes, which meant five or ten minutes each break, and with a little luck they'd smoke some weed, which would slow them down even more. Once they got to the chute they'd have to take the skins off their boards and transition their gear, and Jimmy would light up another cigarette. They'd look at the view for a while and try to scout the chute. If they were smart and brought rope, one of them might rappel down and look at it, but that would have been Lucas, and Lucas was back in town. So two rests and the gear change and he'd have them. There was nothing to worry about except the rhythm of his poles and ski tips swinging back and forth in front of him.

The trail was starting to climb toward the tree line, and the trees had gotten smaller and sparser. So little color in these woods that even the slightest shade of other things replaced color: the ptarmigan tracks coming out of a clump of alder looked faintly gray against the unbroken snow, and the small, deep postholes of a deer wandering around searching for forage were a pale blue-white, but in the narrow range of shades in the forest, his eyes tuned in to them as if they were the yellows and reds of a painting. Even though he was only in a T-shirt, he felt completely comfortable, as if he were skiing through an endless room in an endless house, winter's house, which he hadn't visited in so very long, but which was familiar and welcoming.

The snow was beautiful today. He could pick it up in his hand and blow on it, and it would scatter like sparks. Without effort, he was skiing it already, here among the dark trees, on a steep slope, floating downward through the endless white field below him, dreamlike and timeless. It was infinity compressed into a few moments. No past or future, no worries, only life stripped down to a perfect black-and-white abstraction of itself, crystalline and undying.

In snow like this, anyone could drop that other chute. No Name, or whatever they called it. That winter when he'd thought about doing it, there hadn't been so much snow, and that had been one of the things that held him back. With less snow, the chutes were deeper and narrower, the drops were longer. Now, though, with three feet of fresh on top of everything else, it almost seemed like a shame to go all the way out there and not do it. Unfinished business from twenty years ago, and maybe, in some way, it had taken Jimmie and Jarrod to get him out there and finish it.

He could see it now. Jimmie saying, *Dream on, old man!* in that punk voice of his. Whenever Jarrod got in trouble, Jimmie was always close by, but he could never pry them apart, and the more famous Jimmie got, the more his son looked up to him. That's why the boy had come out here today, even though he'd told him not to. He ought to just wrap his pole around Jimmie's head. Jimmie could ride, though. He'd seen the videos, and it wasn't an accident that his sponsors flew him all over the world. He chose the most difficult lines, with the most exposure, and he made them work in a way that was thrilling, like cutting down a two-foot-wide spine with eighty-foot cliffs on either side, then cutting back to safety at the last possible moment. He did runs that didn't allow for a mistake, and one of these days he was going to make that mistake. Jarrod was more artistic, slow, and almost poetic. He chose less risky lines and pulled the appropriate trick out of each feature. A soaring backflip off a wind-lip, or grinding sideways along a tree overhanging a cliff, then launching off it and spinning a 360 before he hit the ground. It was sheer, frightening boldness versus style, and even though Jarrod had placed well in a couple of competitions, Jimmie was the one with the big life, while Jarrod lived at home. He didn't want to move down to Tahoe, like Jimmie and some of the other kids had, to get into the bigger arena. Jarrod was a hometown kid. He loved his friends and he loved his town, and even if part of him would never stop wanting to be on the cover of a magazine, he was a local. He had his private glory. Except when Jimmie came home to visit. Jimmie riled him up. Jimmie could get him killed.

Harry was angry again, and that made him pick up the pace. The tracks were winding upward at a steeper rate now, and as the trees thinned out, the wind was starting to go through his T-shirt. His bare forearms had gotten numb from the wind and the snowflakes, and he stopped and pulled out a fleece sweatshirt from the top of his pack. How long had it been since he

was alone in the woods on skis? He'd used to do it often, climb up somewhere high and then rip it, alone. Something forbidden in every list of safety
rules. Now it was all about safety and avalanches and obligations to his wife
and children. Go to work on Saturday, pay the bills, fill the truck, cut the
wood, surf the Net, go to bed, eat a bowl of oatmeal.

He probably should have stayed in Jackson Hole. He'd been at the top.
Ranked number 1 for four years running, although probably fewer than
two thousand people in the world knew that. That's what the sport was like
back then. But the owner of the resort at Jackson Hole was one of those two
thousand, and he'd seen him ski. He offered him sponsorship and the kind
of cushy job any skier would want. As a sponsor, he'd be wearing their bib
at all the comps and they'd pay his expenses. When he wasn't competing,
he'd guide the VIPs around the area. Basically, show rich people the mountain, give them some skiing tips, tell them some stories, take them to all
the hidden bowls and glades that only the locals knew how to get to. He'd
done it part of one winter, host to Denver dentists and Wall Street stockbro-
kers, even a couple of celebrities.

He could have stayed in Jackson Hole, probably ended up in management and a whole easy life doing exactly what he loved to do. But he'd wanted
to go home, where everyone knew him, where he could walk down the street
and see friends' kids and friends' parents and know their histories, bad and
good: who'd been a bully, who'd been expelled from school for drugs, re-
deemed cheaters, disgraced politicians, epic tragedies of people lost at sea or
fallen through frozen lakes or off mountains. And maybe knowing those
things about other people was completely insignificant in the big scheme of
things, because they were hardly famous, important people, just people in a
small town. But to him it was what made the world deep.

The tracks came out above the tree line and into a scruff of willows whose
naked gray branches scratched the unbroken white screen around him. He
saw a confusion in the tracks in front of him, and yellow holes where the
kids had taken a leak. From the indents he could see that a couple of them

had sat down and rested. An empty cigarette pack lay in the snow. Jimmie. From here the incline to the ridge got steeper, and their trail became a zig-zagging series of switchbacks. Hard to tell how far ahead they were because the bulge of the ascent hid them from view, but once they topped the ridge, they would have to follow it some ways to get to the chute, and that would be his chance to flag them down, depending on the visibility. The clouds had been raising and lowering like a theatrical curtain all day.

He pushed on a little faster. He was well above the tree line now, and the wind was whipping him harder and piling little deposits of frozen snow onto his sweater. He slipped on his jacket and continued, aware of his own panting as the way got steeper. His downhill ski kept breaking through the track and sliding toward the bottom as he followed their switchbacks. Soft, light snow, not the usual heavy coastal stuff that you could press into a snowball. Powder, avalanche snow. The ridge was definitely getting closer now. A hundred more feet above him, but now it had gotten really steep, the kind of steep where you could take a step and sink right back down to where you started. The snow kept sloughing off below his lower ski, and when he stomped his board, he could see shooting cracks taking off ten feet across the mountain. He was starting to worry that they were too far ahead, started to imagine Jarrod trying to run that chute. He was sweating and his heart was beating fast, but he put it aside and kept trudging upward with a steady, machinelike pace. Twenty more feet, two last switchbacks, and then the trail suddenly straightened out and became a gentle incline. He'd reached the ridge that formed the rim of the Wedding Bowl.

He got a glimpse of them, far ahead, moving, small figures in coats that looked dark gray in the dense, snowy air. He yelled, but they didn't hear him. They disappeared behind a hump in the mountain's contour, heading for the chutes, and he steeled his mind and picked up his pace, his open jacket flapping in the wind, the cold air welcome beneath his arms. He wished for a second he'd brought a flare gun or a whistle. Nearly two and a half hours since he'd left the trailhead, without a rest. His thighs were exhausted, and he felt a blister rising on his heel. Nothing he could do about it now.

The ridge continued upward and became narrower, and the slopes dropped away steeply below him on either side. This was the high world, the rarefied territory that always felt exhilarating and a little frightening. The world of trees was far behind, and the wind moved unbroken across the clean eggshell surface. Below him he could make out the inverted cone of a slide across the bowl, and it looked fresh. Loose, unconsolidated snow that had started as a slough and grown into an avalanche as it made its way down the slope. Far ahead on the ridge he made out his son's group again, clustered next to an outcropping of rock that he knew was the head of the chute they called No Name. He yelled out, and this time they heard him, or they happened to glance over. One of them waved back at him, then, getting closer, he recognized his son's colors: blue jacket, red pants, lifting a wave to him that seemed hesitant, resigned. He cut his pace and kept going. They'd wait for him. He didn't want to arrive so out of breath that he couldn't speak.

He reached them about ten minutes later. The four boys were looking at him: Jimmie, TJ, Brandon, his son. Brandon had roped up to an anchor he'd made by burying his skis in the snow and seemed about to pick his way down to a perch above the chute that would offer a good shot. TJ was ready to belay him. Jimmie was smoking a cigarette, his snowboard still in ski mode. Jarrod had already put his board back together and was ready to ride down. Always that question: *Who goes first?* His son muttered a greeting and looked off to the side. They all knew why he was there.

Jimmie said, "Hey, Mr. Harrington!"

He didn't answer immediately, just skied the last fifty feet in silence until he was five feet away from Jimmie. They were all looking at him.

He didn't raise his voice. He wanted to be angry, but the truth was that he was glad to be on top of the mountain. Winter was all around him.

"Hi, Jimmie. How's the tour going?"

"Great. Just great."

"Good." He didn't say anything. No one else did either. "You trying to kill these guys?"

They all stiffened, and nobody answered. "Brandon? TJ?" He could see their faces become wary and defensive, and he went on. "Did it occur to you that this whole mountain is ready to pop?"

"We wanted to hit this chute while it's full," Jimmie offered weakly.

"Oh, it's full all right!" No one answered. "Jarrod?"

His son looked at him and then glanced away, and Harry could sense how embarrassed he was. He couldn't help feeling bad for him. Even Jimmie, the idiot, looked uncomfortable, because he'd been caught doing something stupid yet again, and not by some remote authority figure but by his friend's dad, who he'd known since nursery school, and what made it worse was that he'd been around enough to hear the old stories, so it wasn't just any dad. Harry looked past them to the edge of the chute, and slid over to it. He looked down it, remembered it again, from this angle. A lot more snow than the last time he'd stood here with Guy for a half hour. Not quite as deep or tight as back then, but the same run. Steep and wide for fifteen feet, narrowing into a chute the width of a doorway that went nearly straight down for another twenty feet, then bore right and turned into a cliff that you had to drop with rock walls at your elbows. That got you halfway in.

As he looked down, he heard Jimmie's voice behind him. "Nobody's ever dropped this one."

He answered without turning around. "I know. You can't really see it all from any angle unless you rappel down into it." They didn't answer him. "But it's pretty much a straight shot down a very narrow chute. Once you're in, you're in. You can't slow down and you can't change your mind. Your slough's getting funneled right behind you, and if you don't outrun it, you're screwed. You've got a little turn; then you've immediately got to drop a cliff, more like a really small mine shaft, maybe ten to twenty feet of drop with about a foot and a half to spare on either side of your body, and if you line it up wrong, you're going to go banging between those rock walls like a pinball. If you do make it through there, you've got ten feet to recover and launch that last drop that's visible from the bottom."

"That one's about forty feet," TJ said.

"Depending on conditions. With all the snow we've had this year, my guess is it's only twenty-five to thirty."

Jimmie spoke. "How do you know all this, Mr. Harrington? Did you scout it?"

"If you're going to Seattle and the wind is coming from the south, the plane banks around right over the Wedding Bowl. If you sit on the left side, you get about a ten-second look right into the chute at low altitude. But you've got to be watching for it."

They were kids, so it didn't occur to them to wonder why he'd be watching for it, year after year. "But I didn't tell you the last part."

"What's that?"

"Play it out all the way: you go down the entry, you cut that little turn and line it up just right and clear the elevator shaft, you get your second takeoff right and land the second drop, and just when you're thinking how awesome you are—surprise, surprise—the whole damned bowl cuts loose on top of you, and then you're tomahawking down with a couple of megatons of snow on your ass."

The exchange died out and they were silent for a moment. The cloud level was above the mountains, so there was a slice of empty gray sky sandwiched between the jagged horizon and the pearly layer of white clouds. He could hear the gentle sizzling of the falling snow around them.

"The only safe way out of here today is back down the ridge, and that's how we're going out." He waited, but no one challenged him. He pulled his beacon out of his pack and strapped it onto his body, turning on the SEND signal. "You guys got me?"

They each looked at their beacons.

"Got you." "Got you, Mr. Harrington." "Four meters: got you."

When he clipped out of his skis he sank thigh-deep into the snow. It was light, cloudlike, with large flakes that lay on top of each other like confetti. Champagne snow, like they hardly ever got up here. He pulled off his skins and rolled them up inside his pack, then locked the bindings down. He put on his goggles. He grabbed his poles again, but he didn't put his hands through the straps. Nobody noticed that. They were busy arranging their gear for the return—putting on extra layers and zipping up packs. Except for Jimmie. He was still sitting on his snowboard smoking his cigarette. "Jimmie? You coming with us?"

He didn't answer, but he threw away the cigarette and slowly took his feet. He started clipping together the snowboard for the ride down.

He'd done it. He'd dragged his ass up here, caught up with them, and kept his son from doing something that had a very good chance of killing him. It was worth doing. His wife would be happy. He'd fulfilled all his obligations.

Harry turned downslope and looked at the chute they called No Name. The wide funnel that was its entry was perfect and untracked, as it always had been, and maybe always would be. He remembered it from twenty-odd years ago. Guy was there—Guy had tried to talk him out of it, at first, but finally stood back and let him decide on his own. Why had he wanted to do it? There were only a dozen people who even knew that chute existed. No film crew, no judges, no videos on the Internet.

Different now. More snow, and he'd seen it from the air. He'd seen bits and pieces from different angles and he had a special talent for reassembling all those views and having a pretty good idea of how it would look as you were going down it, even for the first time. If you didn't have that talent, you weren't going to win every competition in the world for four years running.

He heard Jarrod's voice behind him. "Dad?"

His son trudged the last few steps through the thigh-deep snow and stood beside him. "Don't even think about it."

Harry turned to him. He could see his concern through the mask of teenage apathy that had cloaked him for the last few years.

"No. I was just thinking that with all this snow, it probably wouldn't be that big a deal. I've done harder. And with these new fat skis . . ."

He looked out at the vast, open bowl of falling snow below him, then straight down the chute. It was like staring into the gullet of a beast. Things could go wrong, but that was true on any difficult run, and he'd spent years carefully erasing all the things that could go wrong from his mind. Straight, turn, line it up, drop it, then drop it again. That was all. Take away the exposure, and it wasn't that big a deal. You just had to be all the way in it, not second-guess yourself. Not even for a fraction of a second.

He looked out at the horizon again. The snow was picking up, and it had gotten blurry again. The slope below was tensed as tight as a drum. Jarrod's voice was more insistent. He could hear the fear in it. "Dad, *no.*"

"I don't really think it's that hard."

"I know. But what about avalanches? You said it's dangerous. That's why you came out here, isn't it?"

Harry felt far away from the voice. "Is that why I came out here?"

They heard a soft, deep *whoof,* then a low rumble, like a jet flying down below them. They all listened to it as it echoed around the bowl and reached a crescendo before dying out. "One just let go," his son said. "You hear that?"

"I heard it," TJ said.

"Dad . . ."

Harry didn't answer. He was still looking down the chute. A fifteen-second run, at most. More like ten. He'd be out before he knew what had happened. And the snow below would be so deep and soft that the landing wouldn't feel like a landing at all, just a miraculous transition between the air and the earth.

"You know something? I might have spoken too soon. If you hit this chute, and then land that last drop really as soft as you can, keep a nice, straight line, and don't turn out of it at all, and then, if it lets go, you just cut over to the left, below that cliff. You'd probably be okay."

"Dad!" his son said again. He turned to face him. "You don't even have a helmet."

Now, even Jimmie sounded worried. "Yeah, Mr. Harrington. We know you can drop this. Let's come back and do it when we've got better conditions."

Sure. You could always say things like that. Other people always did. But he knew that if he left now he'd never come back. It was too far. He had too many things to do. He'd gotten too sensible. He edged a little closer to the dropoff, swiveling his skis around so that the tips of them sank into the slope above the chute. Through the snow-softened air he could see the faint dark outlines of the other chutes, and the blackened smudge of the trees far below him. For a moment he thought he could sense the whole slope, straining with the tonnage of the new snow, ready to release. But that was all responsible stuff.

"Dad! Please don't!"

The snow had quickened and the air was buzzing with particles of white so close in color to the sky that the world seemed swarming and alive. It would clear, then it would snow again, the little white disk of sun would sail away, and it would snow all night. It would snow the next day, burying his tracks, burying his deeds, burying his life.

"Fuck it," he said, and with a quick little jump turn he pointed his skis downward into the chute and pushed off.

Nearly instantly the boards sank deeply into the white dust, then surfaced again as he picked up speed. He pointed them straight down then twitched his hips to bring them sideways, and felt the friction slowing him just a bit as he came to the throat of the chute. He felt an instant of panic in his stomach as he sped up toward the two rock walls, but he overcame it and he knew he was going straight in, perfectly lined up. He longed for the chute, leaned into it. He felt himself falling, his skis barely touching the snow and then not touching it at all, dropping like a sparrow between the jagged stone buttresses, in perfect silence because the world of noise didn't exist any longer, it was only the world of snow and stone and frozen air, the rock on either side, the subtle sideways leaning of his body in space, no way to correct it, his shoulder moving closer and closer to the face that would spin him around and break him into pieces, and just as he heard the nylon on his arm begin to rasp against the stone, he was out of it, flying unobstructed through the open air, then blending into the first landing with only ten feet of slope left to recover his balance and set up his next takeoff. His left ski hit first and he forced his body upright, sank his weight down, and used up his landing zone in a fraction of a second. Then the ground disappeared again and he was in that last big drop, falling, falling, tucking up his legs beneath him as he dropped. Closer and closer to the steep slope below him, and then, as he reached the white surface he extended out again, absorbing the blurry impact of gravity with his thighs, melding into the deep, feathery surface, a surface so light and steep that at first it was barely distinguishable from the air. He kept his line straight down the mountain as a blinding explosion of snow came up into his face, and he smiled at the joyful familiarity of the sensation, alone there, under the chute. He heard the compressed-air sound of his own slough thumping off the cliff right behind him, and he darted a quick glance over his shoulder.

He knew immediately that something very bad had happened. Just behind him, the surface of the snow was shattering like a pane of glass. A sickness reached up from the pit of his stomach and tried to grab his throat, but he let it pass and kept his skis pointed straight down. It was going to be a race, if he was lucky. He tucked and put his poles under his arms.

The air began to whiten as the powder blast caught up with him. Suddenly his speed seemed weirdly slow, as if some strange relativity had taken hold. The entire mountain was sliding behind him, liquefied into a boiling field of molten snow. Thick slabs and ice boulders jumbled just above his head, bouncing like coffee beans in the top of a grinder, then everything disappeared into a colorless world of mist. There was no mountain, there was no time, there was no up or down. It was like being in pitch dark, but it was a choking pitch white, its tiny crystals swirling into his nose and mouth, instantly coating his goggles.

He couldn't turn. If he turned, the seething mass would suck him in and crush him like a grape. He had to reach the run-out at the bottom of the bowl, where the slope flattened and the furious wave of frozen rubble would slow and spread. He thought briefly of his son, above, watching, felt a flicker of regret, then pushed it away and braced himself against the chaotic world that raged around him. Ground and air had become a hissing, thumping, blinding smoke of pure motion. It was all by feel now.

He reached up and gave one lens of his goggles a quick swipe with the back of his hand. To his amazement, he could see something ahead. The air was slightly clearer, which meant he was getting ahead of it, but just as he thought that, the ground beneath suddenly slowed and began to shift. He no longer had any speed, because the field of snow he stood on was itself sliding, accelerating down the mountain. The slope had turned to churning boulders that he desperately poked and pushed with his poles in a bid to keep his balance. The front edge of the avalanche was only some fifteen feet ahead. It was all about staying on his feet now. If he stayed up, he might live.

And then, in a horrifying instant, he felt the ground drop away beneath his left ski, and he went pitching to the side, riding the roaring mass with his head downhill of his body. He let go of his poles and began to flail in the snow. People talked about swimming in an avalanche, but there was no swimming in this. Around him he could see ice blocks the size of garbage cans and sofas, bounding down the hill beside him, rolling and leaping end over end with a crazed freedom, and mattress-sized rafts of frozen snow vibrating along. He felt one of his feet release from the ski, and he watched the red tip of it rise up from the mass and then slide along on top. He was sinking. His legs were buried now, and he kept trying to push his upper body out of the snow, but it kept sinking lower, even though the snow was moving more slowly. He was in up to the waist, his head still downhill, then up to the chest, and though the mass below him had stopped, there was still snow moving down the mountain from above, and he felt it closing over his head, deeper and deeper. The world had turned a dark gray. It was almost done now; the snow was beginning to set up, and once it did, it would be like concrete. He took one last gulp of air and expanded his lungs. In one final gesture of desperation or defiance he convulsed his entire body toward the surface, pushing downward with his arms with all his strength, and his head rose one last time three inches above the surface of the snow and stopped. The world was locked into a raw, broken silence.

His arms were pinned downward in the snow and his entire body was gripped as tightly as if he was a fist in cast iron. He was sideways to the slope, and a large boulder of snow sat on his chest, compressing it so tightly that he could only take shallow, suffocating breaths, as if he'd just sprinted a hundred yards and was being held in a bear hug. But it was air, welcome and cool. He was going to get another chance.

Then he thought of Jarrod and the boys up there, and the dread welled up inside him. He'd panicked when Guy had gotten caught; he'd jumped onto the bed of the avalanche and almost been killed himself. They might do that. Or there might have been a sympathetic avalanche that reached all the way to the ridge and sucked the boys down with it, and in that case there'd be no rescue, just five men dying in the cold, broken or smothered or fading out from hypothermia. With that thought, he felt a remorse that nearly made him sick to his stomach. *Jarrod!* He tried to call out but he couldn't muster enough breath, and he heard his voice come out in a muffled gasp. There was only silence. He'd come up here to save his son and instead he'd let everything get fucked up beyond recognition. Like before: tried to be the big man and just wrecked it all! Lost his money. *Lost his son!* His goggles had been ripped from his face, and now the little plugs of snow in his eye sockets were melting and running down his face. He strained to catch sight of the boys, but he was locked in place, and his field of vision was nearly completely blocked by the frozen debris that pinned him. He didn't know how to pray or who to pray to, but he tried to cut some sort of deal, offering things of little value in exchange for everything that mattered.

Some time passed. The snow that had been pushed beneath his coat began to burn his ribs, then to chill them. He thought he heard somebody shouting, but he couldn't make out what they were saying. Then there was silence again. A few seconds later, he saw his son picking his way carefully down the bed of the avalanche on his snowboard, below the chute, and he tried uselessly to call out to him. He lost sight of him behind the debris piled up around his head, heard him yell, "I've got a signal!" then his footsteps scuffling over the debris.

Jarrod's head appeared in the air above his face. "Dad! Dad! Are you hurt?"

"I'm okay," he said. He heard it come out like a whisper, with barely any breath behind it.

Jarrod turned and yelled to summon the others, then slipped his pack off and started taking out his shovel. He was kneeling beside his father. "Hold on. I'm getting you out of there."

He could read a lot in that voice. It was the voice of his son trying to be brave, trying to be a man, but he could sense the terror and the anguish. He wanted to hold him, to reassure him. "I'm not hurt," he gasped. "Just get that thing off my chest."

His son had taken his goggles off, and his father could see the turbulent expression on his face. His eyes were wet and his voice was filled with pain. "Why, Dad? *Why?*"

"I don't know. I really don't." Harry could feel the snow melting down his cheeks, and he realized his son would think he was crying. "I'm sorry."

Jimmie's face suddenly appeared over Jarrod's shoulder. He seemed to assess the situation instantly, and he put his arm across his friend's shoulders and squeezed. "Jarrod, man, it's all right. Your dad's okay." At this Jarrod lost all control and began to sob. "Let it out, man. It's okay. That scared the shit out of me, too." He turned back to Harry's head poking out of the snow. "Mr. Harrington, you are one crazy dude!" He took hold of Jarrod's shovel and offered it to him. "Here. Let's get your dad out of there."

They had him out in less than two minutes. Jarrod said nothing, while the others concentrated on the details of digging or looked for his skis. One had escaped the avalanche and gone down the slope another two hundred yards, and TJ went after it. The other was found through luck: the top six inches were sticking upright through the snow. They never found the poles.

It was just as well, Harry thought. His shoulder was pretty tweaked. The entire bowl had gone: the valley floor was a jumble of shards and boulders for hundreds of yards, an impassable debris field they would have to skirt.

There was silence as they pulled their gear together for the ski out. Snowboards were disassembled into skis again, and skins were stuck back onto their bases for traction. He couldn't separate his skins from each other because of his shoulder, and TJ offered to do it for him. As they readied their gear they would look up at the massive avalanche around them and study it, imagining themselves in its grip, awed at its power. Two-foot-wide trees had been snapped off at the snow line, while ice boulders the size of pickup trucks stood like primitive obelisks hundreds of yards across the valley floor.

"I can't believe you skied out of that," Jimmie offered at last.

"*Almost* skied out of it," Harry answered.

They headed out across the lower part of the bowl, eyeing the slopes above them with a mixture of reverence and fear. It was still snowing. There were still great overhanging cornices capable of breaking loose and thundering down on them. TJ took the lead and Harry followed without his poles. He was weak, and his shoulder hurt him. He was trying not to shake. Not much of a hero now, he guessed. He'd come up here to protect his son, to set a good example, and instead he'd made a complete ass of himself. The story would spread about what an idiot he was, how they'd had to dig him out. Humiliating. And his wife; that was going to be a whole other problem. He'd have to ask Jarrod to let him be the one to tell her.

They got to where the high valley fell downward back toward the trailhead, and they posted up at a safe spot to transition their gear. Skins came off and snowboards came back together. Poles were collapsed and stowed. Jimmy decided to smoke another cigarette, and they all stood looking out across the whitened fuzzy space toward the bowl and the chute he had run. No Name was barely visible through the buzzing air, and he watched as the clouds closed down over it. He knew he had to say something.

"Thanks for digging me out, guys. I'd still be lying there if it wasn't for you."

"Don't mention it, Mr. Harrington," Jimmie said. "I know it'd work the other way around, too."

"It would. But this time it worked this way."

TJ said, "It never would have happened if we hadn't come out here."

"He's right," Jimmie said. "This was my fault."

"Yeah, well . . . we were all a little bit stupid today. But I set a piss-poor example of how to be a man, and I'm sorry for that."

The boys all looked at him. Jarrod was poking the snow beside his ski with his pole, leaving little circles with dark blue holes in the middle.

Jimmie said, "You *crushed* No Name! And then you rode out a fifty-year avalanche event! I wouldn't call that a piss-poor example; I'd call it freak-ing *hero*!"

He suspected Jimmie was just trying to make him feel better, and for the first time he felt genuine affection for his son's friend. But having done something so reckless and gotten away with it, he had the sense that he'd just signed Jimmie's death warrant. He knew it wouldn't be long before someone else worked up the nerve to try that chute, and someone was going to get hurt.

"Nothing 'hero' about wrecking your family trying to prove something." But that wasn't it, he thought. That wasn't what he needed to tell them. That was only part of it. He struggled for the words.

"In a million years, I wouldn't run that chute again. It's a squirrelly, nasty little chute and there's no margin of error. Maybe you could do it, or maybe that particular day you clip your ski on the way in, or you hit a little patch of glaze right at the turn, and then you're fucked. Your friends have to try to save you and somebody has to pay to medevac you out of there, or do body recovery, and the bottom line is, it's not really worth doing in the first place. You can't see anything; you can't style it. There's no joy in it, except to brag that you did it—"

He hesitated as he tried to get to the heart of it. "Some things aren't worth doing. They look shiny and they impress people, but they're stupid. That chute's one of them. You want to do something? Get big air. Fly. Rip some five-thousand-foot line and make it look pretty. Go do something"—he looked for the right word, the unlikely word—"beautiful."

None of the boys answered. They stood in the silence, and the word hung there awkwardly, holding them.

"So what are you going to call it?" Jimmie finally said.

He'd forgotten about naming rights. He looked toward the chute, but it had disappeared now in a bundle of mist, so he could only imagine it back there, a lightning-shaped fissure of black stone pointing at the sky. "I'm not going to call it anything," he said. "It just is."

Behind them, the clouds were starting to lose their light. "We'd better get going," he said, and without another word they pointed their boards back over their tracks and glided down the ridge and into the secret, quiet forest.

⁂

Peter Harrington had been lucky to land, they told him. Most of the other flights had cancelled without ever leaving Seattle, and a couple had left Seattle only to bounce back and forth between Anchorage and Sitka without ever getting into Juneau. The snow was heavy and all the small-plane traffic between Haines and Juneau was grounded, something he'd never counted on as a possibility. There were no roads in this part of Alaska, and the next ferry north was in two days. It suited him.

He was going to a small town north of Juneau called Haines, the seat of a famous heli-skiing operation, where skiers were dropped at the top of big mountains and navigated their way down endless runs of spines and glaciers. The real reason he'd chosen Haines was that he couldn't admit to himself that he'd gone all the way to Alaska with the vague idea of skiing with someone he'd spent twenty minutes with two years ago. Now, if he found him at his hardware store, he could say, *I was going up to Haines to do some heli-skiing. I thought I'd stop by.* His name was Harry. That was all he knew about him. He might not see him at all. Now that he was here, it wasn't that important. When he left Juneau, he would go on to Haines, and then maybe he would leave Haines and go on to Anchorage, then farther north, or farther west, to a succession of places that got smaller and more lost until the whole idea of Peter Harrington disappeared. When he reached the end, he'd go visit his son.

His intention of kicking around tiny towns in Alaska in winter was aimless and weird, but Camille had encouraged him, for reasons that were intuitive to the point of nonsense and that he couldn't resist. On the night before he left, they slept together, which left him more confused about her than ever. He knew he didn't really live in Shanghai anymore. He didn't feel he lived anywhere.

For some reason, as he dropped down into the dark, hostile landscape of Alaska, he sensed he'd come to the right place. The taxi driver took him to a hotel owned by the local Native corporation, and he checked in beneath the gaze of wooden masks and strangely shaped blankets woven into eyes and beaks. For a moment the girl at the front desk seemed to recognize him, and he thought she was going to say something to him, but she finally dismissed it, or decided to keep it to herself. The snow was still falling outside, and he left his things in his room and went out to look around. Maybe tomorrow he'd ask where the hardware store was, but it didn't seem that important anymore.

The town was a warren of narrow one-way streets climbing upward toward the soaring two-thousand-foot cliffs that boxed it in on the land side. The low wooden buildings that lined the sidewalk retained the resonance of the gold rush that had put the town on the map. Christmas lights were still sprinkled in most of the windows, and on the wooden awnings and on the light posts. He passed Juneau Drug and the Ben Franklin five-and-dime, the kind his mother would have shopped at fifty years ago, passed the florist and the bookstore and several modest law offices near the small stately capitol building. Behind the town, he'd read, were miles and miles of ice fields, so the tiny city was closed off from the rest of the world.

It was incredibly beautiful here. The vertical faces of the mountains were covered with frozen waterfalls that dropped a thousand feet, and above them his eye instinctively followed the steep, rounded fields of snow until they disappeared into the white fog. He had coffee at a café and watched the people come in and greet each other, flecks of snow on their shoulders and their hats. He had a second coffee at another place and did the same thing. The citizens dressed simply, in nylon rain jackets and rubber boots, but interspersed with them were the suits and ties of the lawyers and lobbyists who were working the little capitol a few blocks away. Even the politicians looked small-town, like they'd stepped out of an old movie. He imagined

people's errands and jobs, their cars parked along the snowy street, and the
homes they would return to. The children and the dinner pots, the dogs in
their favorite spots, the wet boots, the damp coats hung up by the door. All
those half-imagined worlds.

By three thirty in the afternoon, the sky was dim already. He walked a few
short blocks to the sea and wandered into a restaurant that had giant windows facing down the channel. Mountain after mountain sprang out of the
black water, and he stared at the hypnotic view. He ordered a cup of coffee
and a BLT. A couple of older men were sitting at a booth with a pot of coffee
between them, talking something over in serious tones, and he could tell
from their expressions that if he lived there and knew the people it would
be of the utmost importance. Something about an avalanche blocking the
road to somewhere and how you'd have to be crazy . . . It was good talk.
Meaningful talk. He'd arrived at this strangely perfect place that filled him
with a sense of well-being for no reason he could understand. A waitress
with a pierced nose poured his coffee into a thick white mug with two green
pinstripes and said the sandwich would be out in a minute.

Shanghai felt irretrievably far away now. It was as if he wasn't that person
anymore, that financier. He was just a person in a small town in the distant
north surrounded by mountains and snow, and nobody knew his name.
What he'd regarded as his greatest accomplishment now felt petty and vague,
not something he could measure his life with, or anyone else's. It seemed a
bit silly, when you got right down to it. A fool's errand he'd sent himself on,
thinking it was some sort of quest. The mountain was massive, the mountain
was mist. But at the bottom of the mountain was the town, and in the town
were a thousand other lives, ten thousand, each of them alive and ever changing. Ten thousand far-off countries, ten thousand daydreams. Ten thousand
mysterious journeys.

It was night now, at 4:30. He decided, without really thinking about it,
to simply walk up. He followed Seward Street to Fifth, then walked along it
toward the mountain. He heard the rubbery whine of tires spinning against

the snow, the beeping of the snowplow as it backed up and then scraped forward. As he approached the mountain, it got steeper, and the street ended at a stairway that went much higher, overhung by a single streetlight and the snowy branches of trees. He paused at the bottom of it and looked upward, but he couldn't see beyond the light. He looked backward, and up again, then set his foot on the first metal tread and began to climb. After seven or eight flights he reached another street.

It was a tiny neighborhood tucked away in a cleft in the mountain. All around it crouched the forest. The houses here were small and old and wooden, and some of them had stacks of logs split and piled beneath their eaves or their porches. The street was closed to traffic in the winter, and the children had turned it into a sledding hill. There were a half dozen of them, boys and girls, hurling themselves facedown onto slabs of slippery foam or plastic saucers. They had made a jump and were endlessly refining it with a shovel, building it up and patting it down, all with tremendous energy and purpose. He watched them run and slide, and though they were sliding at a modest speed, he knew that to them, with their noses just above the snow, it felt fast, as fast as a sports car or a ski run, as fast as a private jet. He listened to their boasts and their happy squeals, and he had the sense again of a life that had eluded him. The smell of wood smoke, the idea that in each of these houses was a mother or father cooking dinner, a warm stove, the ties to friends who had seen each other fail and succeed, where success didn't mean amassing eight hundred million dollars but buying a house, cooking a turkey that didn't dry out, building a deck, seeing your letter to the editor in the morning paper with your own name in black print. The air was dark blue here, the lights in the windows buttery and rich. In one of these houses there was probably a wife who suited him: Someone intelligent. Someone nice. He'd walk in and she'd be at the stove in an apron—no! She'd be sitting reading a magazine with a sweater on that had a few wood chips clinging to it from the firewood she'd just chopped. A wife eagerly waiting for him, filled with news of the day and waiting to hear his own report.

He could make out some skis leaning up against someone's porch railing, beside a snowboard and a sled. He walked toward the house. Some of the children were watching him: they said *Hi, Mr. Harrington,* and he said hello to them.

He walked up the wooden stairs of the porch and knocked on the door, not even knowing what he would say, and he heard the footsteps crossing the floor toward him, saw the light go on in the hallway and a woman approaching through the tiny glass window at eye level. She opened the door and smiled at him. She was just as he'd pictured her: blond, in a white sweater with reindeer across her breasts, almost stocky, but in a pleasing way, her face open and luminous as she saw him. "Thank God you're back! I've been worried about you! Why didn't you answer your phone?" She collapsed into him and he held her, feeling her breasts against his chest, but even more, her warmth, her relief, the knowledge that she belonged to him and he belonged to her.

He came into the room. Everything was exactly where it should be. The couch, the pillows on the couch, the wood piled up in the wrought-iron cradle by the stove. The goldfish, her African violet, the painting by his sister-in-law, the cooling rack covered with warm cookies. This was it. This was the life, just as he'd imagined it.

"What happened? Is everything okay?"

He looked into her beautiful face as he put his hands on her hips. "Everything turned out okay."

"Tell me what happened! Did you get to them before they tried to do that chute?"

"Oh, I made sure they didn't do anything stupid. You can bet on that."

She hugged him, smiling. "You're my hero!"

"Yeah . . . Well . . . You'd better wait till you hear the whole story." He'd tell her later, but for now, he just wanted to quietly, secretly rejoice in being alive, in front of the fire. "Where's Lizbeth?"

"She had a late rehearsal. She's on her way now. What about Jarrod? You told him I'm expecting him, didn't you?"

"He'll be home soon," he answered. "He had to pick up something from TJ's."

His wife went out to the porch to get more wood and he shuffled over to the stovetop. She'd made chicken and dumplings; he could smell it. The cast-iron Dutch oven was sitting on the stove with a towel wrapped around the lid. It was bubbling over and a tiny stream of liquid was going into the burner, hissing. He looked inside, saw the dumplings had risen. He turned the dial to OFF.

Yeah, there was going to be a conversation tonight, but right now he was going to sit back down in front of this fire. In about ten minutes, or maybe at dinner, he was going to tell his wife what happened and he'd do his best to make it sound like no big deal, but she'd see through it and it was going to be sharp. His daughter would be upset, and Jarrod probably wouldn't say much of anything, because they'd already said it all on the mountain.

In a minute he'd get up and take an aspirin for his shoulder, but that would be a long minute from now, in which he'd pull open the door of the stove and the orange heat would well up over his wrists and his face. There'd be a brightening of the embers, a pop from the fresh log, a tiny spark flying out, and he'd close the door and sit back, thinking of that chute, how it had almost killed him in his stupidity and his longing, but also recalling the entire run in all its minuteness, from the deep, soft powder at the top to that long, quiet drop at the end and how the whole thing had just been perfect, like now, sitting here, still alive, warm, aching, valued: perfect. He knew, as he never had, that he was going to get old, he was going to ski slower, that all the things that happened to other people were going to happen to him. But it was okay. That was a long time from now. More moments than he could ever count. It was like that song, he thought. He didn't know the name. The one about the man who climbs the mountain and comes home and sits in front of his stove. He comes home and he thinks of all the faraway places he'll never go and the fortunes he'll never have, then he thinks about the perfect snow falling outside his window and the perfect snow falling on the ridge. That man and his wife and his children and the fire. That song. This is how it really sounds.